'Absorbingly atmospheric ...
beautiful and sinister'
The Times

'Haunting and evocative'
Clare Mackintosh

'Obsessive friendship, family tragedy ...
had me hooked from page one'
Louise Candlish

'A haunting story with the moral
ambiguity of du Maurier'
Liz Fenwick

'A beautiful, stirring story of
loss and obsession'
Lisa Jewell

'Completely addictive and utterly compelling'
Hannah Beckerman

'Hugely enjoyable, well written and gripping and clever'
Jane Casey

'A beautifully written, slow-burn of a thriller'
Red

'Immensely atmospheric, with vividly drawn
characters and a set-up fraught with tension'
Lucy Atkins

Amanda Jennings lives in Oxfordshire with her husband, three daughters, and a menagerie of animals. She studied History of Art at Cambridge and before writing her first book, was a researcher at the BBC. With a deep fascination for the far-reaching effects of trauma, her books focus on the different ways people find to cope with loss, as well as the moral struggles her protagonists face. When she isn't writing she can usually be found walking the dog. Her favourite place to be is up a mountain or beside the sea.

Also by Amanda Jennings

In Her Wake
The Judas Scar
Sworn Secret

The Cliff House

Amanda Jennings

ONE PLACE. MANY STORIES

HQ
An imprint of HarperCollins*Publishers* Ltd
1 London Bridge Street
London SE1 9GF

This paperback edition 2020

1

First published in Great Britain by
HQ, an imprint of HarperCollins*Publishers* Ltd 2018

Copyright © Amanda Jennings 2018

Amanda Jennings asserts the moral right to be
identified as the author of this work.
A catalogue record for this book is
available from the British Library.

ISBN: 978-0-00-838619-1

MIX
Paper from
responsible sources
FSC™ C007454

This book is produced from independently certified
FSC™ paper to ensure responsible forest management.

For more information visit: www.harpercollins.co.uk/green

Printed and bound in Great Britain by
CPI Group (UK) Ltd, Croydon, CR0 4YY

To Mum and Dad.
With love as always.

'If one is lucky, a solitary fantasy can totally transform one million realities.'
Maya Angelou

Prologue

You sit and watch them from the same place you always do.

I spy.

With my little eye.

The grass is flattened where your weight rests. A patch of earth revealed where your feet have kicked back and forth to pass the time. The purple foil of a chocolate bar you ate a week ago glints from where it nestles amid the sandy thatch of vegetation beside you. Seagulls cry mournfully, wheeling high in the sky above you, above the breaking waves and the reach of their salty spray, no more than specks.

The house rises up from the windswept cliffs like a chalk monolith. You imagine somebody, God perhaps, has carved it from a giant block of marble, smooth and white with bold lines and straight edges and expansive sheets of glass that reflect the sea and sky like cinema screens. It stands proud and defiant, alien in this coastal place, a place of weathered cottages, ruined mine shafts and precarious birds' nests made of dried seaweed and discarded fishing twine. Its heart beats rhythmically. Drums your ears. Deafens you as you watch them shift like wraiths from one room to another, then outside onto the terrace, their clothes and hair ruffled by a playful onshore breeze.

He sits at the iron table. You hold your breath as you watch him swill his drink around a squat glass with facets cut into it which flash as they catch the light. You are certain you can hear the clink of ice cubes even though you know it's not possible. Your mind is playing tricks. You aren't close enough to hear ice on glass.

Though, of course, you wish you were.

She adjusts her sunglasses and angles her face towards the sun. Her eyes close like a cat as she luxuriates in the heat. You watch her lower herself backwards onto the sun lounger. She stretches her leg out to kiss the edge of the black-tiled swimming pool. Her skin is tanned and silky. It reminds you of toffee and you briefly imagine touching it with the tip of your tongue to taste its creamy sweetness. You feel the chill as she dips her toe into the water. Gentle ripples spread out through the inky darkness which matches the time-blackened rocks that fringe the coast of Cornwall.

You scan the house. The binoculars press hard against your face. You raise your gaze to the top floor windows. Up to the slate roof patched with a yellow mist of lichen. Down to the huge gunnera leaves which loom over a garden awash with vibrant colours, an oasis on the rugged, salt-spritzed clifftop.

I spy.

You focus the binoculars on him again. Run your eyes along the slope of his shoulder. You study the tilt of his head. The way his fingers seem to caress his glass as he concentrates on the newspaper he reads. His legs are crossed. One ankle resting on one knee. Blue leather shoes – the ones you love – cradle his feet like Cinderella's slippers.

Something beginning with P.

She moves and steals your attention. Shifts her weight as she stretches her body and arches her back. One arm reaches over her head. Her fingers rest lightly, stroking something invisible. Waves crash on the rocks below you and the scent of brine hangs in the warm dry air. Two adolescent kittiwakes, new feathers pushing through a haze of down, jostle and screech a safe distance away. You watch them for a few moments then return to the terrace.

To her and to him.

To the white-walled house.

'I spy with my little eye something beginning with P,' you say under your breath.

The man lifts his drink and sips. The woman runs her hand through her honey-blonde hair.

Perfection.

'I spy perfection.'

CHAPTER ONE

Present Day

I lean against the worktop and watch her. Her hands rest lightly on the table. She stares at me, unmoving, impassive. If I didn't know her so well it would be unnerving.

There's a chill in the air and I rub my arms to warm myself. It's good to see her looking so beautiful, her hair shining, skin flawless and eyes bright. Neither of us speak. The silence isn't uncomfortable but I know it won't last. There's a reason she's here.

There always is.

I am unable to hold my tongue any longer. 'Say it then.'

She raises an eyebrow, amused at the sharpness of my tone. 'I was thinking back.' Her voice never fails to take me by surprise, soft and melodic, close to singing.

'To that summer?'

'Yes.' Her face is like a millpond, her expression placid and calm. This is misleading, of course. Beneath the veneer lies a tangle of questions and emotions. 'But my memories are hazy, like half-remembered dreams.'

I turn away from her. Look out of the window. A crack runs diagonally across the glass. Dusty cobwebs are collected in the corners. The paintwork on the frame is peeling and patches of rot caress the edge of the pane. I long to open it. There's a thick smell of mildew in the kitchen and it's catching the back of my throat, but I'm not certain fresh air would be enough to get rid of it, so I leave it closed.

Outside the sky is the colour of a ripened bruise. It hangs low and heavy, threatening thunder. Raindrops spatter the window, run downwards in random paths, merging and barrelling as they grow heavier. I close my eyes and hear the distant echo of Edie's laugh. Remembering her brings with it the smell of seaweed drying in the farthest reach of a spring tide, the tang of salt carried on a summer breeze, the feel of the sun-warmed terrace beneath my feet. My own memories are crystal clear. Each one as crisp and complete as if it happened just hours before.

We met, Edie and I, on the first day of the summer holidays in 1986. Until that moment I didn't know her name or what she looked like. I didn't even know she existed.

But I knew the place she lived.

I knew The Cliff House.

CHAPTER TWO

Tamsyn
July 1986

I sprang out of bed as soon as I woke. It was the first day of the holidays and I couldn't wait to escape.

The house was still. It hung with a silence as thick as pea soup. Mum was at work. My brother was in his bedroom. Door closed. I didn't need to go in to know he was still asleep. Sleeping was pretty much all he'd done since the tin mine shut down. Granfer was also in his room. Although it wasn't really his room. It was Mum and Dad's, but Mum had moved to a fold-up bed in the sitting room when Granfer came to live with us. She wanted him to be comfortable, what with the state of his lungs, she said. I remember when the man from the tip came to pick up the double bed. Jago had dragged it onto the street and the three of us watched as the man and his friend hefted it onto the back of a truck in exchange for a six-pack of beer. Though Mum didn't say, I could tell by her face she was sad to see it go, but, as she said, Granfer needed the space and a chair was more use to him than a bed for two.

His door was open a crack and there he was, in his chair, leaning forward to study the mess of jigsaw pieces scattered on the small table in front of him. I watched him for a minute or two, ready to smile if he noticed me, but he didn't move a muscle, just stared down at the table.

I turned and walked over to the airing cupboard on the landing. Mum used it to keep her stuff in. She'd put the spare sheets and towels in a cardboard box in the corner of Granfer's room, then removed the shelves and put up a hanging rail which she made from a length of pine doweling she picked up from the hardware shop in Penzance. She had to cut it to size with our rusted hacksaw and I remember thinking how well she'd done it despite her not being Dad.

I opened the cupboard door and stared at the clothes inside with her shoes lined up below them in happy pairs. There was a variety of boxes with belts and earrings and her winter hat and scarf on a high shelf above. I ran my finger along clothes on their hangers, enjoying the feel of the different fabrics as I looked for something pretty. Something suitable.

My eyes settled on her rainbow dress and I smiled.

'Perfect.'

A shiver of excitement ran through my body as I took the dress into the bathroom and closed the door behind me. I let my dressing gown fall to the floor and slipped on the dress, smoothing it over my hips and waist, the crepe fabric rough against my skin. Mum kept her make-up in a flowery wash-bag on a wire vegetable rack below the basin along with her shower cap, a soap-on-a-rope we'd never used, and a pot of Oil of Ulay which Jago and I gave her for her last birthday. Inside the wash-bag was a pressed powder she'd had forever, a drying mascara and her lipstick. I took out the lipstick and removed the lid, then turned the base to reveal the scarlet innards. Lifting it to my nose I breathed in. The smell conjured memories of when I was younger, my parents dressed up to go out, perhaps – if it was a special occasion – to the Italian restaurant in Porthleven they loved so much. I pictured her turning a circle for him. Saw him smile, eyes alight, as he leant in to kiss her cheek. It was painful remembering how it was back then. Back then when our house felt like a home.

Home.

Just a memory. Vague and fading. I stared at myself in the mirror above the basin and searched for the ten-year-old girl who'd lived in that happy place. But she was long gone. I drew in a deep breath and touched the tip of my finger to the blood-coloured lipstick, dabbing first its waxy surface and then my lips to add a blush of colour. I dropped the lipstick back into the wash-bag and zipped it up. Then, looking down, I swung left and right to make the rainbow dress swish, imagining my father watching on and smiling.

I went downstairs and glanced into the sitting room as I passed. Her bed was stored neatly behind the settee. The folded duvet and pillow lay on top of it, struck through by a line of sunlight from a gap between the curtains. As I walked into the kitchen I saw two mugs on the table, one with a smudge of lipstick on it, the other without. A sudden sweep of anger washed over me and I snatched them up and marched them to the sink where I turned the tap on, squirted washing-up liquid into the mugs, and reached for the scouring pad. I attacked the one without the red smear the hardest. How had he squirmed his way into the kitchen? I scrubbed, wanting all trace of him gone, then dried the mugs and returned them to the cupboard before squeezing bleach on the table and meticulously cleaning every inch of it, rubbing all the way into the corners and along the edges.

The kitchen hung with the pungent tang of bleach and my mind returned to thoughts of getting out. I stood on tiptoes and reached for the battered biscuit tin on top of the fridge. Inside was a collection of odds and sods, as Mum called them: safety pins, pencil stubs, an assortment of rusted screws and nails, and a variety of keys. Excitement wriggled along my arm and down to the pit of my stomach as I pulled out the key with the green fob. I slipped it into the pocket of the rainbow dress, replaced the tin, then grabbed my bag from the hook in the hallway.

As the front door closed behind me every muscle in my body began to relax. I turned out of our road and headed down towards the Cape, smiling as the breeze took my hair and tossed it playfully about my face. That day the sea was the very same navy as Granfer's favourite knitted Gansey sweater and sprinkled with diamonds of sunlight. High above my head, a handful of seagulls flew in sweeping circles, their distant cries jubilant. An almost perfect day.

As ever my thoughts drifted to Dad. It was impossible to walk down this stretch of road to the Cape without remembering the feel of his hand gripping mine. Or how I'd had to half run to keep up with his stride. I could still picture the book folded into his back pocket, dog-eared, marked on the cover with a single perfect tea-ring. I recalled him reaching for it when he spotted a bird, leafing quickly through the pages before pulling me in close.

Do you see it?

My cheek rested against his stubbled face as he pointed. I didn't care much about the bird. All that mattered was being in his arms.

A golden plover.

Then I'd listen quietly as he told me all about it. That its name came from the word for rain in Latin – or maybe it was Greek – because plovers flock when the weather draws in. After he died, any smidgen of interest I might have had in seabirds waned, but sometimes, when I missed him the most, I'd pretend I loved them and would watch them through the binoculars as they balanced on ledges or dive-bombed for fish, trying to recall their names, population numbers, and the colour of their eggs.

There were only four cars in the car park at Cape Cornwall. It was early though. Later in the day it would be full, vehicles jammed bumper to bumper, with National Trust stickers on their windscreens and woollen picnic rugs folded beneath raincoats in their boots. I joined the coastal path and walked up onto the clifftop where the wind was stronger and my skin spread with goosebumps. I wrapped my arms around my body and told myself off for not bringing a sweater.

The footpath was well worn by walkers who strode from Botallack to Cape Cornwall and on to Sennen Cove in their special boots with canvas sides and long laces double-knotted for safety. My body tingled with excitement as the fields of lush grazing on my left changed to unruly moorland. Pillows of heather and fern stretched away from me in a carpet of green and purple patched with spiky yellow gorse. If I stood still and closed my eyes, I'd be able to hear the rustling of voles and mice which hid from the sparrowhawk circling on the thermals above.

When the footpath bent sharply to the left my body fizzed with anticipation. Four steps until the heart-stone. I counted them. Eyes fixed on the ground in front of me.

One. Two. Three.

Four.

Then there was the stone. The shape of a perfect heart. Grey and polished, with grass kissing its edges like the sea surrounding an island. I placed both feet on top of it then looked up.

My breath caught.

The house gleamed white in the sunshine. A beacon on the cliffs. As always its beauty jolted me like a slap on the face. I saw my father ahead of me, his long legs pounding the path, arms swinging with purpose at his sides. He turned and smiled. Beckoned to me.

Hurry up!

The wind blew his hair and made his eyes glint with weather-tears.

Isn't it beautiful?

'Yes, Dad. It is.'

As he turned to walk onwards, I smiled, then broke into a run to catch up with him.

CHAPTER THREE

Tamsyn
July 1986

I scrambled up the grassy slope that led from the path to the lichen-coated rock on the point. I opened my bag and pulled out my father's binoculars, looping the leather strap over my head and caressing the cool metal with the edge of my thumb.

This was our spot. It was where he took me to watch the sea and the birds. A protrusion of cliff with rocks to shelter us from the wind and weather, and views out to the horizon a thousand miles away, with Sennen Cove to the left and The Cliff House to our right.

It was here that my memories of him were the strongest. Sitting in this spot I could recall him in such Technicolor detail. The patches of sweat which darkened his T-shirt. The individual beads of moisture glistening on his forehead. I could hear his voice telling me to make the most of the sunshine. Warning me the weather wouldn't last. That storms were coming. As I sat and watched the house I felt him beside me.

Isn't it beautiful, Tam?

He jumped to his feet and grabbed my hand, pulling me down to the path and the iron railing which encircled the garden. When he reached over to open the latch on the gate I pulled back.

Are we allowed?

Nobody's home.

Are you sure?

I raised the binoculars to my face and scanned the house and the driveway. There was no movement, no lights or opened windows, no car parked outside. I didn't rush. I gave myself time to make certain nobody was home. When I was sure, I unhooked the strap from my neck and wrapped it around the binoculars and tucked them back in my bag, then stood and walked down to rejoin the footpath.

The white-painted railings were patched with rust, which bled down the uprights in autumnal orange smears. I walked along the edge of the boundary until I reached the gate, then pushed it open enough for me to squeeze through, but not past the point where the hinges creaked. The lawn was the colour of emeralds, soft and mown into stripes by a gardener who came on a Wednesday afternoon and peed in the bushes unaware I was watching. The grass ran from the gate up to the house and was bordered by lush flowerbeds which held plants of every colour and insects that flitted busily between flower heads. I'd looked some of them up in a book of Dad's – *The Comprehensive Guide to the Flora and Fauna of Cornwall and Devon* – and learnt lots of their names by heart. Cordyline, sea pinks, red and lilac poppies, phormium, flowering sea kale, and others I couldn't remember grew amongst copses of bamboo and blue hydrangea. There were ornamental ferns which should have been in the jungle and agapanthus and towering gunnera with giant leaves straight out of *Alice in Wonderland*.

When I reached the terrace I stopped and looked up at the house. It wrapped itself around me like a warm blanket. The air crackled with electricity and the cry of curlews rang in my ears as I drank in its salt-stained white and the soft slips of cloud moving like ghosts across ginormous windows. According to Dad it was something called 'Art Deco', built between the Wars by the heir to an enormous tobacco fortune as a gift for his American wife who'd taken a shine to Cornwall. It was hard to believe that an actual American once lived in St Just. I imagined her walking across this very same terrace, talking American, dressed in pressed white slacks with a silver cigarette case, the spit of Lauren Bacall.

Most of the terrace was taken up by the glorious swimming pool. Rectangular, with semi-circular steps at one end, it was lined with mosaic tiles as black as coal. I walked to the edge of it and trod on my plimsolls to take them off. I heard my mother's voice lecturing me.

Don't break the backs. Undo the laces. No money for more.

The paving stones were warm underfoot. I placed my bag beside my shoes and stared down at the pool. The surface was still. Not even a ripple. It shone like a sheet of black mirror, reflecting the sky like the windows that punctured the house. I bent to put my finger to it and heard the echo of his voice. Saw him smile at me. Saw the glint in his eye. Wavelets spread outwards from my touch and faded to nothing but a shift of light on the disturbed water.

One of her scarves was draped over the sun lounger nearest me. I reached for it. The silk was soft in my fingers. I brought it up to my face and breathed in. It smelt of her perfume, rich and thick, with a hint of coconut suntan oil beneath. I wrapped the scarf around my neck as I'd seen her do a hundred times.

I'd been watching the house on and off since the Davenports

bought it two years earlier from an elderly couple who moved to Spain. I don't know exactly why I first walked up to the point to see the house. Up until that moment I'd avoided it. I'd found the thought of going back to the place too painful. Too much of a reminder of what I'd lost when my father died. But something made me curious. Maybe it was the rumours which had spread through St Just like wildfire. A famous writer. His glamorous wife. Londoners bringing their *fancy ways* to West Penwith. Or perhaps it was hearing the house in overheard conversations, each mention of it bringing a vibrant memory back to me. But whatever the reason for that first visit, I knew within moments it wouldn't be the last. As soon as the house loomed into view it was like a spell had been cast. The connection was undeniable. And then, when I began to watch them – Mr and Mrs Davenport – the connection deepened. As I became increasingly sucked into their lives, going to the house became a heady mix of both memory of my father and dreamy escapism.

I knew their routine well. They only ever came at weekends, arriving late afternoon on a Friday and leaving before noon on the Monday. On as many Fridays as I could manage I'd walk to the point and wait, binoculars primed, praying for the roar of the Jaguar as it careened down the lane. They didn't always appear. There was no way of knowing. Even though Mum went in every week – whether they were coming or not – they never thought to tell her which weekends they'd be there. On the days when they didn't appear I'd feel so let down it physically hurt, deflated by disappointment. It was following one of these no-shows that I braved creeping into the garden, just like I'd done with my dad all those years before.

Adrenalin coursed through me as I walked across the lawn

towards the house. I didn't make it all the way to the terrace before nerves got the better of me and I turned and hared out of the gate to the safety of the footpath. As I paused to catch my breath, my whole body trembled and a bout of excited laughter rippled through me. The thrill of it became an addiction, and while the other kids at school sniffed glue or drank snakebite and black to get their kicks, I walked up to The Cliff House, either to watch the Davenports or explore, depending on the mood which took me.

I stood in front of the window and cupped my hands around my eyes, peering in to double-check it was empty. The sitting room was as spotless as always, not a magazine or an ornament or a picture frame out of place. I thought of my mother dusting and polishing, arranging everything just so, wanting it to be perfect for when they arrived. I felt for the key with the green tag in my pocket and pushed it into the lock. I held my breath as I turned it. There was a loud click. I opened the door and paused to listen. The only sound was the hum of the enormous fridge in the kitchen so I stepped inside and pulled the door closed behind me.

The inside of the house was what I imagined an art gallery would look like. It was cool and quiet with paintings on white walls, unusual pottery dotted about, and a large hunk of grey stone in one corner which was carved into a vague human form. The paintings were oversized canvases with no frames or glass, splashes of colour daubed over them as if someone had poured the paint from a tin instead of brushing it. All were signed in the corner with the name *Etienne* scrawled in an extravagant blue flourish. Truth be told, I didn't think they were that good, but what did I know? There was no way people like the Davenports would put anything on their walls that wasn't the very best. I preferred the photographs, black-and-white close-ups of body parts made to look like the landscape. A woman's breast turned into a hill. A tummy button filled with water to resemble a pool in the desert.

My feet made a soft padding sound as I crossed the room. The polished floorboards shone as if coated with syrup. I walked through the door leading into the kitchen where a central worktop held a neat stack of recipe books, the titles of which I now knew by heart – *Robert Carrier*, *Elizabeth David*, *The F Plan*, *The Complete Scarsdale Medical Diet* – and a pepper mill which was at least a foot tall and the same shade of red as my mother's movie-star lipstick. I struck a pose against the worktop, flicked back my hair, swished my dress.

'Darling?' My voice fractured the stillness. 'Yes, my love? Oh, *darling*, do bring me a Martini. Stirred, if you will. Of course, my love. I'll fetch you one now. Shall I put one of those green things in it, too? I know how you love them so.'

I gave a trill, mimicking the laugh I was sure she'd have.

'*Darling*, you're right. I *do* love them. And, oh, goodness me, isn't it *hot* today? Baking hot. Thank goodness we have the swimming pool. What on earth would we do if we didn't? We'd boil, darling. We'd absolutely *boil*.'

He smiled.

My stomach tightened as he reached out for my hand, then lifted it to his mouth and pressed his lips against my skin.

I smiled and went to the cupboard for a glass, which I filled from the tap. I turned the tap off and the last drips fell against the stainless steel sink with the beat of a slowing clock. As I drank I held my little finger up in a delicate salute. I also took the tiniest sips because people like the Davenports never gulped their water. After I'd rinsed the glass and dried it on my dress, I returned it to the cupboard before walking back through the sitting room and out onto the terrace, where the heat seemed to have intensified.

I walked like a model on a catwalk, swinging my hips from side to side, one foot in front of the other, chin held high. Then I untied the silk scarf and pulled it away from my neck, enjoying the way it caressed my skin. I laid it over the sun lounger exactly as I had found it, watching for a moment as a slight wind ruffled the material and made it dance. I walked over to the swimming pool steps and looked into the water. The blackness was like a dead television screen and for a moment or two I stared at my reflected face, imagined I was floating beneath the surface looking up at the sky. I reached for the zip on my mother's dress and undid it and let it fall to the ground, enjoying the breeze on my sweat-dampened skin.

It was then I felt somebody watching me.

I turned quickly but the terrace was empty and the house still.

I waited. Scanned the house. Searched every window. I'd imagined it.

Nobody's home.

Remembering my father's words reassured me and I turned my attention back to the pool. I took a step into the water. It was heated but not enough to stop goosebumps leaping up across my skin. I rubbed my arms as I waited for the water to settle and when it did, when the ripples had faded to flatness, I stepped down again. Between each step I allowed the wavering surface to still and savoured the growing feeling of calm that enveloped me.

I pushed off the wall and held my head clear of the water, swimming like she did with her swan's neck straight and tall. My strokes were long and slow and as I pulled through the water I focused on the way it soothed my skin. I turned when I reached the end then dived beneath the water and closed my eyes as the silence wrapped around me. I held my breath and waited for the familiar burn in my lungs. As always I allowed the indulgent thought of opening my mouth to pass through my mind.

One breath. Swift and silky. And then…

When the raking pain became too much to bear, I pushed off the floor of the pool and propelled myself upwards. My head broke the surface and I drew a breath in, dragging oxygen deep into my body.

When I heard her voice I screamed.

'What the fuck do you think you're doing?'

CHAPTER FOUR

Tamsyn
July 1986

'What the fuck do you think you're doing?'

My stomach turned over.

There was a figure silhouetted against the sun, features obscured in shadow, standing at the edge of the pool.

My heart pounded as I heaved myself through the water towards the steps.

'I'm… I… Sorry…' The words wouldn't form and my voice stumbled as I clambered out of the swimming pool. I tried to hide my underwear with my hands. Why hadn't I worn a proper swimsuit? Why had I swum in my bra and pants, which were old and baggy and turned see-through with water? 'I'm… I…'

Panic muddied my thoughts. The voice had been female. Who was she? It was a Thursday. The Davenports *never* came on a Thursday. Was it her? Mrs Davenport? Blinded by the sun, it was hard to be certain, but surely that was the only person it could be?

'Answer my question.'

I bent to pick up my dress from the ground and drew it up to my chin to hide my body.

'I'll leave,' I whispered. 'Sorry. I'm sorry.'

She didn't speak. A soft, rhythmic tapping echoed across the terrace. I glanced at the house. The back door was ajar, a breeze worrying it gently against the frame. Everything inside me screamed *run*. I looked down towards the gate and path, my route to freedom.

'Don't even think about it.'

As I looked back at her she blurred like an out-of-focus picture. I swallowed. My throat was dry and my palms sweating, my body numbed by guilt and fear. When she stepped towards me, I readied myself for Mrs Davenport to shriek at me, demand an explanation before calling the police and firing my mum.

But she didn't shriek.

As the figure stepped out of the glare of the sun her face became visible. It wasn't Mrs Davenport. It was a girl, about my own age, maybe a year or two older. She stared at me with her hands on her hips, head cocked to one side. Her eyes were heavily made up with thick black eyeliner dragged upwards into arrowheads. She wore a black skirt that trailed the floor, a black top with holes worn into the sleeves, and a thin leather chord encircling her neck which threatened to throttle her. Her dyed white-blonde hair was cut into an aggressively short bob, framing her elfin face and razor-sharp cheekbones. She radiated an aristocratic confidence that made my breath catch. My mother would have disagreed. She would have hated her make-up and the fact she was so painfully thin. She'd think she looked like an addict. But this girl's skin was too perfect – too porcelain – for that. Eyes too clear. I knew which kids from school did drugs. Their acne, gaunt faces, and wide staring eyes gave them away.

This girl was nothing like them.

Her eyes scanned me as if I were something she was thinking

of buying. I cringed beneath her scrutiny, painfully aware of how spongy and uncared for my body was. Shame swept over me and I desperately tried to arrange the fabric of the dress so it covered more of me.

On her wrists she wore a collection of silver bangles like Madonna and when she crossed her arms they jangled tunefully.

'Who said you could swim here?'

My mouth opened and closed as I grappled to find a reason – any reason – to justify me being there. I thought of my dad. Tried to imagine what flawless excuse he'd have given for our trespassing. Somewhere above me I could have sworn I heard a raven cry and a shiver wriggled through me.

'For God's sake,' she said, tapping her toe against the paving impatiently. 'Put the dress back on if you're that cold.'

I didn't move for a moment or two, but then turned my back and shook out the dress, biting back tears of humiliation as I felt her eyes on my body as I bent to step into it. The fabric clung to my damp skin so I had to tug hard at it, risking tearing the delicate material. I pulled the zip up and faced her. My wet hair dripped down my back as I bit my lower lip to stop myself crying.

The girl raised a single dark and perfectly plucked eyebrow. 'If you don't say something soon, I'm going to call the police and have you locked up.' Her voice oozed with money. 'Who are you and what are you doing here?'

Mum was going to lose her job. I felt sick as I pictured her sitting at the kitchen table, a ragged piece of toilet roll clutched in her fist, red-topped bills surrounding her.

'I'm… I…' My voice stuttered and waned.

The girl looked irritated. 'Well?'

23

Something caught my eye. Eleanor Davenport's silk scarf fluttering in a gust of wind, half-lifting off the sun lounger as if, like me, it was desperate to escape. I glanced at the girl. Her eyes narrowed. Her patience was visibly running out.

'My… mother…'

'*What*? Speak up, for God's sake.'

'My mother,' I said more loudly. 'She… She cleans here. She's the cleaner. I think… I mean, she said… She left her scarf here. She gave me the key.' I pulled the key with the green tag out of my slightly soggy pocket and held it aloft as if this small piece of metal was my passport to being here. 'I looked for it. The scarf. But couldn't see it. I was leaving. And, well, I was hot…' My voice wilted as the little bravery I'd mustered evaporated. 'And the pool… I thought nobody… I'm… I'm sorry.'

For what felt like a century the girl with peroxide hair didn't speak. I shifted on my feet, willing her to send me away with nothing more than a sharp warning never to show my face there again.

'Who were you speaking to?'

'What?' My throat was dry and tight and trapped my voice so it came out in a rasp.

'When you broke in to look for this scarf. I heard you having a conversation. Is there someone else here?' Her eyes flicked from me to the house and back again.

My cheeks burst into flame. 'No… I… I was… Talking to myself.'

'How strange.'

She turned and walked back towards the door. Was this my signal to go? Was I free? I hesitated, about to turn away, but she glanced back with narrowed eyes. 'Don't even *think* about leaving. If you move an inch, you'll be sorry.'

My stomach hardened to a tight ball. Who was she? Why was she here? As I did what I was told and stood stock still, water collecting at my feet, I was hit with the sudden idea that perhaps she might also be trespassing and that in a remarkable twist of fate we'd both arrived at the house, uninvited, at the same time. Perhaps I wasn't the only girl who watched this place from an out-of-sight vantage point and snuck in when nobody was home.

This thought bought a little clarity with it. My mind seemed to demist. Whoever she was, whatever reason she had to be here, the most important thing was to convince her not to tell the Davenports. If Mum lost her job she'd have to do more hours at the bloody chip shop or, worse still, sign on, something I knew full well she'd rather die than do.

The girl walked back out of the door. She held two bottles in her hand and an opener in the other.

'I like your dress,' she said as she neared me.

I wasn't sure if I'd heard her correctly so didn't say anything in return.

'Where did you get it?'

'My dress?'

She made a face like I was stupid. 'Er, yeah, your *dress*.'

'It's my mum's. From the Sixties. She wore it to a Rolling Stones concert.'

'Retro?' Her eyes blinked slowly. '*Très* fashionable.'

I let my breath go with a nervous laugh. I was struck again by how pretty she was. Not pretty like Alice Daley or Imogen Norris – who were universally acknowledged to be the prettiest girls in school, all pushed-up boobs and bum-skimming skirts. No, this girl was graceful and poised and pretty like Princess

25

Di, if Princess Di wore black make-up, a hundred bangles and had a silver stud in her nose.

'*Très*… cool,' she said.

I managed to nod.

'You're very lucky to have a cool mother. Mine,' she said deliberately, 'is very, *very*, *un*cool.'

I thought of the photograph of my parents, the one that had his writing on the back:

Angie and Me. Odeon Theatre, Guildford, March 1965.

In the picture my mum wore the rainbow dress. She was seventeen, not long engaged, delirious with love. Her hair was held back by a thick red scarf, feline eyes outlined with liner, her lips and skin pale as was the fashion. My dad wore a white shirt and a thin black tie. His hair was slicked back and he held a cigarette loosely in his fingers. I closed my eyes for a second, caught a flash of him singing me to sleep, smelt the cigarettes stuck to his skin.

'Would you like a drink?' She gestured to the bottles in her hand. Coca-Cola – the real thing, in curvaceous glass bottles like the ones I'd seen shiny, happy Americans with white-toothed smiles selling on the television.

'Who are you?'

She gave no indication of having heard me. Maybe I'd spoken too quietly. She walked over to the table and put the bottles down, then using the opener she flicked the caps off each in turn, the cola fizzing loudly as she threw them onto the table. One bounced across the iron fretwork and fell with a tinny clink against the paving stones.

'I think I should go.'

'If you leave, I'll tell my mother you broke into our house and I found you rifling through her jewellery box.'

Horror mushroomed inside me so violently I thought I might be sick.

'Your mother?' I didn't understand. They didn't have a daughter. Mum had never mentioned one. There was nothing in the house that indicated they had children – no photos, no clothes, no posters in any bedrooms. Was she lying?

'Yes. My mother. More's the pity.' She sat on one of the chairs and lifted her bare feet onto the table and crossed them at the ankle. I'd never seen toenails painted purple before and never heard of people wearing rings on their toes, but she wore three and her nails were the colour of autumn plums.

'Are they here?' My voice quivered. Why had I been so careless? How stupid could I be?

'My mother's shopping while my father gets something fixed on the Jag. A tyre or, God, I don't know, something dull. My mother will already be in a filthy mood because she won't have found anything worth buying and will be moaning about Cornwall being stuck in the Dark Ages and wondering why anybody ever leaves Chelsea.'

'My mum can't lose her job,' I whispered.

She stared at me for a moment or two, her expression flat, but then her body seemed to soften.

'Relax.' Her voice had lost its sharpness. 'You don't need to worry. I'm not going to tell them. I don't give a shit about you swimming in the pool. I mean, why wouldn't you? It's hot as hell today.'

I could have cried with relief.

'Go on. Stay for a bit. I'm literally dying of boredom. You can leave before they get back.' She pushed one of the bottles towards me. 'Have a Coke.'

'I've never had a real Coke, only the one they do at Wimpy.' And even then I'd only tried it once, though I didn't tell her that.

She furrowed her brow and a bemused smile flashed across her face as she reached for the bottle nearest her and tipped it up to her lips. I inhaled sharply, shocked by how much she resembled Mrs Davenport in that split second. As I stared at her I noticed other similarities between her and her parents. Her face was the same shape as his. The sweeping curve of her neck was identical to hers. How stupid not to see these things immediately. Stupid not to have guessed who she was. Their daughter. Her house. A surge of irrational jealousy shuddered through me like an electric charge.

The girl looked up at me whilst shielding her eyes from the sun. 'For God's sake sit down.' She kicked the empty chair and it scraped against the paving.

The movement jolted me into action and I walked towards her. I hesitated as I reached the table, wondering if it might be a trap and when I sat down she'd laugh and say, 'Ha! Idiot! As if someone like *you* could actually sit with someone like *me*?'

But she didn't. She smiled.

From nowhere a waft of her perfume swept over me. I had a vivid recollection of Truro. The shopping centre. My mother rummaging through the bottles and sprays in The Body Shop. Taking lids off. Pumping scent onto her wrists. Then mine. Ignoring the hard stares of the lady behind the counter.

'White Musk.'

'Sorry?'

Had I said that aloud? 'Your perfume,' I said quickly. 'It's White Musk.'

'You're quite unusual, aren't you? Not that it's a bad thing. I

28

like unusual.' She blew upwards over her forehead. 'Christ, it's hot.' She took hold of her top and flapped it.

We were silent. She didn't seem to mind but it made me itch. When the awkwardness became unbearable I turned my head to look out over the sea. The wind had painted dashes of white across its surface and a small boat sat out near the horizon. So far away. Little more than a dot. I thought of the day my dad died. How quickly the squall had rolled in, turning sunshine and blue skies to driving rain and treacherous waves within moments. A crack of thunder echoed in my ears as I recalled snatching hopelessly at his legs to stop him leaving the safety of our house.

'My name's Edie, by the way.'

She waited expectantly but when I didn't reply I saw her expression fade to boredom.

For God's sake speak.

'I like it.'

'What?'

'Your name. I like it.'

She stared at me for a moment then burst into laughter which sounded like sleigh bells. She tipped her head back. Exposed her throat. Pale and delicate. It struck me how vulnerable that part of her was and I hurriedly banished the thought of my hands encircling it and squeezing until her white skin bruised.

I thought she might let me in on the joke but she didn't. 'My mother chose it,' she said. 'It's short for Edith. Piaf. Eleanor thinks it's glamorous. Anything – and everything – *à la France est très glamoureux, cherie* according to *Maman*.'

The accent she used on some of her words reminded me of my French teacher, Madame Thomas, who came from Widemouth

Bay but turned puce with rage if we failed to pronounce her surname 'Toh-*maah*'. Thinking of ridiculous Madame Toh-*maah* made me braver and I ventured a smile in return.

'And yours?' Edie Davenport lifted her bottle and studied the Coke inside as she tipped it from side to side like a pendulum.

I hesitated. Should I make something up? Re-christen myself something *très glamoureux*? Esmerelda perhaps? Or maybe Ruby or Anastasia?

'God,' she said, rolling her eyes. 'It's not a difficult question. Someone tells you their name then asks you yours and you reply. Didn't your mother teach you any manners between cleaning jobs?'

Edie brushed something, a fly perhaps, off one of her knees. I noticed how smooth and free of blemishes her legs were. Hairless with skin as white as a china doll except for the soles of her feet which were soft and pink like the inside of a kitten's ear. I thought of my own legs covered ankle to thigh in fine hairs bleached by the sun, the skin peppered with scratches from brambles and mysterious bruises, my feet hardened and cracked and my toenails uneven and in need of a trim.

Edie cleared her throat and raised her eyebrows as she sipped her drink. Her eyes were bolted onto me.

Speak.

'Tamsyn.'

'Tamsyn.' She rolled my name around her tongue like the Coke she swilled in the bottle. 'Yes. It's the perfect name for a thief.'

My stomach pitched. 'No! I'm not a thief! I was here to find—'

'Yes, yes.' Edie gave a dismissive flick of her hand. 'The cleaner's scarf. You said.'

'I should go.' My voice trembled and when I lowered my eyes, I saw the tremble mirrored in my quivering hem.

'You can't. I've already taken the lid off the Coke.' Edie gestured at the second bottle on the table. 'You're being rude again.'

'Rude?'

'Yes. *Rude*. I invited you to sit down with me and you haven't. That's *rude*.'

So I sat quickly because the last thing I wanted to be was rude. She flashed me a half-smile and tipped the Coca-Cola to her lips. I'd have given anything to have a fraction of her confidence and swagger, to have what she had, her father's casual indifference, her mother's grace and sophistication.

Even though the silence bore down on us like ten tonnes of lead, Edie didn't seem to care one bit. But I did. I was desperate to speak but it was as if my lips were sewn together with fishing twine which looped through my skin. I imagined wrenching my mouth open so I could say something, the stitches ripping my lips to blood and tatters.

I ran my finger down the length of the bottle, traced the ridges, the gathered condensation wetting my skin.

'Try it.'

I raised the bottle and sipped. Bubbles exploded on my tongue and the cloying sweetness made me smile involuntarily.

She shifted in her chair and tucked her legs beneath her body. 'Have you swum here before?'

'No.' My dishonesty flared hot beneath my skin. I thought of my father and I in the pool. His arms wrapped around me. His eyelashes laced with droplets of water like tiny pearls. 'I didn't know they had a daughter,' I said, wanting to steer away from the subject of my trespassing. Talking about Edie was safer. I just had to keep her talking about anything other than me.

She seemed amused by this. 'Do you know much about them then?'

I shook my head. Another lie. I knew lots. I knew what newspaper he read, what clothes they wore, the position he sat in when he wrote at his typewriter. I knew she turned her sun lounger to follow the arc of the sun and when, every now and then, a sparrowhawk cried out he'd look up and search the sky for it. I knew they let food go to waste. That vegetables were left to blacken in the fridge beside sour milk, and that abandoned bread grew mould in the shiny steel bread bin. I knew they left their bed unmade when they left for London and I knew where they kept the sheets my mother would change for them. I knew what books were piled up on his bedside table and what her night cream smelt like and how soft her silk dressing gown felt against my cheek.

Edie lifted the Coke bottle and drained the last inch. 'To be honest, I wouldn't expect anyone to know they have a daughter. They're barely aware of it themselves. They keep me in a boarding school so they don't have to think about it.'

'A boarding school?'

Edie nodded.

I had visions of great Gothic buildings and *Malory Towers*, hockey sticks and midnight feasts and huge panelled dining rooms where hundreds of these girls, identikit clones, gathered to sip soup from round silver spoons.

'That must be amazing.'

'It's the pits. I *loathe* it. Every single girl there is a bitch and the teachers are idiots. Literally everybody there hates me and I hate them.' She rolled her eyes. 'The head says I'm *trouble*. Rude and difficult. But,' and here she paused and leant forward, 'what the flying *fuck* does *she* fucking know about anything anyway?'

I couldn't help but smile, and as I did the tension I'd been feeling since we first laid eyes on each other finally started to fade.

Then she needled her eyes at me and pointed. '*You* don't hate me, do you?'

'No!' I said quickly. 'Not at all.'

She sat back. 'Anyway,' she said. 'It's probably a good thing the *'rents* keep me in a boarding school. If they didn't I'd be tempted to murder them. Maybe not him but definitely her.'

She smiled at me and I smiled back and as I did invisible strands of friendship began to stretch out between us.

'Where do you go to school?'

'The local comp. It's a dump.'

'I'd give anything to go to a comprehensive. Boarding school is so lame. Being at a comprehensive is cool, isn't it? I bet you don't even have to work. Our teachers are obsessed with results and the girls spend most of their time bingeing and chucking up. You're actually really lucky.'

I thought about my school – teachers drowned out by constant chatting, blocked toilets with permanent *Out of Order* signs on them, the stench of the canteen – and shrugged.

'Anyway, I'm imprisoned here for the holidays which is beyond dull. Are you in Cornwall for the summer too?'

I wondered where she thought I might be going. France, maybe? On one of those exchanges where you swap families? Or New York or Tokyo or India? I didn't answer immediately, allowing myself to enjoy a few precious seconds where as far

33

as Edie Davenport was concerned, I was someone who could have a life beyond St Just.

When the pause grew uncomfortable, I nodded. 'Yes, I'm here the whole time.'

'And presumably you have no friends?'

Her assumption took the wind out of me. I opened my mouth to protest but then decided not to. She was, after all, correct.

'Good,' she said emphatically. 'Then you and I will hang out. We'll be holiday friends. It'll be fun.'

Holiday friends? The thought made my skin tingle.

'I mean, *Jesus*,' she said. 'The thought of being stuck in this place with nobody to talk to for six weeks is unbearable.'

I looked up at the house and wondered if there was anywhere on this planet I'd prefer to be stuck.

Edie gave an impatient sigh. 'Well then?' Her question was laced with irritation. It dawned on me she might be reading my silence as lack of enthusiasm so I nodded quickly.

From nowhere a gust of wind blew. Dust and bits of last year's leaves were lifted off the terrace in a flurry. Eleanor Davenport's scarf again caught my eye as it was scooped up and tumbled through the air. The wind dropped as suddenly as it had picked up and the scarf fell. It floated downwards to settle on the surface of the pool. The material darkened as it sucked in the water and sank slowly until it hung suspended as if trapped in aspic.

As I stared at the scarf, the stillness was torn in two by a screech. The noise was instantly recognisable. I jumped and grabbed the table instinctively, catching the edge of one of the bottles with my hand. It fell and Coke spilled through the fretwork and collected on the paving slabs below the table.

'Oh, I'm... sorry...' I reached for the bottle and quickly righted it whilst casting my eyes about in search of the raven, which I knew was lurking somewhere close.

My skin prickled. I scoured the lawn, the trees, the railings, but there was no sign.

'I have to go.'

'Are you all right?'

'Yes. My grandad. I need to get back to see him. He isn't well.' I glanced up and scanned the sky and the roof of the house. I let out a breath. There it was. The raven. Perched on the guttering of the roof. Black feathers buffeted by the wind coming off the sea. It screeched again and the sound cut through me like a shard of glass.

I had a vivid flash of the raven on the path. The one Dad and I had seen that day as we hurried home beneath a darkening sky, the first drops of rain spattering our faces.

My lungs tightened.

It's just a bird.

I could feel the heat of its eyes on me. Polished black marbles. Charcoal beak shining.

'Will you tell your parents about me?' I said as I stood.

She didn't answer immediately.

'Please don't.'

'I said I wouldn't,' she said a little crossly. 'So I won't.' Then she gave me a teasing smile. 'Not today anyway.'

CHAPTER FIVE

Edie
July 1986

Edie reached out of her window and struck a red-tipped match against the wall. The head burst into flame with a sputter and she held it to the end of her cigarette, the tobacco crackling as it caught. She inhaled then hung her hand out of the window to allow the smoke to curl upwards into the sky rather than into her room. Not that she cared if her parents smelt it. What were they going to do? Send her back to London? Hardly a punishment.

She could still see Tamsyn on the cliffs in the distance. She leant against the window frame as she smoked, her eyes fixed on the girl's retreating figure, knotted red hair trailing behind her like a knight's pennant.

The blazing sun had disappeared behind light grey clouds and it had started to rain. The relief from the heat was welcome. The rain wasn't normal rain but that particular drizzly nothingness Edie only ever saw in Cornwall. More mist than rain. Cornwall had its own weather system as far as she could tell. There was nothing predictable about it at all. She watched the fine spots of water marking the cigarette, tiny dots turning its whiteness a translucent grey, the same grey, in fact, as Tamsyn's childish cotton bra.

Edie had never met anybody that innocent before. That sheltered. It was so striking she wondered if perhaps it was put on. A well-rehearsed act designed to elicit sympathy and ward off punishment for breaking into houses. Clever if it was. Unnecessary though. Edie didn't give a shit about her being in the house. When she'd heard noises downstairs her first thought was she was going to be kidnapped by someone who'd then send her father a ransom note made from newspaper cuttings demanding thousands of pounds, so it was quite a relief to discover a girl her own age as terrified as a rabbit in a snare. Plus she'd literally been about to kill herself with boredom and Tamsyn was a perfect distraction.

When Tamsyn finally disappeared out of view, Edie took a last drag then roughly stubbed her cigarette out on the wall below the window, which stained the paintwork with another charcoal smudge and sent out a shower of tiny sparks. She flicked it and it skimmed through the air and landed on the terrace below. She watched the cigarette end smoulder until it burnt out, a thin trail of smoke wending its way upwards and dissolving to nothing. She lifted her head and looked out over the sea. A handful of boats dotted the blue, and the horizon lay in the distance with exciting lands beyond, each of them offering a different adventure, like chocolates in a box.

She closed the window and shut out the sounds of the waves and gulls, then cast her eyes around the bedroom with disdain. Stuck here for the whole damn summer. Jesus. It was no better than a prison cell. Nothing more than essential furniture – a bed, a wardrobe, a bedside table – and grim cream and grey striped curtains at the window. There were no pictures. No plants in pots. The only thing of mild interest were the four white walls, which changed shade as the sun moved through the day. Edie thought of Tamsyn in the house, her wild hair and regional accent contaminating the designer emptiness which Edie's parents believed to be the height of sophistication. *Minimalism* they called it – *all the rage in New York, darling* – which as far as Edie could tell meant echoing rooms with too much white and expensive pieces of statement furniture chosen to be coveted not used. But in this room, her room, the minimalism wasn't a design feature. This was just a room that didn't matter.

Edie lay back on the bed. She'd had a dismal end of term. Everything had spiralled from bad to worse and now she'd had enough of every single person she knew. If life were a poker game, she'd swap her whole hand of cards. Her father barely knew she existed. Her mother was forever gummed up with pills – pills to wake up, pills to calm down, pills for energy, pills for sleep – all liberally washed down with whatever booze was closest to hand. Edie had been in Cornwall for four days and was already climbing the walls. Most of her time was spent daydreaming about escape. Shoving a few things into a bag and leaving in the dead of night, walking down the moonlit lane to the main road and hitching a lift to anywhere. But of course she wouldn't do it. Everybody knew girls like her who hitchhiked alone got raped or strangled.

Maybe Tamsyn would be enough to get her through the summer. She was certainly interesting. Unusual. Different to the people Edie usually met. She was the daughter of a cleaner for starters. The people Edie knew were all the offspring of doctors or barristers or duller-than-dull bores who ran boring companies doing boring things with numbers. Her own father was something of an anomaly, a well-known restaurant critic turned *New York Times* bestseller. Whilst her mother was a tragic cliché. A failed model turned socialite wife with a penchant for getting off her face. Between them they didn't have one friend who was a cleaner or a shopkeeper or anything remotely normal. They'd sealed themselves in a bubble and floated about in a manufactured world of braying voices, nauseating opinions, and a universal lack of morals. It made Edie's stomach heave. Having no friends was better than having fake ones.

She reached for her Walkman and slipped the headphones on. Yes. Hanging out with Tamsyn, the trespassing daughter of a cleaner, with unkempt red hair and a look of adoration, would hopefully make the purgatory more bearable.

At the very least it would seriously piss Eleanor off.

CHAPTER SIX

Present Day

'*A*re you still scared of ravens?'

My hands instinctively ball tightly. Where did that question come from?

I check my rear-view mirror, indicate, turn the wheel. The back seat of the car is piled up with shopping bags. She sits in the passenger seat. Her hands rest on her lap, motionless, ankles crossed, skirt risen above her knees. Her legs are blemish-free; nothing, not even a freckle marks them. It's as if she's been airbrushed.

We skirt Hayle. Drive past the mudflats revealed by the tide. Sea birds pick over the exposed silt in search of razor clams and worms and the remains of dead fish.

'*I remember how you were back then. Terrified, weren't you?*'

I don't answer. I can't. The familiar dread gathers in my stomach like a sponge soaking up tar. I glance at her. She's staring at me, eyes fixed, challenging me. She won't let this go. She'll push and push. I have no choice but to answer.

'*Yes,' I say.*

'*Because of the one you saw the day he died?*'

I don't reply.

'*Tell me.*'

'You know.'

'Tell me again.' Her voice has dropped to a low angry rumble and my stomach tightens.

'It was on the path,' I whisper. Tears prick the backs of my eyes. I don't want to think about it. 'Black all over. Calm. It had eyes like tiny lacquered marbles. The sky was getting darker and darker, pressing down on us. In its beak…' My voice is choked by a knot of emotion. 'Long thin strands. Like spaghetti. I grabbed his hand. "It's just a raven," he said. Granfer says ravens make bad things happen, I whispered. He saw one at the mine once and the next day the tunnel collapsed and two men were crushed.'

I see my father's face then. He's laughing at me. Telling me not to believe such superstitious nonsense. I try hard to recall the sound of his laughter but it's elusive. If only I'd known it would be the last time I'd hear that noise I'd have listened harder, sucked the sound of it right into myself, etched it onto my brain forever.

'"Don't be daft, Tam," he said. "Granfer's an old fool. Ravens are just birds. Species genus Corvus. He's trying to scare you. Too much of the Hitchcock in that one. Don't you worry."'

'But you were right to worry.'

'Yes.'

We round the bend and I slow to a halt to let a farmer cross with his cows. Their underbellies swing as they walk, hip bones pushing against black-and-white hides, tails chasing away the flies. The farmer raises his hand in thanks. Then he does a double take. Stares. Brow furrowed in vague – or perhaps judgemental – recognition.

I put the car into gear and drive onwards. The farmer lifts

the iron gate into place, stick resting against the dry-stone wall, his fleeting interest in me gone.

'What was in the raven's beak?'

I recall how I pressed myself tight into my father, wary eyes bolted onto the bird, my body flooding with building horror.

'A chick,' I say softly. My hands grip the steering wheel. Knuckles white. 'The entrails of a dead chick.'

Flashes of that small pink body batter me. Flecked with newly emerging feathers. Sodden and bloodied. Its stomach ripped open. Entrails, tiny and thin, spewing from the ragged hole. Its baby head twisted unnaturally, spindly legs broken, wings spread-eagled. One eye bulging beneath a translucent membrane. The other pecked out.

'A kittiwake. A day or two old, Dad said.'

Then without warning the raven had taken flight. Startled me so I squeezed my father tighter. The bird beat the air with powerful wings, dark feathers outstretched, body rising like a phoenix into the bruising sky.

I take a breath and shift my weight as I change gear. I glance out of the window to my right. The sea is silver today. Touched white in places where the wind annoys it. Foreboding wraps around me like a cloak. I pull in to a lay-by. A caravan passes, its driver red-faced, stressed as he negotiates the narrow Cornish lanes and unforgiving locals who speed around corners primed and ready to shake their fists at the tourists.

'You saw a raven the day I left, didn't you?'

I look across at her. She is staring straight ahead. My breathing grows tight as if my lungs are silting up. A gull cries and the shadow of a cloud passes over us.

'Yes,' I say. 'I saw a raven that day too.'

43

CHAPTER SEVEN

Tamsyn
July 1986

I knocked on Granfer's door as I pushed it open and walked in. My whole body was buzzing from my morning. The raven on the roof was forgotten, blanked out so I was free to relish every moment I'd spent at the house.

'Hi,' I said. 'I made you a sandwich.'

Granfer hadn't moved and was still sitting in the worn leather chair he'd had forever. I never understood how he could spend so long staring at the same muddle of jigsaw pieces. It would have driven me mad. But Granfer could sit at the table for hours on end, happy in his own world, poring over the spread of shapes on the table Mum got for him a few years earlier. She'd found the table in the Salvation Army shop in Penzance and brought it back on the bus as proud as could be. It looked like junk to me, with its sun-bleached flimsy laminate top and legs riddled with woodworm, and sure enough, as she set it down in the kitchen, she'd beamed and announced it only cost a pound.

It took her three evenings, a yard of green felt from the haberdashers in Hayle, and a staple gun she borrowed from school to transform it into what she grandly called a *card table*, perfect, she'd said with a wide smile, for holding a jigsaw.

It wasn't perfect, but Granfer loved it. Told her it reminded him of one they'd had when Robbie was small, which they'd use for games of Gin Rummy and Snap.

Granfer's attention switched from the jigsaw to me as I neared him. I put the sandwich on the table, and kissed him on his hair, which was thick and white with a yellow tinge and in need of a wash.

'Fish paste on white sliced.'

'Lovely,' he said. 'I was feeling a… bit peckish.'

'How's it going?' I gestured at the puzzle.

'Got the corners… and that far… edge. But… blimey… it's a bugger.'

'I'll give you a hand.'

I sat on the small stool beside him and leant over the table, resting my chin on one hand to stare at the pieces. His breathing was loud in my ears. Each inhalation a fight to draw air into his lungs which had been ruined by dust from the mines. I tuned out his painful rasping by reliving my encounter with Edie Davenport. I savoured every detail, from the warmth of the paving stones beneath my feet, to the look of admiration she gave my dress, to each delicious elongated vowel which dripped from her lips. It was all so unreal, too unreal perhaps. If it wasn't for the syrupy taste of Coca-Cola lingering in my mouth, I'd worry the whole episode was a figment of my imagination.

A triumphant holler from Granfer intruded on my thoughts. He patted my knee with excitement and launched forward to slot the piece of puzzle he'd found into the space that matched it in the jigsaw. It was a section of sky, half cloud, half blue, and he jabbed it vigorously into place.

'Well… that's one step… closer to finishing. Only another

two… hundred and fifty-seven… to go.' He beamed at me, revealing his crooked stained teeth, and a glint of gold from an ancient filling. 'I'll have… it done in a… jiffy.'

'Would you like a cup of tea?'

'Ta, love.' His eyes drifted back to the pieces again. 'With two and a half… please.'

'Mum says no more than one.'

He made a face.

'So don't tell her, okay?'

He winked and tapped the side of his nose. As he did he erupted into a fit of coughing. Though I'd seen this a hundred times – coughing, spluttering, fingers bent into claws as they dug into the arms of his chair – it still shocked me. You'd have thought I'd got used to it, but each time, with each attack, I was terrified it wasn't going to stop until his oxygen-starved body collapsed dead on the floor.

I reached for his hand and rubbed it helplessly. His eyes widened and the whites turned bloodshot as the effort of pulling air into his ravaged lungs popped capillaries in tiny scarlet explosions. He struggled to get his handkerchief from his sleeve and to his mouth.

I jumped up and went to the bed. Dragged the oxygen tank close enough to get the mask over his head. As I moved his hand out of the way to position it over his nose and mouth, I tried not to look at the blood on the cotton of his handkerchief.

'Breathe, Granfer.' His body was rigid as if somebody was sending an electric charge through him. 'Breathe.' The plastic mask misted and cleared with the breaths he managed to draw in. I chewed my lip, wondering if I should leave him to shake Jago awake, but just as I was about to stand up, the tortured

47

gasps seemed to abate and Granfer's face lost its violent purple hue. I glanced down at the smear of dark blood on the handkerchief. He caught me looking and balled it up to hide it.

When I was younger I used to daydream he had a transplant, that his black and shrivelled lungs were cut out and fresh pink ones sewn into their place. I'd imagine him waking from the anaesthetic with silent breathing, air slipping in and out of him discreetly and without pain. I'd see him flying kites on Sennen Beach with me and Jago, or rowing us out to catch mackerel and ling which we'd later bake into a stargazy pie, little fish heads poking out from the pastry with their eyes cooked to a cloudy grey.

'I've met a friend,' I said, when his body lost the last of its rigidity. 'She lives in the white house on the cliff. You know the one? The one Dad loved.'

He gestured for me to lift up his mask and I did, leaving it on his forehead like a jaunty Christmas party hat. 'Is she as nice... as Penny?'

Granfer had only met Penny once. It was a few years ago when she knocked on our door with a school sweater of mine.

This is Tamsyn's.

My heart had skipped when I recognised her voice. Someone from my school at our house? It felt dangerous and unsafe, as if two planets had veered off orbit and crashed into each other.

She's here... Do you... want to see... her?

No, it's fine—

Tamsyn!

Then he'd collapsed into one of his fits and I'd run out from my hiding place behind the door in the sitting room to make sure he was okay. Penny was eyeing my grandad with thinly veiled revulsion. I noticed he had a globule of mucus threaded with blood on his sweater. I wiped it off with my sleeve then slipped my hand into his and squeezed. I faced her, pushing back my shoulders and raising my chin. She thrust out my sweater.

I picked it up by mistake.

I gave her the evils as I took it but she didn't notice because she'd gone back to staring at Granfer.

Thanks then.

Penny forced a tight smile and stepped backwards off the doorstep.

Mum said to say hi to yours.

Then she was gone like a dog from the traps. Penny was the only person from school who'd ever come to our house and because of this Granfer had decided she was my best friend.

'She's nicer than Penny,' I said.

'Must be… a cracker then.' He smiled and lowered the mask and went back to the jigsaw pieces, with the sound of oxygen hissing softly in the background.

I left his room and stood outside Jago's door. I paused to listen. I wanted to wake him so he could tell me not to worry about Granfer's fit. He always managed to calm me. But I knew if I dragged him from sleep he'd be cross and would probably refuse to talk to me, so instead I went back into my box. I called it *my box* because that's what it was. A room with only enough space for a bed and a small bedside table. The door didn't open fully and hit the bed before it was even halfway. There was a shelf that ran around the top of the room which Dad had made before I was born, when they decided to use the box room for my cot rather than make Jago share with a baby. It held my clothes and although I could only get to it if I stood on my bed it was fine as long as I kept them in neat folded piles. My underwear was under the bed in a wooden crate that had once held oranges from Spain, and beside it was another box which contained all my other bits and pieces including my scrapbook.

I slid the box out and retrieved the scrapbook then sat cross-legged on the bed and slowly leafed through it. There was the yellowed newspaper cutting that made the announcement of the date and time his memorial plaque was to be unveiled at the RNLI station in Sennen. Then the small red flower I'd picked from a bush at the churchyard on the day we buried him, which was now dry and crispy. There were photographs too. One of me on his shoulders, his hands clasping my ankles, the remains of an ice cream smudged over my face. My favourite was the one of me and Jago, arms around each other, heads tipped close with Dad behind us, all posing beside the sandcastle we'd built and smiling at Mum behind the camera. Three sets of happy eyes squinting into the sunshine.

I made the scrapbook when I was twelve. Nineteen months and twenty-three days after he died. Mum had taken me to the Cape surgery, desperate for anything which might help me sleep through the night.

She has nightmares.

Mum had paused and rubbed her face hard, tears welling in her exhausted, bloodshot eyes.

The doctor glanced at the clock on the wall and cleared his throat impatiently. He leant forward, elbows on knees, close enough to suffocate me with his nasty aftershave and told me to fill a scrapbook with things which reminded me of Dad. Happy things. Memories. Mum was unconvinced and grumbled about the *quack doctor* all the way to Ted's as I jogged to keep up with her. But she did as she was told and bought a scrapbook made of coloured sugar-paper and a glue stick. It didn't stop my nightmares but I loved making it and when I felt tense it definitely calmed me. I was glad the doctor suggested it.

My brother's door creaked open and I heard his footsteps going towards the bathroom. I closed the book and slipped it beneath my pillow for later, then went into his room. I sat on his unmade bed – still warm from his body and smelling of cigarettes and unwashed sheets – to wait for him.

'Morning, half-pint,' he said as he came back in, hair ruffled, eyes gummed up with sleep.

'You know it's after lunchtime, don't you?'

He ignored my comment. 'First day of the holidays?'

I nodded.

'Bored already?'

'No.' I reached for the copy of *Playboy* which lay on the chest of drawers beside his bed and idly flicked through it while he dressed. I paused to look at a dark-haired girl with wet lips the colour of bubblegum who splayed her legs to reveal her privates without any shame at all.

'Blimey,' I said. 'Not leaving much to the imagination is she?'

'Get off that,' he snapped, as his head emerged from his faded AC/DC T-shirt. He snatched it from me then opened his top drawer and stuffed it under his pants and socks.

'Why do you want to look at pictures like that anyway?'

'I don't look at the pictures. I buy it for the stories and articles.'

I laughed. 'Yeah, *right*.'

His irritation slipped for a second or two to reveal a brief smile. He smiled so rarely these days, which was such a shame

51

because when he did it made his eyes sparkle and he looked even more handsome. His eyes were definitely one of his best features. They were hazel, and the exact same shade as his hair. Colour-coordinated, according to Mum. But they were nearly always dulled by sadness. Laughter replaced by melancholy. His spirit sucked out, leaving just the pretty packaging. Dad dying was bad enough, but then the mine closed and took his job and in the months since then he hadn't been able to find work. The guilt bore down on him. Dad had been big on work and responsibility, believed with passion that everybody should pay their own way in the world.

Graft, he called it.

Graft. That's all I expect. You can't hold your head up if you're not willing to graft.

Mum had tried to hide her fear when Jago told her the mine was done for. White-faced, she'd sat at the table and leafed through the red-topped bills to work out which ones needed paying soonest.

It'll be okay, love. You'll get another job soon. I know you will.

Wracked by the weight of responsibility, his face had fallen. I'd seen that look on him before. The day after our father died. I'd walked into the kitchen and found him huddled on the floor with his arms clutched around his legs and his cheeks stained with dirty tear-tracks. I was ten, mad with hunger, and even though I'd knocked and knocked, Mum hadn't come out of her room. I told him I was starving but he didn't reply. He didn't even move, not a muscle, and it scared me. It was as if he and Mum had stopped working. As if their batteries had run out.

Jago?

I knelt down next to him and put my hand on his knee.

Jago? Can you hear me? It's like rats gnawing my belly up.

Maybe it was because I used Dad's words – what he used to say to us when we were starving hungry – because Jago seemed to click back on. He turned to look at me and I could see his brain whirring behind his eyes. Then he gave a purposeful nod and stood. I sat on the floor, stomach rumbling, and watched him silently walk to the cupboard and get out a pan. Then he took a wooden spoon from the drawer and three eggs from the rack, and set about scrambling them, cracking each into a mug and whisking them with the fork. After he'd heated the eggs on the gas he tipped them onto a slice of toast on a plate and put the plate on the table with a fork beside it. Then he walked back to me, reached for my hand and led me to the table. I stared at the eggs. Two tiny bits of shell decorated the top.

He noticed me looking and picked them out with his fingers.

Eat up, Tam.

The eggs weren't bad, but I couldn't take more than a mouthful. I think my tummy was hurting because of crying not hunger, because the food was too hard to swallow and got stuck in my throat like lumps of rock. Jago squeezed my hand and we both sat and stared at the cold egg.

I'm the dad now, aren't I?

His whispered voice had cracked the silence in two.

I often look back and wish I'd told him, *No, of course not, you're a child who's lost his father.* But I didn't. I was frightened and sad and missed my dad so much I could hardly breathe.

Right at that moment, having Jago as my dad was a better prospect than having no dad at all. So I looked at him and nodded solemnly.

Yes, you are. You're the dad now.

Jago and I heard the front door open then close, and then Mum call up to tell us she was home.

'Right, I'll see you later, half-pint. If she asks just say I'm doing a shift at the yard, okay?' He grabbed his jacket and pouch of tobacco from the chest of drawers.

'When are you going to tell her?'

'Tell her what?'

'That you don't actually have a job at the yard.'

He stopped dead, defences up as if I'd flicked a switch. He glared at me. 'You serious?'

'You shouldn't lie to her.'

'I'm not lying to her.'

I raised my eyebrows.

'I'm giving her money, aren't I? She doesn't need to know where it comes from.'

I didn't reply, hoping my silence would convey my disapproval.

'Jesus, Tam. What? You're the honesty police all of a sudden?' He gave me a look. 'I know you lie too, so don't get all high and mighty.'

I had a flash of the key with the green tag which I'd slipped back into the tin and the rainbow dress that hung in her wardrobe, still damp from my swim, so I relented, nodding, and said, 'Sure, if she asks me, I'll tell her.'

Mum's footfalls sounded on the stairs and he swore under his breath. The door opened and he moved to go past her with muttered words I couldn't decipher.

She stepped in front of him. 'Can I have a quick chat?'

'I'm late.'

'Jago—'

But he was gone, feet hammering down the stairs, ears closed to her. The front door slammed and the walls around us shuddered.

'Don't slam the door!' she shouted. Then she turned to me and forced a light smile. 'What's he late for?' Mum was trying her hardest to sound casual and disinterested.

'The yard.' I fixed my eyes on the floor.

'Again? That's good. Maybe Rick'll offer him something full-time.'

I nodded, knotting my fingers into the duvet on his bed, then glanced up at her. She stared at me for a moment or two, waiting, I think, for more information, but then she took a weary breath and gave a quick nod.

'Cup of tea?' she asked as she scooped up an empty mug and a sausage roll wrapper from his chest of drawers.

'That would be nice.' I was relieved we were safely off the subject of Jago and Rick. Tea was safe. 'I said I'd get Granfer one, but I haven't made it yet.'

I followed her out of his room but as we reached the stairs she glanced back at me briefly with a sudden air of awkwardness. 'Gareth dropped me home. He's come in for a cup too.'

My stomach leapt up my throat and I stopped dead. 'But why?'

'It seemed rude not to ask him in.' Her eyes flickered from

side to side avoiding mine as her lips twitched with obvious discomfort.

I suppose I shouldn't have been so shocked. Gareth had spent years trying to wheedle his way into our house and he'd clearly succeeded in wearing her down.

'Oh, love, no need to look like that. It's not for long.'

'You know, I don't want the tea now. I fancy a walk. Will you put two sugars in Granfer's tea?' Emotion sprung up and choked my words so I had to fight to stop from crying. 'I know you don't like him having more than one, but I promised. And he… he had a pretty bad turn earlier so—'

'Tamsyn—'

'It's fine. I need some air, that's all.' I tried to move past her but she grabbed my arm. We looked at each other, neither of us said anything for a moment or two, until finally her eyebrows knotted and she forced a weak smile.

'It's just a cup of tea,' she said softly.

Biting back tears, I eased my arm out of her grip, and ran down the stairs. As I passed the kitchen, I caught the shape of him out of the corner of my eye, and bolted my gaze to the floor as I grabbed my bag off the hook.

'Tamsyn!' Mum called.

As soon as I was safely out of sight of the house, I leant back against the wall and kicked it a couple of times with my heel.

It's just a cup of tea.

Irritation needled through me. I'd been so excited coming back from The Cliff House and now all I felt was angry. Gareth bloody Spence in our bloody kitchen having a-bloody-nother cup of tea.

I pushed myself off the wall and walked back to the corner

of our road. Our front door was closed with no sign of Mum looking for me and Gareth's crappy car was still parked outside. They were probably sitting at the kitchen table having a good old laugh about teenagers and hormones and slamming doors.

'Get out of our house, Gareth *bloody* Spence,' I whispered through gritted teeth.

I wasn't going to go back. Not while he was there. No, I was going back to The Cliff House.

The car park was now filled with vehicles parked in obedient rows. I made sure to keep my eyes on the floor as I passed people. I had neither the time nor desire to exchange pleasantries with idiot visitors whose only concern was whether they'd prefer a pub lunch or pasties on the beach.

Relief flooded me the moment I pressed the binoculars against my face. Gareth bloody Spence was gone and she was there, Eleanor, on the terrace of The Cliff House.

'Hello,' I whispered. 'I met your daughter this morning. Isn't she beautiful? Just like you.'

Eleanor was lying on her sun lounger with a glass beside her and a glossy magazine in her hand. I twisted the dial to make her bigger, then refocused on her outstretched legs, which were scattered with beads of water like glitter. Her scarf was wrapped around her body and I felt the phantom touch of the silk against my skin. I imagined lying beside her, my leg bent like hers, my toe stroking the lacquered surface of the pool.

A movement over by the house caught my attention. It was him. Max Davenport. My stomach knotted as I watched him stroll over to her. He wore a pink collared shirt, beige shorts, and his blue shoes, and he carried a newspaper tucked under one arm. He stood above her, speaking words I couldn't hear. She tilted her head to look at him, raised her sunglasses on top of her head.

'You look comfortable, darling,' I said under my breath. 'Oh, I *am*, darling. Isn't it *bliss*? Would you like me to fetch you anything? No, my love, I'm perfectly happy. I *do* love you so. Oh *darling*! I love you too. Who in the world could be happier than us?'

Eleanor Davenport lowered her sunglasses and returned to her magazine and he crossed the terrace to sit at the table where he shook open his newspaper.

Then I remembered Edie.

I lifted my sights to the windows on the first floor. Scanned them from left to right. Which was hers? I knew the one with the largest window on the far left was her parents', but which of the other three rooms was Edie's?

I moved the binoculars across and inhaled sharply. She was there. Standing at the window two along from theirs. Her palm rested against the glass. Was she looking at me? I dropped the binoculars as if the metal was molten and threw myself forward to flatten my body against the grass. I held my breath and, keeping myself hidden, I slowly lifted my head and raised the binoculars up again. I parted the grasses and manoeuvred so I could see through the vegetation for a better view of her window. I focused on her face. I exhaled. She wasn't looking at me. She was looking down at her parents on the terrace below. Her gaze fixed. Face blank. As I watched she turned away from the window and slipped backwards into the shadows behind her.

I rolled onto my back and stared up at the sky. White clouds raced across the blue. I rested the binoculars on my stomach and coiled my fingers into the grass. I closed my eyes and the sun danced in patterns on my eyelids as I listened to the seagulls and insects scurrying in amongst the heat-dried grasses. I conjured Edie and allowed my mind to drift into daydream. I pictured her back at the window and instead of slipping into the darkness she caught sight of me and waved. Then she opened the window and leant out to call my name. My chest swelled with joy as I waved back at her. Then she beckoned to me. I heard myself laughing as I skipped down the grassy slope and ran along the path to the gate. I threw it open and strode up the lawn. Edie burst out of the house and ran down to greet me whilst Mr and Mrs Davenport stood arm in arm, her with the silk scarf wrapped around her, him in his soft blue leather shoes. They were telling me to hurry up. Telling me how pleased they were to see me. Then in the background I saw my father. He was sitting at the table on the terrace. He held a cigarette in his long slim fingers, a ghostly trail of smoke wending its way upwards, the sun draping him, lighting him up like an angel.

He smiled at me and, as I approached, he nodded his approval.

CHAPTER EIGHT

Tamsyn
July 1986

All I could think about was going back to The Cliff House to see Edie again. Reasons to go tumbled over and over in my mind as I lay in bed and stared at the cracks that fractured the ceiling.

Perhaps I could tell her the green-tagged key had fallen out of my pocket and my mother was furious and had ordered me to retrace my steps? Or I could tell her I'd lost a ring, or a bracelet, or a pair of socks. Maybe I could offer to show her around? Be her guide. Take her to Porthcurno and the Minack, to St Ives and Logan's Rock, to Land's End, or to Penzance to buy paper bags of penny sweets and watch the helicopters take off on their way to the Scilly Isles. I imagined walking her around St Just, our postcard-pretty town. Imagined my patter: *Population four thousand, most westerly settlement in mainland Britain, until recently home to a thriving mining industry…*

But even if I found the perfect excuse I still couldn't go. It was Friday morning and on Friday mornings Mum cleaned at The Cliff House in preparation for their possible arrival. Of course, she had no idea they were already there, that they'd arrived early and with a daughter she didn't know they had.

I lay on my bed and watched her through my open door as

she got dressed on the landing. She took her cleaning clothes out of the airing cupboard, her stone-washed denim jeans, white T-shirt, a grey sweatshirt over the top. For work she always tied her hair into a tight ponytail, high enough to be out of her way, and her earrings were simple gold hoops. She didn't wear any make-up, just some briskly applied Oil of Ulay.

'You okay?' she asked with a warm smile as she caught me watching her.

I turned on my side on the pillow and nodded.

'You look happy snuggled up there,' she said. 'I wish I could come and jump in with you. But' —she sighed— 'no rest for the char lady.'

I was desperate to share the fact they had a daughter. A girl with white-blonde hair who was called Edie after *très glamoureux* Edith Piaf. But I stayed quiet. If I told her, she'd ask questions and I might let slip I'd been taking the key and letting myself in, which I knew would send her mental.

She closed the front door and I listened to her footsteps ringing on the pavement until they faded to nothing. My immediate thought was to get out to the rock with my binoculars and watch her in the house with them, but it wasn't worth the risk. She knew about the spot where Dad used to take me. He'd taken her there too. Even as a boy it had been his favourite place to watch the sun set over the sea and spy on the gulls and kittiwakes and choughs. The chances of her glancing in the direction of the point were significant and if she saw me I'd have to explain why I was there. So I tried to ignore the gnawing lure of the house by keeping myself busy. I cleaned the kitchen, washed up and dried, changed the sheets on Granfer's bed then sat with him a while, listening to him attempting to breathe whilst grumbling about the godforsaken government who murdered the tin mines and this being the hardest jigsaw he'd ever tried to do. Then I made him a cup of tea with two and a half sugars in, which made him wink and flash me his gap-toothed smile.

When I finally heard the latch click and the front door open, I ran to the top of the stairs, desperate to hear about the house and the Davenports and Edie.

She was hanging her coat on the hook.

'Hi,' I said. 'Good time?'

'Cleaning?' She raised her eyebrows and wiped her forehead with her hand. 'It's hot today. And I nearly missed the bus and had to run.' She paused, stared up at me, her brow knotted. 'The Davenports were there.'

It was then I noticed she held an envelope.

'What's that in your hand?'

She looked down as if confused by it. 'It's for you.'

'For me?'

She hesitated. 'Their daughter asked me to give it to you.'

'What?' I squealed and ran down the stairs taking them two at a time and when I got to the bottom I thrust out my hand.

She didn't give it to me. Instead her hand moved fractionally closer towards her body.

'Can I have it then?'

She furrowed her brow. 'I didn't even know they had—'

But I didn't let her finish. 'I can't believe she wrote to me!' As I grabbed the letter from her an electric charge shot through me. I stared down at my name which was written across it in the neatest writing I'd ever seen, all the letters even and rounded and perfectly joined up. I beamed at Mum but my smile faded when I saw her expression.

'How do you know each other?' she asked with forced indifference.

I gripped the letter hard as my brain turned over and over.

'Oh. Well, yesterday…' I hesitated. 'You know… when you were working at the chip shop? It was a really nice day so I went for a walk. On the cliffs. And, well, I ended up going past their house, and, this girl – their daughter, it turns out – was on the terrace. And I smiled at her. Like you always tell me to. I mean, you're always saying I should smile more, aren't you? Anyway, I did smile and she said something. Hello, I think. Then she said something about the weather. Isn't it sunny? Or maybe something about rain coming. Anyway, we sort of got talking and then she asked me to come in for a drink. A Coke. One of the fancy American ones from the adverts. I think her name's Edie. Something like that.'

Mum nodded vaguely, her face slick with mild confusion.

'She's here for the whole summer,' I said.

'Yes, Mrs Davenport told me today. Christ, I nearly jumped out of my skin when I opened the door and the woman was sitting there. I wish I'd known. I'd have worn something a little nicer. You should have *seen* the way she looked me up and down. Snooty cow. I hated cleaning with her there. So much nicer when it's just me. Can you believe she actually followed me round? I swear she ran her finger along a windowsill after I'd cleaned it. I mean, even though I know I cleaned it I was terrified it would come up covered in grime.' She sighed. 'She said Mr Davenport is finishing a book. Can't be in London, she said, because it's too noisy or too crowded or something like that. So they're here until the end of August. Anyway… ' She took a breath and smiled. 'Whatever the reason, she's given me more hours. Three times a week plus more at the weekend if they have guests.'

'That's good,' I said, relieved she seemed happy enough with my garbled account of meeting Edie.

'It's come just when we needed it, to be honest. I don't think we've ever had this little money.' She rubbed her face. 'Maybe Gareth will advance me some this month.'

The letter throbbed in my hand. All I wanted to do was tear it open and I willed her to let me go.

'Mrs Davenport said they need some help in the garden. Painting the railings. She asked if I knew any local tradesmen who might be able to do it. I was cheeky and suggested your brother. Obviously he'd have to fit it in around the yard, but he's only there every now and then, so it would be ideal. She wants to meet him first to make sure he's *suitable*. Whatever that means. Is he still asleep?'

'I don't think so. I saw him up earlier.' A lie. He hadn't emerged from his room yet but she hated him sleeping past eleven and I didn't want her to storm up there and wake him just so they could fight about it.

I stroked the envelope with my thumb.

'How's Granfer doing?'

'Nearly finished the sky.'

'He'll be pleased about that.'

We stood in silence for a few minutes. She glanced down at the envelope with an expectant look on her face. I held it behind my back and she nodded imperceptibly then turned to go into the kitchen.

Clutching the letter to my chest I shot up the stairs like a bullet from a rifle. With the door to my box closed, I fell onto

65

my bed, tore open the envelope and unfolded the single piece of heavy cream notepaper.

Dear Tamsyn

Can you come over later? Max is doing a barbecue for supper. I asked if I could invite a friend and he said YES. Your mother didn't know if you were busy or not.
I REALLY hope you aren't!!
Please say you'll come! I am LITERALLY going out of my mind with the boredom. I think I might DIE of it soon!
Call me on Penzance 3483 to arrange.

Edie x

To make sure I hadn't misread a word of it, I read it three times over. Then I held the notepaper up to my face and kissed it. This was the single most exciting thing that had ever happened to me. Had she really called me a *friend*? I read the note a fourth time to make sure while a heat burnt inside me like a bonfire. An invite to a barbecue? I couldn't believe it. I'd never even had a barbecue. But there I was – me! – with a proper invitation in blue fountain pen on watermarked paper. No more sneaking around. No more fear of getting caught. I was going to The Cliff House as an invited and welcome guest. It was – as Edie would say – *literally* a dream come true.

'Mum! *Mum!*' I called as I ran down the stairs. 'Can I borrow ten pence?'

I grabbed her bag from the hook and took out her purse then

hared out of the front door. She called something after me, but I didn't hear what she'd said so I lifted a hand and shouted, 'Back in a sec!'

When I reached the telephone box on the corner I yanked open the door, recoiling a little from the smell inside. Jago said it was where drunk men peed after the pub closed. So disgusting. Breathing through my mouth and not my nose, I pushed my hair off my face and blew sharply upwards against my sweating brow, whilst retrieving a coin from Mum's purse.

My hand shook as I picked up the receiver and placed it between my shoulder and cheek. Holding the letter up to read the telephone number, I carefully turned the dial for each digit. As I waited for the numbers to click through I had the sudden fear that this was an elaborate practical joke, that perhaps the number she gave me was made up and she was hiding nearby, watching me make a fool of myself with tears of laughter pouring down her cheeks. My stomach churned so ferociously I nearly slammed the receiver down. But then it began to ring. Two rings in my ear. Two in The Cliff House. Two in my ear…

I pictured their phone on the hall table. Black and new-fangled with buttons like a calculator. I imagined its ring echoing around the house and Edie walking towards it with her hand outstretched. Nerves catapulted around my body. What on earth was I going to say? I had to keep calm. I'd been invited for tea. If I wanted to go – and, oh *God*, I did – then I had to get through this.

Someone picked up the phone. Then the phone beeped demanding its money. I swallowed and pushed in the coin. It dropped into the box and the beeps silenced.

'Penzance three four eight three?' said the poshest voice I'd ever heard. It wasn't Edie. It must be her. Mrs Davenport with her creamy skin and honeyed hair. My stomach pitched.

'Erm, hello…' My throat constricted, forcing my words into a strangled squeak. 'It's… Tamsyn.'

'*Who?*'

'Can I… speak to Edie?'

There was talking in the background. Muffled. The receiver must have been smothered by a hand as the voices became faint. Then distant footsteps. A muted 'It's for you.'

Then Edie's voice. 'Tamsyn?'

'Hi. I… got your… letter.' My finger went to my mouth and I chewed on my nail, now certain this couldn't be real and she was about to explode with cruel laughter.

But she didn't.

'Can you come?' she said.

I closed my eyes as relief flooded me. 'Yes,' I breathed.

'That's great.'

'I'd love to. I really would. And I've got nothing planned. Nothing at all.' I was aware I was speaking too fast, tripping over my words in my desperation to get them out.

'Excellent. Max thinks he's God's gift to barbecuing, so I apologise in advance for any weirdness. And bring your swimming costume. I'm not sure your bra and knickers are appropriate.'

She laughed and a prickling heat swept over my neck and cheeks as I relived hauling myself out of the pool in my translucent underwear while she looked on, clothed and beautiful.

'Come as soon as you can, will you? I wasn't lying when I said I was dying of boredom. I have no idea how you exist down here. *God*, I miss London.'

The beeps signalling the end of my ten pence began to chirrup. 'Okay. I'm walking, but I'll leave now.'

'When you get here we—'

The line clicked dead so I missed the end of her sentence.

Despite being delirious with happiness, the claustrophobic atmosphere in our dark cramped house closed in around me in an instant. I hated it. There used to be a time when this house felt like the safest place in the world. When the air rang with laughter, not devastated silence. It had been a place of bedtime stories and playing Snakes and Ladders in front of the fire. Now it was cold and unwelcoming, any joy snuffed out by loss and worry.

My mother stepped out of the kitchen as I came in. She held a packet of Jaffa Cakes. 'Want one?'

'Jaffa Cakes? What are we celebrating?'

'My extra hours.'

'Maybe later,' I said, as casually as I could manage. 'I'm going to the Davenports' for a barbecue supper.'

'A what?'

'Supper.'

'Supper?' Her face clouded in confusion again.

'Tea. A barbecue tea. Edie asked me. That was what was in the letter. I checked. Just now on the phone.' Saying the words aloud made it all seem even more thrilling and I beamed. 'She said bring a swimsuit.'

A look crossed my mother's face which I couldn't read. 'Why?'

'For a swim.'

'No, I mean why's she asked you for tea?'

'Supper not tea. And I already told you. We met yesterday and she likes me.'

My mother shook her head. Her brow knotted. 'She *likes* you?'

The way she kept repeating everything I said whilst looking so bloody suspicious made me want to scream, but I took a breath and kept my voice level. 'It is possible for people to like me, you know.'

'I know. I'm not saying... It's just...'

My irritation boiled over like a forgotten milk pan. '*What?*'

'Well, they're... I don't know. It's...'

'It's *what?*'

'They're different. To us.'

'What are you talking about? They're not royalty.'

'They might as well be when it comes to the likes of you and me.' She sighed and rested her hand on her forehead. 'Look, he's rich and famous, in and out of the papers, and they've got so much money.'

'That doesn't mean anything anymore. Things aren't like they used to be. People aren't so stuck in their places.'

'I'm their *cleaner*.' My mother looked down at her hands and regarded them as if she wished they weren't her own. 'I'm not sure about it.'

'Edie knows what you do and she doesn't care. So why should we?' I crossed my arms and jutted a hip out.

She sighed. 'I suppose you're right. She's bound to be bored being an only child in that big empty house. I can see why she'd want to spend time with someone her own age. But be careful, okay? I'm not sure about any of them, if I'm honest. Especially Mrs Davenport.' She put the packet of Jaffa Cakes on the side, then smiled at me. 'I'll save a couple for you. Granfer and Jago will be on those like weevils. Will you tell her – Mrs Davenport

– that I'll send your brother up in a bit? Remind her it's about the painting. And say nice things about him, that he works hard and he's *suitable*.'

When she said the word *suitable* she wrinkled her nose. I could tell she was implying something, that there was some sort of meaning hidden beneath the words she spoke, but I decided not to pick up on it. I didn't have time. I had to find something to wear for a barbecue at The Cliff House. I wished more than anything I hadn't already worn Mum's rainbow dress. It would have been perfect, but I'd read a copy of *Cosmopolitan* in the doctor's waiting room once which said you could never wear the same dress twice, so I'd have to search out something else.

CHAPTER NINE

Edie
July 1986

Edie walked through the double doors that led out to the terrace and pulled her cigarettes from her pocket. She removed one from the box and paused to light it, shielding it from the breeze with a cupped hand.

The lawn was soft underfoot and the flowers flanking it teemed with bees and butterflies which flew busily from one bloom to the next. The wind was too slight to dilute the dry heat. She leant over the railings and the sun beat down on her, reflecting off the surface of the sea so it shone like a polished silver salver. The gulls were so high they were no more than specks in the cloudless sky and their incessant screeching was barely audible. Edie watched the path and chain-smoked until Tamsyn finally appeared round the bend. As soon as she saw her she stubbed her cigarette out on the railing and dropped the end into the spiky thatch of gorse on the other side of the boundary.

Tamsyn hadn't seen her and Edie noticed she was walking with a strange sense of purpose, like a soldier marching towards the front line. The wind was clearly stronger on the brow of the cliff and buffeted her hair in a glorious knot of red as if the strands were fighting their tethers in an attempt to escape. Edie waited for her to notice her, but she was too intent on striding the path, concentrating as if she were counting her steps.

When Tamsyn pushed open the gate, Edie called down to her.

The girl looked momentarily surprised but then her face cracked a shy smile and she waved, using her whole arm like a flag, a childish gesture which accentuated how immature she appeared in her denim shorts and shirt tied at the waist. The outfit could have been sexy and grown-up but the shorts were too baggy and there was something wrong in the way she'd knotted the shirt. Too innocent. More *Jackie* mag than Daisy Duke. Edie made a mental note to tell her that if she tied it tighter and higher to reveal more stomach, and undid an extra button to show some cleavage, she'd look a hundred times better.

'My father hasn't even lit the barbecue yet so I thought we could listen to some music in my room,' she said as soon as Tamsyn was near enough.

Before Tamsyn could answer Edie turned to walk inside. She checked over her shoulder and was pleased to see the girl following like an obedient puppy.

'What music do you like?' Edie said as they walked up the stairs.

'Anything.'

Tamsyn didn't follow Edie into her room, but hovered at the doorway, her fingers twisting around each other, eyes glued to the floor. Her reticence was annoying and Edie wondered if she'd made a mistake and spending time with this girl was going to be more tedious than diverting. Where was the girl who'd broken into the house and stripped off to swim in their pool? That was the girl Edie liked. This timid version didn't interest her at all. She picked up her Walkman from her bedside table and sat on her bed, crossing her feet at her ankles, deliberately not looking at the girl in the doorway.

'I like your room,' Tamsyn said then. 'Mine's tiny.'

Edie looked up. 'Smaller than this?'

Tamsyn nodded. 'Way smaller. Only room for my bed. I can't even open the door properly.'

Edie shifted over on the bed. Tamsyn seemed to take the hint and walked over and sat down beside her. Edie pressed play on the Walkman, then pulled each of the foam headphones off in turn. She pressed one against her ear and offered the other to Tamsyn.

'Do you know The Cure?'

Tamsyn shook her head.

'You'll love them. Robert Smith is a total sex god. Sexy in a way that isn't really sexy but is, if you know what I mean? This track is "Killing an Arab".'

Tamsyn held the headphone to her ear.

'What do you think?' Edie asked, watching her face carefully.

'I like it,' Tamsyn replied, sounding as if she was telling the truth. 'I haven't heard anything like it before but it's brilliant.'

Edie rested her head against the back wall, pulled her knees up and draped her arms over them. Tamsyn copied her, adopting exactly the same position, except with her head turned towards Edie. The girl's eyes were bolted to her. Edie tried to ignore it for a bit, assuming she'd eventually look away, but she didn't and it became irritating.

Edie pressed the stop button on the Walkman and the music quietened with a loud click.

'Are you all right?' She turned to face Tamsyn.

'Sorry?' Tamsyn's lips twitched nervously.

'You're staring. It's unnerving. And a bit weird, if I'm truthful.'

Tamsyn's face flushed fuchsia, clashing horribly with her hair. Edie was hoping she would laugh and say something cool or even combative, but she didn't, she just clammed up and mumbled apologetically. Dull. Boring and dull.

Edie knelt up and shuffled to the end of her bed and climbed off. She wrapped the headphone wires around her Walkman then faced Tamsyn with crossed arms. She was going to tell her to leave. This wasn't fun. This was worse than being alone. She'd tell her the barbecue was off and her plans for the summer had changed and didn't include her anymore.

But as she opened her mouth, Tamsyn swung her legs off the bed and looked up at her, eyes fixed and unwavering. 'My dad died.'

Edie raised her eyebrows. A dead father definitely made her interesting again.

'I think I come over a bit weird because of it.'

Edie didn't say anything.

'Sorry. Maybe I should have told you sooner. I—'

'How old were you?'

'Ten.'

Edie felt a small twist in her stomach. Ten years old. A little younger than the age she'd been when she first found her mother passed out on the floor, pale and still. For a while she'd been convinced she was dead and it terrified her. She'd sat beside her for ages, holding her hand, stroking her, begging her to wake up. Then her father appeared and sent her out of their bedroom. As she left she heard him muttering crossly, saying 'at this rate she'd be dead before Christmas.' Shortly afterwards Edie returned to school and every night she went to bed convinced she'd get a message in the morning that this time her mother hadn't woken up.

'What happened to him?' she asked, sitting down beside Tamsyn on the bed.

'He drowned.'

Edie rested her hand on Tamsyn's knee.

'He was a volunteer with the RNLI.' She hesitated and glanced at Edie. 'The lifeboats? He was called out in a storm that had come in too fast. There were a couple of tourists who'd got caught in a dinghy. Idiots. They died too. His body was washed up the next morning a few miles down the coast.' She paused and blinked slowly, then whispered: 'Sometimes it hurts so much I can't breathe. I miss him every day.'

Tamsyn became animated as she talked about her father's death. Her shyness evaporated. Her raw grief was palpable, but so was the inner strength which Edie had seen a flash of the day before.

'That's dreadful. I'm so sorry,' Edie said. And she meant it. 'You poor thing.'

Without thinking she put her arm around Tamsyn and for a while they sat like that, peaceful, no sound except the lilt of the breaking waves which rolled in through the slightly open window.

CHAPTER TEN

Tamsyn
July 1986

There had been a moment in Edie's room, when she caught me staring at her, that I'd thought I'd ruined it all. I'd been distracted by her. Carefully studying the slope of her nose, the tiny silver stud that glinted in one nostril, her flawless eyeliner drawn into extravagant sweeps on each eyelid. But when she challenged me I noted the sudden cooling in her. I'd seen the look she gave me before, many times, on the girls and boys at school. It generally came with a dismissive sneer and a silent promise not to be seen dead with me.

When I saw it on Edie's face I panicked.

Offering up my father's death as an excuse was risky. It could have easily scared her off. She might not have seen it as an explanation. She might not have cared. I was trading information for a second chance. But the gamble paid off and within seconds her face softened and her body opened up like a flower in water, arms uncrossing, fists unclenching, eyes widening.

I'm so sorry. You poor thing.

Then she held me and let me rest my head on her shoulder. Of course, I froze like a marble statue. There was no way I was going to move for fear of spoiling the moment. Nobody had ever shown me sympathy like that. Especially not people my age. At school his death was a topic to be avoided in case it made me cry or shout or punch a wall.

Eventually she stood up. 'Come on,' she said. 'I'm hungry.'

As I followed her down the stairs the reality of where I was, and how I'd come to be there as an invited guest, made me light-headed. I was so used to being in the house illegally with the constant threat of being discovered hanging over me. Being there legitimately was suddenly a little overwhelming and for a moment I had to pause, grip hold of the banister, and take three deep breaths to steady myself.

We walked through the living room and towards the back door. The windows were open and the gauzy curtains danced like ghosts in the billowing breeze. A wall of late afternoon heat hit me as we stepped outside. I gasped when I saw the table. I hadn't noticed when I arrived, too intent, I suspected, on following Edie up to her room to listen to music. I'd never seen anything like it. The iron table was laid up as if for a banquet. A white tablecloth had been laid over it and there was a large glass bowl in the centre which was piled high with a rainbow of exotic fruit I'd never even seen before. There was a small dish of butter which had softened in the sun and rolled-up serviettes encircled with silver rings and a silver bucket on a stand which held ice cubes and two bottles. The table had been set for four places and my stomach turned over with the thrill of realising one of them was for me.

'Typical. Wine but no water,' Edie said. 'Wait here. I'll go and get some.'

As she left a movement caught my eye. I looked across the gleaming surface of the pool and saw Max Davenport. He stood with his back to me in front of the brick barbecue in the far corner of the terrace, poking a pile of smoking charcoal which sent clouds of sparks into the air with each prod.

I decided to try to talk to him. My stomach fizzed as I neared him and I focused on the voice in my head which was telling me to *be brave, be brave, be brave*.

He must have heard me and turned, face broken in half by a smile, and raised his tongs in greeting. A film of sweat coated his forehead and there were two patches of damp in the armpits of his snow-white shirt, which was open to his stomach revealing white skin with a light thatch of greying chest hair. He wore long red shorts with a crease ironed down the centres of the legs and on his feet the soft blue shoes. I'd seen them a hundred times through the lenses of my dad's binoculars, but had never noticed the two gold coins slipped into slots in the leather on the tops of the shoes.

He must have seen me staring at them. 'They're penny loafers,' he said, with an unmistakable glint of amusement. 'You're supposed to put a penny in them, but I put pound coins in mine.'

'Like a wallet?'

He laughed. 'For decoration.'

I hadn't realised money could be used for decoration. When I looked back down at the coins they seemed to shine like the beams from a lighthouse.

'Mum's not sure about the new coins,' I said. 'She likes money you can fold, not pockets weighed down with shrapnel.'

'Your mother sounds supremely sensible.'

I smiled. His voice was different to how I'd imagined it. Posher and gravelly as if he'd swallowed a handful of sand before talking.

'What's your name?'

'Tamsyn Tresize.' I hoped he wouldn't notice me blushing.

'A good Cornish name.' He smiled again. 'And pretty too.'

'It's nice to meet you, Mr Davenport,' I said, remembering my manners.

'Max,' he said. 'You must call me Max.'

As he spoke I was hit by the peculiar sensation of being separated from my body and sitting up by the rock, watching Max Davenport talking to a girl with long red hair who looked identical to me.

'Max? Are you ready to cook yet?'

The voice catapulted me back onto the terrace. I turned to see Mrs Davenport walking out through the door. She was dressed in a voluminous kaftan in peacock greens and blues, which was edged with gold and wafted out behind her as she moved. Oversized white-framed sunglasses concealed most of her face and her hair was piled into a bun on the top of her head, revealing heavy pearl and gold earrings at each ear.

'You must be Tamsyn,' she said.

Her voice was soft with a slight slur as if her words had melted into each other. She smiled and showed perfect white teeth and when she sashayed over to me with her hand outstretched, I almost didn't take it, worrying that if I did I'd make it dirty.

'Lovely to meet you. Your mother is an absolute *godsend*. I have literally no idea how we'd survive *sans elle*.'

'Her mother?' Max asked.

Mrs Davenport smiled. 'The cleaner, darling.'

I swallowed as my reality bit at my ankles like a vicious dog. My eyes flicked over to Max. I watched for his reaction. Wondered if he now thought my name less pretty.

'Amazing woman,' he said and I beamed.

Edie came out of the house holding a green bottle and sat down. She beckoned to me and I went to her, though part of me wanted to stay and talk to Max about his shoes.

A short while later we were all sitting at the table and my cheeks ached with smiling. It was all I could do to stop myself laughing out loud. I thought of all those times I'd hidden myself in the sandy grass on the cliff and watched the Davenports eating – either out on the terrace or inside at the round white table in the sitting room – and sucked up every movement, every mouthful, every sip of every drink. It was all so familiar, the way she placed her knife and fork down precisely as she chewed, how he leant back in his chair to look out over the ocean, how he poured wine and she tipped her face to the sun. It was like I'd fallen into my favourite film.

'Your mother was kind enough to lay up for us this morning. Of course, she did it for three not four. Edie didn't tell us you were coming until just before you arrived so I had to lay the extra place myself.'

Edie rolled her eyes. 'It's not exactly hard to put out another knife and fork, Eleanor.'

'It's really nice to be here, Mrs Davenport,' I said quickly, sensing something between them.

Eleanor smiled at me as she lifted a bottle of wine from the ice bucket and topped up her glass, though I could tell that she was annoyed, and I wished Edie hadn't mentioned the cutlery.

Max Davenport stood and excused himself quietly before walking back to the barbecue. He picked up the tongs and waved them about like a sword as he turned steaks as thick as the Bible.

'So, Tamsyn,' said Eleanor Davenport, dragging my attention

away from Max and the barbecue. 'Are you pleased it's the school holidays?'

'Oh, yes. Very. I've just had exams so last term was pretty hard work.' I thought back to all the hours I'd stared blindly at my books whilst daydreaming and then the exams in which the words had swum and I'd struggled to even remember my name let alone how to long divide.

'O levels?'

'CSEs.'

'CSEs?' Eleanor placed her glass down on the table. 'The ones you take if you aren't bright enough to do O levels? How many did you take?'

I swallowed and a wave of hot shame swept over my body. 'Just five.'

'Do we have to talk about school, Eleanor? I mean, *God*, that's the last thing Tamsyn and I want to think about.'

'My apologies,' Eleanor said. 'I was interested, that's all. Aren't you always saying I need to be more interested?'

I wracked my brain to think of something to say. 'I really like this tablecloth.'

'The tablecloth?' Eleanor laughed. 'Thank you. It's an old one we don't need in London anymore.'

'I've never eaten at a table with a cloth before. I don't think we even own one.'

'Really?'

'Mum would worry about staining something so pretty.' I fingered the cloth, which was made of fine white cotton with exquisitely embroidered daisies dotted across it. I imagined my mum lifting it up into the sky so the sun lit its whiteness and the wind caught hold of it like a ship's sail before allowing it to float back down to the table. I saw her hands smoothing it. Saw the care she'd have taken to make sure it was centred properly, everything perfect, wanting to please Mrs Davenport. Then I heard her voice.

They're different to us.

And she was right, she and Eleanor were as different as two people could be. Eleanor reached for the salad bowl and I studied her hands. Soft. Blemish-free. Unlike my mother's which were blotched red and rough, unpainted nails trimmed short for practicality. Mum might have been right about her being different but she was wrong about me. Sitting at that table I didn't feel out of place or as if I shouldn't be there. I felt as if I belonged.

'Do you want some water, Tamsyn?'

Edie was holding the green glass bottle and without waiting for my reply she leant over to pour some in my glass. The water fizzed as it went in. I didn't even know they made water fizzy and wondered briefly if it came up from the ground that way. Before Edie had finished filling my glass, however, Eleanor reached over and lifted the neck of the bottle with her finger to stop the flow.

'Champagne surely, girls? What do you think, Tamsyn?' Eleanor retrieved the second bottle from the ice bucket and tore off the gold foil then untied the wire caging. 'Do you like champagne?'

'I've never had it before.'

'*Never?*'

I shook my head.

'Then you absolutely must try some.' She eased the cork out and it popped like an air rifle.

She poured the sparkling pale liquid into a tall, thin glass

85

and passed it to me. I lifted it up to the light and watched the bubbles race to the surface in a million effervescent pinpricks.

'I can't believe your mother hasn't let you have half a glass before. It's not right you've got to this age and not even tasted it.'

'I don't think she's ever had it either.'

Eleanor looked genuinely horrified.

'Vile stuff,' Edie said then.

'Ah, my darling daughter,' Eleanor said, whilst sipping from her glass. 'The very measure of sophistication.'

Edie rolled her eyes and made a face, and I looked away quickly, not wanting to be caught in collusion. Edie's chair scraped back on the terrace with a loud screech and she disappeared inside the house.

Eleanor drank most of her champagne in one go then topped up her glass. We sat in silence until Edie arrived back at the table with a carton of orange juice. She poured a glass for herself and offered it to me, but I shook my head and sipped the champagne, which wasn't as nice as I'd hoped it would be, too acrid and not very thirst-quenching.

'By the way, Edith, if you have to smoke, can you at least put your cigarette ends in the bin? I found three on the terrace this morning.'

How could Edie say Eleanor Davenport wasn't cool? Letting her smoke? That was definitely a cool mother. I tried to imagine what mine would have said if she'd found out I'd been smoking.

'The wait is over!' Max called over. 'The steaks are done!'

He returned to the table and with an air of triumph he placed the white serving plate down. The four steaks bled their red and brown juices all over the china. I grinned. Steak for tea. Granfer wasn't going to believe his ears.

Someone's birthday?

No!

Just any old tea?

Yes. Any old tea. Steak and champagne. Can you believe it?

'I hope it's cooked as you like it,' Max said, as he lifted a whole steak onto my plate.

'Thank you. Yes.'

Max began to vigorously cut into his steak. 'I must say, it's lovely to have you with us, Tamsyn. A real treat to have a proper local as our guest. Especially such a lovely one.'

Then he smiled at me and I smiled back because it was possibly the nicest thing he could have said.

Eleanor reached for her champagne glass and drained it.

'Be careful not to drink too much in this heat, darling,' he said to her.

Eleanor ignored him and took a mouthful of steak. She grimaced. 'Christ, I can't eat this,' she opened her mouth and pulled out the piece of meat which she put on the side of her plate. 'It's tougher than leather.'

'Why don't you have half of mine,' Max said coolly as he took a sip of wine. 'It's incredibly tender.'

'I'm not hungry.'

I momentarily considered asking if I could take it home to give to my grandad, but decided against it. Eleanor rapidly tapped her perfectly painted fingernail against the table as if punching out Morse code, then she reached for the carton beside her plate. She opened the lid to reveal cigarettes inside which were unlike any I'd ever seen before. Each one a different colour with a filter of shiny gold foil. She selected a red one and lit it.

Eleanor drew on her cigarette then turned to look at me

before leaning forward and jabbing my shoulder a couple of times.

'If you sat up straight and pushed your shoulders back you'd look much more elegant at the table.'

This drew a sharp glance from Edie. 'For God's sake,' she muttered.

'Don't be silly. I'm helping, that's all.' She smiled at me. 'You don't mind do you, Tamsyn?'

I shook my head. I didn't mind at all. In fact, I was grateful to Eleanor. Yes, her manner was a little brusque, but I was happy to have her point out the things I did wrong. I glanced at Edie who was looking fixedly out to sea, then sat up in my seat, straightening my back and pushing out my shoulders, aware of my chest rising.

Eleanor smiled and sipped her drink. 'You see, Edie? Now your friend doesn't look completely like *Le Bossu de Notre Dame.*'

Max cleared his throat. 'So, Edith, tell me.' He pressed his serviette to his mouth then placed it carefully on the table. 'While I'm finishing this *magnus opus* of mine and your mother is enjoying our little piece of Cornish heaven, how are you planning to use your time while we're here?'

'Well, *Max.*' She drew out his name and leant towards him. 'How about I shut myself in my room all day to avoid my family like you do and enjoy a triple vodka for breakfast like she does. That sound okay?'

I inhaled sharply and glanced at Edie in horror. If I used that tone with my mother I'd be sent upstairs before I'd finished my sentence, but Eleanor Davenport merely ignored her so I could only assume she hadn't heard properly.

Edie stood then picked up a couple of plates and left the table.

It turned out Eleanor Davenport had heard her daughter. 'Tell me, Tamsyn,' she said. 'Do you speak to *your* mother like that?'

I had no idea what to say. 'I, well, I—'

'Of course she does, Ellie.' Max grinned at me again. 'She's a teenage girl. That's how they speak to their mothers. You wouldn't want a wallflower for a daughter, now would you?'

Eleanor stared at Max over the rim of her glass. 'And you'd know all about teenage girls, wouldn't you?'

There was a jagged edge to Eleanor's comment and I watched Max's eyes narrow with anger for the briefest of moments.

Eleanor turned to address me. 'Tamsyn, do forgive me.' She stood, stumbling as she did, then steadying herself on the table. 'I've a headache. Max was right about wine in the sunshine. I need to go indoors.'

Max and I watched her retreat back to the house. Without Eleanor or Edie an awkwardness crept over us and I wondered if I should also excuse myself and try to find Edie. I glanced at Max and forced a smile.

'I'm sure Edith will be back soon.' He reached across the table to the bowl. His fingers lightly traced the fruit and then settled on a large red apple. He placed it on a small plate to the side of him, then took the knife he'd used for his steak and ran it through the folds of his serviette, leaving a greasy brown mark on the white. He carefully sliced the apple into quarters, then held each piece in turn, made two cuts to remove a triangle of core, and one lengthways to divide each piece in two.

He placed his knife down and held the plate out towards me.

'Have some,' he said. 'They're delicious. Bought from the farm shop yesterday. Sweetest apples I've ever tasted.'

I hesitated but he nodded so I reached for a slice and bit into it.

Max looked at me expectantly. 'Well?'

He was right. The apple was the sweetest and juiciest I'd ever tried. I smiled at him and took another.

'What's your book about?' I asked as I broke the second slice of apple in two and put half in my mouth.

'I never talk about my novels until they're finished. I'm convinced that if I do, I won't ever finish them. Superstitious nonsense, I know.'

'You must really like writing.'

This made him laugh though I had no idea why. 'Hemingway said *there's nothing to writing, all you do is sit at a typewriter and bleed*. It's an obsession. If it wasn't, we wouldn't do it. But then again, I know I'm lucky to earn so much money doing something I love and not have to tread the hamster wheel for peanuts in an office somewhere. Plus,' he said, taking another piece of apple and gesturing at me with it, 'writers have fictional worlds to escape to, which I'm certain stops us all going completely batty.'

I knew exactly what he meant.

'Here's a pearl of wisdom for you. In life always remember you're the author of your own story.' He smiled. 'Don't let life be something that happens to you. Write it yourself.'

It was the type of thing my dad would probably have said to me. Edie was lucky to have her father still. To have him alive and eating apples, not drowned and buried in a coffin in the ground.

Max patted the table then stood. 'Anyway,' he said. 'Enough of that nonsense. My book calls.'

'Thank you for supper,' I said, pleased I'd remembered it was supper not tea.

'Not at all. Please do stay and enjoy the pool.'

I needed no persuading. The thought of having to go back to St Just and our small damp house filled me with cold dread. Everything about it was grey and unwelcoming. But here, at The Cliff House, the colours were exaggerated, the light brighter, the smells, tastes and sounds richer. Was it just because I had happy memories of my dad here and sad ones back there? Or was it more than that? Was this place possessed with some kind of magic?

I watched him walk across the terrace and through the double doors into his study, then tipped my head back to enjoy the sunshine on my face.

'Thank fuck that's over,' said Edie from behind me. I turned in my seat to see her emerging from the house.

'Your parents are really nice,' I said.

'Ha! Nice? What the hell are you *on*? Oh my God,' she said through her laughter. 'Tamsyn, you're hilarious.'

Her laughter cut through me and my skin flushed. I stood, mumbling about needing to use the toilet.

'Sure,' she said, remnants of her amusement still lingering. 'It's through the living—' She stopped herself. 'Hang on. What am I saying? You don't need me to tell you, do you? I forgot you've been here before.'

Her comment annoyed me. What if Max or Eleanor had overheard? Was she ever going to stop going on about it?

The downstairs toilet was small and white with old-fashioned silver taps and a picture of a naked woman drawn on the wall. I washed my hands and dried them on the fluffy white towel, unable to resist burying my face in it to enjoy the smell of fabric conditioner and the cotton wool softness. It was bone dry too.

It struck me this was one of the differences between rich people and poor people. In our house there was nowhere to hang towels apart from a hook on the bathroom door and with no drying machine, and the fact the house was always so bloody damp, they never had time to dry properly so there was always a mustiness to them. One day I'd have fluffy white towels. Dry ones. Cupboards overflowing with them.

I walked out of the toilet and almost bumped into Eleanor Davenport. She was carrying a drink in one hand and in the other was a small brown bottle with a prescription label on it, which I presumed were pills for her headache.

'I just used your toilet.' I've no idea why I said that and felt immediately foolish.

Eleanor ignored me. She slipped the bottle into the pocket of her kaftan and climbed the stairs. A few moments later came the sound of her bedroom door closing.

Outside Edie was lying on one of the sun loungers. She had put on some round mirrored sunglasses which reflected the sky, and her face was serene and untroubled. As I was about to sit down I noticed a daisy which was growing between two paving stones. I bent to pick it. It was perfect, the petals evenly spread, white and tinged with pink, the centre a brilliant yellow. I dropped it carefully into the breast pocket of my shirt, then lay down on the lounger beside her and closed my eyes. The sun flickered orange on the backs of my eyelids and my head swam in a champagne haze.

'So here's a question,' she said then.

I opened my eyes and turned my head to look at her.

'If you had to – if your actual life depended on it – do you think you could kill someone?'

'In real life?'

She nodded.

'And if I didn't, I'd die?'

She smiled. 'Yes. You'd die *horribly*.'

As I thought about her question, about whether I could kill someone, I imagined reaching over and putting my hands around her neck, imagined squeezing harder and harder until her face turned blue and her eyes bulged from their sockets. I pictured the look of horror on her face as she realised she was going to die and heard the sound of her mirrored sunglasses smashing on the paving stones.

I pushed the image away.

'No, I don't think so.' I paused. 'Could you?'

She nodded. 'Yes, if I had to. If it was her or me. In that situation you have no choice, do you?'

'Her?'

'Or him,' she said with disinterest. 'Whoever.'

I closed my eyes and drifted away whilst listening to the lulling noises around me, the rhythmic waves below us, the gulls, and the sound of Edie's easy breathing...

Eleanor Davenport came out of the house. Her kaftan billowed out behind her. As she approached the pool she peeled it off and dropped it on the floor. Underneath she wore nothing. I tried not to look at the dark triangle of hair between her legs or her breasts with their nipples standing proud. She walked down the steps like a queen. Her skin turned a pale, yellowy-green in the light which bounced off the pool walls. She appeared dead. Bled dry. Then as she swam the atmosphere darkened. Something was watching her. I glanced up to see the raven back on the guttering. Its shining eyes fixed on the figure in the water. My heart raced. It was then I knew something bad was hiding beneath the surface of the pool. The hairs on the back of my neck sprang upright. My skin prickled. I should warn her but I couldn't move or speak. As I watched, helpless, whatever malevolent thing that lurked grabbed hold of her. Her face twisted in panic as it tried to drag her downwards. Her hands clawed the air as she fought to stay above the surface. But her struggling was in vain. She was pulled downwards. And as the water closed over her head, her fingers grasped at nothing…

'Tamsyn? Tamsyn?'

I opened my eyes and snapped my head round to look at Edie. It took me a moment or two to work out where I was. Her hand rested on my arm.

My heart pummelled my ribcage.

'Are you all right? You shouted out.'

'I'm fine…'

'You look like you've seen a ghost.'

'No… I…' I looked over at the pool. The early evening light threw a golden haze across its stillness. There was no kaftan on the terrace. No Eleanor in the pool. And, when I checked the guttering, no raven watching.

CHAPTER ELEVEN

Tamsyn
July 1986

Edie sat up at the noise of a motorbike coming towards the house and turning into the driveway. When the doorbell sounded I sat up too. Through the bank of sitting room windows we watched Max emerge from his study and head towards the front door.

A few moments later my brother walked into the house. He seemed uncertain, tentative, his head lowered and nodding. The two of them talked for a minute or two. I wished more than anything I knew what they were saying. I remembered then I was supposed to have told Eleanor that Jago was coming up to talk about the painting she wanted doing.

Max Davenport appeared at the terrace door with Jago following him. My brother caught sight of me and looked expectant, as if I might jump up to see him. But I didn't. I didn't want him there. Him standing uneasy and awkward in his ripped jeans and scuffed Doc Marten boots was a stark reminder of where I came from, a cramped terraced house with peeling wallpaper and a sofa covered by a blanket to hide the holes and ancient stains. With my brother there it was hard to escape who I really was and I didn't want to be me. I wanted to remain the girl who sunbathed beside a pool with steak and champagne in her belly in the company of people who shone as if varnished.

'I wonder who that is?' said Edie, lifting her sunglasses off her eyes and squinting.

'My brother.'

'Your *brother*?'

I nodded. 'He's come to talk about doing some work. I was supposed to tell your mum but I forgot.'

'He's beautiful, isn't he?' She lowered her sunglasses and glanced at me.

I shrugged. 'He's my brother. I don't know if he's beautiful,' I lied.

Edie laughed. She bent one leg and her skirt slipped down to reveal her thigh.

'How old is he?'

'Nineteen.'

'Back from university?'

'University?' Nobody I knew had been to university, let alone my brother who left school after failing all but three of his CSEs. 'No. He doesn't go.'

'What does he do?'

'He's unemployed. He used to work at the tin mine, but it got closed down. He's not worked since. Bugger all jobs down here.' As I repeated his words, my brother's voice resounded in my head, heavy with all the anger and frustration which drove his fights with Mum whenever she pushed the classifieds across the table towards him. Tiny adverts for jobs he'd never get ringed in red biro that made his fists ball. 'There's nothing for us down here. Cornwall might as well not exist. London doesn't give a shit.'

'I knew about the coal industry. We learnt about it in Geography. But I didn't know anything about the tin.'

'They marched in Westminster. Jago went on a coach overnight. I helped him paint a sign saying *Save Cornish Tin Mines*. But the day they marched the space shuttle blew up so nothing got in the papers. He said it wouldn't have made any difference because mining was already dead. And he got to see Big Ben so it wasn't a wasted trip.'

'Tamsyn?' It was Max calling. 'Can you come here a moment?'

I stood and walked over to them, retying the ends of my shirt which had worked loose.

'Hey, Tam,' my brother said.

'Hey,' I said, shielding my eyes from the sun.

'I'm afraid I don't know anything about the work Eleanor mentioned to your mother.' Max cleared his throat. 'And unfortunately she's had to have a lie down because of a migraine.'

Edie arrived beside me. She held out her hand towards my brother, sunglasses perched on her head. 'I'm Edie,' she said.

Jago regarded her hand, unsure, I think, what he should do. I watched as he seemed to work it out, and after wiping his hand on the back of his jeans he shook hers. 'Jago,' he said quietly.

'Cool name.'

Jago dragged his hand through his hair. 'Most people think it's weird.'

Edie raised her eyebrows. 'I'm not most people.'

I suddenly felt excluded. It was as if I'd been banished to my spot on the cliff and I touched my cheek in response to the phantom pressure of the binoculars. I suddenly wanted to shout at Jago. Tell him he was trespassing and that if he wanted to sunbathe beside a pool, he had to find his own. This one was mine.

'I need to get back to my work, but I think it best you come back as we discussed. I'll tell Eleanor you'll be up tomorrow with your mother. If you're sure that suits you?'

Jago nodded then looked at me. 'Mum said to bring you home.'

'I'll walk.'

'You've got to see Ted.'

'Shit,' I said under my breath. 'I'd forgotten. Okay. I'll leave in a bit.'

'She wants me to take you back on my bike. He's only there until six then he's off to the Men's Club.'

I swore under my breath.

'Your bike?' Edie said. 'As in motorbike? I thought I heard one.'

Edie followed us out. When she saw my brother's bike she whistled through her teeth. 'Oh, how cool! Jesus. The *freedom*. You could just leave whenever you want. Go anywhere. God, I'm so *jealous*.'

Jago didn't respond to her, but passed me his helmet which I strapped on before climbing up behind him.

Edie put her hand on my arm. 'Will you come up tomorrow, Tamsyn?'

Almost as if a switch had been turned on, my disappointment at being told I had to leave was replaced with intense excitement. I grinned at her and nodded. Jago turned the engine on then revved it unnecessarily.

'Great!' She had to shout to be heard over the bike's racket. 'We're going to have such a brilliant summer!'

I wrapped my arms around Jago's waist and he let the throttle go and we roared out of the gate and onto the lane. I smiled and rested my chin on his shoulder. I hardly ever got to go out on the bike with him. He'd passed his test a couple of weeks after his seventeenth birthday.

Want a ride on it?

But Mum had cried out in horror.

She's not going out on that thing. She's only just fourteen!

Her eyes had settled on the bike and misted with tears.

Later, after Mum left for work, he'd grabbed my hand and yanked me into the hall. For the first time since before our dad died he looked excited, as if someone had lit a fire behind his eyes. He slid his helmet onto my head and tightened the chin strap, then touched his finger to the tip of my nose.

There you go, Tam. All safe and sound.

He'd felt solid and strong like Dad and the wind rushed so fast into my face my eyes watered and even though I felt a bit scared I didn't want the ride to ever end. When we got home I watched him wheel the bike into our small yard and run his hands over it lovingly. Then he walked back to me, cheeks ruddy, hair windblown. I handed his helmet back and thanked him, and he put his arm around my neck and pulled me close to him.

As if I'd take Dad's bike out without you.

CHAPTER TWELVE

Present Day

*I*t's the anniversary of my father's death. I spend it, as I always do, at our rock on the point looking over the house.

Even though the raw pain of it has dulled a little, years later I still feel it. The grief is a vein of quartz running through me. I walk along the path and climb the salty grass. The wind is blustering, unable to make up its mind which way to blow. I have a rucksack packed with a Thermos of tea and some fruitcake. I have his book on birds, the pages so worn in places the writing is unreadable, the tea-ring on its cover faded to a mere shadow.

I lie back and knot my fingers into the grass. The sky is dull. No discernible colour. I listen to the hateful sea. The sea which filled up his lungs so he could no longer breathe. The waves break below me like a metronome. I imagine the sound of his heartbeat and imagine I'm lying with my ear against his chest to hear it.

On this anniversary I can't keep the raven from my thoughts. Or, indeed, the kittiwake chick torn to bloody shreds in its beak. Or how the sky had darkened to a blackish-purple, inching down to crush us as the rain advanced across the sea in a threatening sheet. Or the wind which angered the waves, forcing them larger and larger, each one crashing heavily on the rocks and firing spray up in deafening explosions.

Then later, when we made it home, the relentless rain had lashed the windows and the walls trembled as if a giant was shaking the house like a rattle.

Decades have passed but I can still see his face as clearly as if he was with me now. The concern in his eyes as he crouches to blot my tears.

Don't go, don't go, don't go.

Lying here on this anniversary I imagine a parallel universe. A universe where he didn't leave, but instead took me in his arms and walked me into the kitchen, drew the curtains to shut out the weather and lit the stove and made mugs of Ovaltine in which we dipped digestives. Safe and alive.

But then I hear his voice as it really happened.

Listen, Tam, he says. There are people out there, lost at sea, and if I don't go they'll die. Do you understand?

I didn't understand but I didn't say anything. I stayed quiet. Watched him button his heavy yellow oilskin and pull on thick rubber boots. He kissed my mother. Whispered something in her ear. Her fingers briefly touched the side of his face. Then he left.

I ran after him, of course. Yanked the front door open wide. I was hit by a rush of wind and driving rain that burnt my skin. Everything around me – the curtain, the coats on the hooks, the letters on the small table – was blown into an angry maelstrom.

When I screamed his name my voice was lost, whipped from my mouth and stolen by the storm. My mother pulled me back inside and closed the door. Everything stilled. It was as if death had danced through our house and followed my father out.

My mother's scream woke me from my dream about the

raven with the kittiwake chick gripped in its talons. Except it wasn't the chick in the raven's grasp. It was me. My body that was twisted and bent. My eye pecked clean. My insides trailing from its glistening beak.

I recall the way my heart hammered at the sound of her scream and the remnants of my nightmare. The light beside my bed glowed softly. Tiny china figurines frozen forever in their tree-trunk house.

No.

I am there again. Ten years old. Climbing from my bed. Tying my dressing gown. I am crouching at the top of the stairs. Looking down on my mother who is by the door. A man stands in front of her. He wears the same yellow coat as my father. The door is open behind him and I am struck by how still the air is, quiet and peaceful, content after eating my father, dozing like a sated monster. I can't hear what the man is saying. He has huge hands. One rests on my mother's shoulder. The back of it is covered with fine black hairs. I think how heavy it must feel on her and that perhaps it is the weight of his hand which makes her collapse on the floor.

I open my eyes and stare up at the sky. A bird flies overhead. I think of my brother. Of how he arrived beside me at the top of the stairs, sleepy, yawning, his hair stuck up in all directions. His voice echoes in my head.

What's happened?

Daddy died.

Then something catches my eye from The Cliff House.

It's her.

She is walking across the terrace. I hold my breath and don't move, hoping she won't see me. But she stops. Looks up. She *knew I'd be here. Our eyes lock. She raises a hand and waves and as she does a shiver cuts through me like a sharpened blade of ice. Her hair catches in a gust of wind. She tucks it behind her ear, then turns and walks back up the lawn, across the terrace, and disappears into the house.*

CHAPTER THIRTEEN

Tamsyn
July 1986

'Hello, young Tamsyn.'

The shop was dark. Ted didn't believe in electric light during the daytime despite the windows being mostly obscured with the adverts, fliers and wanted signs which he let people stick up at no cost but a ten-minute chat. My eyes took a moment or two to adjust to the gloom after the glorious late afternoon sunshine that draped the day. As they did, Ted came into vision. He was wiping the door of the freezer cabinet with a blue rag which was so dirty it left smears in sweeping arcs on the glass.

'Well, don't you look like the hen that got the corn! Good day?'

'It's the school holidays. That's worth a smile.'

'Holidays again? I can't believe it.'

I nodded and waited for what was to come: *Time flies. But my, time flies.*

'Time flies, Tamsyn Tresize. But my, time flies.'

There was something reassuring about Ted's predictable patter. He loved a saying and a proverb, and his chirpy, non-stop conversation was reliably punctuated with cats and dogs that fell from the sky and time waiting for no man.

'So how many hours do you want then?'

'Mum says as many as you've got.'

The corners of his mouth turned down. 'Things are tight for all of us.'

I nodded and ran my fingers over the brightly coloured packs of sweets and chocolate. I'd been working at Ted's shop on Saturday mornings for two years, apart from my last term, when I'd taken a break in order to give me more time to study, or, as it transpired, stare out of the window in my box or through a pair of binoculars trained on The Cliff House. On my fourteenth birthday, before I'd even swallowed my last mouthful of cake, Granfer had announced it was time to bring some pennies in.

Your dad would want you to pay your way in the world.

During the school holidays I did a couple more days a week. I don't think Ted needed the extra help, but like so many of the men in St Just he had a soft spot for Mum. I'd seen how they acted around her, neatening themselves, standing tall, taking their caps off or standing aside to let her go in front of them in a queue.

The work was easy but dull, unpacking boxes of chocolate and crisps, counting coins into small plastic bags for the bank, sorting through things in the fridge which had gone over their Best Before, then moving them into the freezer section with a reduced price scrawled on their label in marker pen.

'How about Monday, ten until four, and Wednesday mornings, and starting back with your Saturdays now exams are done with.'

'Sounds good.' I didn't push for more. I had Edie and the Davenports now and the last thing I wanted was to be cooped up here arranging bags of Wotsits and Discos when I could be at The Cliff House eating slices of apple and lying by the pool.

'Right, I should be getting to the club now, but I'll see you tomorrow. I'll look forward to it. It'll be good to have company again.'

'Tomorrow?' A mild panic took hold of me. I was supposed to be going up to The Cliff House. 'Would it be okay if I started on Monday? I've got something on tomorrow which I can't really get out of.'

'Something exciting?'

I shrugged.

He dropped the filthy cloth into the bucket beside him and the sudsy grey water slopped up the sides and splashed onto the discoloured vinyl floor. 'I heard your mother's got more hours at the white house?'

I nodded.

'London folk,' he said, then wrinkled his nose as if he'd smelt something nasty. 'Licence to print money where they come from.'

'Do you know them?'

'She comes in here for cigarettes and a bottle of something every now and then. The cigarettes I have to order in specially. Coloured like a box of felt tips and wrapped in gold. Normal fags too common. More money than sense some people. He came in with her once. Didn't want to talk. Cock-of-the-walk type. I borrowed one of his books from the library a while back.' Ted picked up the bucket and pushed through the fringe of red and white plastic strips that marked the doorway into the back room. 'You know,' he called back. 'To see what all the fuss is about.'

He tipped the bucket down the sink and it glugged loudly as it went down the plug. I imagined the particles of dirt collecting on the stained porcelain and silting up the U-bend.

'*The Bird Sang Twice in Winter* or something. Or maybe it was *Cried Twice in Summer*. Some noise made by birds and a season. Anyways,' he said, as he walked back through the plastic strips, 'doesn't matter what the damn thing was called because it was a load of stuff and nonsense.'

Ted walked past me and went behind the counter. I absent-mindedly straightened the chocolate bars on the shelf nearest me so their edges were perfectly in line.

'*Her heart wept for the relentless march of time*,' he said with all the melodrama of a village pantomime. '*A race to nothing. The continuous desire to freeze fractured moments of grabbed perfection. Stepping stones to eventual non-existence*.' He looked at me with a knotted brow. 'Who has time to sit and read rubbish like that? Page two, that was. Nearly three hundred pages all like that and not a story to speak of.' He shook his head. 'Give me a Dick Francis or a Harold Robbins any day. Books without a story aren't worth the paper they're printed on.'

'You memorised it though.'

'Sorry?'

'His writing. That bit. You memorised it.' I was surprised at how defensive I felt, how much I wanted to protect Max, remembering him telling me that writing was like bleeding.

'Took me bloody ages. I kept forgetting the word *continuous*.'

'Well, he's got awards for it and makes a tonne of money so some people must love it. Also, they have a daughter. Did you know that? She's really nice. So,' I said, 'they can't be that bad if they've got a nice daughter, can they?'

He didn't look convinced. 'Never trust London folk. Your grandpa'd say the same thing. I dare say your dad would too.'

Ted turned away from me and I gave his back a hard stare.

'Right, I better get going. There's a quiz tonight and I'm feeling lucky. See you Monday.' He opened the till and retrieved a bunch of keys as heavy as a prison guard's. 'Give that mother of yours a hello from me.'

Despite Ted trying to make me feel bad about the Davenports, it wasn't long before the spring in my step returned. Eating with the Davenports had been incredible: new drinks, delicious food, in the company of glorious people from a different world. On top of that, Ted had given me some hours, which meant money in Mum's pocket, the sun was still shining, and the summer holidays stretched out ahead of me with the promise of more time at The Cliff House.

'I'm back!' I called as I burst in through the front door. I was brimming over with stories I wanted to share with Mum, but when I charged into the kitchen, it wasn't her I came face to face with but Gareth. *Bloody*. Spence.

There was no sign of Mum. Just him. And now me. I glanced at the clock on the wall. It was nearly seven o'clock. What on earth was he doing here at seven on a Friday bloody evening?

'Hello, Tamsyn.' At least Gareth had the grace to look awkward as he shifted uncomfortably and pulled on one of his shirtsleeves. I noticed then he was holding the seagull mug and my body tensed.

'That's not your mug.'

'What?' Confusion screwed his eyes into little piggy slits.

'Put the mug down.'

'Your mother—'

'I don't care. You're not to touch that mug. *Ever*. Do you hear me?' Tears spiked my eyes and I bit my lip hard to stop them falling. 'Well, *do* you?'

I walked over to him and reached for it. He gave it to me without protest or question. His skin reddened as he clasped both hands behind his back. I tipped what was left of his tea into another mug, then squeezed dish soap into the seagull one and scrubbed it all over.

I passed him the new mug but he didn't take it.

I hated him. Hated how he wouldn't leave my mother alone. Hated how his lecherous eyes watched her move around the room. How they hunted her like a hungry wolf desperate to swallow her up. I'd seen him watching her when she wasn't looking. Stealing glances at her as she wrapped fish, desire oozing out of him. I knew what he was thinking, what disgusting things he wanted to do to her, and it made my skin crawl.

'Why are you here?'

'We're – your mum and me – we're going out.' He passed his palm over the side of his head to flatten his sandy hair, then dropped his pale eyes to the floor and began to tap his foot.

'Are you sure?'

'Sorry?'

'That you're going out. I mean, I can't imagine she wants to. We'd planned to watch the television tonight. *Dallas*. We even circled it in the *Radio Times*. We always watch it.'

'Oh. Well. Your mother and I arranged to go to the pub.' His neck and cheeks were the colour of raspberries. 'For scampi.'

My mother came into the kitchen and kissed my forehead like I was eleven. 'Hi, love.'

Just like that. *Hi, love*. No embarrassed muttering or surprise at seeing Gareth. Just a cheery *hi, love*.

Gareth smiled with relief and scooted his finger around the inside of his shirt collar.

'Gareth says you're going out for scampi.' I made no effort to hide my annoyance. 'I thought we were watching the television tonight.'

'Did we say that?'

'*Dallas*. It's circled. We circle it every week.'

She hesitated and a flash of doubt passed over her face.

'But if you've got something better to do…' I left my sentence hanging.

'It's no problem, Ange. We can go another time.' Gareth made a sighing noise like a deflating beach ball.

'Oh, and I'd prefer you didn't let him use the mug I gave *Dad*.'

'Tamsyn, it's just a—'

'No! It's special and I don't want it broken.'

She shook her head and sighed. 'Let's not do this now.' Her words were delivered with a warning tone intended to remind me Gareth was a visitor in our house and that raising my voice and getting upset was unacceptable.

I didn't understand why she didn't tell him to get lost. I'd told her that was all she had to do a hundred times. She didn't owe him anything and it wasn't right he pestered her at work. It should be against the law for a boss to do that, to come on to her and make her feel awkward for saying no. I didn't understand why she couldn't see him for what he was. A horrible lecher. Why did she thank him for the flowers he bought her when they were clearly cheap and nasty and almost certainly from the bucket in the petrol station on the A30. He had a cheek. It wasn't as if he'd never met my dad either. They were at school together. He knew what type of man he was. How could he think she'd ever be interested in a puny chip shop owner who wore a shiny blue suit with the sleeves rolled up like a ratty Don Johnson after she'd been married to a man like him?

'I should go.' Gareth reached for his jacket from the back of the chair.

My body relaxed a bit, triumphant that I'd been successful in chasing him out of our house.

'No,' my mother said then. She smiled at him. 'I was looking forward to it. I can't remember the last time I went out.'

I opened my mouth to protest, but she spoke before I had the chance to.

'Tamsyn, can I talk to you a minute?' She gestured to the door with a couple of sharp nods of her head.

I followed her out of the kitchen, shooting Gareth a look over my shoulder, a look that said: *I see you. Don't think I don't.*

'Tam,' my mother whispered, her mouth close to my ear. 'I'm sorry about the mug. I wasn't thinking.'

I wrapped my arms around my body and dropped my eyes.

'Maybe you should keep it in your room. It'll be safe up there. You can keep pens in it or what-have-you.'

I nodded as I bit back tears.

She rested a hand on my elbow. 'I'd like to go out tonight. I know he's not your favourite—'

I scoffed a little.

'But it's just a drink.'

'Stop saying that!' I said too sharply. 'You keep saying "it's just a". It's *just* a cup of tea, it's *just* a mug, it's *just* a drink. And anyway, it's not *just* a drink, it's scampi too. He said you're going for *scampi*!'

Her face fell and a wave of guilt washed over me. I didn't want to make her sad.

'Please,' she said. 'I'll only be an hour or two. You watch *Dallas* with Granfer. Like you planned. You don't need me. I'd only be doing the ironing anyway and I'm not in the mood to do it tonight. I was looking forward to a night off. Is that okay?'

She blurred in my tears and I managed a nod.

'He's a good friend.' She looked as if she might say something else but if she was intending to she stopped herself. She squeezed my arm and smiled with a gratitude that made my knees crumple. I wished I could press a rewind button and take back the things I'd said.

'I hope the scampi is nice.'

Then she left me in the hallway and walked back into the kitchen, and in a bright voice I could tell she'd manufactured said, 'Come on, Gareth Spence, let's paint this sleepy little town red.'

I didn't want to be in the hall when Gareth came out of the kitchen, so I ran up the stairs, then knelt at the top to watch them through the banister. He took her coat off the hook in the hallway and held it up for her to put on. Then he opened the door and gestured for her to walk out in front of him. When his hand went to rest in the small of her back, I flinched as if it were me he'd touched.

Granfer must have been downstairs already as the television burst into life. The *Dallas* theme tune swam up the stairs, but rather than draw me down, it drove me into my box. I closed the door and the music dimmed to a gentle thrum through the floorboards.

I dragged the *Encyclopaedia Britannica Volume III* and *Complete Book of Birds of the British Isles* from the crate beneath my bed, and took the daisy I'd picked from between the paving stones at The Cliff House out of my pocket. I twirled it between my fingers so it turned like a ballerina. Though it was wilted, and the petals were limp, the spongey yellow centre was still radiant.

I opened the back cover of the encyclopaedia and took out the two pieces of blotting paper I kept there; then I laid the daisy between the sheets, pressed gently, and carefully repositioned the blotting paper. I closed the back cover then rested the second heavy book on top of it and slid both into the gap between the crates beneath my bed to let the daisy dry. Then I lay on my bed and waited for my mum to get back.

It was late when I finally heard their voices. The sky was black and the moon high and full, and my room was dipped blue by the light which fell through the window. I knelt up on my bed, and keeping myself hidden from view I peered around the edge of the window frame at the street below. The two of them stood facing each other beside our low granite wall. I held my breath, my hands clenched into fists, fingernails digging into my palms.

'Don't kiss her,' I whispered. 'Don't kiss her.'

Don't kiss her.

When she rested her hand on his arm my stomach pitched. He reached out to tuck a stray strand of hair behind her ear. I watched helplessly as she smiled and nodded. For a moment they didn't move and I held my breath.

When she dropped her hand and turned away from him I exhaled with relief, and rested my head against the cool glass and said a silent *thank you*. I looked down again and saw her walk through our gate. She paused to glance over her shoulder and raised a hand to him before rummaging in her bag for her key. He stood with his hands in his pockets and watched her. It was only when the front door closed with a gentle thud that he finally turned away and retreated up the street.

'Yes, that's it, you prick,' I whispered. 'Leave us a-bloody-lone.'

Then I turned away from the window, covered my face with my hands, and shook.

CHAPTER FOURTEEN

Tamsyn
July 1986

Mum was catching a lift up to the house on the motorbike with Jago. She was insistent they arrive together so she could be there to introduce him to the Davenports. Jago joked that she obviously didn't trust him to get there alone, which she tried to laugh off but not very convincingly.

I was happy to walk. It was a beautiful day and it meant I had an excuse to get out of the house early. I cut myself a slice of bread for my breakfast and spread it with butter before setting off.

I went up to the rock first. It was a clear day and the waves were calm. I looked over to Sennen Cove in the distance. At the cottages which crept up the hillside, the sea wall dotted with fishermen, and the car park above the bay which held cars in neat lines that glinted in the sunshine.

I'd hoped I might catch the Davenports eating breakfast on the terrace. The two of them in contented peace, the glass pot of coffee with its golden dome between them. A bowl of fruit from which Eleanor would select a piece to cut into segments whilst Max ate toast, perfectly golden, always with marmalade. But the terrace was empty. Perhaps they'd already eaten or maybe they hadn't woken yet. I felt a rush of excitement as I pictured them warm in their bed, her head on his chest, white cotton sheets tangled around them, sunlight falling through the slatted blinds throwing lines of shadow and gold across their silken bodies. I shifted position to get a better view of their bedroom through the thatch of grasses, but the morning sun glared off the window so even if they were in there they were shielded from sight.

I checked my watch which read a quarter to ten. Jago and Mum would soon be arriving so I wrapped up the binoculars and dropped them into my bag then walked down the slope. When I reached the gate I pushed it wide open. No need to worry about creaking hinges anymore.

'What do you mean *work*? It's the holidays. Do you *have* to?'

Edie sat on the windowsill in her bedroom and looked out of the window.

'I need to help Mum out with money and stuff.'

'But you said you were free to hang out.'

'I'm only doing Mondays, then Wednesday and Saturday mornings.' I tried to sound upbeat.

Edie craned her head to look at something down below. Her hand went to her ear and she fingered her earring absent-mindedly. 'Your brother's arrived.'

'To see your mum. She wants to interview him.'

Edie laughed. 'It's only painting a fence, you know. Not a proper job. She just wants to make sure he's not going to take her jewellery. She's paranoid about people wanting to steal from her. She's insane.'

Edie glanced down at the terrace again then pushed herself off the windowsill and headed out of her room.

I didn't follow her immediately but instead moved closer to the window and looked down to see Eleanor and my brother on the terrace. She was pointing down towards the railings and he was nodding, holding his arm, head dipped. I didn't need to be able to hear him to know he'd be talking in monosyllabic grunts. Hopefully this wouldn't put Eleanor off.

Edie was in the kitchen pouring blackcurrant into a jug. It was dark purple, thick like single cream, proper Ribena, something we never had at home. She topped it up from the tap then opened the freezer and took out an ice tray. I heard voices from the utility room. One of them was Mum. The other was a man so had to be Max. My stomach turned over. I didn't want her cleaning The Cliff House today. The place felt different with her and my brother there. Not as relaxed. I wanted it all for myself.

'You know, we should go to the beach today,' I said. 'To Sennen. You'll love it.'

Edie filled a glass and held it out to me, whilst giving a throwaway shrug. 'I thought we could hang by the pool.'

As I took the drink from her she walked out of the kitchen with the jug and an empty glass.

'I'd love to show you the beach.' But I don't think she heard me.

I trailed behind her as she walked over to Jago. 'I thought you might like a drink,' she said. 'It's so hot today.'

He mumbled, 'No thanks,' without looking at her, before refocusing on the instructions Eleanor was giving him about what she wanted him to do with the railings.

'The sanding should be enough for today,' she said. 'You need to take all the rust off. Don't cut any corners or it'll bleed through the paint.' Then she seemed to have a sudden thought. She looked at Edie. 'Edith? Where's your father?'

Edie gave her a withering look. 'How on *earth* should I know?'

Eleanor glanced up at the house. Her eyes narrowed and then her mouth set hard. 'Jago, go down and take a good look at the fence. Make sure you understand what you're going to be doing. I need to go inside for a minute.' She turned and marched up towards the house, walking quickly and with purpose. 'Girls,' she called over her shoulder as an afterthought. 'Please don't distract him.'

Edie crossed her arms and scowled at her mother's retreating figure. 'Why does she keep calling us *girls*?' she grumbled as she walked over to the table and put the jug and glass down. 'How old does she think we are? *Ten*?' Edie shook her head and rolled her eyes as she sat down and put her feet up on the table. 'And, Jesus, *how* unfriendly is your brother?'

The tone of her voice lit a fuse and I jumped to his defence without thinking. 'He's nervous, that's all. Probably worried he's not *suitable*.' I heard the edge to my voice, so added, more gently, 'He's nice. I promise.'

Edie shrugged and kicked her heel against the tabletop. 'Fuck this. We might as well go to the beach. Anything to get away from this hellish place.'

She didn't move. I stood and waited, unsure if I should sit down or not. At last, she sighed heavily, kicked the table again, and got up. She glanced down towards my brother once more, then made a huffing noise and began to walk back towards the house. She didn't ask me to come with her but I followed anyway. We walked inside and crossed the sitting room, making way for Eleanor who stomped down the stairs with a face like thunder, and went through the kitchen to the utility room.

Thankfully, my mother was no longer in there. I really didn't want Edie to see her with the box of cleaning stuff, in her work clothes and slippers.

Edie bent and opened the drying machine. A warm smell of fabric conditioner filled the room. Inside was a jumble of clothes. She pulled them out and rifled through them, discarding things she didn't want on the floor. When she'd found what she was looking for she took her jumper off and dropped it on the pile of clean clothes from the dryer. She wore a black bra with a simple lace trim. I didn't even know they made normal underwear in black. I looked up at the ceiling to avoid staring at her.

She put a T-shirt on, a vest top with skinny black straps and a marijuana leaf stencilled onto it in white, with a scooped neck that showed off the multitude of silver and black necklaces that hung at different lengths around her neck. She stepped out of her skirt and left it on the floor with the other clothes then climbed into some shorts, denim cut-offs like mine only tighter and so short they grazed the curve of her buttocks. Then she reached into her bra and adjusted her breasts, pulling them into the middle to make more of a cleavage.

'Beachwear,' she said, answering a question I hadn't asked.

CHAPTER FIFTEEN

Angie
July 1986

Angie rang the doorbell and tried to neaten Jago while they waited. She sighed. Grey faded jeans with rips on the knees, scuffed Doc Marten boots, and black leather cuffs around each wrist was hardly the outfit she'd have chosen for him.

'Couldn't you have worn something a bit smarter?' she whispered.

'Like what?'

'I don't know. *Anything* else?'

'I'm painting a garden fence for them. You want me in a pin-striped suit for that?'

'You're not painting it yet. She wants to make sure you're suitable, remember?'

The door opened and Eleanor appeared. She wore white three-quarter length trousers and a striped top with her hair tied into a low bun at the nape of her neck.

'I thought you had a key?'

'Oh, I do.' Angie's cheeks grew hot. 'But it didn't feel right using it with you home.'

Eleanor looked past her and smiled at Jago.

'Come on, then. I'll show you what needs to be done. There's some sandpaper on the sideboard there.'

'You mean he's got the job?' Angie couldn't keep the surprise from her voice.

'I can't see how I'm going to find anybody else,' Eleanor said to Angie. 'Christ, as long as he can follow simple instructions, he'll be fine. It's not rocket science.' She smiled but it wasn't what Granfer would have called an honest smile.

'Angie, could you start upstairs and work down? I'm going to take a moment to sit down with a magazine as soon as I've got Jago going on the fence and it would be lovely to have a bit of peace and quiet.'

'No problem. I'll quickly change my shoes, get my stuff and head up.'

But Eleanor had turned away before she finished the sentence.

'Come on then, Jago,' she called as she walked away from them. 'Let's put you to work.'

'Did you *smell* her?' Jago whispered. 'Jesus. She must have had a skinful last night.'

'Shush.' Angie's eyes widened and she swallowed a laugh as she batted him on the arm. 'She'll hear.'

'Hear what?' The voice came from behind them.

Angie's heart stopped and she looked around to see Max Davenport standing in the doorway through to the kitchen.

'Nothing. Sorry.' She glanced at her son who didn't seem remotely worried about the possibility of having been overheard. 'Jago, love.' She grabbed the packet of sandpaper from the sideboard and thrust it out towards him. 'Go out and join Mrs Davenport.'

Angie smiled briefly at Max Davenport and eased past him

into the kitchen then hurried through to the utility room. She bent down, trying to work out the likelihood of Max Davenport having heard them, and opened the cleaning cupboard. She reached in for the bag she kept at the back and the plastic box of cleaning products, willing Max Davenport to walk away.

'We haven't been formally introduced. You must be Angie.' She turned and looked up to see him approaching her with his hand outstretched. 'Max Davenport. I understand you're the angel who swoops in and makes our house gleam before we arrive each weekend.'

She stood and reached into the bag for her indoor slippers, which she placed on the worktop.

'I'm not sure about being an angel, but, yes, I'm the one that cleans your house, Mr Davenport.'

'Max.'

Angie unzipped her pixie boots, grey suede with a pointed toe and a small heel, then slipped them off and put them in her bag.

He smiled and his eyes wandered over her. It didn't bother her; she was used to it. Yes, she had two children who were nearly grown up, but she kept herself looking nice. And, anyway, men were men, weren't they? It wasn't hard to get their attention. Wanted or otherwise.

'Mrs Davenport says you're down here to finish a book?' She got her Marigolds out and laid them on top of the cleaning box. She kept them hidden in the bag with her slippers as she hated the idea of wearing rubber gloves other people had used, even though she was sure Eleanor Davenport had never worn a pair in her life.

'Yes. But I've been desperate to spend a decent amount of time here since we bought the place. It's tiring driving back and forth in a weekend and I never feel like I really get to enjoy it. You live in a beautiful part of the world, Angie. The sea air is spectacular.'

He smiled at her. It was a smile Angie could tell he'd used a thousand times before on a thousand different women. Angie knew men. This one might have a posh voice and creases ironed into the front of his jeans but he was no different to any of the others.

She rested her hand on the worktop to balance herself then bent each leg in turn to put on her slippers.

'Well,' she said. 'I should get on. I'm going to start upstairs.' She hesitated. 'That won't disturb you, will it?'

'No, I'll be shut away in my study doing battle with a blank page. Though you would be a welcome distraction, I'm sure.'

'Going into battle? Sounds messy. I hope you don't expect me to clean up after you?' She kicked herself for the playful tone she'd used. It was complicated enough having one employer in pursuit of her without encouraging a second.

'No actual blood and guts to deal with thankfully.' He leant closer to her. 'Unless I murder the lady of the house, of course, in which case I'll need you on hand with the bleach.'

Angie smiled despite knowing she shouldn't. She decided she liked him, despite the flirting and the fact his mouth was stuffed full of plums. He had kind eyes, and kind eyes went a long way.

'Angie?'

Angie jumped and looked around to see Eleanor standing in the doorway.

'When you do the bathroom,' she said, 'can you make sure you give the floors a proper wash? I don't know when you last did them but they are in dire need of attention.'

Angie's stomach twisted. 'Oh... I... I did them last week. Did I do them wrong—?'

'No need to discuss it, but I'd like you to give them another going over. They're really quite filthy.' Then she turned on her heel and marched out of the room.

'I'll let you get on,' Max said.

'I cleaned them properly last week. I promise I did.'

'I'm sure you did.' He smiled again. 'If you're going to use her toothbrush to clean the loos it's the green one, not the orange.'

Angie wanted to laugh, but she suspected Eleanor might be listening from the kitchen, so instead she picked up the box of cleaning products and hurried towards the stairs.

Angie started in the bathroom as she'd been told. She examined the floor when she went in. It was spotless. Nothing more sinister than a fine film of dust, but she would have expected that after a week. As she rested the box of cleaning products on the windowsill her eye was caught by the two girls walking down the lawn towards the coast path. Though she couldn't put her finger on why, this new friendship made her nervous. She had the overwhelming urge to build a brick wall around her daughter to protect her from these people. Perhaps she was being overdramatic. Different wasn't a bad thing. Yes, the Davenports were from another planet, but it didn't mean they weren't nice people. It was just there was something about the way Tamsyn spoke about them, how she looked at them, adoration in her eyes and voice, plus the fact she seemed to think the house gave her some sort of connection to Rob. It made her uneasy. He should never have told her they'd live there one day. Silly nonsense. As if they could ever have afforded a house like this on Rob's salary. That was him, though. Always a dreamer.

Rob had loved the place since they were children and used

to drag their group over to play in the garden back in the days when it was owned by the absent granddaughter of an American tobacco merchant who'd built on the land well before the planners had any say over who and what could ruin the natural beauty of a place. She once made the mistake of telling him it gave her the creeps, so he'd dared her to run up the lawn and touch the surface of the pool. Just before she was about to creep through the gate he told her the pool was turned black by the souls of a hundred drowned sailors.

Don't be a wimp, Ange. You just have to touch it.

And the rest of them had crouched behind the fern and gorse as she pushed open the gate, heart hammering, hinges creaking as the house loomed over her. She'd run as fast as she could towards the pool filled with the ghosts of dead men. Of course one of the group had decided to split the air with a scream to scare her. It had worked and she'd half jumped out of her skin before escaping the house as fast as she could. When she caught up with them, they'd all laughed hysterically as they hared back along the cliff path towards St Just. Seeing Tamsyn walking through the same gate, history repeating itself, treading the same footsteps Rob and she had trodden two decades earlier, hit her with a pang of nostalgia.

She watched the girls until they disappeared from sight, then picked up a cloth and the bottle of Jif. Her son was on the other side of the garden, sanding the railings. Her heart tightened as she watched him. He was so deflated, so altered, and with each day that passed he seemed to lose a little more of his spirit. Rob's death had left a hole in all their hearts, but with Jago it was as if his fire had gone out. He wasn't robust enough to cope with the stress of the mine closures and the dearth of jobs on top of it. Tamsyn was different. There was a furnace inside her. Granfer said it was the red hair. Fiery and strong-willed. But Jago? Too sensitive, too delicate, and she worried he would wither to nothing if he carried on the path he was following. She knew he smoked marijuana and God only knew what else. So many of the kids took harder drugs too. He promised her he didn't touch stuff like that but she suspected he was lying to her. She didn't blame them though. What else was here for them? It was all so bleak. Though it would break her heart she wished he'd come down the stairs one morning with his rucksack packed and announce he was leaving for London. There was nothing for the young in this forgotten corner of England with its deserted mine shafts and boarded-up high streets. But she knew he wouldn't go. He was a home-bird like she was. As a child all he'd wanted was cuddles and while his sister was out with Rob climbing cliffs and building fires, he'd be curled up with her on the armchair, happily reading his motoring mags while she stroked his hair and breathed him in.

Four hours later she'd finished the house. Eleanor Davenport was drinking what Angie suspected was a gin and tonic on the white leather settee in the sitting room. Angie cleared her throat as she approached and the other woman turned her head to look at her.

'I've finished,' she said. 'I gave the bathroom floors a good scrub.'

Eleanor nodded.

Angie looked down towards the railings. Jago had removed his top and tucked it into the back of his jeans. He was crouched down, sanding one of the iron uprights, muscles working hard beneath his tanned skin.

'Do you need him to stay for a bit?'

'Until he's finished what he's doing, yes.'

'I was going to get a lift home with him. Would you mind if I called a friend to pick me up?'

Eleanor waved a dismissive hand in the direction of the telephone.

Angie rang Gareth at the shop and spoke as quietly as she could. 'Can you get here soon? I'll wait on the lane.'

Angie was happy to be free of the house. Eleanor Davenport made her anxious. She was unpredictable and one of those women who thought an awful lot of herself.

Angie leant against the gatepost and breathed deeply. There was nothing like the Cornish air. She'd only been out of Cornwall once, when she and Rob had gone on their honeymoon. They'd taken the train from Penzance to Blackpool. It had taken nearly nine hours to get there and as soon as she stepped onto the platform she missed the air of West Penwith. They were young and in love so obviously stayed mostly in their room. They only left it to see the lights on the pier one night and make trips out for chips when hunger got the better of them. She smiled when she remembered Rob kissing her stomach whilst reaching over her to get two chips – one for her and one for him – and the rest going cold as lust overwhelmed them yet again.

'What are they like, the Davenports?' Gareth asked as he flicked the indicator to turn off the lane onto the main road.

'I don't know them really. They aren't usually there when I clean. I've met her a couple of times. She's uptight and very...' Angie paused to choose her word, 'polished.'

Gareth nodded, his face serious. Angie tried not to think of Rob then, of him behind the wheel, his strong hands gripping it lightly, the sun catching his eyelashes and the side of his face. He would have glanced at her and laughed at her comment.

She imagined him replying. Pointing out how the two of them could have done with a polish.

In need of a polish but happy, eh, Ange?

Though years had passed he was still with her every moment. It tended to be only the good things she remembered. His laugh, the dimple on his left cheek when he smiled, the muscles on his chest that were covered in a fine down of strawberry-blonde hair she liked to kiss, the taste of fresh sweat on his skin. She looked out of the car window. Focused on the sea in the distance, hazy with the promise of rain on the horizon. The things that had driven her mad about him, made her scream with anger and frustration, had faded. They'd become irrelevant. How she regretted the arguments over silly things of no consequence. Who cared whose turn it was to put the bins out when all that mattered was pressing her lips to his downy chest?

She leant her head against the passenger side window and watched The Cliff House retreating in the wing mirror. Such a ridiculous house, brash and shining white, all straight lines and huge windows, as conspicuous as a chalk carving on a grassy hillside. Her house would have fitted into it five times over and it wasn't even the Davenports' main home. When Angie had gone for an interview for the cleaning position, Eleanor Davenport told her their 'principal residence' was in somewhere called Holland Park. She said it as if Angie should have known where that was. She didn't but she nodded anyway, just in case not knowing where Holland Park was could cost her the job.

'It was nice last night.' Gareth's voice cut into her thoughts. She pulled her head away from the window and looked at him. He glanced at her with a shy smile.

'It was.'

'Can I take you out again tonight?'

'Oh, well, I was thinking… I might have a night in.'

'Because of the kids?'

She recalled Tamsyn's disapproval, the hurt in her eyes, looking more like Rob than she'd ever done before.

'No,' she said. 'I'm tired. That's all. I'd planned a bit of telly in my pyjamas.'

Gareth dropped his head like a child who'd been told Christmas was cancelled.

Angie suspected he knew she was lying. That it was, as he guessed, because of her children. He would never be able to understand how hard it was for them. They only knew their own grief. For them Rob could never be replaced. That was all they could see. They were blinkered. They could never appreciate how lonely she was. How lying in her foldaway bed in the sitting room, the silence echoing in her head like funeral bells night after night after night, was eating away at her. Cutting her adrift on a lonely piece of wreckage.

They pulled up outside her house and Gareth stilled the engine.

'Thanks for the lift.'

'No problem.'

Her hands rested in her lap and he leant over and laid his on top of them. They held eyes for a moment then she eased away from him and opened the car door.

'If you change your mind about tonight let me know.'

As she watched him drive away, his exhaust spluttering small coughs of black fumes into the fresh sea air, she wished he'd asked to stay for a quick cup of tea.

CHAPTER SIXTEEN

Tamsyn
July 1986

We walked along the path in single file and, even though it was supposed to be me showing her the way, Edie walked ahead. I noticed she had a small cross on her left shoulder, black and uneven, as if it had been drawn in felt tip pen with a shaky hand.

'Is that a tattoo?'

'Yup. I got it when I was fourteen.' She glanced back at me briefly. 'I did it myself.'

'Yourself?'

She nodded.

'What did your mum say?'

'One of the plus points of boarding school is no parents watching and plenty of opportunity to break the rules.'

'God, mine would go mental.'

Edie stopped walking and turned. There was a mischievous glint in her eye. 'You know, you should totally get one. Shall I do it for you?'

'Really?'

Edie nodded vigorously. 'Yes. Really. I'd love to.'

It was a nice idea, the thought of Edie etching my skin with ink, but there was no way I could get a tattoo. I wasn't joking about Mum going mad. She thought tattoos were disgusting and couldn't understand why anybody would want to deface their body in such a permanent way. 'I can't. She really would kill me.'

'You're such a good girl, aren't you?' Her eyes narrowed a fraction and her voice had a sudden unkind edge, as if being a *good girl* was the very worst thing I could be.

She started walking again and I fixed my eyes on the mark, picturing it on my own skin, matching, like hers.

We walked down the steps, a sturdy construction of thick wire, wooden slats, ropes and heavy stakes driven into the sand. The ground was sheltered from the harsh onshore winds here, and orange lilies and delicate pinks grew amongst lush fronds of fern which tumbled down the sandy slope in a glorious carpet of colour. When I stepped onto the beach, I pulled off my shoes, and dug my toes into the sand, pushing them through the layer of hot and dry to the cool damp beneath. We walked down towards the sea and stopped at the reach of the break, where we stood side by side, the waves running up to kiss our feet with spume.

I crouched and my fingers searched the sand for a few stones. I threw one in a high arc into the sea. It fell into the churning water with a splash before sinking down to the seabed below. Jago and I had spent hours doing this when we were younger. Dad would walk up onto an outcrop of rock nearby with his binoculars and bird book to scan the cliffs and sky, and we'd sit beside each other on the sand with a small pile of carefully selected stones between us. Then we'd throw them, counting down from three so they released at the same time, and see who could throw theirs the furthest. Sometimes I'd win and when I did, Jago would pat me on the back and say, *Good throw, that*.

Looking back on it I knew he'd let me win on those occasions and I had a sudden rush of warmth towards him.

I turned and stared up at The Cliff House which stood like a monument, a temple perhaps, on the expanse of empty cliff. The sunlight fell on it in such a way that it appeared to glow, its windows blazing, a haze of light splayed around its outline.

'You're so lucky to live there,' I said to Edie as I threw a pebble.

She wrinkled her nose. 'I *hate* it. I've got no way of getting out, even for a day. I'm *literally* trapped.'

'You should see where we live.'

'What's it like?'

'Tiny. Dark. Horrible.' I threw another stone out and watched it splash and disappear. 'When Dad died it stopped feeling like home. And now Mum's got this guy hanging around and every time he comes over it feels like we're being invaded.'

'Do you think she'll marry him?'

Her question hit me so hard in the stomach I felt physically winded. 'No!' I said sharply. 'No. Of course not. She barely knows him. And, anyway, she loved my dad too much.'

'But he's dead. And she's so pretty and young. It must be awful for her to have lost the love of her life. God, we'll probably all die soon anyway, catch AIDS or get nuked by mad Soviets or taken over by aliens. We might as well squeeze as much love out of this crappy life as we can, don't you think?'

My fists clenched. I was overcome with wanting to scream at her. Take her face in my hands and press it into the sand until she promised she'd never say anything about Mum marrying Gareth bloody Spence again. If I had to choose between that and crisping to death in a nuclear war I'd choose the nuking without

135

hesitation. Edie didn't get it. Her father was alive. He didn't drown at sea. He wasn't rotted to bones and wisps of hair in a box in an overcrowded graveyard. Edie's life was dipped in gold. How could she ever understand? So I blocked out her comments about Gareth bloody Spence and thoughts of pushing her into the sand, and walked onwards in the direction of Sennen.

The two beaches – Gwenver, the one we were on, and Sennen Cove, the one we were heading for – were wide and sandy, and separated by a small inlet and a rocky outcrop which cut the two bays off from each other at high tide.

'The tide's on the turn,' I said, as she caught up with me. 'We haven't long before the route back is under the sea.'

She was playing with a handful of sand, allowing it to trickle through her fingers like an egg timer. 'What type of girl does your brother usually go out with?'

'No idea,' I said, surprised by the question. 'He's never brought a girl back. I don't even know if he's had a girlfriend.'

'Really?' she said. 'He's had sex though?'

'Edie! God, I don't want to think about my brother having sex, thank you very much.' I shuddered and she laughed. I cast her a sideways look and said carefully, 'Have you?'

'Have I what? Had sex?'

I nodded.

'Of course I have. Haven't you?'

I flushed with embarrassment at both the question and my own naivety. 'No. Not really. I mean, there was this boy. We…' I hesitated, '*did* things. But it wasn't very good.'

'I'm not sure it ever is. What happened?'

I decided not to tell her what happened. It still made me die inside. So instead I shrugged. 'Not much.'

'What's his name, this boyfriend of yours?'

'He's not my boyfriend,' I said.

She laughed. 'You made him up, didn't you?'

'No, of course not.'

'So what's his name then?'

My skin felt hot and red. 'Kevin,' I said at last, wincing as I did. 'Kevin Chambers.'

'Kevin?' She exploded with laughter. 'Oh my God, Tamsyn. You actually got it on with someone called *Kevin*?'

I crossed my arms and tried to push away the recollection of kissing Kevin Chambers, horrifyingly wet, his tongue circling my mouth like a washing machine, his stubby probing finger slipped down into my pants in a dark corner of the school disco.

'I lost my virginity two years ago. It was with one of the beach staff at the Four Seasons in Florida. I don't know why I'm laughing at the name Kevin. My guy was called Chuck Junior. Can you believe it? Anyway, I can't say the earth moved but he looked like Rob Lowe and bought me tacos afterwards.'

I didn't like to ask what tacos were.

She stopped suddenly and bent down. Her slender fingers reached out to close around something on the sand. She stood up and outstretched her arm. Between her thumb and forefinger was a piece of sea glass. It was a brilliant aquamarine, smooth, opaque, without imperfection, and weathered to a perfect oval. She held it up to the sun and shut one eye to look at it. The light passing through it made it glow. Then without a word she gave it to me and walked on.

The sea glass sat in the centre of my palm like a turquoise pearl in an oyster shell. I held it up to my lips and rubbed it against them, closed my eyes to marvel at its silkiness, then I slipped it into my pocket and jogged to catch up with her.

The beach became increasingly crowded as we neared Sennen and, by the time we reached the concrete ramp which led up to the car park, scores of pink-and-white tourists patchworked the sand. They sat so close to each other there was barely room to pick our way through. There was a buzz in the air, screams of joy, mothers telling children not to throw sand, fathers grumbling as they battled with deckchairs and inflatables, excitable laughs and angry shouts at thieving gulls who scoured the holiday chaos for chips to steal.

'Is Florida anything like this?'

Edie laughed. 'Not exactly. I mean parts of Florida are like this, only hotter. But where we go has its own private beach so there are fewer people. And there are white sunbeds with white towels and a waiter with the name of the hotel stitched to his shirt to bring you drinks. And obviously, because it's America, everywhere you go people tell you to *have a nice day*.'

Her American accent was perfect and as I walked up the ramp I repeated the words in my head and tried to mimic it.

'It's boring though. Max is always writing, Eleanor spends all day dousing herself in gin and baby oil and turning herself to sozzled leather. The last time we went I saw this father playing with his kids, you know, bat and ball, throwing them up in the sea, reading to them, and all I could do was look at my parents and think how fucking shit they were.'

As she told me this story I pictured my own dad. He was the father playing with his kids who Edie had watched with jealousy. If we'd ever had the chance to go to Florida I know he'd have played with me all day long.

'Come on, don't look so glum. Let's get an ice cream.' Edie grabbed my arm. 'We'll eat them on the walk back.'

We joined the queue of children with rubber rings clutched under their arms and dads in T-shirts stretched over their bellies. When we got to the front, Edie asked the lady for a scoop of vanilla and a flake, then she turned to me. 'What do you want?'

'Oh,' I said. 'No. I'm okay.'

'You sure?'

'I don't have any money on me.'

'My treat.'

'Really?'

'Of course.' She looked up at the lady and said, 'We'll have two of those, please.'

'I get paid next week. I'll pay you back, I promise—'

'Oi! Tamsyn Tresize!' called a voice from somewhere behind us. 'Who's your lezzer girlfriend?'

We turned in the direction of the voice. It had come from a group of boys who were leaning against the wall of the car park, Choppers and BMXs discarded in a mess around them. I groaned when I realised who they were.

'Idiots from school,' I whispered.

The boys, who were all smoking, a few holding cans of lager, nudged each other whilst smirking at the boy who'd shouted. He was a thick-necked skinhead with a busted nose and pockmarked skin called Billy Granger.

Edie gave the lady behind the counter the money then handed me my ice cream. We both took a lick and smiled. It was delicious, creamy and sweet. I couldn't remember the last time I'd had an ice cream.

'I'd love a lick of your girlfriend!' called Billy Granger, causing the others to fold in half with laughter around him.

'Ignore them,' I said quietly. 'They'll get bored soon enough.'

Edie threw the boys a contemptuous look then took hold of my wrist and pulled me after her back towards the ramp.

'Oi! I was talking to you!'

I glanced over my shoulder to see Billy chuck his cigarette onto the sand behind him and push himself off the wall to follow us. He thrust his hands deep into his pockets and swaggered side to side like a listing boat. The rest of the group trailed after him. My heart was thumping. These weren't nice boys. These were the type of boys who stole dinner money at the school gate and shoved first years in the playground. I stared straight ahead and focused on The Cliff House up ahead.

The boys drew alongside us and fell into step.

'Hey, blondie,' Billy said. 'I know you're a lezzer but I reckon I can turn you.'

More sniggering. More jeers.

'You want me. Admit it, you slag!'

I considered breaking into a run, but knew it wouldn't work. They were faster than us and would catch up easily and when they did things would be worse.

Edie stopped dead in her tracks then turned to face them, squaring her shoulders and raising her chin in defiance.

'Leave it, Edie,' I whispered. 'Let's just get back.'

'No.' She spoke loud enough for them to hear. 'These little boys are rude and annoying and are ruining our walk.'

'Making it better, you mean,' Billy said. 'Offering you a *ride* when I know you're gagging.'

The boys had stopped walking. They jostled and nudged each

other. Whispered. Waited to see what this new girl was going to do. I glanced at a family beside us on the beach. The man was reading a newspaper in a colourful deckchair while his wife bounced a baby on her lap, sand coating his pudgy hands and chin where he'd been eating it. There was a second child. She wore a frilled swimsuit and banged an upturned bucket with a small blue spade. The woman was staring at us.

'You know, that's exactly what I meant,' Edie said. 'We were literally just saying, weren't we Tamsyn, that we really hope we get the chance to screw a guy on the beach with a great big dick.'

I gasped and Billy smiled at his mates like he'd won a prize.

'But,' she said in a breezy voice, 'I heard *you* have one this size.' She wiggled her little finger in the air and gave a regretful shrug. 'Which is *such* a shame.'

She stood with one hand on her hip, ice cream in the other, eyes shining with bravery. The woman beside us muttered, disgust on her face, as she exchanged looks with her husband who momentarily glanced up from his paper.

Billy Granger's smile slipped away as he visibly attempted to process what she'd hurled at him. His friends tried not to laugh, but two of them didn't manage it and were forced to smother their sniggering with fake coughing and dropped heads.

His mouth twisted into a snarl as he fought the bristling humiliation. '*What* did you say?'

My stomach rolled with nerves. I swallowed. My mouth had dried up, the taste of vanilla ice cream now cloying and sickly.

'Come on, Tamsyn.' She pulled on my arm as she turned. 'These babies are boring me.'

We took a couple of paces, then her body lurched forward

as he shoved her from behind. 'I *said* – you ugly bitch – what did you say?'

She stopped. Turned again. Stepped close to him.

'And *I* said, your dick is so fucking *tiny* I'd need a microscope to find it.' She spoke deliberately and clearly, giving each word time and space to sink in. 'So I won't be having sex with you.' She moved her face so close to his he was forced to lean away from her. 'Do you understand, moron?'

The corner of his top lip twitched as his fists clenched and unclenched like two beating hearts.

Edie stepped back from him then raised the ice cream to her mouth. She stuck her tongue out and, with her eyes bolted to his, licked the ice cream slowly. 'Now,' she said, her voice as sweet and smooth as honey. 'If it's okay with you, my friend and I were enjoying a nice walk on the beach.'

I held my breath as we walked away from them and carefully picked our way through the sea of people, who stared at us whilst muttering to each other, tutting and exchanging glances. But Edie didn't care. She was magnificent.

'Stuck-up cow!' Billy shouted after us.

Edie swung around as she walked and flicked her middle finger up at him then collapsed against me and we both started to laugh uncontrollably.

'Oh my God! His *face*.' I could barely talk for laughing. 'That lot are never going to let him live it down. They'll be wiggling their little fingers at him for weeks.'

She laughed and licked her ice cream. 'Stupid idiot. I mean, this ice cream is delicious, as if I was *ever* going to give him a lick.'

Then she hooked her arm though mine and we strolled

through the crowds as if we'd been friends for years. My chest swelled with pride and at that moment, with the ice cream slipping down my throat and my arm linked with Edie's on our way back to The Cliff House, I couldn't have been happier even if I was the Queen of England.

But then the air was sliced through by a bloodcurdling scream.

We both stopped giggling and spun around in the direction of the noise. There was a woman running down towards the sea. She was screaming over and over. The picture-perfect holiday scene of a few moments before changed before our eyes. Other people began to run after the woman. There were shouts. Worried faces. Everybody looked out across the water. Shielding their eyes. Searching the waves for the source of her anguish. Gradually, like a building storm, the rumble of concern grew. Edie grabbed my wrist and pulled me towards the commotion. We joined the gathering crowd in time to see the lifeguard throw his loudhailer onto the sand and sprint down to the water. The breaking waves were large, rolling up and over, crashing down vertically. There was a steep shelf not far from the shoreline, and at certain points in the rising tide the water deepened there and caused a mighty undertow.

The crowd were talking, exchanging information, and it was clear within moments of joining them that a child had been pulled under and out to sea. My stomach turned over as I saw the figure struggling and I felt the warm rise of bile in my throat.

'It's a boy. The man's got him,' Edie said. We watched the lifeguard hook his arm under the boy's shoulders and swim back to shore, his free arm powering through the waves. 'I don't think he's moving.' The thrill in her voice grated. Her eyes shone and she reached for my hand with excitement.

The lifeguard was buffeted left and right as he scrambled out of the break. In his arms was the boy. The child was around nine or ten. His head lolled backwards. Arms hung limp. There was sand stuck to his body, which was white and dipped blue with cold.

'Stand back!' a man's voice shouted. 'Give them space for God's sake!'

Edie pulled me forward, pushing us through the crowd until we reached the front of the semicircle which had surrounded the spectacle. Men and women clutched each other, hands over mouths, eyes fixed on the boy as he was laid down on the sand. The lifeguard's face was contorted with worry. He flapped his hand angrily in the hope of people moving back. If anything they seemed to inch closer. Someone behind me asked whoever they were with what the hell the parents were thinking to let such a small boy out of their sight for a second.

'Hush,' said another voice. 'It could happen to anyone.'

'He's dead.' Edie made no effort to lower her voice and right then I wished I wasn't standing anywhere near her. 'You can tell. Look. He's definitely dead. His lips are purple and there's seaweed in his mouth.'

The small boy was motionless. His hair was wet, plastered over his cheeks and eyes. I pictured his lungs filled with salt-sharpened water, no more room for air, tiny particles of sand floating around in them like astronauts in space. I tore my eyes off him and looked out over the waves, searched the sea for my father. We were only a mile or so from where he died. I imagined how he had fought to keep afloat. Shouted for help. How his head had disappeared beneath the surface before the waves closed over him. My body collapsed from the inside, the horror of what was unfurling on the beach dredging up every memory associated with losing my dad to the sea. I wanted to turn away but I was held rigid by fear and agonising grief, my eyes wide, bolted to the lifeless figure of the child.

Be alive. Please, please be alive.

The lifeguard was crouched over him. He held his face in his hand. With his other hand he pinched his nose closed. He tipped his chin up and pulled open his mouth, then pressed his lips to him. Two breaths. Another two. Forcing air into him. Another two. Short and sharp. The woman we'd watched run down to the sea screaming knelt beside them. Tears streaked her stricken face. There was a man behind her with his hand on her shoulder with a small girl in his other arm whose head was tucked into his neck.

'Why's he bothering?' Edie said. 'You can see the kid's dead.'

Shut up.

'God, Tamsyn. Can you believe we're seeing this? I've never seen a dead body before. It's insane.'

Shut up. Shut up. Shut up.

The lifeguard pumped the boy's chest with both hands, hard enough to snap his delicate ribs like twigs. I dug my nails into my palm. I saw my dad's face, eyes glazed, mouth filled with salt water and grit. If he'd been with us on the beach he'd have saved the boy. I knew it for sure and I wished then he was there, that he hadn't died, that he'd been with us, buying us ice creams, near enough to help these desperate people.

Horror seeped into every part of me as I watched the lifeguard push two more breaths into the child's listless body. More compressions. A hushed, expectant silence had settled over the crowd, the quiet only broken by the occasional sob or concerned whisper. One by one those watching started to lower their heads sadly. A few turned away, head in their hands, tears forming in their eyes.

But then the boy coughed.

Water sprayed out of his mouth. Another cough. A breath in. His head rolled to one side. Water sputtered from his mouth as if he were vomiting. The crowd seemed to exhale in unison. Somebody laughed. A few people cried out with relief. Then there was clapping. The lifeguard fell back on his haunches with his hands on his thighs. He tipped his head back, eyes closed, body heaving with relief. The mother fell on her son and pulled him close. Her arms knotted around him as her body gave way to shuddering sobs. The man behind her sat down on the sand and held his other child tightly to him as he cried silently.

'Come on, let's get out of here.' Edie sounded disappointed as she turned and walked past me, pushing her way through the people.

My legs were so wobbly I wasn't sure I could make it back.

'Jesus,' Edie breathed. 'Can you imagine if he'd died? And we'd seen it?'

She sounded exhilarated, unaffected by what we'd witnessed. My head rang with the screams of his mother. The sight of his father weeping. The exhausted lifeguard desperately trying to expel the water from the child's saturated lungs and fill them with air. I couldn't speak. My whole body tumbled with fear and emotion and I trembled uncontrollably. With every step I worried I might collapse. I couldn't clear my mind. All I could see was the boy laid out on the sand. His limp limbs. Mouth filled with water and weed. Beside him my father's lifeless body flickering in and out of focus. I tried to block it out. Breathed deeply. Focused on the words I'd been told at his funeral – God knows who by – that drowning was the best way to die.

Like dreaming. Painless and peaceful. Just slipping away.

They lied. That boy hadn't looked peaceful. He'd looked weak and broken, the wrong colour, battered and twisted having done battle with the sea.

'Are you okay?'

I held back my tears and nodded.

'It'll be nice to get back for a swim,' she said. 'It's so damn hot.'

We walked back in silence. Edie strode ahead. I dragged behind. I couldn't comprehend how she was so unshaken. Was this what they taught them at boarding school? Taught them to be tough and without emotion. Army officers, politicians, heads of business, and Edie Davenport, all of them blessed with the ability to handle any situation without batting an eyelid?

The walk up from the beach was a steep one, hot and sticky, and I couldn't seem to stop shaking. I had to keep reminding myself the boy was fine. He didn't drown. He was safe with his parents, wrapped up on his mother's lap, people around him all fussing and loving and thanking God. But it was only when we got back to The Cliff House, when I stepped onto the lawn, that my trembling body began to calm. The gate clanged shut and as it did I felt safer, the clamp around my stomach easing, my breaths coming more steadily.

Jago was still working on the fence. He was shirtless with his top tucked into his waistband. His tanned torso shone with a film of sweat highlighting his muscles which flexed beneath his skin as he rubbed the railings back and forth.

'Hey,' Edie said as we neared him. 'Looks like hot work.'

'It's okay.' He glanced at her briefly but then looked at me. 'Mum's gone home. I can give you a lift when I'm done here.' Then his face fell in concern. 'Hey,' he said, stepping towards me, his hand resting on my arm. 'What's up? You're white as a sheet.'

'She's fine,' Edie answered. 'A boy was pulled out of the water and needed the kiss of life but it had a happy ending. He didn't die.'

Jago ignored Edie and pulled me in for a hug. 'Jesus,' he breathed. 'Fuck.'

'I'm okay,' I whispered.

'Honestly, there's nothing to get worked up about,' said Edie. 'I mean, he's probably running around demanding fish and chips right now. It's fine.'

Jago squeezed me. 'Do you want me to take you home? I can leave this.'

'No!' Edie said with too much enthusiasm. 'Don't go, Tamsyn! Not before you've had a swim. Jago, you should come too. My father has spare swimming trunks if you'd like to cool off before you go home.'

I shook my head and gave him a pretend smile. I wanted to stay. I didn't want to face the brutal world outside the fence.

He stared at me for a moment then addressed Edie. 'She can stay and swim. I'm okay though.' Then he returned his attention to the railings.

Edie told me to wait in the living room while she went up to put her swimming costume on and grab one for me to borrow as, in my haste to leave that morning, I'd stupidly forgotten mine.

I sat on the edge of the settee and noticed how clean it was. Mum was good at her job. Didn't cut corners and cared about the detail, plumping up the cushions, cleaning the white

148

leather with furniture spray which turned it slippery, polishing its chrome feet to a mirror-shine. I leant forward and breathed on the glass coffee table top, then with my finger I drew a cross like the one that marked Edie's shoulder. Then I pressed my forearm against the underside of the table so the cross appeared to be on my skin. It faded quickly and I sat back to wait for Edie to reappear.

She came down the stairs with a towel wrapped around her. She threw a black swimming costume at me. 'It's my school one. Regulation, I'm afraid. I borrowed one of Eleanor's so you can use it.'

'Thank you,' I said.

'No big deal.' She smiled then walked towards the door to the terrace. 'You can change in the downstairs loo.'

I changed quickly then folded my clothes and put them on the table in the hall. Edie was standing by the pool steps. When I saw her I inhaled sharply. She was wearing a hot pink string bikini. Gone were the leather bracelets and bangles. The only piece of jewellery she wore was a silver necklace with a heart on it. The scraps of material which comprised her bikini drew attention to her small but perfect breasts. I squirmed, feeling horribly self-conscious in the low-rise black one-piece made of thick itchy material that smelled of stale chlorine. I fought the urge to bolt back indoors and get dressed into my clothes again.

Down by the railings Jago was staring at her. When he caught me looking at him he dropped his eyes and turned his back to us. Edie squealed and dived in, her feet perfectly aligned, hands clasped over her head, toes pointed. She made barely a splash. For a moment or two I felt a creep of panic crawling over me. All I could think of was the water seeping into her lungs, that she wasn't going to come up, that if I stepped closer to the edge I'd see her hanging lifelessly in the water. My heart sped up. She was under too long. I looked down at my brother. Wanted to call out to him but couldn't form words.

Then she appeared. Her head pushed up through the surface. She swam to the end of the pool and heaved herself half out then leant on her arms.

'It's lovely!' she called to my brother. 'Are you sure you won't come in?'

He looked at her, seemed to hesitate, but then shook his head and went back to his sanding.

She turned and beckoned to me. I forced my legs into motion. Moving one then the other until I reached the steps. It felt odd to be swimming with someone else in the pool. Wrong. Unnatural, almost. But the water was crisp and cool and as I stretched out to swim towards her she smiled at me. I drew near her and noticed her mascara had run, which gave the impression of her crying black tears.

'Does your mum mind you borrowing her bikini?'

Edie laughed then pushed herself off backwards to float on the surface to reveal her perfect breasts and taut stomach the colour of cream.

'As long as she doesn't have to *deal* with me she doesn't give a shit.'

'Deal with you?'

'You know, be an actual mother.' She outstretched her arms then kicked a couple of times and drifted slowly to the other side of the pool. She righted herself and pushed her hair back with both hands. 'She's annoyed because I've been told I can't go back to school. *Expelled for bad behaviour*. They've paid thousands and I'm not allowed to finish my A levels.' She was watching something behind me. I glanced back and saw my brother was putting his T-shirt back on.

'What will you do?' I said as I swam closer to her in an attempt to get her attention back.

It worked. She looked back at me and gave an exaggerated shrug. 'Who knows? I'm basically a problem now. Like Maria. How *do* you solve a problem like Maria?' Then she trilled with laughter and dived backwards, twisting her body under the water and swimming beneath the surface, a pink fish glistening in the blackness.

As she broke the surface, her body brushed against my hand, which sent an electric charge skittering though me. She smiled at me. Jago walked past the pool. She gave him nothing more than a cursory glance, then looped her arms around my neck and whispered in my ear, her breath hot against my water-cooled skin: 'I'm glad we're friends.'

Then she flipped over like a seal and swam to the end of the pool.

It was as if a fire had been lit inside me. Every cell of my body sang as I took a breath and ducked beneath the surface. The water closed over my ears. Blocked out the sound. I opened my eyes and watched the slashes of sunlight cutting through the water and the reflected ripples which danced like water piskies, finally safe from the horrors of the episode on the beach.

In the distance was a flash of pink. I pushed off and glided over to her, then broke the surface, emerging just in front of her.

Then I smiled.

'I'm glad we're friends too.'

CHAPTER SEVENTEEN

Jago
July 1986

He sits with his grandfather and makes a show of trying to find a home for a piece of the ridiculous puzzle. The picture he's trying to make is of a grassy field with sheep and cows, idyllic, with butterflies in the blue sky and a white picket fence and a lamb in the foreground with a ladybird on its back.

All he can think about is her. The moment he caught her looking at him and dropped his head to avoid her gaze.

Don't be stupid, says the voice in his head. *Why would a girl like Edie Davenport be interested in you? You're a waste of space. Good for nothing but sanding railings.*

They are from different worlds.

And yet...

Did he imagine her half-smile? Or the way her eyes lingered on him? He had tried not to watch her swimming. Had torn his eyes off her body when she floated in the black water. Didn't want to be a creep.

But how exquisite she is. Out of his league. Forbidden fruit from a world of red braces, striped suits and Swiss bank accounts. He's seen them on the news, those educated men in cavernous rooms filled with screens and rolling numbers, red sports cars parked outside London mansion blocks, portable phones like bricks.

Not his world.

Not his world of broken men with blackened lungs, who scream in pain and carry bloodied handkerchiefs. Bent backs. Fingers so ingrained with grime that years would never see them clean. His world is one of rusted boats and silent engine rooms and men who spend their days in betting shops or the pub or at home, staring at the wall, waiting for a job.

Any fucking job.

He thinks of his father. Imagines him looking down from wherever he is. His dad. The lionheart. The *hero*. Honoured with a brass plaque. A town in mourning. The sad talk of pubs and shops and dinner tables. Robert Tresize. Courage of a hundred men. Heart of an angel.

And his son? A waste of fucking space.

You? You're Rob's son? Are you sure?

The sceptical strangers are right. How can they be father and son? So different. On and on go the whispers behind his back. On and on. Speaking their truths.

Why would a girl like her look at someone like him?

His grandfather hacks as he reaches for a piece of jigsaw. He tries it for size, but it doesn't fit, so he replaces it back with the others.

'What are we... having for tea?' he says. 'Did she... tell you?'

'Fish,' Jago says, ignoring his grandfather's rasping. 'Gareth gave her a couple of bits of haddock.'

Gareth. The prick. Trying to buy them with fillets of fish.

Granfer grins. 'Love a... bit of haddock.'

Cough, cough, hack.

Jago doesn't move until the wheezing calms, just sits and stares at the jigsaw.

'How was…' *Cough. Hack.* 'The fence painting?'

'Easy enough.'

'Your mum'll be… pleased.'

Jago nods.

'Shame your dad isn't… here.'

He nods again.

'He was a good man, that one. Clever, too. Different from… the likes of me and… you.'

He watches as Granfer's eyes mist over with tears for his dead son.

His mother calls up to them.

'Tea's ready,' Jago says and places the homeless bit of jigsaw back on the table.

'Lovely,' the old man says, licking his lips. 'Nice bit of haddock.'

'Hi, love.' His mum smiles as he walks into the kitchen.

'Granfer's on his way down.'

Jago opens the fridge.

'Don't eat anything now. You'll ruin your tea.' She sounds weary today. 'I'm about to put it on the table. Fish. From Gareth.'

'Prick,' Jago whispers under his breath as he shuts the fridge door.

'All good today? You got on okay at the Davenports?'

He nods. 'Though I don't like the way Tam is with them. She's not herself with them, acts weird.'

'Hush,' his mother says. 'It's good she's found a friend. Don't piss on her chips, love.'

He thinks of his dad. Of how he'd have frowned.

Don't say piss on her chips, Ange. Not in front of the kids.

And his mother would have laughed and rolled her eyes behind his back, and he and his sister would have glowed inside because she'd said *piss*.

'I'm going out.'

'But tea—'

'I'm not hungry. Granfer can have mine. He loves haddock.'

'Where are you going?' He avoids looking at her, but not before he catches her lips pressed tight with disappointment, shadows settled in her eyes.

'Just out.'

'I thought we could eat together.'

He turns his back on the sadness in her voice.

Before he leaves he reaches into his jacket pocket. Pulls out some folded notes. Leaves them on the kitchen table. 'Rick paid me yesterday,' he says. 'Sorry it's not much.'

His mum smiles at him. Takes the money. Plants a kiss on his cheek. 'Thanks, love. You're a good boy. I know it's been tough these last few months. Your dad would be proud of you.'

He walks out without replying.

CHAPTER EIGHTEEN

Tamsyn
July 1986

Mum had tried to persuade me not to go to The Cliff House on a Sunday but I'd told her it was fine.

'They don't mind. Eleanor said I was welcome whenever.'

'Yes, love, but Sunday? Sunday isn't for disturbing people. Use the telephone first, at least.'

So as soon as the clock hit eleven – Mum said I was absolutely not to call any house on a Sunday before eleven – I borrowed ten pence from her purse and ran up to the box.

Edie answered.

'Hi,' I said breathlessly. 'It's me. Tamsyn.'

'Oh, hey.' She sounded as if she'd only just woken up and I was pleased I hadn't called earlier. 'You okay?'

'I'm fine.' I hesitated, suddenly feeling unsure about inviting myself over. 'Are you busy today? I was wondering…' My voice trailed away.

'You'd like to come over?'

I grinned. 'Yes,' I said quickly. 'Is that okay?'

'Of course.'

'Should you check with your parents?'

And Edie laughed.

Eleanor was sitting at the table on the terrace when I walked up the lawn. I waved and she lifted her sunglasses off and squinted at me, then smiled.

'Hello, Tamsyn,' she said as I approached. She was filing her nails. There was a gold bag in front of her with scissors and nail polishes visible within. 'What a surprise to see you again.'

I said hello, then paused to catch my breath having walked over at quite a pace. 'Thanks for letting me come.'

Eleanor smiled. 'E-*dith*!' she called. 'Tamsyn's here!'

Edie shouted from the house to say she'd be there in a second. I saw her standing at her window. She pointed at her wrist and gestured to tell me she'd be down in five minutes.

I hovered, not sure what to do, but then Eleanor patted the other chair. 'Do sit.'

'Your nails are nice,' I said after a moment or two.

She laughed as if I'd told a hilarious joke. 'Would you like me to do yours?'

I splayed my hands in front of me and grimaced. 'They're awful. I'm not sure you can do much with them.'

She flicked her hand a couple of times indicating I should show her. When I did she made a face. 'Good God, child. Give them here.'

It tickled as she filed and I had to fight to stop from flinching and pulling my hand back. She worked quickly, stopping every now and then to inhale from one of her gold-tipped cigarettes, which smoked in the ashtray to the side of her.

It wasn't long until my nails were neat and round and even in length.

'Better,' she said. 'You should look after yourself. You're a pretty girl. I'm amazed your mother doesn't insist on doing them for you if you aren't going to do them properly yourself.'

'She's never done my nails.'

'Really? How old are you?'

'Sixteen.'

'Goodness, at sixteen you should have a manicure at least every six weeks.' She rifled in her bag and retrieved a soft coral-coloured polish. 'You'll see such a difference when I've finished.'

My chest swelled with joy as she grabbed hold of my finger. I was mesmerised by the way she painted each of my nails, rhythmically drawing one stroke down the centre, then one to the left, then one to the right. No mistakes. No smudges or wrinkles. Not a spot of colour smudged my skin.

'Thank you,' I said when she finished. 'I love them.'

'My pleasure, *cherie*.' She screwed the lid back on to the varnish and dropped it into her bag.

I held out my hands and tipped them from side to side to admire them. They looked like they belonged to somebody else, as if they'd been cut from another person and sewn onto me.

'It's perfect here, isn't it?' I said, without thinking. 'Like heaven on earth.'

'Perfect?'

'Yes. All of it. You. Mr Davenport. Edie.' I paused. 'The house. You're so lucky.'

She took a long draw on the cigarette before pressing it forcefully into the ashtray to extinguish it. 'You'll need a top coat on that or it'll ruin. Give me your hand.' She selected another bottle from her bag and held my hand tightly as she added a coat of clear varnish to each of my newly coral nails.

'God. Leave the poor girl alone, Eleanor.'

I turned to see Edie walking towards us.

'Why? We're both happy, aren't we, Tamsyn? And it's nice to have someone who'll actually let me do her nails.' She smiled at me and I thought I might explode with ecstasy. 'Anyway, it's a tragedy to see someone so beautiful not making the most of herself.' Eleanor stared pointedly at Edie who rolled her eyes. 'If Tamsyn spent a bit of time on herself she could be a real hit with the chaps. We could even take her up to London and show her off a bit.'

London? With the Davenports? The thought of it was both thrilling and terrifying. I'd never stepped a foot further out than Truro. London was like another country with its golden pavements, towering office blocks, and punks in Sid Vicious T-shirts loitering on every corner.

'I'm sure now you've done her nails,' said Edie, her words tinged with a diamond edge, 'she'll finally get to go all the way with *Kevin Chambers*.'

My insides turned to ice. Edie glanced at me mischievously as shame thumped me in the stomach. Why would she do that? Why would she tell her mother about Kevin? I lowered my eyes, unable to conceal my dismay.

'Kevin Chambers?' Eleanor gave a small trill of laughter. 'Well, what a *très* lucky *garçon* the young man is.'

I cringed as I recalled how Kevin had pushed away from me to return to his group of smirking friends. How, frozen with horror, I'd watched from the darkened corner of the hall as he held his fingers beneath their noses, watched them grimace in unison then recoil laughing. The feeling of wanting to die of shame was still as vivid as it had been then. I should never have let him touch me like that. I should never have been so foolish as to think he actually fancied me. How pathetic to be so desperate to be liked.

'We're not together. It's not like—'

Edie groaned. 'Who cares? Come on, let's go up to my room.'

I didn't follow her. I felt inexplicably hurt by her telling her mother about Kevin. I'd told her about him in confidence. Her betrayal skewered me and I wished more than anything I'd never told her about him. 'Er, Tamsyn? Are you coming then?' She snapped suddenly. 'God, don't look so wounded. Eleanor doesn't care. Seriously.'

I glanced at Eleanor who'd lost interest in us and was rummaging around in her gold bag.

'Come on, I've got something for you. A present.'

Edie turned and walked back to the house.

I stood. 'Thank you for doing my nails,' I said.

Eleanor reached for her cigarettes. 'Don't touch anything for fifteen minutes. If you catch them, they'll smudge.'

I was nearly at the back door when she called to me.

'Yes?' I walked back towards her.

'I meant to ask you, we're having a party the weekend after next and I was wondering,' she said with a smile. 'Are you free?'

'A party? Here?' My knees threatened to give way. 'Yes. I am. Definitely.'

Eleanor beamed. 'Wonderful!' Then her attention returned to her nails.

A party at The Cliff House? Oh my God. I tore inside and ran up the stairs, Kevin Chambers now forgotten. I had far more important things to think about. Edie hadn't *meant* to hurt me anyway. I was being oversensitive. Mum was always telling me

I was far too oversensitive. And, seriously, who even cared? I'd been invited to a party at The Cliff House!

Edie was standing in front of her window looking out.

'Your mum just asked me to come to a party,' I said. 'It's so exciting!'

Edie turned and raised her eyebrows. 'Yes, she told me she was going to ask you. They throw good parties. She'll be happy to have you there.' Edie sat on her bed. 'Sorry about mentioning that boy.'

'It's fine—'

'No, it's not. It was unkind. I didn't realise until I saw how upset you were. It's just… Eleanor, she and I… I shouldn't have said anything.'

'It's fine. Honest.'

'Look,' she said then. 'I made you this. Last night.' She took a cassette case off the windowsill and held it out towards me. When I didn't take it immediately, she waved it at me. 'Go on then.'

The plastic was warm where it had been lying in the sunlight. There was a list of songs and bands on the back. Words written in the neatest handwriting, tiny capitals, perfectly formed, and not one thing crossed-out.

The Cure, Depeche Mode, Siouxsie and the Banshees, The Jesus and Mary Chain…

But it was the title that caught my breath.

For Tamsyn.

'It's a mix tape,' she said.

'Yes,' I breathed.

'You said you liked The Cure the other day, so I thought I'd give you a tape with all my favourite tracks on.'

I didn't know what to say. I stared at the tape. Read and reread the list on the back. The letters blurred as my eyes misted with tears. Nobody had ever done anything like this for me before. I turned the tape over and on the other side, in larger black capitals, the words *For Tamsyn* were repeated, and around them Edie had drawn exquisite doodles: flowers, paisley and skulls.

'You're so good at art.'

People didn't just *make* mix tapes. Mix tapes took time. Care. They *meant* something. The only mix tapes I'd seen were the ones passed from school bag to school bag by the best-looking boys to the girls who showed the most cleavage.

'Thank you,' I said quietly. I swallowed, trying not to let my voice crack with emotion. 'It's the best thing anybody's ever given me.'

Edie laughed. 'Jesus, you've had some crappy presents.'

Holding the cassette in my hand I was hit hard by how isolated I'd become. A friendless loner at school. It was difficult to be anything else. You have to work quite hard to get friends when you're infected by death. That's all they saw. I might as well have had festering sores all over my skin. Nobody wanted to be anywhere near me. They feared the sudden onset of tears, uncontrollable outbursts which sent me straight to the headmaster's office. My grief made me unpredictable and that made them uneasy. Made them look at their feet and turn their backs on me. I told myself I didn't care. That I wanted to sit alone at lunchtime. That I had no interest in having company at breaktime. That their airhead chatter irritated me. I had, after all, more important things to worry about than whether *Smash Hits* was cooler than *Just Seventeen* or if I'd prefer to get

163

off with George Michael or Billy Idol. I'd built a wall around myself for protection. If I didn't try to make friends there'd be no chance of rejection. But the cost of this was loneliness and getting excited because Kevin Chambers had asked me to dance only to find out he'd fingered *the freak* for a dare.

CHAPTER NINETEEN

Tamsyn
July 1986

I spent most of the morning unpacking chocolate and sweets in Ted's shop and silently grumbling about not being up at the house.

Ted's voice had become a low hum of background noise, like a mistuned radio you eventually grow immune to. Every now and then I nodded or mumbled a *yes* or a *no* or something which could be either.

A steady stream of people came in and out of the shop. Tourists mainly, there to buy sticks of lurid rock and boxes of fudge, postcards and small kegs of mead to take back for people they felt obliged to give gifts to.

'Fairings,' a woman said to her husband who huffed and puffed impatiently. 'Audrey's partial to a ginger nut so she'll love a Cornish Fairing.'

'Does Audrey really need something? We've only been away three days.'

'She watered the plants yesterday and I'm sure she'll have picked the post up off the mat. That deserves a Fairing at the very least.'

The woman then leafed through the postcards on the

revolving stand. Some of the cards shouldn't have been there anymore, curled and yellowed with sunlight, a fine layer of dust dulling their sheen. The woman chose one of Cape Cornwall, two of Botallack and two of the war memorial clock tower in the centre of St Just, which was a copy of a photo taken in the sixties. She looked up from the cards and caught me staring at her.

'Such a quaint little town, isn't it?'

I didn't reply.

'Do you live here?'

I nodded.

'Lived here long?'

'Yes.' But I couldn't be bothered to expand, so I turned my back on her and took another handful of Marathons out of the box and arranged them on the shelf so the letter Ms lined up.

'Bit rude,' the woman whispered loudly to her husband. 'There *are* some rude ones down here you know. You wouldn't expect it, would you? Not in such a pretty place.'

She marched past me and set her rock, postcards, and the tin of Fairings on the counter with such force I reckon she must have broken the rock all the way through. 'John, bring the box of fudge over here and let's get it paid for. If someone's going to come and open the till, of course.'

'Tamsyn, can you ring that up?' Ted gestured in the direction of the till as he carried a couple of empty boxes through to the storeroom.

I went behind the counter and smiled at the woman, but she wouldn't look me in the eye.

'Careful,' I said, lowering my voice. 'Most of us are witches.'

You don't want to go and upset us.' She glanced at me and I winked at her and began to ring up the shopping.

Her eyes grew wide and she rested a hand against her chest, her mouth making a perfect O-shape.

'John,' she said. 'We're leaving.'

She grabbed her husband by the arm and scurried out of the shop, eyeing me over her shoulder as she went.

I poked my tongue out.

'What's up with them?' Ted emerged through the plastic strips in the doorway carrying a full box of crisps. 'Changed their minds?'

'*Londoners*,' I said, unsure if they were or weren't, but knowing Ted wouldn't question the lost business if they were.

As predicted he rolled his eyes and tutted.

The day dragged. I couldn't stop thinking of Jago working up at The Cliff House. I wanted to be there. I wanted to be lying on the terrace with the water lapping gently at the black walls of the pool as Eleanor drank champagne and Max barbecued. I imagined my brother painting the railings. Shirt off. Sun on his back. Edie taking him a glass of blackcurrant. Ice clinking. I gently kicked the base of the display cabinet to ease the resentment I was feeling. Why should he be up there while I was stuck here stacking shelves with nothing to do but tease tourists for entertainment?

I leant back against the counter and held my hands out in front of me to admire my nails. The colour was gorgeous, exactly the same shade as the inside of a conch shell. I hoped they would last until the party or, if not, that Eleanor might do them again. I was determined to grow mine like hers, long talons, which I'd paint a brilliant red, the colour of postboxes. I'd loved Eleanor doing my nails, her hand holding mine, the look of concentration on her face as she lavished me with attention. I wondered what other things I was missing out on which Eleanor and I could do together. So much, I was certain. Mum worked pretty much all the time and when she wasn't at work, she was doing the housework or the ironing or weeding the backyard. And when she wasn't doing that she was sleeping, more often than not, in her clothes on the settee, her camp bed still folded next to the wall, the ten o'clock news on, an untouched cup of tea held loosely in her hand. Though it was awful to admit it, if I had to choose one of them to spend time with, I think I'd have chosen Eleanor over Mum. Though, of course, I'd never tell Mum that. Or, indeed, Edie.

CHAPTER TWENTY

Edie
July 1986

Edie had gone outside as soon as they started fighting, but the doors from the study to the terrace were wide open and she could still hear every single word. She sat at one of the chairs on the terrace and glanced down towards Jago, wondering if he could hear them as well. Thankfully, it appeared not, as he was focusing intently on sanding the last few uprights.

'Why the hell are you lying?' cried her mother, drawing Edie's attention away from Jago and back to the shouting.

'I'm not.' He sounded more weary than angry. 'I told you it was a publishing event.'

'Yes. You did. A *publishing event*. To which you decided to turn up with an *unnamed brunette* instead of your wife?'

'You didn't want to come. I asked you. You said it would be boring, and that – and I quote – *all the parties I go to these days are dull and full of puffed-up idiots who only want to talk about books and the view up their own arses*. Which, incidentally, is pretty bloody accurate.'

'Not on this occasion. I mean, Christ, look at her? How old is she? Twenty-one? Twenty-two?'

'I have absolutely no idea. She works at the publishing house.'

'God!' she shouted bitterly. 'It's so *humiliating*, you pranc-ing about town with girls young enough to be your daughter while you abandon your wife at home. How everybody must be laughing!'

'Don't be ridiculous.'

'I'm being *ridiculous*, am I? You, Max Davenport, are a grade-A *arsehole*! And why do you never take *me* out anymore?'

'I don't take you out because...' He stopped himself. Edie knew what he was going to say. Of course she did. Taking Eleanor out always ended badly.

'Because *what?*'

He hesitated. 'It doesn't matter.'

'What? Because I'll *embarrass* you? *Shame* you? Cause a *scene?*'

'Stop it, Eleanor—'

'No, I won't stop it. You have no idea what it's like for me. You and a seemingly endless tide of young women who are no more than a pair of tits on legs. It's pathetic. If it's not some tart from the publishing house, it's your secretary or the au pair or fucking *Etienne*—'

Her mother's voice choked with emotion and Edie drew her knees tight up to her chest and hugged them.

'—and I have to be in this *horrible* house filled with her dreadful bits of so-called art which remind me every day about what you did.'

'How many times do I need to tell you, nothing went on between me and Etienne—'

'Ha! You expect me to believe that? You bought six of those hideous paintings because you actually like them?'

'Yes. That's exactly it. I told you—'

'Yes, I know, I *know*! You got talking to her in Cannes and somehow felt compelled to spend *thousands* of pounds on her work out of the goodness of your heart to help an up-and-coming artist.' Eleanor spat out a bitter laugh. 'Of course, the fact that she was twenty-eight with long dark hair and a thirty-six inch chest had nothing to do with it.'

'You're being hysterical, Eleanor. Try and pull yourself together.'

There was a silence then. Edie pictured her mother's seething face. Anger building like a pressure cooker. Perhaps muttering about wanting to drive a knife into his philandering heart.

Edie had no idea how many of Eleanor's continuous accusations were true – if, indeed, any – but what she did know was that as her mother aged, her insecurities and jealousies and irrational explosions grew more and more intense. Her father only had to look at another woman for the raging ire which hovered beneath her surface to ignite.

The internal door to the study flew open and her mother burst into the living room. Eleanor walked over to the sideboard and bent to open the doors. When she stood she was holding a full bottle. Brown liquid. She slammed the cupboard door shut then caught sight of Edie watching her from the table on the terrace. They held each other's stare for a moment before Eleanor turned on her heel and marched up the stairs.

Edie got up and went into the house, pausing at the door to her father's study. He was sitting at his desk, an expansive glass table that held nothing but the vintage typewriter he'd picked up at a literary auction for a vast sum of money. He was staring at the piece of white paper protruding from the typewriter, oblivious to her presence, his lips moving silently. A moment later he swore and yanked the sheet from the roller, screwed it up and balled it aggressively, before throwing it into the corner of the room where it missed the wastepaper basket.

Edie walked across the room and bent to pick it up and deposit it in the bin.

'Edith, I didn't see you there.' He hesitated. 'I'm sorry if you had to listen to that.'

She shrugged. 'I'm used to it.'

Edie approached his desk. There was copy of *Tatler* lying open on the society page, a double-page spread with a collage of photographs of famous faces taken at prestigious events. She picked it up and scanned the pictures until she found the one which had set her mother off. It didn't take long. It was a photograph of him within a small group of people. He was smiling at the camera, shirt open at the neck, his jacket sporting a flamboyant silk handkerchief tucked into his breast pocket. He stood with his hand around the waist of a girl in a red jumpsuit and vertiginous white heels who could easily have been a model. She was gazing up at him, her perfect teeth exposed as she laughed at whatever he'd just said. The caption beneath read: New York Times *bestseller Max Davenport and unnamed brunette at celebrity Knightsbridge haunt San Lorenzo for post-awards dinner for winner Kingsley Amis.*

'She works with my editor.' He concentrated on winding another sheet of paper into his typewriter. 'It was a party. I don't even recall her name.'

Edie discarded the magazine on the desk then moved to leave the study. Before she reached the door, she stopped, and glancing over her shoulder said, 'Eleanor took a bottle of whisky upstairs.'

He didn't reply. Instead he nodded. Then he sighed and stood up. He walked past her and out of the study. She followed him and watched him pick up his car keys from the table in the hallway before going out of the front door. A moment later his car engine fired. Edie went and lay down on the sofa. With her hands tucked beneath her cheek she stared through the window at the boy in the garden as he worked on the fence.

Edie must have dozed off. The next thing she was aware of was a knock on the door which made her sit up with a start. It was Tamsyn.

'I'd forgotten you were coming,' Edie said a little sharply which made Tamsyn flinch and look downcast, so Edie added, 'I'm glad you're here though. How was work?'

Tamsyn rolled her eyes. 'I nearly *died* of boredom.'

They lay on the grass and talked. Edie found it hard not to watch Jago working. He was undoubtedly beautiful and Tamsyn's chatter faded into the background as she studied the slope of his shoulders, the way his hair brushed the neck of his top, his delicate wrists encircled with worn black leather cords. He wore faded jeans which hung off his narrow hips and DM boots, scuffed and dull, and every so often, when he reached down for something, his T-shirt lifted to reveal a strip of tanned skin above his waistband. She had to remind herself he'd shown no interest in her at all and that she had no intention of lusting after someone she had to fight to attract. Total humiliation.

'Edie? Did you hear me?'

Edie realised Tamsyn had asked her a question. 'Sorry?'

Tamsyn laughed. 'You haven't been listening.'

Edie nodded. 'I have. Just not the last thing you said.'

'I was saying that one day I'd love to stay the night. Maybe we could watch a horror film or something. I've never seen one before. Jago has a few in his room we could borrow, though they're Betamax not VHS, but maybe you've got a Betamax somewhere? They're pretty full-on. What do you think?'

Her face shone. Eyes bright. She was like a Labrador puppy now she was relaxed and her confidence had grown. Edie thought about the evening ahead. Her father and mother not talking. Her mother drinking herself to sleep. The hours Edie would spend alone in her room, staring out of the window, wishing she could walk along the corridor of moonlight on the sea.

'All right,' she said. 'That sounds cool.'

'Tonight? I don't have to be at the shop tomorrow, so it doesn't matter what time I get up. I could even stay for lunch.'

'Yeah, okay. But I should probably check with Eleanor. Make sure we're not going out for supper or anything.'

Edie pushed herself up and went into the house to ask her mother about Tamsyn staying over before she got too drunk to care. She went up the stairs, pushed open the door into her room then stopped dead.

'Fuck,' she whispered under her breath. 'Fuck.'

She ran down the stairs, taking them two at a time and back out to the garden.

'Sorry. You have to leave.'

Tamsyn's face fell. 'But I don't—'

'I'm sorry. I forgot I have to do something. You need to leave.'

'But—'

'You have to fucking *leave*!'

Edie noticed Tamsyn's lip trembling and her eyes welling with tears.

'I'm sorry. I didn't mean to swear. Please,' Edie said, trying to control her voice. 'I just need you to go. We'll do the film and stay-over another time, okay?'

When Tamsyn tried again to protest, she almost lost the plot, but using every ounce of control, she repeated her request as calmly as possible. 'Look, why don't you come back tomorrow? We can go back to the beach. Or listen to music. But, please, right now, I just need you to leave.'

CHAPTER TWENTY-ONE

Jago
July 1986

When he sees her rushing out of the house he can tell immediately she's upset. Her arms are tightly crossed and wrapped around her body as if she's trying to keep warm. He pretends to sand the railings but watches her with Tamsyn. Sees his sister's face fall. Edie doesn't look her in the eye. She's twitchy. Then her voice raises in volumes and he hears her tell Tamsyn to go home.

Of course, Tamsyn doesn't want to leave. She's glued herself to this place and these people. He knows it's because of their father. She told him once, a few years after the storm, that the two of them had been at the house the day he died. They'd walked out to the point. Eaten a picnic. Broken in. Swum without permission. That kind of thing was typical of their father, rebellious and brave, scaling fences, sticking two fingers up to the *rules*.

Tamsyn nods then turns. She walks down the garden to the gate and he notices she is crying. He wonders if he should go after her, but then he sees Edie's face, tight with anxiety. As soon as the gate bangs shut Edie spins around and runs back inside.

Something's wrong.

He hesitates, lays the sandpaper down on the grass, then hesitates again before following her into the house.

At the door he pauses. Listens.

'Hello?' he calls.

Nothing in reply. He walks into the house. Takes a couple of tentative steps towards the stairs. Before he calls to her again there's a strangled cry from Edie. He runs up the stairs and follows the noise, turns right at the top, then goes along to a room at the end.

Edie is crouched on the floor.

'Is everything okay?'

She whips her head around. Tears streak her face. He sees then that her mother is lying on the floor, half concealed by Edie. 'Go away,' she snaps, swiping angrily at her tears. 'Leave us alone.'

But he steps closer. Looks down at Eleanor Davenport. Her head lolls to one side. Her eyes are open but out of focus. Her chin is wet with vomit. There's a pool of it on the floor beside her. The stench hits the back of his throat and he gags. When he turns his head away he sees the bottle of whisky on the bedside table next to a brown medicine bottle, lid off, lying on its side with a couple of pills spilled out.

He steps closer. Slowly. Then kneels beside Edie and rests his fingers against Eleanor Davenport's neck. She's alive. Breathing easily. Her eyes focus on him. She slurs something unintelligible.

Edie sobs.

'What's she had?' he asks Edie.

Edie lowers her head. 'Whisky,' she says softly. 'About half the bottle. Those are Valium. Not that many are gone. I counted them. Maybe one or two. The Xanax hasn't been touched. It's still in the bathroom cabinet. She's just drunk.' She shrugs helplessly. 'She gets like this. She doesn't know when to stop.'

'We should call an ambulance.'

'No!' Edie says. 'No. She won't want us to. Please. I'll sit with her. She's done it before. Loads of times. She's just fallen asleep. That's all.'

He hesitates but then nods. 'We should clean her up.'

'No,' she says, almost too quietly to hear. 'I'll do it. You don't need to help.'

He stands, grabs the glass from beside the bed, and goes to the bathroom. He turns the tap on and rinses the glass, then fills it with water. He takes a towel off the rail and holds it under the stream of water to wet it. Then he carries both back into the bedroom.

'Take off her top,' he says gently. 'It's dirty.'

Edie nods. She won't look him in the eye. As she eases her mother's top off she chews her bottom lip repeatedly. Eleanor complains. Tries to smack her away. Calls her a bitch then vomits again. He passes Edie the towel and she wipes her up. He returns to the bathroom for a fresh one, wets it as before, then returns to Edie and holds it out to her.

He is struck by how tender she is as she cleans her mother's face. Eleanor starts writhing. Again, pushes her daughter away.

When she is clean, Edie tries to hook her arms under her mother's, but after a few futile attempts to lift her, she sits back on her haunches, defeated.

Jago rests a hand on her shoulder. 'Let me do it.'

She still doesn't look at him, but wearily nods. He bends and lifts Eleanor, slides one arm under the back of her knees, the other under her shoulders. She smells of alcohol and puke. Her forehead is slicked with sweat, eyes and cheeks smeared with make-up. Edie pulls the sheets back on the bed and he

179

lays Eleanor down. As her head touches the pillow she seems to relax. She moans softly. He steps back from the bed so Edie can cover her with the sheet. Within moments she's snoring softly.

'We should turn her on her side.' he says. 'My dad taught me that. Stops her suffocating if she's sick again or swallowing her tongue.'

Edie's eyes grow wide and she reaches quickly for her mother. He helps her manoeuvre Eleanor then arranges her arms so she can't roll back.

'Don't leave her for a bit. Even like that there's a chance she can choke.'

Edie doesn't reply. She sits with her back against the bank of wardrobes, knees pulled up to her chest, chin resting on them like a little girl.

He goes downstairs and fills the kettle. Finds teabags. A mug. He adds three spoons of sugar.

'It's sweet,' he says, when he comes back into the bedroom. He holds it out to her. 'My grandad says sugar is good for shock.'

At first she doesn't take it, but then she looks up at him and smiles weakly. 'Thank you,' she says. 'For helping me.'

He shrugs.

He sits down as well. Not too near her though. His hands are clasped and rest between his knees.

'She used to be so much fun, you know. I liked having her as my mum and not one of the other boring ones,' Edie says. 'I have memories of her always being the first to start dancing. When they had parties I'd lie in bed upstairs and listen to her laughing. Always louder than everybody else. She'd light up any room she walked into. Even though I was young, I remember that. I used to think she was a princess.'

Jago doesn't say anything. He lets her breathe. Gives her space to talk.

'But then it changed and it wasn't fun anymore. There was one Christmas Day when her hangover was so bad she spent the whole day in bed with the curtains shut. She only got out of bed to throw up. My father said she had a tummy bug.' Edie glances at him and gives him a tight rueful smile. 'I used to mark the levels of liquid inside the bottles in the drinks cabinet so I could measure how much she was drinking. Not that I knew what to do with the information. So I just left AA leaflets on the kitchen table.'

Edie sips the tea then bends over to rest the mug on the floor beside her. She stretches her legs out and tips her head back.

'Then last year she turned up to a school event totally wasted. She was lurching around the place and had an argument with another mother. Accused her of flirting with Max. She slapped this other woman in front of everybody.' She shakes her head, laughs a little. 'Actually *slapped* another mother in front of the whole school! Can you believe that?'

Edie takes a deep breath and her smile falls away.

'After that, school was a nightmare. The few friends I had stopped talking to me. The teachers whispered behind my back, some even sniggered as I walked past. I fucking hated it, so I did everything I could to get chucked out. Started missing lessons, was rude to the staff, spiteful to other girls, didn't do any homework or write any notes in class, and eventually they had no choice but to chuck me out. There's only so much bad behaviour a school can take, even if your father is a *New York Times* best-fucking-seller.' She stops speaking and screws up her face. 'God, I'm sorry. I'm talking too much.'

'No problem.'

Edie stands and walks over to her mother's bed. She looks down at her for a moment or two then picks up the medicine bottle and replaces the pills that have fallen across the bedside table before screwing on the cap. She turns to look down at him. Her eyes are filmed with fresh tears and it's all he can do to stop himself jumping up to put his arms around her.

'Thank you for helping. Please don't tell anybody about this. Especially not Tamsyn or your mother. I don't want them to think badly of her.'

He is moved by Edie's desire to protect her mother. He identifies with it. He feels the same.

He nods and stands. 'Will you be okay?'

She smiles as she pushes her shoulders back and lifts her chin. Then she affixes a wry, defiant mask to her face and nods.

'Yes,' she says. 'I'll be absolutely fine.'

CHAPTER TWENTY-TWO

Tamsyn
July 1986

My stomach churned all the way home.

Why had Edie flipped like that? What had I done? I went over everything I'd said, desperate to work out what I should apologise for. She'd been so angry, but hadn't given me the chance to find out why.

As I sat with Granfer on the settee while he waited for *Coronation Street,* I bit down on my lip, well past the point where it hurt; then, to take my mind off the pain in my lip, I dug my fingernails into my thighs as hard as I could.

Mum appeared as soon as the theme tune blared out. The two of them never missed an episode. The world would have to be ending before they allowed that to happen. She pulled the basket of laundry out from behind the settee and sat folding sheets and pairing socks, while he grumbled about the soap opera's *shenanigans,* his rasping breaths coming in an uneven rhythm.

I tried to focus on the comings and goings in Weatherfield, but I couldn't get Edie out of my head. Anxiety snowballed in my stomach until I could no longer sit still. I ran upstairs to my box and closed the door, then reached beneath my pillow for the mix tape. I stared at it. Ran my fingers down the list of songs.

Mix tapes took so long to make. There was no way she'd have made it for me unless she really cared. Maybe she'd suddenly felt poorly. Yes. That had to be it. Or maybe it wasn't? Maybe I had done something wrong. Was I too forward in inviting myself to stay over for the night?

There was a knock on the door. It opened. Mum's face appeared. 'I thought I'd make sure you're okay. You didn't fancy *Corrie* tonight?'

'I'm tired.'

She nodded. 'I've got a bit of ironing to finish then I'm going to turn in too.' She hesitated then asked casually, 'Any sign of your brother?'

'I think he went to the pub.'

'Do you know how he got on at The Cliff House today?'

I shrugged. 'I didn't talk to him, but he was doing the fence like they asked him to.'

She said goodnight and closed the door. I heard her and Granfer having a brief conversation about his jigsaw on the landing and then her footsteps descending the stairs.

I lay on my bed and stared straight ahead. I wanted it to be tomorrow so I could get back to Edie. The minutes ticked by with a stubborn lack of haste. My room was damp and colder than it should have been in the middle of summer. As dusk turned to darkness, shadows formed on the ceiling and the floorboards creaked as the timbers cooled. I could hear the sea faintly, the crashing of the waves against the rocks reduced to purring by the distance. I couldn't get rid of the image of Edie rushing out of the house and chasing me away.

When insomnia finally beat me, I reached over and pressed the button on my clock to illuminate its face. Seven minutes past three. I reached beneath my pillow for the mix tape again and stroked my thumb over its smoothness. Then I climbed out of bed and crept out of my box and across the landing to Jago's room. I trod carefully. Heel to toe, distributing my weight evenly so as not to make any sound.

My brother's door was covered in the black marker pen graffiti that my mother had turned a blind eye to when he'd decorated it in a fit of anger aged fifteen. I stood in front of it and listened for noises from within. There were none, so I turned the handle as quietly as I could. The door creaked as I pushed it open. I held my breath, expecting him to wake, but he didn't stir. I stepped into his room. The smell enveloped me, stale smoke and musty clothes, deodorant and leather boots, sweat and the sweet tang of joss sticks. He slept silently and heavily, covers half off his body, chest bare and lit by the moonlight pouring in through the window. I wondered what images flickered in his head. Was he helping Dad with his motorbike? Or dreaming of his bloated, drowned body?

I went to his chest of drawers and tapped the flat of my hand over its surface which was strewn with Jago's tobacco and Zippo, coins, a packet of gum, motorbike magazines and two overflowing ashtrays. My fingers closed around his Walkman. I lifted it silently then backed out of the room and pulled the door closed.

Back in my box, I slipped Edie's mix tape into the Walkman and lay back on my bed. I closed my eyes and, as her music played, I imagined myself walking along the footpath to The Cliff House. I pushed the gate open. Walked up the lawn. The plants swayed beside me in a gentle salty breeze, leaves a brilliant green, a kaleidoscope of flowers towering over me. The house seemed to pulse in time with the music and then as I watched it became fluid. The walls reached out to wrap around me until I was fully enclosed. It was only then, feeling warm and safe, that I finally fell asleep.

CHAPTER TWENTY-THREE

Angie
July 1986

'Angie. Could I talk to you for a moment?'

Eleanor Davenport's face was blotched with red. She wore sunglasses. Her hair was pulled back into a tightly twisted bun. She wore no make-up and her hands wrung anxiously around each other.

Angie nodded and set down her cloth and the bottle of Jif. Her stomach bubbled with nerves. She had a sinking feeling she was about to get the sack. As she wracked her brains trying to think of what she could have done wrong, a shot of fear passed through her as she realised it might not be her at all, but one of the children. God, she'd kill Jago if he'd mucked things up.

'Is everything okay?' she asked hesitantly.

Eleanor straightened her shoulders and lifted her chin, girding herself for whatever she was about to say. 'I want to apologise for the way I spoke to you the other day. Max said that I might have come across badly when I mentioned…' She drew in a deep breath and closed her eyes. 'When I mentioned the bathroom floors.'

Angie picked up the cloth and squeezed some of the white cream onto it. 'I can't remember that, Mrs Davenport,' she lied.

'And anyway, you're well within your rights to tell me if you don't think something's been done right. You pay me, after all. It's important I get things as you want them.'

'Yes. But,' she hesitated, her mouth twitching, 'the floors were fine. I was angry, but… well, I shouldn't have taken it out on you.' Eleanor took a breath as if to say more, but instead she turned swiftly and walked out of the kitchen.

Angie watched her retreating up the stairs and listened to her footsteps cross the landing. There was a strangled sob and the sound of her door closing. For a moment Angie wondered if she should follow her up and make sure she was okay. But she decided not to. The woman was prickly at the best of times. If she'd wanted to talk, Angie reasoned, she'd just had her opportunity.

Angie ran the cloth beneath the tap, squeezing out the water which ran cloudy with cream cleaner, then turned. She jumped with shock when she found Max Davenport was watching her from the doorway.

'Sorry,' he said. 'I keep doing that, don't I? I don't mean to sneak up on you, I promise.' He smiled at her.

Angie glanced over his shoulder and up the stairs. 'Mr Davenport—'

'Max, please. You sound like my bloody accountant when you call me Mr Davenport.'

'Sorry. Max. I think…' She hesitated. 'Mrs Davenport – Eleanor – she might be a bit upset? She's upstairs and I'm not sure, but I think she might be crying. I wondered if I should check on her but I didn't want to step out of line.'

Max walked past her and opened the fridge without registering any reaction. He took out a bottle of wine. The label was classy looking with a fine gold border, scalloped corners, and foreign writing on it in fancy curling letters. He took a corkscrew from the drawer and proceeded to remove the cork, which pulled free with a soft popping sound.

'Would you like a glass?'

She hesitated, confused and wrong-footed by the question. Had he not registered her concerns about his wife? And an offer of wine? It wasn't even midday.

She shook her head. 'No, thank you. I shouldn't when I'm working.'

He laughed. 'Yes, sorry. Of course, it's only writers who can legitimately drink whilst on the payroll.'

He leant past her to retrieve a glass from the cupboard. Had she imagined his hand brushing hers? He poured the wine then set the bottle down. Angie watched a dribble of wine run down the glass and pool on the worktop.

'Don't worry about Eleanor. She's fine,' he said. 'I'll check on her though. It's kind of you to be concerned but, honestly, don't burden yourself. My wife can be' —he hesitated— 'delicate sometimes. In London she has a professional to talk to. I'm not sure how much it helps. I have a sneaking suspicion it's merely an exercise in draining my bank account.' He drinks from his glass. 'She feels isolated down here. Especially when I'm writing and *in absentia* so much. It's a shame because I love it. I'm desperate to move down. London is' —he paused— 'exhausting for me now. I've outgrown it. Or perhaps it's outgrown me. But here, well, here is quite magical, isn't it? I was hoping that if we spent the summer down here she'd fall in love with it too, be happy to move here permanently. It would give her some space from all the temptations in London.' He held the wine up to the light and studied it for a moment or two before looking back at her. 'My wife is the embodiment of a cautionary tale. She pursued me relentlessly, but perhaps being the glamorous, party-loving wife of a bestselling writer isn't all it's cracked up to be.' He drank again, his face flinching with undisguised regret. 'Be careful what you wish for,' he said. 'That's what they say, isn't it?'

She flushed with heat. He shouldn't be talking about his marriage so candidly. It wasn't right. If Eleanor knew he was discussing her with the cleaner she'd be horrified.

Angie smiled tightly. 'I should get on.' She bent to pick up the bucket of cleaning products off the floor. 'Would you like me to do your study quickly?'

Max stared at her with a look of wry amusement. 'Why not? It does have a tendency to get rather unsavoury in there.' He didn't move. But remained leaning against the worktop, wine in hand, studying her with intense scrutiny.

She dropped her eyes to break his stare.

'I think I'll make the most of the break and drive to St Just for a paper. Do you need anything?'

She wasn't sure what he thought she might need, but thanked him anyway and excused herself, hurrying out of the kitchen and praying his increasing flirtatiousness was imagined. She went into his study and over to his desk, and sprayed its surface with glass cleaner and wiped vigorously as she listened to his car pull away from the house.

She straightened the tartan blanket which was hooked over the chair in the corner, then went to draw the curtains. Sunlight poured in through the French windows and flooded the room. The view was breathtaking. The double doors opened straight onto the terrace, exactly opposite the swimming pool, and his desk was arranged in the centre of the room, so that when he was at his typewriter all he had to do was lift his head and he would see the pool stretching away from him, merging with the sea and the horizon beyond. She opened the doors to let the fresh air in, and the room filled with the sounds she'd grown up with: the rolling waves on the shore, the calls of the gulls, the curlews and choughs, and the wind blowing over the clifftop.

When she finished in the study she carried three used teacups to the kitchen. She walked through the sitting room and found it hard to ignore the muffled sobbing coming from Eleanor's room upstairs. Angie's stomach pulsed with a gnawing guilt as she ran the tap to wash the cups. She wished she'd been more sympathetic. Maybe Eleanor Davenport had needed to talk to her?

Angie turned the last cup upside down on the drainer, and walked to the bottom of the stairs to peer up the stairwell. She took a tentative step then another, and continued tiptoeing lightly until she was at the top. She walked towards their bedroom, careful not to make any noise, and stood outside with her breath held and head tilted close to the door so she could hear more easily.

There was definitely sobbing, raw and guttural noises, that left Angie in no doubt Eleanor was more than a little distressed. She reached for the door handle, but hesitated. The sobbing had stopped. She dropped her hand. Worried that Eleanor was coming out of the room, Angie turned and made a run for the stairs, but then there was a heart-stopping crash and the sound of glass shattering.

She went back to the room and knocked softly.

Nothing.

'Mrs Davenport?' She knocked again. Turned the handle. Through the half-opened door, she could see Eleanor Davenport crouched on the floor. Angie hesitated, unsure if she should go in. Eleanor looked up at her. Her eyes were raw with crying. Cheeks puffy. When she saw Angie she turned away and her hands went to cover her face. She rubbed a couple of times then re-tied her hair as she stood.

'I heard a noise.' Angie realised then that the crash had been caused by the mirror from the dressing table. It had fallen from the wall and was broken and scattered in glinting shards across the wooden floor.

'Yes,' said Eleanor. 'I knocked the mirror off the wall.'

'I'll fetch the dustpan.'

Angie returned with the dustpan and brush, and some newspaper, which she laid out flat on the floor.

'Are you…' Angie asked hesitantly, 'okay?'

Eleanor nodded. 'Yes. Yes, of course, I am. Why wouldn't I be?'

They held each other's gaze for a number of seconds. Eleanor's eyes appeared to soften and her mouth twitched as if she might be about to speak. But she said nothing.

Angie crouched down and began to put the larger pieces of mirror in the dustpan. Then Eleanor did the same and the two women worked in silence to clear up the mess. Angie winced as she caught Eleanor's haunted reflection repeated many times over in the pieces of broken mirror, her eyes bloodshot, skin blotched and lips taut. Angie wrapped the newspaper around the bits of mirror then swept the area thoroughly to clear it of smaller slivers and glass dust.

When she was done she sat back and looked at Eleanor. 'Can I get you anything?' she asked.

Eleanor turned her gaze on Angie. Any softness that might have been there a few moments before had retreated and her eyes were glazed with familiar hardness. 'Like I said, I knocked it by mistake.' Then she stood and looked down at Angie. 'Please hoover the floor. We walk around with bare feet up here and don't want to get cut.'

CHAPTER TWENTY-FOUR

Tamsyn
July 1986

As usual I watched the clock all morning and as usual it limped around like a wounded soldier. 'Hurry up,' I whispered, but it didn't move faster; if anything it seemed to slow.

I needed to see Edie. I'd phoned yesterday to see what time I should go up and she'd said she was shopping with her mother. Apparently Max had to meet with his editor in Exeter, and she and Eleanor were going too, in the hope of finding some half-decent shops. I had suggested I come up for supper, but Edie had said they might stay the night in a hotel because the publisher was paying after all. She must have picked up my fear because she then added she would definitely see me on Wednesday after work. When I put the phone down my vision blurred with a fizzing worry. I went back to our house and grabbed my bag with the binoculars, and spent the rest of Tuesday with my sights trained on the The Cliff House, praying they'd decide not to stay in Exeter and I wouldn't have to wait another day.

At work I passed the time by wiping a cloth over the tins and bottles without enthusiasm and flicking through *The Cornishman*. I idly turned the page, past news of a proposed leisure centre to be built above St Ives and an article on why the tourist industry was suffering because of sunshine on the Costa Brava, which I didn't understand because it hadn't rained – not enough to put off the tourists – for what felt like weeks. I turned the page and was confronted with the picture of a man I recognised.

It was the lifeguard. The one who'd dragged the young boy out of the sea at Sennen. He was standing on the beach, in black and white, and smiling broadly. There was a child beside him. It was a boy. They held hands, raised above their heads like boxers at the end of a fight. Of course. The boy was the child who'd nearly drowned. I had a flash of his face, lifeless, sand stuck to his blueish skin. Body like a rag doll. If it wasn't for the man standing beside him who battled fatigue and fear and the pressure of a gathered crowd to literally breathe life back into him, he'd be shut in a drawer in the morgue. I touched my fingers to the lifeguard's face. A hero. Just like my dad. Yet, unlike my dad, alive to pose for a newspaper photograph.

I closed the paper and looked up at the clock. Midday. Or near enough. I whipped off my navy-and-white striped apron and hung it on a peg in the storeroom.

'Bye, Ted.'

'See you Saturday!' he called as I ran from the shop, the little bell tinkling as the door opened and closed. 'Say hello to—'

I didn't wait to hear the end of his sentence.

The wind was up. It was blustery but sunny, and the smell of the sea was strong. I half ran along the path, my heart pounding with adrenalin. If I could have sprinted the whole way I would have done. I was desperate to get there, to see Edie, to make sure everything between us was all right. I was feeling brighter though. Perhaps it was seeing the little boy smiling happily in the paper, alive and well, and proud as punch to have a story to tell. I was certain that things were going to be fine. The nearer I got to the house, the stronger I felt, until – and it is no exaggeration to say – I was feeling quite buoyant.

I saw Edie as soon as I rounded the first bend after passing the heart-stone. She was standing below the terrace on the lawn near the railings. She wore a long black skirt and a black vest top, bangles halfway up her forearms, mirrored sunglasses covering her eyes. I waved but she didn't see me. So I shouted out to her. My words must have been stolen by the wind because she didn't look my way. I walked on and she momentarily dropped out of sight as the path dipped. When she came back into view I saw she was talking to my brother who held a paintbrush in his hand and was daubing the railings white.

I dropped to a crouch before either of them noticed me. My insides solidified as if my stomach had filled with concrete. Keeping low, I crept to a place on the path where I could watch them both whilst remaining obscured by the brambles and gorse. God. Why hadn't I brought my binoculars?

Edie was talking animatedly. Jago nodding. Turning his head every now and then before bending to dip his brush into the paint. What were they saying? Was she inviting him for a barbecue? Talking about Dad and the night he died? Was she going to tell him he could spend the summer hanging out with her at The Cliff House?

My jealousy erupted and I screamed out, 'Edie! I'm here! I'm here!'

At last she heard and turned to look in the direction of my

shout. I waved and she waved back, then spoke to Jago, who glanced down towards me then continued with his painting.

I carried on along the path, tucking my hair behind my ear as wind tossed it about my face and trying to ignore my fear that she was going to tell me to leave again, which had now come back with full force.

I needn't have worried.

She was at the gate to meet me and when I got close to her she smiled and kissed me on the cheek, happier to see me than she'd ever been. We linked arms and walked up the lawn.

'How was Exeter?'

'Oh, you know,' she said. But I didn't and wished she'd told me.

'Come and sit.'

On the table was an ashtray with a number of cigarette ends pressed into it. Some – but not all – had a kiss of lipstick in the same shade of maroon that stained her lips. A couple had the small telltale tube which was torn from the packet of cigarette papers to form a roach. I was pretty certain this meant they'd been smoking 'gear' as Jago called it. It struck me that Max and Eleanor might not be that happy to know Jago had been using marijuana at their house, let alone sharing it with their daughter. For a brief moment I considered telling Eleanor and pictured Jago being marched away from the house so I didn't have to share it, but I didn't allow that nasty thought to linger long in my head.

Edie sat with both feet on the table. She ran a hand through her hair then glanced down at my brother who was concentrating on slapping white paint onto sanded ironwork.

'It turns out your brother and I have exactly the same taste in music,' she said. 'And – oh my God – he plays the guitar!'

I furrowed my brow and looked over at him. 'No, you don't. Not really. It's not like you've had lessons or anything.'

'It's not that hard,' he said, pointedly avoiding my eyes. 'I bought a book of chords from the second-hand shop.'

'I'd love to play an instrument,' Edie said. 'Eleanor wanted me to play the harp but, seriously, what good is that to anybody? And teaching yourself is way cooler than having lessons. Hendrix and Bowie both learnt that way.'

Hendrix and Bowie? I smothered a laugh and cast an amused glance at Jago who had the grace to look sheepish.

'Jay was telling me about the disused mines. The ones at Botallack?'

'Jay?'

'It's what I call him. It suits him, don't you think? Anyway, he said I'd love the mines so I thought we could walk out there. I know it would take a while, but it might be fun, we could take a few beers. What do you think?'

My heart sank. I didn't want to go anywhere. I wanted to stay at the house. I wanted to swim and eat slices of the sweetest apple and lie with the sun on my face and my toe trailing in the inky water with the smell of coconut suntan lotion suspended in the air around me.

'Can't we stay here?'

'No,' she said. 'I want to get away from this bloody place. It's so fucking depressing.'

Why wouldn't she look at me while she was talking? Why was she so fascinated with watching Jago paint?

'You know what? I'm going to walk to Botallack,' she said with sudden resolve. 'It sounds amazing. Balancing right on the cliff edge with the sea crashing below? He was telling me about the Knockers which haunt the shafts.' She laughed. 'You have crazy names for spirits around here. Will you come, Jay?'

'Piskies, not spirits,' I said. But she ignored me.

'Yeah.' My brother had his back to us. His arm moved back and forth, and spots of white paint had spattered his skin, which glistened with sweat. 'I'm done here, I reckon.'

'Really? That's great. I mean, I'd have been fine on my own but much better to have company.' Edie's eyes glinted.

A cloud passed overhead, its shadow moving quickly, momentarily dulling the glare of the sunshine.

'Fine,' I said. 'I'll come.'

'You don't have to. Not if you don't feel like it.'

'No, I want to.'

But Edie wasn't listening. She had already started walking towards the house. 'I'll grab a few cans then we can get going.'

I watched her go inside then looked down towards my brother, who had put the lid on the tin of paint and was pressing it down with his foot.

'Don't you have to tell Eleanor you're stopping?'

'I told her this morning I'd work until two.'

I checked my watch. 'It's only quarter-to.'

'She's not here, so she'll never know.'

'I could tell her.'

He smiled at me but I didn't smile back.

His face fell. 'Jesus, Tam. Calm down. I'll do an extra fifteen minutes next time, okay? What's up with you anyway?'

I sighed and picked at a flake of paint on the wrought-iron table. 'Nothing. I slept badly last night. You know I wouldn't tell Eleanor anything bad.' I traced my finger over the fretwork. 'I thought you hated walking.'

'Why do you say that?'

I shrugged. 'I can't remember the last time you went for a walk on the cliffs.'

'It wasn't that long ago. I do things without telling you, you know.' He picked up the paint pot. 'Anyway, I fancy it today. You know, if you're feeling tired, maybe you shouldn't walk that far.'

'I'll be fine.'

Edie emerged from the house holding a carrier bag, lager cans visible through the thin white plastic. She smiled broadly.

I smiled back.

It was only when she got closer I realised she was looking at Jago, not me.

CHAPTER TWENTY-FIVE

Jago
July 1986

The girls walk ahead. They each hold a can of lager. Edie smokes. He listens to them talking and studies her.

The whiteness of her skin is exaggerated by the black she wears. Her skirt billows in the breeze and occasionally lifts so she is obliged to push it down to keep herself covered, but not before he gets a tantalising glimpse of her legs beneath. Soft thighs. Narrow calves and slender ankles. Heavy boots emphasising their slightness, like delicate saplings rooted in clods of earth, he thinks.

She stops briefly to pluck a head of lilac heather and, as she walks, she crumbles the heather between her fingers and lets the tiny pieces of colour fly off in the wind. This picture of her is almost more bewitching to him than the one of her in the pink bikini which has filled his thoughts these last few days. Since helping her with her mother he hasn't been able to get her out of his head. The desperate vulnerability in her eyes when she'd looked up at him from the floor, the way she talked so frankly, the pain in her voice, had pierced him.

'How far is it, Jay?' She throws the naked heather stalk away and glances over her shoulder at him.

If anybody else called him Jay he'd hate it, but from her it sounds right. Her own personal name for him. She is mesmerising and he is impossibly attracted to her.

When she came out onto the terrace that morning, he'd angled himself so he could watch her while he worked. It had taken a while for him to pluck up the courage to ask what she was reading.

She held the book up to show him the front cover.

L'Etranger by Camus.

He'd never heard of it and felt stupid and uneducated.

It's French. It means stranger.

Then she told him this book – *L'Etranger*, she repeated, her voice honey-coated with an exotic accent – was the inspiration for 'Killing an Arab'.

Do you like The Cure?

He lied.

Yes.

Now, on the cliff, he lowers his eyes when she looks back at him. He doesn't want to be caught spying on her, even though this is what he's been doing all day, stealing glances at every opportunity, his body firing at the slightest thing, a revealed shoulder, her hand brushing a fly from her knee, a shift of weight in her chair.

'Not too far,' he says, in answer to her question.

'Our dad loved this walk,' Tamsyn says, but Edie doesn't respond to her.

They walk down past Cape Cornwall. The water is wild and angry, pummelling the rocks and throwing fireworks of spray into the air. They stop to watch for a while, face the sea, close their eyes as the water catches on the wind and spritzes their faces.

'You see those rocks?' His sister taps Edie on the shoulder and points out towards the twin peaks that break the surface of the sea a mile or so offshore.

Edie squints. Follows the line of Tam's arm. Then she nods. 'I see them.'

'They're the Brisons. People race to them.'

'In boats?'

'Swimming.'

'But it's so far.'

'My dad swam it once.'

Jago doesn't correct her. He doesn't say, *You mean* our *dad. You might have been his favourite, but he belongs to me too.*

'Have either of you?'

Edie looks at them both. He doesn't say anything, but Tamsyn shakes her head, says no, she doesn't really swim in the sea.

Not anymore.

He watches Edie's face move from confusion to comprehension as she remembers how their father died.

'You know that boy?' Tamsyn says then. 'He was in the paper.'

'Which boy?'

'The one that nearly drowned.'

'Why's he in the paper?'

Tamsyn looked confused. 'What do you mean?'

'I mean, it's not really *news* is it? *Boy Goes In the Sea and Doesn't Die.*' Edie smiles but Tamsyn doesn't. Instead she separates herself from Edie, and walks over to the sea wall, leans on it and stares out at the sea, or perhaps at the seabirds which fall like rocks from the sky in search of fish.

He looks out over the water too. It is a greenish-grey today.

The Cornish word for the colour of the sea is *glas*. *Glas* can be green or blue or grey, or any shade between, whatever colour describes it at that moment. A fisherman's joke. So today the sea is *glas* and touched with tufts of white.

He's about to join his sister when he hears her voice.

'Jay?'

He turns to find her standing beside him. The wind has hold of her hair and blows it over one eye. She smooths it back from her face and he notices the black polish on her bitten nails is chipped.

'Can I borrow your lighter?'

He reaches into his jacket for his Zippo.

She takes it and for a fraction of a second their fingers touch. 'Did you know the US Army issued these to their troops?' she says. 'Because they're completely windproof and stay alight in any weather.'

He nods. He knows this. Everybody knows this.

They lean against an outcrop of rock and he rolls a cigarette. Edie lights her Camel Light. He puts the cigarette between his lips and takes the lighter from her. Lights up. Knocks the Zippo shut against his wrist. It clicks loudly and he slips it back into his pocket.

They finish their smokes and walk on. He has a flash of vivid recollection. The last time he walked here. With his father and Tamsyn. He hears the echo of her crying. She'd fallen while running along the path and grazed her knee on a rock. She was fine until she realised it was bleeding. The sound of her crying was grating but their father didn't shout or sound irritated. He stopped still and bent down. Told her the three of them were explorers discovering magical lands that were yet to be mapped.

Her crying had ebbed and through the remnants of her tears she asked if there were tigers. He laughed. Said yes. Then scooped her onto his shoulders to keep her safe from the tigers' teeth. As he did she squealed with delight.

Jago pushes the memory away and walks on. The path becomes steeper. The three of them, him following Edie and Tamsyn, walk solemnly, as if on a pilgrimage. Their footsteps beat a steady rhythm. He wonders where his friends are. Imagines they are down at the dock, kicking the walls, moaning about the mines and London wankers and the price of weed. Tamsyn's right. He doesn't walk the cliffs enough. A mistake. The air up here is good for the soul.

They come to a steep section in the path. Tamsyn rests her hand on a rock and lowers herself down. Then Edie looks around at him. He steps close to her. Holds his hand out for her to steady herself. When she is down safely she turns to say thank you and it skewers him. She smiles and lets go of his hand and he has to pause to catch his breath.

The mine shafts of Botallack rise out of the moorland. Ruined chimneys. Walls that now are only piles of stones. Arches standing like sculptures. The cliff path is rough here. Loose pebbles scatter the way. Scars of rock cut into expanses of earth and cushions of heather. They walk on towards the engine houses set low on the cliffs. The remains of the arsenic-refining works. He's amazed at how much he remembers. His father was a good teacher.

The path narrows and heads downwards, drawing closer to the sea. The cliff falls away at colossal speed to their left and waves crash angrily at the foot of the vertical face.

Edie gasps. Her hand reaches instinctively for the rock to her right.

'Don't slip,' Tamsyn calls back.

Tamsyn stops in front of what's left of the engine house. She pulls herself up onto the wall.

Edie looks hesitant. 'Is it safe?'

'No,' he says, then jumps onto the wall and follows his sister.

Edie climbs up too. They step carefully then haul themselves up onto the wide ledge beneath the glassless window in the ruined wall. There's no roof. The timbers rotted away decades before. Looking upwards, the hole where the roof should be creates a picture frame for the sky. Grass has grown over the floor of the ruin and makes a soft carpet. The three of them lean out of the window. The cliff falls away. A drop of forty or fifty foot. The sea boils white like a witch's cauldron, swirling and crashing in from all directions with a low rumbling in which he hears his father's voice.

'Get ready for a big one,' Jago says.

And moments later the swell rolls into a giant white-topped monster which breaks hard against the rocks.

'How did you know that?' Edie's voice is filled with wonder and it twists his stomach.

'He counted,' his sister says. 'Every seventh is a big one.'

They sit down on the grassy ledge. Backs against the wall. Edie is between him and Tamsyn and every part of him is aware of her, her body against his. Being this close to her he realises how slight she is, like a porcelain doll with flawless skin and limbs like glass that might snap in his hands.

Jago reaches into his pocket for his tobacco. Edie gets her own cigarettes out and offers the packet to Tamsyn who shakes her head. Edie passes a can of lager to each of them. The lagers foam when they crack them. They smoke and drink. Edie pulls her knees close to her body and rests her chin on them.

He steals a look at her. Her profile is perfect against the dark walls of stone. The way she holds the can makes his blood pound. He notices her hair has gathered together in clumps where it has dried after being wetted by sea-spray at the Cape.

He imagines leaning over and putting the strands of hair in his mouth to suck out the salt.

CHAPTER TWENTY-SIX

Edie
July 1986

'I can't tell you how good it feels to get out of that house.' Edie drew on her cigarette and exhaled heavily.

'I don't get why you don't love it.' Tamsyn spoke quietly, as if part of her didn't want to be heard. 'If it were my house I'd never want to leave.'

'I hate it. It's like a cage. Claustrophobic and quiet, and, oh *God*, so bloody white.' Edie stubbed her cigarette into the tufts of grass at her feet and flicked the end into the centre of the engine house floor.

'How can you say that?' Tamsyn seemed to be cross, her mouth set, words clipped. 'I think it's lovely. In fact, if I were you I'd be happy I had the perfect life.'

'Perfect?' She looked at Tamsyn and narrowed her eyes. 'You've no idea, do you?'

She knew she was sounding too defensive, but nobody got it and it pissed her off. Everybody thought money made people happy. They didn't have a clue. It didn't matter how rich a family was, if things were broken, they were broken, and they certainly wouldn't get fixed by a fancy holiday home in Cornwall.

Tamsyn didn't say anything, which annoyed Edie. Her silence implied disagreement.

'Seriously, my life is far from perfect. You know nothing about me.'

Edie leant her head back against the wall and banged it gently a few times. Privilege was a poisoned chalice. People only saw the golden coating. Anything looks beautiful when it shines, but you didn't have to dig too far to find a rotten centre. 'You know,' she said. 'I actually wish we didn't have money. I wish we were normal. Lived like normal people.' She kicked her leg out, banged her heel against the grass. 'I can't wait to get away from all the bullshit.'

'But you have so much to make you happy, a beautiful home, a mum *and* a dad, who both love you—'

Edie snorted with bitter laughter. 'Oh, yeah, they *really* love me. So much so they packed me off to boarding school when I was eight? You remember being eight? Now think about being stuffed into a car and dropped with a load of strangers who hit you across the hand with a ruler if you dare to say you're sad. My *so-called* mother would rather be shopping or having her hair done than looking after me. And that's before we even get to the bloody pills and drink. He's not much better. Always tapping away on that stupid typewriter or jetting off to New York or LA. Parties every other night. Flirting with anybody in a skirt. They're pathetic. Neither of them could even spell *parent* and I know they both wish they'd never had me.' Edie blotted an escaped tear on the sleeve of her top, then wiped beneath her eyes in case her make-up had run.

'But at least you're getting this great educ—'

'Tam.' It was Jago, quiet but firm. 'Leave it.'

His low warning tone and the care in his voice dug into Edie and almost pathetic gratitude spread through her like wildfire.

'I'm trying to help. To make her see she's okay.' Tamsyn's voice cracked with emotion. 'That her life is good—'

'That's not how it works,' he said, interrupting her. 'You can't tell people what they *should* be feeling. They feel what they feel.'

Edie swallowed. This was the first time anybody had ever stood up for her and she was struggling not to collapse into full-blown sobbing.

'When Dad died,' said Jago, 'how many people said in time you'd get over it?'

Edie bit her bottom lip hard. She became aware of his body beside hers. Heat radiated out from where they touched.

'Or that he was a fucking angel God needed back? Or that you shouldn't be sad but be grateful you'd had him in your life?'

'I… I just…' Tamsyn's cheeks had flushed pink.

'Things aren't always what they seem,' Edie said. 'That's all.'

'I didn't say—'

'Leave it. It's fine.' Edie hadn't meant to snap so sharply.

Jago stood. Her body became suddenly colder. She stared up at him. His face was lit in the afternoon light that fell in a shaft through the window opening. She thought he might look down at her, so she could smile, mouth a thank you, but he didn't. He stared at his sister for a moment or two and then walked to the edge of the ledge and jumped down.

Edie stood too. She followed him and carefully climbed out of the hole in the ruined wall. She glanced back at Tamsyn who didn't move, but just sat and stared at her hands.

Outside the engine house, Jago was leaning against the rock face and rolling a cigarette.

'Thanks for—'

But he interrupted her. 'She was trying to be nice.'

'Sorry?'

'Tamsyn.' He gestured with his head towards the ruin. 'Just then.' He spoke in a low voice to shield his words from his sister who still hadn't emerged from the engine house. 'I know she said the wrong thing, but she doesn't get it. She looks at your life and wants it. I don't know if she's told you, but our dad loved your house. It means something to her.'

Edie looked at the floor.

'She likes you. A lot.' He ran the tip of his tongue along the edge of the cigarette paper. 'Don't hurt her. Your parents aren't her fault.' He put the cigarette to his lips, lit it and drew smoke into his lungs deeply. 'She needs a friend.'

Even though he didn't say the words in black and white, she knew what he was asking. She nodded.

Tamsyn appeared from the ruin. Her shoulders were hunched, mouth turned down at the corners, her arms crossed protectively around her body. Jago cast Edie a brief glance before turning and starting back up the path.

She went over to Tamsyn and reached out to rub her arm. 'Sorry for snapping just then. I know you were trying to be kind.'

Tamsyn looked at her, relief visibly melting her anxiety away. 'I'm sorry,' she said.

Edie smiled. 'All forgotten.'

Tamsyn's eyes shone and she broke into a wide smile then began to chatter, her words coming thick and fast.

Edie looked up to where Jago was standing on a small rocky outcrop. He faced the sea, the muscles in his arms were clearly defined as he cupped his cigarette to protect it from the wind. She thought he resembled a classical statue and imagined walking up to him and taking his face in her hands and pressing her lips to his.

If Tamsyn hadn't been there, she was certain that's what she would have done.

CHAPTER TWENTY-SEVEN

Tamsyn
July 1986

Edie Davenport had no idea how lucky she was. Had she had to bury her father? Did she have to watch her mother work herself to the bone or her grandad cough his bloodied guts up twice a day? Did she have to listen to other people go on and on and on about Florida when she'd never even been as far as the Tamar Bridge? If I were her I'd never complain. I'd be thankful every single day.

As I stared into the darkness, my box room feeling even more claustrophobic than ever, I tried to work out if I'd actually be friends with her if she lived somewhere different. I wasn't entirely sure I would. But then I remembered the mix tape and reached under my pillow to stroke it with the edge of my thumb. As I did so, I recalled the feel of her hand holding mine on the walk back from Botallack and tasted the phantom sweetness of real Coca-Cola.

I had to be sensible. If I wanted to be included in the Davenports' life – and I did – I had to stop expecting Edie to be perfect. It wasn't fair to hold her up to such scrutiny. I'd pushed every friend I'd ever had away because they did or said something wrong, but this time there was so much more to lose.

Now I'd been a welcome part of the house, I couldn't possibly go back to stealing the key from the tin and breaking in when nobody was there.

It took ages for me to fall asleep and when I did it was fitful. The air was hot and still and I was plagued by a terrifying dream I was unable to climb free from...

I was at The Cliff House. Eleanor Davenport was on the roof, crouched with her toes curled over the guttering. There was a cry that sounded like a seagull, but when I looked it was Edie and Jago who were trapped in a cage on the table. Why were they in it together? They should be in separate cages. The cage was too small for two. It was then I noticed the water from the pool. It was rising, bubbling up, spilling over the edges and onto the terrace like black lava. Jago shouted. Edie shook the bars of the cage. I had to free them. My fingers searched the cage for a catch, anything that might open it, but there was nothing. They started to scream and the sound stabbed my head. I rammed my hands over my ears and looked down. There was a padlock. *Where's the key?* I cried. Then there was another noise. A screech. It came from Eleanor on the roof. Six or seven ravens were huddled around her. I looked at her feet in horror. Not feet at all. Black talons. Clutched in one was an old-fashioned key.

That's it! cried Edie.

Grab it! cried Jago.

But as I reached for it Eleanor snatched it away.

I want something in return.

What? What did she want? I had nothing to give.

But then I realised what it was. I knew. I walked back to the cage and stood in front of Edie. I reached out and pushed my hand through the bars. Then corkscrewed into her chest until my fingers found her heart. Edie's face twisted in fear. Her eyes bulged. Her mouth dropped open.

Don't be scared. It's okay. Your mother wants it.

My fingers clamped around her heart and I pulled back. Her chest tore open. Then I turned to Eleanor and presented the heart, pink and pulsing, on my outstretched palm. One of the ravens swooped down from the roof and clasped hold of the heart. He carried it up to Eleanor and she grabbed it. As she did, she dropped the key which fell through the air. I caught it but then the heart began to change. It grew darker and darker, shrivelling as its moisture was drawn out of it. Eleanor's face contorted in rage. I spun around and desperately tried to push the key into the lock before she came for me.

I'll get you out. I promise. I will.

But the key vanished into thin air. Eleanor had gone. The ravens too. All that was left was the dried-up husk of heart which lay twitching on the terrace.

I woke sharply from the nightmare. Fright wriggled inside me like a thousand burrowing worms. I was sweaty and hot. My bedclothes were twisted around me. A clamp around my lungs had expelled the air like a wrung-out cloth.

I clutched my pillow to me as I concentrated on slowing my pulse. I didn't search my dream for meaning. I'd stopped doing that a long while ago. I couldn't remember a time when I wasn't plagued by these terrifyingly surreal nightmares – so vivid and impossible to shake. I was that sort of child. A child who saw monsters in the shadows and spirits in graveyards and heard voices calling from the centre of a windstorm.

When I was young I'd wake screaming and call for my father. He'd be with me in moments, holding my head to his chest, the flat of his hand cradling my cheek, whispering over and over that I didn't need to cry, that he was with me, that I was safe. I placed my pillow back on the bed and lay down, pulling the duvet tightly around me. I missed him stroking my fear away so much it hurt.

CHAPTER TWENTY-EIGHT

Present Day

My eyes snap open. I can feel her watching me. As my mind adjusts to wakefulness I tell myself it's not possible. That she isn't there. She can't be. But nevertheless I turn my light on to check. Beside me he grumbles in his sleep, turns, pulls the sheets over his head.

The bedroom is empty.

My skin crawls with sweat and my throat is tight and dry. Yet another nightmare. I try to recall it, but only the shapeless shadow of it persists, floating around the edge of my mind, evading me.

I get out of bed and put on my dressing gown, turn the light off, then quietly leave the room. For a moment I think I can hear her breathing. I turn around expecting to see her but there's nothing. My footfalls are silent on the stairs. Just the odd creak of timber. I go into the kitchen. The tap drips on the sink and echoes like a tolling funeral bell. I make myself a cup of warm milk, add a spoonful of sugar, stir it and watch the liquid swirl. I wait until the surface of the milk stills. When I've finished the drink, I turn on the tap to wash the mug. I up end it on the stainless steel drainer, cloudy with age, marked with smears.

I unlock the back door and walk out. The clouds are thick and black and obscure the moon. The sea and sky have merged into one dark mass.

'Where are you?' My whispered voice cracks the silence.

I wait and listen. Strain my eyes. See the outlines of the overgrown bushes that encroach the grass. Something scampers through the hedge beside me. An owl screeches further up the lane.

'I know you're there!' I shout this time.

But still there's nothing.

I don't want to go back indoors so I lie down on the unkempt grass, pull my knees in tight. I know I won't sleep. I don't want to. I'm scared.

When dawn breaks I sit up. I'm cold and stiff and wince as I unfurl my spine. I stretch backwards and hear the crack of joints. The sky is lit with a hazy blue light and the grass is sprinkled with dew. There's no wind and the waves are silent. The first seagull mournfully greets another day.

It is now I realise she is beside me. Sitting on the grass. There's a heavy smell, like turned milk, and I know her skin will be sallow, her hair unwashed, lank, eyes dull. I don't look at her. I hate seeing her like this. It fills me with guilt and I can't face that. Not today.

I stare straight ahead, wishing she'd take the hint and leave me alone.

'What are you doing out here?' Her voice is thin and strangled.

'I'm allowed, aren't I?'

She doesn't reply.

'I needed some air,' I say reluctantly.

'But you've been out all night. You could have caught your death.'

'I couldn't sleep, that's all.'

'Not because of me I hope.'

Tears form and spill down my cheeks. I blot them away but she notices.

'Aren't you happy?'

I don't answer.

'You should be. Your life is perfect, isn't it?'

'Can't you leave me alone?' I whisper. 'Isn't there anywhere else you can go?'

She doesn't acknowledge my question and I wonder if I even spoke the words aloud.

CHAPTER TWENTY-NINE

Tamsyn
July 1986

Edie was lying on the lawn on a brightly coloured beach towel. She wore her mum's bikini and her mirrored sunglasses. Her skin gleamed with suntan oil and the smell of coconut hung heavily in the air. She had her Walkman on and didn't notice I was there until I stood right over her, blocking the sun so a shadow fell across her.

She lifted her sunglasses up and pushed herself up on her elbows to see who I was.

'Hi,' I said.

'Hey,' she replied and lay back down, repositioning the sunglasses over her eyes.

I sat on the grass beside her. It had grown longer and the lush green was dotted with daisies. I thought of the daisy drying between the heavy books in my box room and made a mental note to check it when I got back.

I looked down towards the fence. My brother was still painting, but he'd nearly finished. He'd done a good job, or at least it looked like a good job to me. The rust had gone and the iron railings gleamed with their new coat of white. I noticed that someone had been in to weed the garden and sweep the terrace.

The pool sparkled as if sprinkled with diamonds. The whole picture could have been a shot from a travel brochure.

Jago looked up at us and nodded a greeting at me. I half raised my hand and smiled.

'The fence is nearly finished,' I said.

Edie sat up and looked down towards Jago. 'Yes,' she said. 'I told my father we needed more work done in the garden, that maybe Jay could stay and help out, but he said there's a man who comes in already.' She sniffed and looked around the garden. 'I don't think he's very good, do you? I mean, look at the grass.'

'It looks like he spent time on the terrace. Maybe he'll cut the grass next week. Anyway,' I said, 'my brother knows nothing about gardens.'

Edie leant forward and picked a daisy. She held it up and twirled it between her thumb and forefinger, so it looked like a tiny spinning plate.

Max came out of the house and waved at me. I waved back.

'Lovely to see you, Tamsyn!' he called over. 'Do swim if you'd like to. It's such a beautiful day.'

'Thank you,' I called back.

He smiled at me and my tummy glowed with warmth.

'Urgh,' Edie said then, as she cast the daisy aside. 'He's *such* a lech. I mean, look at him. The way he's leering at you. And why's he gurning like that? He looks fucking deranged. I know he only wants you to swim so he can perv at you in your swimming costume.'

'That's not why. He's just being nice.' I looked over at Max, wondering if Edie was right.

She made a guttural sound and mimed putting two fingers down her throat. 'He's so embarrassing. *Jesus.*' She lay back down and put her headphones over her ears.

I watched Max sit down at the table and swill his drink around his glass. He glanced at me again and flashed another smile which I returned, before settling back on the grass and closing my eyes, basking in the warmth on my skin and inside me.

I was aware of Edie moving beside me. I half opened my eyes and saw her sit up. She had picked another daisy and was picking off individual petals, her mouth moving silently. I tried to read her lips, but it was impossible.

'Do you know how to make chains?' I asked her then, shielding my eyes from the midday sun.

She discarded the petal-less daisy and picked another. 'Of course. Everybody knows, don't they?'

I grinned and sat up. Then we crossed our legs and gathered daisies, putting them in a pile between us and taking one at a time to knit our chains. The sun was warm on my back and surrounding us were the sounds of gulls and songbirds, Max turning the pages of his newspaper, occasionally clearing his throat, and Jago tapping the edge of the paint can with his brush.

Edie and I didn't talk. We didn't need to. Our silence was comfortable as we pressed our nails into the stalks of each flower and threaded another stem through the hole, pulling ever-so-gently so as not to tear the delicate eye.

After a while she sighed heavily and threw down her chain. 'Bored of that.' She looked down the garden towards the fence. 'I keep breaking them.'

'Oh,' I said, concealing a stab of disappointment. 'That's okay. You can have mine.'

I threaded the last daisy stalk and finished the circle, then got onto my knees and leant over to lower it onto her head like a crown. She was looking over my shoulder. I glanced back to see Jago smiling at us.

'Thanks,' she said. 'I feel like a princess.'

I sat back on my haunches. 'You look like a flower child, a hippie from Woodstock or something.'

She smiled and held up her hands, her fingers making peace signs either side of her face. 'I'd have been a great hippie, I reckon.' She flapped her hand near her face to shoo away a fly. 'I love travelling to exotic places and always go barefoot when I can.'

We lay back on the grass and I searched the clouds for faces as they drifted above us in the sky.

'If you could get on a plane now, where would you go?' I asked her.

She didn't think for long. 'India. And I'd get one of those red dots of paint on the centre of my forehead and wear a sari in emerald green. Or maybe black if they make them.' She turned her head to look at me. 'You?'

'I'd stay right here.' I patted the ground either side of me.

'Here?' She snorted. 'Are you nuts? You have the whole world to choose from and you'd choose to stay in a place you've never left?'

I think she thought I meant Cornwall, but I didn't, I meant The Cliff House. It occurred to me then that Edie wanted me to say something fanciful, an out-of-reach fantasy I could never make real. So I lied. 'I'm joking!' I said with a laugh. 'I'd go to America. To Florida.'

She laughed. 'Thank God for that. For a moment I thought you had no dreams at all!'

We were interrupted by Eleanor calling my brother's name

from the back door and simultaneously we looked in her direction. Her hair was held back by a royal blue scarf tied at the nape of her neck, the ends trailing one shoulder, and she wore an off-the-shoulder white T-shirt and tight white trousers that reached her calves. On her feet were delicate gold sandals. I was ready to wave but she didn't seem to see us.

'Jago!' she called again. 'Have you finished yet?'

My brother, who was gathering up the paint-spattered sheet, glanced at her briefly and nodded. Then he bent to pick up the paint pot and walked across the terrace towards her. He glanced over in our direction. Edie ran her hand through her hair.

We watched them talking but couldn't hear exactly what they were saying. Jago looked our way a few times. Then he looked down at the floor. Nodded. Kicked his heel against the paving stones. I could tell by the way his body tensed, the clench of his free hand, the set of his mouth, that whatever she was saying to him was making him angry.

'Maybe she thinks he's done a bad job?' I said.

Edie jumped to her feet and went over to them. Her hips swayed from side to side as she walked, her bottom pert and firm and inadequately covered by the pink bikini bottoms.

Jago didn't look up as she approached. Eleanor was stony-faced and said only a few words to her, before turning back to Jago and thrusting out a brown envelope towards him. He folded it and slipped it into the back pocket of his jeans then made to leave. Edie faced her mother. Hands on hips. Glowering. She said something and Eleanor shook her head. Edie spoke again but her mother turned her back on her and walked back into the house.

'What was all that about?' I asked as Edie returned.

'No more work for him.'

'That's what made you cross?'

'I'm not cross, but, God, she's such a cow. I'd told him he could swim before he left and she interrupted me and said she didn't think that was appropriate.'

'He's not that bothered about swimming. Remember?'

She ignored what I said. 'You two are close, aren't you?'

'Me and Jago?'

She nodded.

'Sure. He's annoying sometimes. Like any brother, I suppose. We're definitely close though. I mean, I can tell him anything.'

As I spoke I felt guilt expand inside me. Guilt that I got so angry with him for getting involved when I was talking to Edie at Botallack and for being irritated with him being at The Cliff House. After all, he was working, not there to see Edie or have barbecues.

'I was wondering if maybe the three of us can hang out again. I enjoyed the walk to the mine the other day.'

'I suppose so,' I said. 'He has friends his own age though.'

Again, she ignored what I'd said, which I had begun to find annoying.

'I was thinking we should do your tattoo, too.'

'I can't. But thank you. I really did mean it when I said Mum wouldn't let me.'

'You're sixteen, Tamsyn. You don't *have* to do what your mother tells you to anymore. Anyway, we'll do it somewhere it'll be covered, so she won't even see it.'

'Edith!' Eleanor was standing at the back door. 'Did you remind Tamsyn about the party?'

'She's sitting right here, Eleanor. She can hear you.'

But Eleanor had disappeared indoors.

'I need to remind you about the party. Can you still make it?'

'Yes! Definitely. I can't wait.'

'I wouldn't get too excited. My parents' friends are vile. You'll need to wear something smart. A skirt, maybe?'

Every time I thought of the party it made my stomach fizz. My mother didn't seem to share my excitement when I told her. Rather than be interested or happy for me, she'd come over all suspicious again.

But why?

Why what?

Why would she invite you?

So I gave her a hard stare and asked why she *shouldn't* invite me. Mum had given a vague shrug and tried to smile. Which had made me angry, so I crossed my arms and narrowed my eyes.

I hate that you can't just be happy for me!

She then reached out to lay a palm against my cheek, which I batted away before running upstairs to my box room.

I'd no idea what was wrong with her. My invitation to the Davenports' party was the most thrilling thing that had happened to me and, whatever Mum thought, I knew I was going to have the best time.

CHAPTER THIRTY

Angie
August 1986

They sat at a table in the corner of the Moon and Stars. A couple of men played darts beside them. Serious faces. Pints of ale on the mantelpiece and bellies protesting against their waistbands. At the window hung a greyed net curtain with a pretty star pattern on it. There were a few tiny holes in the top right corner which Angie recognised as moths. The net fluttered every now and then as the wind pushed itself through a small gap in the frame. Pictures hung on the beige textured wallpaper: the pub in years gone by, black and white streets, fishing boats stranded by the tide, fishermen in thick sweaters with tousled hair and toothless grins.

It was a filthy night outside, with rain battering the town and the sea whipped into angry waves. The sky was far darker than it should have been on an early summer evening. She hated storms since the one that took Rob, and it was comforting to be in the pub, with the weather kept at bay behind closed doors, surrounded by chattering voices and protected from inevitable recollections of the night he died.

Angie was distracted though. She couldn't help thinking of Tamsyn, worrying about her and the Davenports. She didn't understand why they were so keen to have her hanging around all the time. And now this party? Tamsyn had erupted with such anger when Angie asked her about it and now she was even more convinced it was going to end in her daughter's tears.

Tamsyn had struggled since her father's death. She'd never really found her place and, though it was tough, Angie had been forced to accept her daughter was a loner. This fixation on the Davenports was unnatural and Angie worried she was opening herself up to being dreadfully hurt. She wished they'd stop with the champagne and the manicures and the bloody party invites.

The Davenports' world wasn't their world. People like them could only ever be temporary visitors and there would come a time when the Davenports would pull up the drawbridge and shut Tamsyn out. Yes, at the moment Tamsyn seemed happy, but Angie wished more than anything the family had rejected her at the beginning. Because when they eventually did – and they undoubtedly would – she was going to fall hard.

'This is nice,' said Gareth.

'Sorry?'

'Being in the pub. With you. Like this.'

'It is,' she said. Then she hesitated. 'Your beer good?'

'Spot on.'

She sipped her lager shandy.

'Fancy some crisps?'

'Yes please,' she said, with forced enthusiasm. 'That'd be lovely.'

He smiled at her and stood. Wiping his hand on his trousers, he reached into his pocket for his wallet and then crossed the pub to the bar.

Angie had known Gareth so long he was like a brother. He'd

been in the same class as she and Rob at Cape Cornwall School. Rob and he had even been friends, until they got to secondary school and Rob became football captain and Gareth started working evenings and weekends at his father's chip shop.

She smiled self-consciously at him as he sat back down and put two packets of Salt 'n' Shake on the table.

'Thanks,' she said.

'Angie—' He hesitated.

She reached for a packet of crisps and pulled it apart, then fished out the little blue envelope of salt and tore off the corner.

'I've got something important I want to tell you.'

Her heart missed a beat.

No, things are fine as they are. Please don't say anything important.

But Gareth couldn't hear her thoughts.

'I care about you, Angie.'

She kept her eyes focused on the crisps as she tipped the salt into the bag. He reached over and stilled her hand.

'Did you hear what I said?' he asked softly.

She looked up at him and took a deep breath. This wasn't what she needed. All she wanted was a drink in the pub and a few hours away from it all.

'I fell in love with you when we were nine years old.'

'Don't, Gareth—'

'No,' he said firmly, raising his hand like a traffic policeman. 'Let me finish. You were in my thoughts all the time. Got my heart broke fair in two at the Penzance Social when I saw you dancing with Robbie Tresize and the look on your face.'

She had a vivid flash of that night. June 1963. They were fifteen. She remembered it like it was yesterday. Ned Miller playing 'From a Jack to a King'. Rob Tresize, best-looking boy in Cornwall, if not the country, chin resting on her head, hands in the small of her back, body pressed against hers, her heart beating so hard it threatened to tear right out of her chest into his.

'And I don't mind telling you, I cried the day I got your wedding invite. Turned it down. Told you I had to visit a poorly aunt in Plymouth.' He smiled then. 'I never had an aunt in Plymouth. Let alone a poorly one. Couldn't face seeing you marry him, see? I hated him and it burnt like a furnace in me.'

Angie opened her mouth to speak but Gareth ploughed on.

'I'd never wish death on anybody. Can't say I was as upset as everybody else, but I don't mind admitting I did get choked up.'

Angie recalled the squall of grief which had torn through the county from Redruth to Land's End. People united in mourning her man. Newspapers, church services, schools, everyone talking about the night Robert Tresize went down on the *Bess Sellen*. His bravery, his sacrifice, their loss.

Gareth had been there for her from that first moment. Knocking on the door with a beef stew or fish pie he'd cooked himself. Flowers. Chocolates, even. But she hadn't been able to see him. Didn't want to talk to anybody. Didn't want to hear any words designed to make her feel better. As if she could ever 'feel better'.

'All I wanted to do was take care of you, Angie.'

'I know,' she whispered. 'You've been so good to us.'

She recalled sitting in the living room, hearing Granfer open the door to him.

I thought some company might cheer her up?

I don't think so, lad. Doubt much could cheer her, save you bringing our boy back.

236

Will you give her these peonies? And say I'm here if she needs me.

And then the money had run dry. Word got out they were struggling. Ted put a small box on the counter. *Fund for the family of local hero, Robert Tresize*, it said on its side in permanent marker. After that, Gareth had come round again.

I want to help, Angie.

I won't take your money. It's bad enough the whole town talking about our affairs, let alone taking charity off individuals. It's the last thing Rob would have wanted. Thank you... But... I just... can't take your money.

I'm not here to offer you money. I'm here with a job. Only part-time, mind, but yours if you want it.

She'd worked there since. Three days a week. Things were tight but it was enough to put food on the table and keep the electricity connected and make sure the kids could go on the odd school trip. In all those years, whenever he'd asked her to go for a drink – and she'd lost count of how many times that had been – she'd always said no.

Then one day, when the thought of another evening watching *Coronation Street* with Granfer whilst dealing with an overflowing basket of ironing made her heart sink, she said yes. He had beamed and told her it was five hundred birthdays come at once.

'I'm not asking for much, Angie. I don't need to marry you. Or even share your bed.'

Angie dropped her eyes, shifted on her chair, then checked around to make sure nobody was listening in.

'I'd love to have a meal with you every now and then,' he went on. 'Maybe watch a bit of telly. Fix things for you...' He paused and reached for her hand to squeeze it. 'What do you say? You think we could do that? Spend a bit more time together outside the shop?'

She looked at him. His skin a mix of pallid white and ruddy pink, sandy hair, eyelashes so fair they were barely there, thin face, gaunt cheeks. It would have been easy to say no for the umpteenth time, but there was a part of her that liked the sound of what he said, liked the idea of having somebody who wanted to spend time with her, who was interested in her, who looked at her in the way he looked at her. Like a woman, not a mum or a daughter-in-law or a skivvy.

'Thank you, Gareth. I'll think on it.'

'Good enough for now.' And he patted her hand.

After they'd finished a second drink, Gareth pulled the net curtain aside and peered out of the window. 'Weather's passed. We can get you back now.'

The rain had stopped, just the sweet lingering smell of it and drops falling from the pub's guttering. Puddles filled indentations in the pavement and potholes in the road, and in the distance white horses danced on the sea. Bats flew from the church eaves across the street and the moonlight turned everything to shades of wet pewter.

They walked back in silence. They didn't hold hands. She crossed her arms around her body. They turned into her road and walked up to the house and there they both stopped and faced each other.

'May I kiss you goodnight?' He lowered his eyes and she was glad he couldn't see her deliberation.

'Yes.'

His head lifted and he smiled at her before leaning forward to press his mouth to hers. His lips were dry, skin roughened by day-old stubble. As the tip of his tongue touched her mouth she was aware of him tensing with urgency. A little alarmed, she pulled away from him and as she did she caught a movement from an upstairs window. She looked up.

Nobody there.

'Thank you for a lovely evening,' she said, then turned from him and walked up the path.

'Goodnight, Angie.'

As soon as the door closed behind her, she put her head in her hands and breathed the trapped air. Her body began to tremble. She listened to his footsteps echo on the pavement. Leather shoes, his best, worn only for church and special occasions.

A brief kiss. Nothing more. She could smell him on her. Aftershave. Strong. She thought about his lips on hers and shook as she walked up the stairs.

She went straight to the airing cupboard and reached for her cardboard box. Inside were a few of Rob's things. A small pile of clothes folded neatly. His belt. A hip flask, battered, engraved with his father's name. His watch wrapped up in a cotton handkerchief. A couple of his T-shirts – her most prized ones – remained unwashed since he died. His smell was still detectable, faint, a mere shadow, but there nonetheless. She leafed through them, not allowing her tears to fall on anything in the box. Nothing was allowed to contaminate what remained of him.

When he was alive, before the sea took him, she would lie beside him, tucked under his arm with her cheek resting on his chest, head turned to breathe him in. She always loved the smell of him. She used to say it was his smell that attracted her, as if they were scientifically matched, two chemicals which reacted perfectly to create something beautiful.

She chose the grey T-shirt and carefully eased it from the pile. She held it up to her face and closed her eyes and smelt it deeply. He was there. On the wide stretch of yellow beach at Sennen Cove, his favourite beach. He walked ahead of her holding Tamsyn's hand in his. Jago ran up in front of them, his bare feet making dents in the sand which shone silver in the low-set autumn sun, his hands clutching his red bucket and fishing net.

Angie watched this scene whilst breathing in the faintest hint of her husband from that day, his tanned arms, strong and smooth, fingers lightly holding his daughter, jeans rolled up to below the knee, brown legs, a dusting of golden hair, calves defined. She breathed in again and imagined bending down and placing her mouth against his calves, first one, then the other. Kissing upwards, over his jeans, lifting up his grey shirt to reveal his stomach, firm and taut, pushing her lips against him.

I miss you.

She went into the bathroom and brushed her teeth, slipped her nightie on over her head, then went back downstairs. She dragged the foldaway bed out and made it up, before closing the curtains and climbing beneath the duvet in a trance-like state.

She lay in bed and held the T-shirt in her hand, unable to keep her thoughts away from Gareth, his face coming in to kiss her, his tongue pushing between her lips.

His smell, so alien, so unfamiliar.

And yet the feel of another person caressing her, desiring her, was tantalising.

Her stomach filled with a sudden and overwhelming guilt. She squeezed her eyes shut and held Rob's soft grey T-shirt against her face.

Wherever I am.

His words warm on her skin.

Wherever I am. However far away. I'll always love you.

'This far?' she whispered into the T-shirt. 'Did you mean this far?'

She pulled the duvet around her. It was their duvet. Too big for the single bed she now slept on, but she'd never use anything else. The duvet was one of the first things they'd bought together. Bought from a department store in Truro. Giggling with each other. Touching each other. Laughing at the disapproving looks from two old ladies pretending to look at china teacups whilst they tutted and sniffed.

This house, everything in it, each piece of furniture, each photograph, each mark, the carpets and chairs and table lamps. The two children. The old man. All of it wedded to her husband.

May I kiss you?

Gareth's words rang in her head. She tried to ease Rob away. Thought about Gareth. Waited for his kiss. When it came it had surprised her. It was so different. Not unpleasant, just…

Different.

Rob reappeared. His eyes bored into hers. Hands either side of her face, readying himself to kiss her.

Angie snapped her eyes open and threw the T-shirt down towards the foot of the bed and away from her. She banged her fist against the pillow.

Leave me alone. I need to move on. I'm so bloody lonely.

His face fell and he drew back from her.

You mean that?

Angie sat up and stretched forward to retrieve the T-shirt. She clasped it to her chest and began to cry.

'No,' she sobbed quietly. 'I don't mean it. How could I? Stay with me, Rob. Never, ever go. Please. Stay with me.'

CHAPTER THIRTY-ONE

Tamsyn
August 1986

Their footsteps drummed the pavement. Lowered voices. The whole time they'd been gone, I'd lain in bed, eyes fixed on the ceiling, and listened to the storm with the thought of them together gnawing at me like a pack of James Herbert's rats.

They stopped outside our front door and I knelt up on my bed to look out of the window, whilst keeping myself concealed behind the curtain. They were down there, obscured somewhat by the crack in the windowpane covered by a strip of masking tape, which my mother attached to stop the glass blowing in during storms. He wore a sweater over a shirt. The moonlight glinted off whatever product he'd used to tame the flyaway strands of his thinning hair. They faced each other. Her hands were clasped in front of her. He said something. She looked at the ground. He nodded. Then he put his hand on her waist and she looked up.

No.

The flat of my hand went up to the glass.

No. *No!*

But then it happened. He leant forward and kissed her.

My insides screamed out as if the kiss was a knife in my belly.

Get off her. Get. Off. Her.

I dropped the curtain and I curled myself into a ball on my bed, my hands scratching at the sides of my head. All I could picture in my head was my father, out there in the crashing waves, crying out as he struggled to stay above the water, his eyes stinging with salt water and tears. My bedroom grew colder and our house more toxic.

The front door closed. I heard feet on the stairs. Only one person. No whispering voices. Just her. She was on the landing. The airing cupboard opened. Then I listened to her going into the bathroom. The tap. The toilet flush. Her feet padding back down the stairs.

I stared into the darkness for some time. I've no idea exactly how long. My skin itched and the claustrophobic air in my box room became harder and harder to breathe. It was as if I'd become allergic to what used to be my home.

I needed to get out.

I grabbed my jeans and sweatshirt from the floor and pulled them on. I took hold of my trainers and crept downstairs, and let myself quietly out of the front door.

I walked along the coast path in the dark as if being dragged by an invisible rope. There was enough light from the moon for me to see, but the ground underfoot was sodden after all the rain. A couple of times I slipped, and once fell, banging my elbow on a large stone at the edge of the path. However, as soon as I was seated at the rock, using my bag to keep the wetness from soaking my jeans, the tension immediately seeped from my body. It was like a drug, calming my anxiety, smoothing my head out.

The moonlight bounced off the house and turned its whiteness spectral. The windows were dark apart from Max and

Eleanor's bedroom and the sitting room. The curtains and blinds were open and the lit windows turned to cinema screens showing Eleanor asleep on the settee. She rested her head on her arm. Her legs were curled beneath her. White trousers. White top. The blue headscarf discarded on the floor beside her golden sandals. Max walked down the stairs. I wondered why he was still up. Maybe he'd fallen asleep then woken to find she wasn't there, come down to look for her. As he stood over her I imagined him gazing on her beauty, remarking to himself how perfect she was. He bent to pick her up, an arm under her knees, the other hooked beneath her shoulders. Her hair trailed over his arm as he walked her up the stairs. They were out of sight for a moment or two then appeared in their bedroom. He walked her to their bed and lowered her onto it as if she were made of glass. After he'd covered her, he left the room and moments later the living room light went out, then a little after that the one in their bedroom. The house plunged into darkness.

I waited sufficiently long for sleep to take hold of them. Then I walked carefully along the coast path and pushed through the gate. I held my breath when the hinges creaked. The image of my mum kissing Gareth filled my head but I chased it away. I didn't want their treachery anywhere near me. Not here. Not at The Cliff House.

Stepping onto the lawn immediately eased me. I felt close to my father. Felt able to reassure him I was no part of her betrayal. The house was where I felt him the strongest. Once, when Jago and I were sharing one of our long chats into the night, he asked me if I'd swap a year of my life for one more day with our father. I didn't even hesitate. I'd have traded ten years for just a few hours with him, and those few hours would be the ones we spent at The Cliff House, our last afternoon together, swimming in a pool that wasn't ours, the sun on our faces, the murderous incoming rainstorm held at bay on the horizon.

I walked silently up to the terrace. The pool shone like oil. I stood at the end of it and undid my jeans. Took off my shoes and sweatshirt. Then I sat on the edge of the pool and lowered myself into the water. I pushed off, making barely a ripple, not a sound. I turned on my back, spread-eagled my arms, and floated, suspended, so the water covered my ears and dulled my hearing and shut out the world.

I looked up at the sky, at the millions of stars which spiked holes in the sheet of navy, and wondered which one my father was watching me from.

CHAPTER THIRTY-TWO

Jago
August 1986

He hesitates outside the door for a minute or two. He's late. He said he'd be back by five to eat with them. It's now after ten. He can see the two of them at the sink, behind the net curtain, light on, her washing, Tam drying. He can see by the way his sister's face is set, how she's snatching at the tea towel, pushing it around the pan roughly, that she's upset about something.

He opens the door as quietly as he can. Steps inside. Holds his breath as he eases the door shut and creeps towards the stairs.

'Jago?'

He freezes. Mutters under his breath. He considers ignoring her and climbing the stairs anyway, hiding in his room with the door closed. But he doesn't. He has missed tea. He should at least say sorry for that.

He sticks his head around the door and Tamsyn smiles at him so he knows her mood is nothing to do with him.

'Where have you been?' His mother is making an effort to keep her voice light, trying to keep the recrimination hidden, though he can hear it as clearly as if she'd shouted through a loudhailer. He knows full well she's doing it to avoid 'setting him off' and he feels his anger ignite.

'I went out,' he says. Hands in his pockets. Eyes on the floor.

She doesn't reply and he glances up briefly. 'With Adam. We were in Penzance. The Turk's Head.'

'You said you'd be here to eat.'

He kicks the base of the kitchen units gently.

His mum takes a deep breath and runs a hand though her hair. She gestures to the kitchen counter, to the right of the sink. 'It's under the cloth if you want it. It's cold though.'

He looks over at the red-and-white cloth that covers a plate of uneaten food.

'Egg and chips,' she says.

Cold egg and chips. He stares at her and catches a flash of challenge in her eyes.

Go on then. Eat your cold egg and chips.

'I'm going up. Unless you're not okay with that?' It comes out of his mouth with more edge than he'd intended and he wishes he could snatch the words out of the air and shove them back down his throat.

He sees Tamsyn glance over her shoulder to check their mother's reaction.

But his mum doesn't seem to have noticed. Instead she rubs one arm with her hand above the elbow. 'Did you ask Mrs Davenport about more work?' That tone again. Soft and appeasing. Trying not to jab the python in its hole.

His body turns rigid and he swears under his breath, fist clenching as he holds fast, fighting the urge to punch his fist through the wall. Mrs Davenport. Her voice still in his head.

There's no more work for you. I've seen you looking at her. Don't think I haven't. It's no longer appropriate for you to be here.

Then that touch on his arm. A squeeze. The alcohol on her breath as she leant closer to him.

You're a good-looking boy, Jago. I can certainly see why she'd be tempted.

'Because I could ask when I go up there on Friday—'

'She said there wasn't.'

'And she actually said that?'

'For God's sake, leave it!'

'Don't raise your voice. There's no need. I just—'

'Look,' he says, getting himself back under control. 'She gave me money for the fence and said there was no more work up there. They have a gardener who's doing extra hours. Okay?'

'It sounds like you could have pushed more, that's all.'

'That's not all though, is it?'

She furrows her brow. 'What does that mean?'

'I mean, it's not *all*. It's not about me pushing, it's about you thinking I'm a waste of space.'

'What?'

'That woman thinks it too. Not good enough. And she's right, isn't she?'

'I don't think Eleanor thinks that,' his sister says from behind them. 'She's really nice.'

'For fuck's sake, Tamsyn. Open your eyes.'

Her mouth drops in shock and he kicks himself for losing his temper with her. It's not her fault she's been taken in by their airs and graces. He knows he should say sorry, but instead he just gets angrier.

'You think I'm good for nothing. All of you!'

His mother tries to form words, but he's too quick for her.

'I'm lazy, aren't I? Gutless, too.'

'Jago, I—'

'A layabout. That's what you think, isn't it?' His body is tensed, muscles quivering.

Her face drains of colour. 'No, I—'

'You think I'm a fucking loser, don't you? No job. No exams. No backbone.'

She shakes her head. 'Jago,' she says then, her voice quiet and laced with sadness. 'Why are you so angry?'

Her question punctures him. His fists unclench and he swallows against a lump of emotion which has lodged in his throat. 'I'm angry because' —he pauses, takes a breath— 'because I can't make you proud of me and I can't look after you.' He hesitates. 'I'm angry I'm not like him, because if I were we'd be okay, wouldn't we?'

Tears film her eyes. She reaches out to him but he steps back. 'This has nothing to do with your dad.'

Jago laughs a bitter snort of laughter as his own tears burn the corners of his eyes. 'It has *everything* to do with him. Without him you're so bloody worried you can't think straight. You're hanging out with that prick Gareth. Tam's prancing around that fucking house as if she lives there. And me?' He spits his words out with bitter self-loathing. 'I'm just a cunt without a job, who'll never be the hero his dead father was and every fucker knows it. Especially *you*. I should just leave, shouldn't I? Then you wouldn't have to pretend not to be so bloody disappointed in me all the fucking time.'

His mother's hand has shot to her mouth. Tamsyn is staring at him with a furrowed brow, half sympathetic, half angry.

'Don't speak… like that…'

Jago turns to see his grandfather standing behind them, a

250

smear of dried blood on his cheek. His pyjamas are spotted with reddy-brown spatters.

Jago needs to get out. He doesn't need this. He doesn't need their disapproval. 'You know what? Fuck this.'

'If your father… were here… he'd—'

'Yeah,' Jago whispers, nodding bitterly. 'I know.' Then he turns on his heel and pushes past his grandfather, punching the door on the way out, and slamming the front door behind him so the walls tremble.

Clouds move fast across the sky, concealing then revealing the moon in snatches. He hears the sea in the distance, a rumble as it crashes against the jagged rocks of the Cape. He turns right, away from the coast, and walks towards the centre of St Just. He passes the pub and hears the voices inside. Laughter. Warm yellow light spills through the netted window and falls across the pavement. The smell of chips and beer creeps out from the gap beneath the door. He crosses the road. Shoves his hands in his pockets. Walks up to the church and through the opening in the granite wall. The wooden gate rests permanently open, its loose hinges in need of fixing, a faded sign pinned to it requesting nobody touch it.

He walks along the path around the church. His feet crunch on the gravel. There's enough light to make out the rough shapes of the headstones either side of him. He walks across the grass, picks his way between the graves, knows the route well enough to avoid tripping. He comes to a halt beside his father's grave. Pulls out his tobacco. Rolls and lights a cigarette. It crackles as he inhales, the tip of the cigarette flaring momentarily and turning everything else black.

He stands and stares at the grave. The moon is full and in

spite of the clouds there's enough light to make out the jar of fresh flowers, a mixture of heather and cow parsley and one or two carnations she's bought from the store. She refreshes the jar every week. Takes it home to wash it out. Scrubs away the grime and dirt. A pointless ritual that he imagines she'll never stop doing.

Why are you so angry?

He winces as he recalls her voice. The look on her face. Why had he shouted at her like that? Used such filthy language? None of it is her fault. He hates himself for taking it out on her. Needling her. She doesn't deserve it.

All he has to do is take care of them. His mother, his sister, his crumbling grandfather. One promise he made. Instead he wastes his days, unemployed, sleeping and rolling joints, while his mum runs two jobs, bags beneath her eyes, blisters on her fingers.

I promise.

He promised. That's what he did – when they put his father in the ground, clods of soil falling on the coffin, their thuds drowned out by the sobs of those gathered around – he promised. He rolls another cigarette and lights it from the first, then flicks the end into the longer grass that fringes a neighbouring grave.

He watches the ember burn to nothing.

I promise I'll look after them.

Lies. Empty lies. He feels his father's disapproval seeping up through the cold damp earth. He wants to cry but what good would that do?

Jago stubs his half-smoked cigarette out on a stone at his feet and slips it back into his tobacco pouch, then turns and walks back across the graveyard.

By the time he gets back to the cottage it is dark and quiet. A cat startles and scoots up the road. The downstairs window in the house next door flickers with light from a television. He opens the door. Peers into the gloom in the kitchen. Everything is clean. The tea towel is folded over the tap to dry. The plate with the cold egg and chips is still on the side with the cloth laid over it.

The only sound is the ticking of the clock on the wall.

As he passes the sitting room he looks in. He expects to find her asleep, but instead she is sitting upright on the edge of her foldaway bed, nightie on, hands lightly clasped in her lap.

'Are you okay?' Her voice is soft.

He has so much he wants to say to her. To tell her he wants to make her proud. That he wants her to look at him from across a crowded room and point him out to anyone who'll listen. He wants to be able to buy her nice clothes so she can throw her old ones away when they get holes and not have to stitch them up in front of the three-bar. He wants to surprise her with chocolates. Wants her to only eat the ones she likes and not care about wasting the coffee creams.

He wants to tell her he loves her.

'I'm sorry.' It's all he can manage. The other stuff is lodged inside him.

He drags his feet up the stairs. He can never be the man he knows he should be. A man his father would be proud to call his son. While his mother worries about red-topped bills and food in their bellies, what does he do? Kicks around feeling sorry for himself. Moans about unemployment and the government and Tory wankers who live up their own arses. He smokes weed he can't afford. Apathy is his constant companion, his Peter Pan shadow, sewn to his heels so he can never escape it. It's like he's slipped into a waking coma. He is numb.

He wishes he'd told her how much he loves her. He considers going back to her. Sitting beside her, wrapping himself around her, feeling her breath on his skin. But he doesn't.

Instead he retrieves the half-smoked cigarette from his pouch, brushes off the strands of tobacco, and lies back on his pillow to smoke it.

CHAPTER THIRTY-THREE

Tamsyn
August 1986

'Does it hurt?'

Edie nodded. 'Of course it does. But you need it to hurt. If it didn't hurt everybody would do it and then what would be the point?'

I'd made up my mind to ask Edie to do the tattoo for me when I went up to bed after Jago and Mum's last row. My shock and sadness at seeing Mum kissing Gareth bloody Spence had solidified to a stubborn underlying anger. If she was going to do something to upset me like that, then I no longer had to worry about upsetting her by getting a tattoo. And anyway, Edie said she'd do it somewhere hidden, so Mum wouldn't even know.

I had to wait a few days as Edie and her parents had to visit a godfather in Herefordshire or something. The days without her passed so slowly it was painful, not helped by two of those days being blighted by incessant rain, the type that kept me confined to the house and climbing the walls. Too wet to sit at the rock with my binoculars. Too wet, even, to enjoy a swim. By the time Tuesday came round, and with it the planned tattooing, I was champing at the bit to get back to The Cliff House.

I sat on Edie's bed and crossed my legs, my tummy jumbled

with nerves, hoping it wasn't going to be so painful I'd cry. Edie
had her back to me and was rummaging around in the pile of
clothes on her wardrobe floor and then turned and thrust out
a three-quarter-full bottle of vodka.

'Get that down your neck. I'll be back in a sec.'

I hesitated but then remembered Gareth's hand squeezing
Mum's waist as his ugly sandy head bent over hers. With that,
I grabbed the bottle, unscrewed the lid and tipped it to my lips,
wincing at the taste of the vodka as it hit my mouth.

Edie's room was such a tip. Everything she owned which
wasn't shoved into her cupboard was scattered over the floor.
The pillow had half escaped its case and there were smudges
of black make-up all over the sheet and duvet as well as balled
tissues littering the top of the chest of drawers and the area of
carpet around the bin. Dirty coffee mugs were dotted along the
windowsill and bedside table. There was something sophisticated about the state of it. My mother would never have stood
for it and the fact I did as I was told, and kept my box tidy, made
me feel childish and trapped. I couldn't wait to get the tattoo.

'Nearly ready.' Edie came back into the room and chucked
a white slip of cardboard onto the bed. It was wrapped around
in different coloured threads with a couple of needles, a button
and a safety pin tucked into them. 'From one of Max's book
tours. He collects souvenirs from the places he stays. Drink,'
she said, tapping the bottle.

As I drank, I picked up the sewing kit and read the writing
on it. *The Astoria Hotel, New York*. I drew the tips of my fingers
over the threads, marvelling at how much further they had
travelled than me and yet still they'd ended up here.

Edie scooped up a bag from the floor beside her bed and

fished around inside it. She took out a pencil case on which words and shapes were doodled in blue and black biro: her name written multiple times in spiky writing, hearts, skulls, CND signs and a few band names I recognised. She unzipped it and took out a bottle of ink. I stared at the black liquid which could have been drawn from the dark pool beneath her bedroom window.

'Indian ink is the only type you can use,' she said, shaking the bottle vigorously.

'Why?' I asked as I lifted the vodka to my mouth and swallowed.

She shrugged. 'No idea. Maybe the other stuff is poisonous.'

She walked over to a small red and black radio cassette player on top of the chest and pressed a button. There was a loud click then music.

'A bit of Depeche Mode,' she said. 'Perfect to get us in the mood.'

A haunting dirge of voices filled the room followed by an echoing noise like a knife tapping on a milk bottle. She walked over to me and reached between my legs for the bottle of vodka. She took the lid off and threw it aside. It skimmed across the floor and bounced against the wall. She smiled as she drank. When she lowered the bottle from her mouth I saw her chin shone with vodka and it crossed my mind to lick it off.

'Martin Gore is a total *God*,' Edie said over the noise, closing her eyes and tipping the bottle to her lips again. The song filled the room and she swayed in time. 'It's called "Black Celebration",' she said. 'It's the track Jay likes.'

The music vibrated through my body. Edie threw her arms in the air and waved them as she turned around and around, eyes still closed, head nodding in time with the beat. She was mesmerising. Every part of me wanted to stand and dance too, but I was shackled by self-consciousness and unable to move. Her hips rotated as she circled, neck tipped back, mouth half opened. Then without warning her face changed. She became pale and peppered with sand. Bits of seaweed stuck to her blueish lips and water flooded her mouth and throat and soaked her lungs like the boy on the beach. I closed my eyes and dug my fingernails into my palms to force the lie away. Edie wasn't drowned. She was alive and dancing for me.

When I opened my eyes she smiled and held the bottle out towards me. As I took it our hands lingered on the glass. I inched my finger up to graze hers and a flash of heat flared where our skin touched. She turned and danced away from me, and I had the strange sensation The Cliff House was sealing itself up, the locks turning, the windows gluing themselves to their frames, as if it was trying to keep me inside.

'Make sure you drink,' she said over the music, gesturing at the bottle and breaking me from my thoughts. 'If you don't it'll sting like *crazy*.'

She sat down beside me and reached for the sewing kit. Using her fingers like tweezers she eased one of the needles out then unravelled some red cotton. She wound the thread around the tip of the needle leaving a couple of millimetres exposed. I leant back against the headboard and closed my eyes.

'Drink more.'

I lifted the bottle and swallowed. The liquid didn't burn anymore but slipped down bitter-smooth. My head floated higher as each pump of my heart forced the alcohol into my bloodstream. It was intoxicating to feel so distanced from my reality, protected by the house. Not just from Mum and Gareth bloody Spence and Granfer's blood-specked handkerchief and my brother's hopeless gloom, but also the grief which throbbed beneath my skin and the nightmares waiting in my sleep.

'So what tattoo do you want?'

As I turned to look at her, my head swum. 'A cross. Like yours.'

She rolled her eyes, but nodded. 'Sure. It's the easiest thing to do anyway.'

'On your shoulder?' She tilted her head and raised an eyebrow. 'That's where mine is after all.' She laughed.

'Yes. Where yours is.' Maybe it was the vodka or the music or just being in her company but I no longer cared about keeping the tattoo hidden. If Mum saw it, well, she'd just have to deal with it.

'Take your top off then.'

I hesitated, recalling the agony of the last time she'd seen me in my underwear, dripping wet, caught trespassing, shivering with humiliation beneath her piercing gaze.

'Seriously, you need to relax. I went to a girls' boarding school. We hang out starkers all the time. It's just skin. I mean, if you're that worried, I can pull your collar down but the tattoo will look shit and you'll get blood on your top.'

She spoke in that tone that made me feel like a kid who was wasting her time, so reluctantly I took a breath and unbuttoned my shirt. Heat spread over me like melting butter, but when I glanced at her she was studying the tip of the needle not me.

When the door opened without warning I jumped. It was Eleanor. She stood in the doorway, hands on hips, face like thunder. My cheeks burst into flame and I grabbed my shirt and held it up against my chest. Eleanor was wearing a dressing

259

gown in sky blue silk which grazed the floor. Her hair was in a ponytail. She had no make-up on and her skin, which shone with night cream, was criss-crossed with red capillaries and smudged greyish-yellow beneath her eyes.

'You're drinking?' She looked from Edie to me and then to the bottle.

Edie snorted. 'You're joking, right?'

Eleanor crossed her arms. 'Well, are you?'

'No,' Edie said flatly. 'We're not drinking.'

Eleanor looked back at the bottle of vodka between us and narrowed her eyes.

'Did you bring that, Tamsyn?' she said, her voice slurred.

Horror flooded me. I wanted to scream, *I didn't bring it here! I don't drink! She made me!* But instead I sat there with my mouth opening and closing in silence.

'It's mine.' Edie turned away from her mother and pretended to yawn. 'I mean, obviously it's yours, but it was me who took it from the cupboard. Don't worry,' she said, reaching for the ink. 'There's plenty more. You won't run out.'

Eleanor's face hardened. I wanted the floor to open up and swallow me. She glared at Edie. I braced myself for her to explode and send me home, but instead she blinked twice and marched over to Edie's chest of drawers and snapped the music off. 'Keep the music *down*. If you don't, I won't let Tamsyn stay the night again.'

I tried to smile at her, aware that I was sitting half naked in her house, a bottle of stolen alcohol on the bed at my feet. But she didn't soften, just stalked out of the room and slammed the door.

Edie closed her eyes briefly and shook her head. 'Sorry you had to see that,' she said. 'She's such a nightmare.'

'Should we go and say sorry to her? For the music?'

Edie furrowed her brow. 'Why?'

I shrugged.

Edie leant forward and pushed the bottle towards me. When I tipped it to my lips I only pretended to drink.

'Who's coming to the party?' I said, wanting to take my mind off Eleanor's anger.

'The party?'

'The one I'm coming to.'

'Oh. Just friends of my parents who are staying for the weekend.'

Edie pressed her finger against the point of the needle. Her skin compressed, the flesh whitening around the point, until finally the needle pierced her skin. She held her finger up in front of her face and squeezed with the other hand, staring at the bubble of blood that grew.

'Do you need to sterilise it?'

'Yeah, actually that's probably a good idea.' She took hold of the vodka bottle and tilted it until the liquid lapped at the opening, then she dipped the tip of the needle into it.

She stood and went over to the tape machine and pressed play.

'But your mother—'

'God, don't worry about her. She doesn't really care. That was her playing at being *la maman*. You know? Doing the whole routine. *Don't be late. Turn that racket down. Make sure you brush your teeth before bed,*' she mimicked. 'It's an act. She doesn't give a shit. She'll swallow a couple of yellows and a skinful of whisky in a minute and be out for the count.'

'What's a yellow?'

261

'Benzodiazepine. Benzos. To stop her going hyper and help her sleep and stuff. The doctor gives them to her like sweeties. Private GPs make the best drug dealers. Right,' she said brightly. 'Let's ink. A cross like mine, yes?'

I nodded and turned my back to her, then pulled my hair to one side and allowed my head to fall forward. When Edie rested her hand on my back, Eleanor's intrusion was quickly forgotten. I gasped at the pain of the first prick of the needle and Edie laughed. She stroked her hand over my back. Her touch was electric. I imagined her hand encircling my neck, running over my shoulder, and along my collarbone. The needle pressed into me again and interrupted my thoughts.

With each prick a shiver ran through me. As the needle broke my skin white heat radiated outwards. I bit down on my lip as the pain grew more intense. I tried to distract myself by thinking of Dad. I wondered what he'd thought of tattoos. Would he have been angry like Mum would undoubtedly be or admired my rebellion? Losing him when I was young meant I didn't have all the information. I was limited to memories and second-hand observations which came from Mum and Granfer. The rest, the between bits, I was forced to make up. He was like a jigsaw with some of the pieces missing and if I wanted the whole picture I had to fill in the gaps myself. As Edie leant over to dip the needle into the ink, I decided he'd have liked the tattoo. This was, after all, the man who broke into a house to swim in a pool which wasn't his.

After what must have been a thousand pinpricks and when the pain was becoming intolerable, she finally sat back on her haunches. 'There. All done.'

I stretched my back as she got up and went to her chest of

drawers. She got hold of her make-up mirror then returned to me. She knelt behind me and held the mirror up at an angle so I could see it. The cross had a slight kink in the middle, but I didn't care. I'd have it forever, a reminder of the house, always there, etched into my skin. 'Oh I love it,' I breathed. 'Thank you so much.'

Edie opened the drawer of her bedside table and took out her cigarettes. She offered me one. I shook my head. She lit up and tapped the ash into her open pencil case. The room quickly filled with smoke and I prayed Eleanor had taken the yellows.

'So what should I wear to the party?'

'Oh,' she said with a dismissive shrug. 'Something smartish. Don't worry too much.'

'What are you wearing?'

'A skirt but I'll be maxing out the black make-up and going heavy on the jewellery. I like to give their friends something to gossip about on their way home. And the Davenports' wayward daughter is always a popular subject.'

'I've got a nice top and I can borrow a skirt from Mum.'

'Eleanor might give us a few things to hand round.'

'Things?'

'Canapés.'

'What are canapés?'

Edie looked at me quizzically and laughed. When she realised I wasn't joking she said, 'Tiny food.'

I nodded and my stomach fizzed with anticipation. Saturday couldn't come quickly enough.

CHAPTER THIRTY-FOUR

Tamsyn
August 1986

The tattoo was itchy and felt bruised to the touch. Edie told me that was normal and that it would be tender for at least a week. I regretted not asking Edie to do the tattoo in a more discreet place. To prevent Mum from seeing it, I covered it with a large plaster, one designed for grazed knees. When the ache got unbearable, I found I could relieve it a little by pressing the flat of my hand against it, but other than that I left it alone. It was too tender to interfere with and Edie assured me it was fine to leave it be.

As soon as I got back from Ted's I went into the bathroom and locked the door. My tummy was a mush of excitement and nerves. I assessed myself in the mirror. There was lots to do. My skin was dull and a little grubby and my hair was a tangled mess in desperate need of a wash. I leant closer and stared at the unruly hairs between my eyebrows. Those would certainly have to go.

I ran a hot and deep bath and prayed Mum wouldn't hear it running. We weren't allowed more than a few inches of water. It was a hangover from when Dad was alive. He had grown up sharing bathwater between him and his four siblings. He was the youngest so always got the cold dregs with everybody else's dirt in. Because of this, Mum said, he had never really thought much of a bath, preferring instead to run a sink of hot water and wash himself over with a flannel. Mum would do the same to us. I'd have to stand in the freezing bathroom when I was a child and she would roughly wipe me then rinse me off, the water running down my body and soaking into the bathmat she made me stand on. After he died she let us have baths, but only shallow ones or else she'd feel guilty.

While I waited, I lined the shampoo, soap and Jago's razor for my legs on the side of the tub. After I'd scrubbed every inch of myself, I got out and put my dressing gown on and wrapped my hair in a towel. Once that was done, I unlocked the bathroom door and went onto the landing.

'Can I borrow a skirt, Mum?' I yelled as I opened the airing cupboard door and began to grab anything which looked vaguely *smart*.

I heard a mumbled reply which I took to be a *yes* then spent the next hour trying everything on three or four times.

When I finally went downstairs, Mum smiled at me. 'You look lovely.'

'Thanks. I'm a bit nervous.'

'Parties always used to make me nervous. You'll be fine when you get there and start chatting to people.'

Just then there was a knock on the door. Mum glanced at me then went to open it.

'Hello, love.' It was Gareth.

'Gareth said he'd drive you,' she said, before I had time to protest. 'I know you'd asked Jago to take you—'

'No, it's—'

'You've done your hair so nice. We don't want you turning up like Worzel Gummidge.'

I was about to press on with my protest when I stopped myself. Of course she was right. I'd used her hairdryer and dried my hair so it was straight and shining like a sheet of copper. It had taken ages and I knew that ten minutes on the back of the bike would destroy it so I nodded reluctantly.

Mum beamed and kissed me on the cheek. Her face grew hesitant but she forced her smile to stick. 'Enjoy yourself, love.'

'Come on, Cinders,' Gareth said, 'let's get you to the ball.'

As I walked past him to the front door I narrowed my eyes and glared.

Gareth tried to talk on the way over, filling the air with irritating quips and dull observations. It was obvious Mum had set this up and that it was some sort of plot to get us talking and make me like him. Well, I wasn't falling for it, so I set my jaw and crossed my arms and fixed my gaze out of the window until he got the message and shut up.

Eventually we reached the road that led up to The Cliff House. As soon as we turned onto it, I asked him to stop to let me out.

'But the house is further on.'

'I'd like some air.' I didn't want to risk any of the Davenports seeing me with weasel-faced Gareth bloody Spence.

'Oh, Tamsyn!' cried Eleanor when she opened the door to me. 'Thank goodness, you're here!'

I grinned as Eleanor put her drink on the console table then rested both hands on my shoulders and kissed me on the forehead. I winced as the pressure of her hand pulled at my skin and made the tattoo sting. I looked over her shoulder expecting to see a room full of people but there was nobody there.

Eleanor was wearing a purple silk dress with a wide gold belt and pads on her shoulders that made them twice as wide as they were. There was a slit in the side of the dress which went almost all the way up to her knickers, and the front was cut into a low V. It was hard to tell without staring, but I was pretty sure she didn't have a bra on. Her make-up was flawless, the blemishes I knew were there were covered up with immaculate foundation, her eyes outlined with blue, lips a glossy red, and on her cheeks were two matching stripes of pink blusher. Her hair had been teased into an extravagant mass around her face like blonde candyfloss. On her wrist was the most beautiful bracelet. Fine gold twisted into a rope with vibrant red stones set in intervals around it.

'It's sweet, isn't it?' she said, catching me staring at it. 'Rubies and rose gold. A present from Max. 'Now,' she purred. 'Edie *did* warn me you might need a bit of help with your clothes.'

'I'm not dressed right?' The skirt I'd borrowed from Mum was her navy one, quite plain but certainly *smart*, which she'd bought to go to the party in the church hall to celebrate Prince Charles marrying Lady Di. In the end I'd paired it with my best top, a soft green sweater with a line of sequins sewn around the hem and sleeves.

'It's fine, Tamsyn, but I think I have something better you can borrow. Come on, let's sort you out.' She rested a hand against my cheek for a moment. 'Such a pretty girl. And, *oh*,' she groaned, 'that *hair*!'

I smiled self-consciously and followed her up the stairs. I adored their bedroom. I hadn't been in it since Edie and I met and I realised how much I'd missed it. The bed was huge, and set with a multitude of tasselled cushions and a gold-stitched bedspread. There was a large rug at the foot of the bed, which was soft and white, and resembled a circle of freshly fallen snow. There was a dressing table in the corner. I noticed that where there was usually a mirror, it was gone, leaving only a faint shadow outline of where it had hung.

'Why don't you sit down?' Eleanor gestured to the stool in front of the dressing table. 'I've got time to put a little make-up on you. We could take the heavy black stuff off your eyes and do something that will bring out your natural eye colour. Would you like that?'

She wiped my eyelids with cotton wool soaked with cream that smelt of roses. 'You look better already,' Eleanor said. 'That heavy black doesn't suit anybody. You need colour.'

'What are you doing?'

We both turned to see Edie at the door. She stood with her arms crossed and a surly frown plastered over her face.

Eleanor smiled at me and rubbed a blusher brush into a compact. 'Getting ready for the party, darling.' She glanced at her daughter. 'I could do yours, too, if you'd like.'

'I've done it.' Her tone made me wince.

Edie was wearing a black dress and black cardigan, heavy fishnet tights with a hole above one knee, her DM boots, and about ten silver necklaces in differing lengths. Her eyes were encased in huge black sweeps, the corners reaching almost to her hairline. Her lips were black, too, and she wore a foundation that was at least one or two shades lighter than normal. Her hair was slicked back on one side with gel as if the wind had blown and it had been frozen mid-gust.

'Yes, so I see,' Eleanor said. 'You've made yourself up to look like you're dead.'

Edie huffed and turned around. Moments later her bedroom door slammed.

'Don't worry about her.' Eleanor smiled. 'She doesn't like our friends, but she'll be fine once the party gets going.' Then she picked up her blue eyeliner. As she applied the eye make-up I breathed her in. I knew the thick, sweet smell. Poison, by Dior. I'd sprayed it on my wrists many times before.

After she finished, she smiled again. 'You look beautiful. And I was right, the blue really picks out your eyes.' She stood. 'Now let me find that top for you. You'll be far too hot in that woollen thing.'

Eleanor made me feel like a princess. Her attention was like the beam from a lighthouse. When I followed her over to the bank of cupboards that ran along one wall, I felt as if I was walking on cloud.

She handed me a crisp white shirt. 'You can change in the bathroom if you want. I'll see you downstairs.'

The bathroom was tiled with marble and had a large tub in the corner with gold taps, and a mother-of-pearl shell to the side of them. The shell contained a number of soft coloured balls which were full of scented oil, as I'd discovered once after squeezing one too hard. I looked at myself in the mirror. My make-up was similar to Eleanor's, though the colour on her cheeks not as pronounced and she'd left my lips pale. Never in my wildest dreams could I have imagined I'd look like this. I struck a pose, put my hand on the side of my head and pouted like one of the girls in Jago's magazine. 'Max, darling,' I mouthed, as I buttoned up the white shirt. 'Would you open a bottle of champagne?'

I walked down the staircase with as much grace as I could

manage. My hand trailed the banister. I'd heard the expression *I feel a million dollars,* but had never known what it really meant until that moment.

'Have you done many parties?' Eleanor asked as I joined her in the kitchen.

'Sorry?'

Shopping bags lined the kitchen worktop and Eleanor topped up her glass from a bottle of wine on the side. 'Doesn't matter. Right – first job is to unpack the bags and put the bits and pieces away. Then the next is to boil and peel the quail eggs. Do you think you can manage that?'

'I… I'm sorry… I don't understand?'

'What? Boiling eggs?'

'No… I mean… I thought…' The air in the kitchen grew hot and heavy.

'Oh dear,' Eleanor said, dragging the words out. 'Did Edith not explain you'd be working?' She sighed. 'Goodness, she's useless. I did nag her to make sure she fully brief you.' Eleanor then pressed her hands together as if she were praying. 'God, please, *please*, tell me you can cook, Tamsyn. I'm sure you can. You lot are so much more capable than us.'

I felt as if I'd been kicked in the stomach. 'Cook?' I repeated weakly.

'Yes,' she smiled. 'Cook. And a bit of waitressing and washing-up. I did ask Edie to talk to you about it.'

My cheeks burned as if I'd been branded. An uncomfortable lump formed in my throat and I blinked rapidly to keep tears of hurt and humiliation at bay. As I fought to control myself I began to feel angry. Angry she'd allowed me to think I was good enough to be a guest at her party. Angry that my mother was right. Angry that Eleanor was smiling, laughing in mock exasperation at her useless daughter who hadn't passed the message on to the poor confused cleaner's daughter who thought she was actually *invited*. There wasn't even a hint of remorse or apology or any indication she knew she might as well have cut my heart out. Edie was right. She was a bitch. Why hadn't I listened to her? It was all I could hear over and over in my head. You bitch. You bitch.

Bitch.

She smiled, showing her white straight teeth, and I briefly imagined smashing them into the worktop.

I cleared my throat. 'She said something about canapés.'

The make-up on my face felt thick and clown-like. The shirt she'd leant me, white and starched like my school uniform, was constricting and rubbed against my skin. I crossed my arms, held them tightly around my body and looked down, my hair hanging in curtains either side of my face, providing a shield of sorts. The itch of my tattoo had turned to a persistent ache. I wanted to leave. Tear the shirt off and throw it at her. But if I left I'd have to face Mum and her inevitable *I told you so* and risk seeing Gareth. And what would I do? Sit on the sofa staring at some shit on the television wishing I were back at The Cliff House. My anger began to dull. I realised some of the fault lay at my own feet. I'd jumped to conclusions and assumed I was invited. I should have checked. Listened to Mum. I had a flash of her then, sitting in the kitchen counting the pennies on the tabletop.

'And you're paying me?' I said, raising my head and looking Eleanor directly in the eye.

'Of course. Good money, too. I always pay my staff more

than fairly. I've a name for being a generous employer up in London. And Edie will be helping too. Well, she *should* be. But no doubt she'll emerge as everybody arrives and do the bare minimum and demand twenty pounds. To be honest, I gave up on her helping a long time ago.' Eleanor rested a hand on my arm and squeezed. 'That's why I hire people I can rely on.' She reached for her glass of wine and drank half of what was in it then refilled it with the rest of the bottle, which she left on the side. 'Edith told me things haven't been easy for your family financially since after your father died. I'm just glad we can put a little your way.' Eleanor smiled but not kindly.

She gestured vaguely in the direction of the shopping bags. 'So if you get on with the unpacking first, then cook the eggs. You'll need to drop them into a bowl of cold water to avoid that hideous black ring on the yolk, and when they're cool you need to take the shells off them. But you need to be terribly careful you get the shell off without damaging the white. They're wildly expensive.'

I eyed the tiny eggs warily and nodded.

'When you've done the eggs, you need to spread the bread – the sliced brown – with a thin layer of butter and pop a slice of smoked salmon on top. Then cut the crusts off and cut them into four. Triangles not squares. Put them on a large plate and then cut some lemons into quarters and put a couple of sprigs of parsley over them. Then peel the carrots and cut them into batons.' She paused and stared at me. 'You know what a baton is, don't you?' She didn't give me time to answer, before adding, 'Long fingers. Whatever you do, don't cut them into those awful common rounds. It's done *à la France* nowadays. Nobody eats round carrots anymore.'

Eleanor walked over to the fridge. She reached in and took out a bowl covered in foil. 'I made a Roquefort dip earlier today. You need to put that in the centre of a big platter and arrange the batons around it.'

'And Edie will—'

'My daughter will appear when she appears.' Eleanor gave an indulgent laugh. 'She's such a pain.'

Eleanor left me and I started to unpack the bags whilst biting back tears that came and went. When I'd done that I put the water on to boil and started to butter the bread. Eleanor was right, the eggs were fiddly and it was impossible to get the shells off without tearing the white beneath.

'Hey,' came Edie's voice behind me.

I glanced over my shoulder to see her leaning on the door-frame.

'Are you okay? You look like you've been crying.'

I turned to hide my face from her and swiped my hand across my cheeks. 'I'm fine.' I went back to the chopping board, picked up the razor sharp knife, and glanced at it. My face was reflected back at me, distorted, out of shape, a vague suggestion of me. I picked up a carrot and cut the carrots into what I hoped Eleanor would call *batons*, then added them to the plate with the others, which I'd arranged in a fan around the bowl of dip she'd made, making sure the ends all lined up with each other, like tiny bodies all in a line.

'You're quiet.'

'I didn't know I was working,' I whispered.

'What was that?'

I opened my mouth to repeat what I'd said, but then stopped myself. What was the point? She'd only say she told me about handing around the food and she'd think I was an idiot for assuming I was invited as a guest. So I kept my anger in and forced a smile.

'When are the people arriving?'

Edie shrugged. 'One couple is staying near Mevagissey, there's a grandmother there or something, and the others are here already. Max picked them up from Penzance Station yesterday. They're probably lying in their rooms waiting for the sun to go down so they can come out of their crypts without bursting into flames.'

Edie reached over and took one of the carrot batons, causing the neighbouring ones to fall out of line. I carefully rearranged them so they were straight again.

There were voices outside the kitchen. Laughing. Eleanor welcoming whoever had walked down the stairs.

Then Max appeared in the kitchen.

'Evening,' he said, with a wide smile. 'Thank you so much for helping us out.'

I smiled back and tucked my hair behind my ear. 'No problem,' I said.

'You look lovely, by the way.' He stepped closer to me and leant his face near my ear, and when he spoke I felt his breath on my skin. 'That shirt looks far better on you than on Eleanor.' He straightened himself then winked. 'Don't tell her I said that, of course.'

I smothered a smile as he went to the fridge and took out a bottle of champagne and tore the foil off the top.

'Would you mind bringing those flutes out?' He pointed to a tray of glasses beside the sink.

'Is it okay for me to come out of the kitchen?'

He smiled. 'Well, you're allowed to, though after you've seen that lot you might feel you're better off in here. It would be great to have a hand passing the drinks around.'

In the sitting room there was a collection of the most beautiful people in the world. There were eight of them including Eleanor and Max. The women shone as if they'd been polished and dipped in gold. They all spoke and laughed at the same time, their voices merging into one high-pitched screeching mass, almost drowning out the music that was playing.

'Oh, how lovely! Champagne!' exclaimed one woman who wore a bright blue trouser suit and thick red jewellery around her neck and wrists.

'About time,' said a man. 'A bloke could die of thirst around here, Maxie Boy.' He wore a white shirt with too many of the buttons undone and had unmoving blonde hair, like a golden sculpture swept across his forehead. He and the woman in blue touched each other in a way that told me they were together. They reminded me of Barbie and Ken dolls.

As Max poured each glass he passed them to me to hand out. I walked within the group, trying hard not to spill anything as I delivered the drinks, and making sure I didn't look at Eleanor. The throbbing in my shoulder had grown more intense and the tattoo felt hotter, with the skin stretched tight around it, and every time I reached out a sharp pain shot up my arm.

One of the group, a man in a green collared T-shirt with a red logo stitched onto the left chest, winked at me as he took a glass. 'Max,' he said loudly, his eyes bolted to me. 'I have to commend you on your waitress. That hair is like one of Lautrec's Parisian doxies. She's quite lovely, isn't she? And a figure to make a man weep.' He raised his eyebrows at me. I dropped my eyes. Part of me thought I might die of embarrassment, the other part glowed undeniably at the compliment. Was this what Alice Daley and Imogen Norris felt like when the boys drooled as they sashayed into the dinner hall with their hips and boobs swinging?

When I glanced up, he was still watching me and I held his stare for a moment longer than I might have ordinarily.

'Oh, Freddie, *stop*!' trilled a woman in a white shirt that was studded with sequins and diamonds. 'Honestly, leave the poor girl alone. You're *incorrigible*.'

'Nothing wrong with telling someone she's pretty is there?' He smiled at me and leant close. His breath was sweet and warm with drink. 'What kind of world is it when a man can't tell a woman she's desirable?'

I cast a nervous look at the woman who'd spoken to him, who I assumed was his wife. She watched me with a wry smile on her face and tipped her glass back and forth between two fingers like a pendulum. I could still feel his eyes on me and imagined walking up to him and kissing him in front of them all, their mouths agog, eyes wide with shock.

'Desirable?' she drawled. 'She has potential, perhaps.' She turned her back to me. 'But too plain for my tastes and she needs a haircut.'

The woman's words, her dismissive tone, skewered me and any delight I'd felt from the man's attention evaporated, leaving me feeling exposed amongst them.

'Play nicely, Jilly,' said Max. 'Tamsyn's a friend of the family.'

I have never been as grateful to anybody as I was to Max right then.

I looked at him and smiled and when he smiled back my heart sang. I noticed then how kind his eyes were, how the creases at

277

their edges made them warmer and more welcoming than I'd realised. He turned away and walked over to top up the Barbie doll's glass. I picked up two empty bottles and hurried back to the kitchen before anybody else could speak to me.

I was arranging more carrots on the plate when someone entered the kitchen. It was Max. He went over to the fridge and retrieved another bottle of champagne, which he opened. The cork popped loudly and he discarded it on the worktop. He poured a glass then held it out to me, gesturing for me to take it.

I hesitated, checking over my shoulder.

'Have some, for God's sake, you deserve it.'

I took the glass and put it to my lips. As the champagne fizzed on my tongue he reached out and touched my arm and rubbed it in a fatherly way.

'I want to apologise for Freddie. The man's a fool who thinks he's a hit with the ladies.' I grimaced and Max laughed which made me smile. 'Exactly! He's the village idiot so pay no attention. And his wife? An absolute pain.'

Max pushed himself off the counter and grabbed the bottle of champagne. 'He also knows nothing about art. Your hair is pure Titian and not a bit Lautrec.' Then he smiled. 'And don't you *ever* cut it. It's glorious.'

'We were wondering where you'd got to, Max.'

I snapped my head around to see Eleanor at the door. I hastily went back to rearranging the carrots, head down, eyes fixed on the plate, heart thumping against my ribcage.

'I came in to get another bottle, darling. We seem to be getting through the stuff like water in a drought.'

'Tamsyn, there are people out there who are desperate for a quail egg. Take the tray out please.'

I wiped my hands on my skirt and glanced up at Max who winked at me, then I picked up the platter of tiny eggs and scuttled out of the kitchen, avoiding Eleanor's eyes as I passed.

'Where's the lovely Edith?' asked a dark-haired man with a full moustache, who was dressed in jeans and a blue V-neck sweater and looked a lot like Burt Reynolds. A woman sat beside him on the settee in a purple floaty dress, her bosoms spilling over as if trying to escape. Her hair was scraped back into a tight bun, which dragged the sides of her face up, pulling at the skin.

'God knows, David. I thought she came down but she's disappeared again,' said Eleanor. As she spoke she frowned at me as if it were my fault Edie wasn't around. I dropped my eyes and offered the platter to the two on the settee.

'Teenagers, eh?' David chuckled and reached for an egg, which he popped into his mouth in one.

'I'm at my wit's end with her at the moment. She's nothing but trouble. Don't even talk to us about Hartwood House. They're refusing to take her back. I mean what the hell are we supposed to do with her?'

'Children,' said the Barbie doll, 'are a constant source of disappointment.'

'That's why we send them away,' said David. 'Can you imagine having to spend term time with them as well?' He laughed.

'David Christie, *don't*!' said the woman with the escaping breasts. 'The poor girl looks horrified. Max, what's her name again?'

'Tamsyn.'

'Tamsyn, *darling*, we adore our offspring, I promise you. Ignore everything you hear tonight. We're all totally full of shit!' The woman laughed and the rest joined in, clinking glasses, sipping champagne, seemingly congratulating themselves on being full of shit.

'Max,' Eleanor said, as the laughing died down. 'You seem to have topped everybody else up but forgotten me.'

She smiled and pushed her glass out towards him.

He hesitated, then tilted the bottle and poured.

'Tamsyn,' he said. 'Would you mind fetching another bottle from the fridge?'

I carried the empty bottle into the kitchen and found Edie leaning against the worktop, smoking. When I came in, she pressed the cigarette onto one of the plates to extinguish it.

'Can you imagine how desperate Max and Eleanor must be to hang out with people like that?'

'I have to take more champagne in to them.'

She made a face at me. 'Why are you being so grumpy?'

I hesitated. Then said carefully, 'I just wish you'd told me Eleanor wanted me to work tonight.'

Edie furrowed her brow. 'What did you think she wanted?'

I lowered my eyes and shrugged my shoulders.

'Look, if I've done something wrong, I'm sorry.'

I lifted my head and forced a smile. I didn't want to talk about it anymore.

Edie took out a bottle of champagne and popped the cork. 'I'll take this one round. It's time I entertained them with my Child of the Night impression.' She opened her eyes and made a face like a ghoul and I couldn't help smiling.

The party grew increasingly raucous as they drank more. At one point, Eleanor, Barbie and Ken disappeared into the toilet together. They were in there for a while and when they stumbled out they were laughing like hyenas.

'We need proper music!' Barbie screeched, as the three of them lurched across the living room. 'Get this crap off and put on something we can dance to!'

Barbie tottered over to the hi-fi and rooted through the music collection. 'Yes, let's change it. Max's bloody jazz is so bloody boring.' She picked up a shining silver compact disc and narrowed her eyes. 'You know they said these things were indestructible. Such bollocks. One of ours was scratched before we'd even played it. I can't say they'll catch on.'

'Better than having to pick fluff off needles.'

'Not if the damn things don't play,' she said. She slid the disc into a small plastic drawer, which glided back into the machine as if it were possessed.

Moments later, the sounds of ABBA filled the room and collectively they all began to dance, apart from Max, who watched from the settee, eyes fixed on his wife.

I walked over and stood near to him. 'I liked the other music,' I said quietly.

He looked at me and nodded his head whilst raising his glass to me. 'Then, young Tamsyn, you have *impeccable* taste. Miles Davies. One of the greatest.'

I turned my attention back to them all as they danced and screeched and smoked and drank. I was mesmerised by it all and relieved I'd stayed and not run back to St Just. This world was Wonderland and I was Alice. The characters around me were as weird and wonderful as the Queen of Hearts and the smoking Caterpillar and the Cheshire Cat's floating smile. I thought of my father, heard the voices he used when he read me that story. Saw his face twisted into the manic grin of the Mad Hatter as he poured tea on the Dormouse. As I watched them they seemed to grow more fantastical. Their expressions more animated. Their clothes brighter and more outlandish. I watched them pop whole eggs into their mouths, the eggs so tiny it gave the illusion they were giants.

'Come on,' Edie said, sidling up behind me. 'Let's get out of here.'

'Don't I need to ask your mum?'

'Look at her. She wouldn't be able to tell you what day it is, let alone who's around to cut fucking carrots up.'

Reluctantly I followed Edie upstairs. She put some music on and sat on her bed. We listened to it, but I wasn't sure I liked it. Plus, it quarrelled with the ABBA coming up from downstairs.

'We could sneak out,' she said. 'Go and find your brother and his friends. Do you know where they are?'

'No idea. Maybe the Nags Head or the dock. We'd need a car to get to Penzance though. The buses won't be running at this time.'

Edie rolled her eyes and lay back on her bed. 'Jesus, it's so fucking backward here. Look, I'm knackered. I'm going to go to sleep. Are you staying?'

'If that's okay.' She shrugged dismissively like she didn't care either way, and left the room to get me a pillow and a blanket.

Last time I slept over – after the tattoo – we'd slept head to toe. I'd lain with my shoulder smarting and my head swimming in a vodka haze enjoying the warmth of her body, but this time she put the pillow on the floor. She turned her light off and said she wasn't in the mood for chatting, and it wasn't long before her breathing deepened and I was left with only the sounds of the party for company. I concentrated hard to try to separate the voices, the laughs, putting them to the faces of the people down below. I imagined joining them. Dressed myself in a red satin dress which trailed the floor. On my wrist was Eleanor's gold and ruby bracelet. I told stories and they all laughed, hanging on my every word and, as I spoke, Max smiled and poured me champagne.

Soon the voices shifted to the terrace. I got up and moved to the window. They were circling around the swimming pool. The women were dancing and twirling, and then one by one, they undressed, pulling silk and satin over their heads, bodies lit from the light within the house. They reminded me of druids dancing around a fire, writhing to music, hands in the air. Two of the women stripped entirely. One of them was Eleanor. Both leapt into the water with shrill shrieks.

The men were laughing. Three of them were smoking. Freddie, the one who'd said I was pretty, put his drink down and threw his burning cigarette into the darkness. He took off his jacket and shirt then his trousers. Soon Ken followed suit. Then, with the women whooping hysterically, they ran and jumped into the blackness of the pool. They didn't re-emerge for what felt like ages and I wondered if the pool had swallowed them up.

Max sat at the table. He waved a dismissive hand at the women who'd climbed out of the pool and now pulled on his arm, dripping wet and giggling. The man who looked like Burt Reynolds – David – shook his head, too, but they didn't let him off so easily. The women, including Eleanor, ignored his protestations and started to forcibly undress him. Like dogs on a carcass, they pulled at his clothes as if they were bits of flesh, discarding them as they came free. Then Eleanor ran back into the house, her arm placed ineffectually across her chest, her small bosoms bouncing as she ran. The other three women were dragging David, now dressed only in his underpants, towards the pool.

When they saw Eleanor they gestured for her to hurry up. He started to shake his head, laughter beginning to take hold of him. The women huddled around him. I couldn't quite see what they were doing, but then I noticed Eleanor was holding a black handled knife from the kitchen. I watched as she slid it up and down inside the band of his underpants. My heart raced like a train. The women cheered triumphantly as they held the cut material aloft. David was stark naked but rather than look embarrassed he flourished a bow.

All of them, apart from Max, were in the pool now. Two of the women held bottles of champagne, and all were squealing and laughing. I carefully let the curtain drop and tiptoed back to the makeshift bed on the floor.

I don't know how long passed, but eventually the music quietened, and voices said goodbye and an engine started up. Then a car drove away and voices and footsteps came up the stairs. Stage whispers. Giggles and shushes. Smothered laughs. Then finally there was silence as each of the bedroom doors closed.

There was no chance of sleep and, after a while, when my buzzing mind and body became unbearable, I sat up. I knelt close to Edie's face. Studied her. Without her make-up she looked younger. She was sleeping peacefully – no ravaging nightmares for her – with a soft whistling sound coming from her as she breathed. I watched the rise and fall of her chest, allowed my breathing to fall in time with hers.

Reluctantly, I decided to go back to my box room. The floor was too hard to sleep on and I wasn't sure I wanted to wake in the morning and come face to face with David or Barbie or any of them actually, not without clean clothes or a hairbrush, both of which I'd forgotten in my excitement to get there.

The sitting room was like a war zone. Empty bottles lay on their sides. Food, clothes, wet towels and spilled wine. It stank of cigarettes and alcohol. A tiny expensive egg was squashed into the sheepskin rug.

The door was unlocked to the outside. I walked through it. Closed it quietly. The sky was cloudless and punctured with bright dots of light. A shaft of moonlight reflected on the mirrored surface of the pool and there was an imperceptible breeze which ruffled the water enough to shimmer the light. Everything was quiet. There was only the sound of the waves breaking gently on the shoreline below. I breathed the air in, soft and warm, salty with the hint of drying seaweed.

The table was covered in glasses, cigarette ends, and mostly empty platters of food, the blue cheese dip, half-eaten, the surface beginning to crust.

And there was the knife.

It lay quietly in the middle of the carnage. The moonlight bounced off the metal like it did the surface of the pool. I reached out. My hand moved slowly through the air. I watched my fingers stroke it as if they belonged to someone else. Saw them clasp the handle. I imagined Eleanor's hand on it. Touching where mine did. I could feel her smoothness. Like silk. Perfumed and soft. I could smell her then, her scent around me, her perfume, hairspray, the creams she rubbed into her face and hands, the way she'd looked at me when she told me to unpack the shopping.

I lifted the knife and tilted it. Caught the moon so it flashed. Pressed the blade flat against my cheek. I felt something then.

Someone – or something – watching. I dropped my hand with the knife so it hung at my side and turned around. But there was nobody there. Nobody on the terrace. The living room was empty. No faces at any of the windows. I squinted and scanned the house.

Then I saw it. The raven. Perched on the edge of the roof. Black eyes fixed on me. But it couldn't be real, could it? Ravens didn't come out at night. I laid the knife back on the table. Took a couple of steps closer to the house. Blinked twice. Looked again. Squinted into the darkness.

Nothing there.

I took a step backwards and my foot brushed against something which made a light metallic sound. I bent down. It was difficult to see. My fingers patted the paving stones in search of what I'd kicked. Then my hand touched something. I picked it up and shifted position so the moonlight fell over my hand. It was Eleanor's bracelet. I stared at it, at the rubies which looked like drops of black blood on the fine chain. So beautiful. The most beautiful piece of jewellery I'd ever seen.

I laid it on the table beside the knife then looked out over the sea, my body swaying slightly in time with the rolling waves.

CHAPTER THIRTY-FIVE

Angie
August 1986

She'd never seen anything like it.

What had Eleanor said? Eight of them? It might as well have been an army on leave. Angie surveyed the living room – the rubbish, broken glass and food trodden into the floor, the discarded clothes and shoes – and tried to decide where to start. She caught sight of the terrace though the living room window. The mess was even worse out there. When Eleanor had said she'd pay her time and a half, Angie had told her not to worry, that her usual hourly rate was fine, even on a Sunday morning, but now she was glad Eleanor had insisted.

'The kitchen's in a godawful state.' Eleanor was behind her. Her voice was quiet and croaky, her eyes hidden behind her huge white-rimmed sunglasses. 'Our friends will be down for breakfast soon and right now I can't even *see* the coffee percolator let alone use it.'

'I'll start in there then.'

Angie sighed when she walked into the kitchen. She didn't feel like cleaning today. She promised herself a walk when she was finished. Maybe she would catch the bus out to Zennor and climb up to the Quoit. As she ran the hot tap to fill a bucket, she recalled the day Rob asked her to marry him. They'd walked up the tor, heading for the ancient burial chamber, five large rocks supporting a huge slab of granite, and got caught in biblical rain. Soaked through, they'd run the last hundred yards, laughing and slipping over wet stones and grass. They reached the Zennor Quoit which, he told her eagerly as they marched up the hill, had been built over three thousand years earlier and was one of only eight remaining quoits on the West Penwith moor, and he leant her back against it. How warm his lips had felt on hers. How hard his chest through his sodden shirt. She'd laughed through tears of joy when he dropped to his knee in the mud and pulled a small velvet box out of his pocket. The ring inside had a tiny perfect diamond on it.

I'm sorry it's not bigger, Ange.

'You daft sod,' she whispered as she squeezed some Fairy into the bucket. 'I'd have been happy with a plastic one from a Christmas cracker.'

She stared at the hot water as it rose and foamed and listened to footsteps crossing the living room. Then Max's study door opened and she heard Eleanor say something to him, though it was too quiet to make out what. More hushed whispers. Then the door closed.

Angie got on with the binning, wiping, and spraying until gradually order began to return. She tried to ignore their rising voices but it quickly became impossible.

'An *embarrassment*?'

'You. And the others. On David like a pack of rabid dogs.'

'Ha! As if you can talk? Flirting with that girl! A *child* for God's sake!'

Angie froze. She put down the cloth she was holding and

moved out of the kitchen and stepped into the living room in order to hear better.

'Flirting?' he exclaimed. 'What on earth are you talking about?'

'There's something going on with her. I know there is.'

He gave a bitter snort of laughter. 'I can't believe I'm hearing this.'

'Don't you dare deny it. I saw you together in the kitchen. When I walked in you pulled away from each other as if I'd burnt you. And she's always here. Always hanging around. *Why?* It's not as if Edie likes her that much. I can tell the girl bores her rigid.'

Angie's stomach pitched; they were talking about Tamsyn.

'No. You've got that wrong. Edie's fond of her. Have you seen her with everybody else? Tamsyn's about the only person she actually gives the time of day to.'

'She's always staring at you.'

'She's always staring at all of us! She's imprinted on us in some way. Enjoys being here. I've seen how she relaxes as soon as she walks in. Maybe things aren't good at home? She often arrives looking tense. Maybe this is some sort of escape for her?'

'Don't you throw your writer's psychobabble bullshit at me.' Eleanor spat the words out like globs of battery acid. 'I saw how you were with each other last night. Everybody did, for crying out loud. Jumping to her defence, winking at her, smiling at her when you thought nobody was looking.'

'I *smiled* at her because last night she was a fish out of water and the poor girl needed reassurance, and I *jumped to her defence* because that boorish friend of yours was – as per usual – being a wanker and needed to be put in his place.'

When Eleanor next spoke Angie could detect a very obvious note of underlying weariness in her voice. 'She's sixteen, Max. *Sixteen*. Even by your standards, that's a little *young*.'

Angie lifted her hand to her mouth and chewed on her fingernail. Surely there was no way Tamsyn could be involved with Max?

'What – exactly – are you accusing me of, Eleanor?'

'It's not as if you don't have form.'

He was silent.

'Everybody in London knows what you get up to. All those literary events and society parties? Girls hanging off you. Weekends away.'

'That's enough.'

Then the voices went low again.

Angie rubbed her face with her hands, straightened her shirt with a brisk couple of rubs. She was weak with nausea, and helpless, unsure what to do. She walked slowly back into the kitchen and ran herself a glass of water. A moment later, the door to the study opened and footsteps crossed the living room. Eleanor screamed with angry frustration. Then there was a crashing noise and another cry from her. Another banging noise. Wood splintering. Angie tucked herself behind the doorframe. Her footsteps approached the kitchen.

Eleanor loomed in the doorway. Her face was twisted in indescribable rage. Anger faced her. Eleanor stared at her, chest heaving, face blotched red, her sunglasses gone to reveal bloodshot eyes that bored into her like blades. 'Leave. My. House.' Her words were low but thick with unhinged malevolence.

'I don't—'

'Leave now,' she said with forced control. 'And tell that *slut* daughter of yours that if I ever – *ever* – see her again, I'll kill her.'

290

Angie's hand flew to her chest and her mouth dropped open in shock. Eleanor's simmering anger was terrifying, like some psycho from a horror film.

'She's not a slut,' Angie whispered.

'Yes. She is.' Eleanor leant her face close to Angie, breathing the warm stale fumes of alcohol across her. 'She's a filthy little slut and you know it. Now get the hell out of my house.'

Angie wanted to tell her to shut up. She wanted to shout in her face, tell her to stop talking about Tamsyn like that, that at sixteen, legal or not, she was a child, and that if anything *was* going on between them then it was Max Davenport who needed killing. But she couldn't speak. It was as if someone had cut out her tongue. Tears prickled the backs of her eyes as she turned and went into the utility room to grab her boots and bag from the cupboard. When she had hold of them, she hurried out of the kitchen, passing Eleanor Davenport who stepped to one side whilst averting her stony eyes.

As Angie walked across the living room she saw what had caused the crashes. One of the paintings – one of the infantile ones with colourful paint strokes on white – had been taken off the wall and smashed against the corner of the coffee table. There was a large, jagged hole in the canvas, the wooden cross-brace broken, the edges frayed where the fabric had torn.

With her head down, she walked quickly towards the back door, desperate to get out to the safety of the coast path. Her mind raced. Outrage mixed with confusion and anxiety. How dare that woman speak about Tamsyn the way she did? But was there any truth in what she accused her and Max of? Was that why Tamsyn was always at the house? Was her friendship with Edie just a cover?

She thought of Rob. Would he expect her to confront Max? No. No, he'd have kept calm. Made sure of the facts. Spoken to Tamsyn first. He definitely would not have marched into Max's study and beaten him with his fists again and again and again…

'Angie.'

Max was standing at his door.

She stopped walking, then after a hesitation turned cautiously to face him. His hands were in his pockets and his shoulders stooped a little. Was it guilt she could see? He didn't speak immediately. The air between them crackled and she found herself battling to keep from crying.

'Nothing's going on—'

'Mrs Davenport asked me to leave.' Angie dropped her eyes and started towards the door again.

'You must believe me, Angie. She…' He hesitated again. 'She makes things up. Lives in a dream world. She's not in her right mind. None of what you heard is true.'

Then from somewhere Angie found some strength. Perhaps it was the recollection of Eleanor's vile words or the stench of alcohol that had accompanied them. Or the idea that people like her said whatever they wanted to without thought for anybody else. Or perhaps it was the idea that this entitled, conceited man might have been doing God-only-knew-what to her daughter.

'Good,' she said, looking him straight in the eye. 'Because if I find out you've laid a finger on her, then I won't be responsible for what I do.'

Then there were voices on the upstairs landing. Not voices she knew. The Davenports' friends. Whispering. A smothered laugh. Angie glanced up at the staircase. Max swallowed and blinked slowly. Straightened his shoulders. He opened his mouth to say something but Angie didn't give him the chance.

'Keep your hands off my daughter.'

Then she flung the back door open and walked down the lawn towards the gate and out onto the coastal path. She kept her head high with her shoulders back and made sure she strode. When she reached the point where she was out of sight of The Cliff House she finally gave in to raking sobs, crouching low, a hand resting on a rock at the side of the path for support.

She hadn't been there long when someone cleared their throat behind her.

Angie snapped her head around to find Edie standing a few feet away. She wore pink and white spotty pyjama bottoms and a Mickey Mouse T-shirt, with bare feet. Her face was clean of make-up and there was no gel in her hair, and her eyes, which seemed so much smaller without the black outlines, were rheumy from sleep.

The girl glanced back towards the house before dropping down beside her.

'It's not true. What she said.' She rested her hand on Angie's shoulder. 'I promise. Tamsyn has been coming to see me. Not him. Eleanor's crazy.'

Angie released a sob of relief and held both hands over her face. She swiped her tears dry, passed her flattened palms over her hair to smooth it. Edie stood and held out her hand, which Angie took. Edie helped her up then reached out her other hand, in which she held a letter with Tamsyn's name on it.

Angie shook her head. 'She can't come back here, Edie. Your mother… I don't think it's safe.'

Edie nodded. Without her rebel armour – the make-up, black clothes, statement jewellery – her vulnerability was plain to see. Young and hurting, no more than a child desperately trying to keep afloat in a family that had long since fractured.

'Will you tell her?' Edie glanced out across the sea and the wind blew her hair off her face. 'What my mother said?'

Angie didn't answer immediately. She hadn't thought about it, not properly, but what choice did she have? Eleanor had forbidden Tamsyn to go to the house again. She would ask why. And what could Angie say that would sound convincing? Tamsyn was going to be broken-hearted and Angie felt a bitter wave of anger sweep through her. She'd predicted this would happen. Saw it plain as day. And who would have to pick up the pieces? Not Eleanor or Max or Edie, but her, and the thought was exhausting her. More emotion. More tears. More confusion overwhelming her youngest child.

'Will you give her this note?'

Angie regarded the envelope warily. She wanted her family to have nothing more to do with the Davenports.

'Please?'

There was that vulnerability again. It melted Angie's resolve. 'Yes. I'll give it to her.' And she reached for the letter.

Edie turned without another word and walked back to the house, her arms crossed tightly, bare feet padding along the grassy path, and the wind catching her pyjama bottoms like boat sails.

As Angie began the walk home to St Just, she opened her bag to put the envelope in, and there, among the detritus, was the green-tagged key to The Cliff House. She turned to call back to Edie, but she was already gone.

'I'm not going back,' she muttered under her breath.

They would have to come and collect it. Or Gareth could drop it back for her. There was no way on earth she was setting foot in that nuthouse again.

CHAPTER THIRTY-SIX

Tamsyn
August 1986

'How long... are you going to... be, love?'

'Only a few minutes!'

I didn't get back from the party until the small hours, and when I fell into my own bed, I slept heavily and late. I woke with a burning pain in my shoulder. The site of my tattoo pulsed as if angry creatures were trapped beneath the skin, scratching to escape.

I winced as I took off my T-shirt. I leant close to the mirror, angling myself so I could see my back, then I gingerly picked at the edge of the plaster with my fingernail. Each flick pulled at the skin and sent a pain firing down from my shoulder to the tips of my fingers. I squeezed my eyes shut, took hold of one edge and yanked sharply to rip it off. My head swam with the agony and I grabbed at the sink to steady myself.

What was revealed was horrific. The skin around the tattoo was a scarlet balloon, tight and shining. The dark lines of Indian ink were crusted bubbles of yellow which oozed in places. The smell was like off milk, and when I pressed my finger to the edge of the sore a globule of creamy pus seeped out.

I took the surgical spirit from the medicine cabinet and tipped it onto a ball of cotton wool then carefully dabbed at the blood and crud that had hardened in places. It was too sore to clean all the gunk off, so instead I decided it would be best to slather it with Savlon and re-cover it. The lint in the centre of the plaster was soaked with yellow and black so I decided it couldn't go back on my skin. The box of plasters had none of the huge ones left, so I cut a section of a fabric one big enough to cover the tattoo – albeit with some of the adhesive part touching the sore – and positioned it over the cross. I gasped at the stab of pain as I pushed the plaster into place then exhaled with relief that I'd seen to it. Afterwards, I buttoned up my shirt then splashed my face with water.

'All yours,' I said to Granfer, as I came out of the bathroom.

'Thanks, love.' Granfer wheezed heavily and I noticed how yellow and dry his skin was today. 'Takes... time to pretty myself up in the... morning. And...' He smiled at me, revealing his brown-stained teeth. 'Got to keep... these boys pearly. You up to much... today?'

I shook my head. 'Not today. I don't feel great. I got back really late from the party so I didn't get much sleep. Is Mum here?'

He shook his head. 'At the white house. Said she'd be back around two.'

'Really?' My heart missed a beat. Why hadn't she told me she was going? Surely she should have mentioned it. I looked at my watch. It was just before eleven.

'Cleaning... after the... party. Was it fun?'

I recalled the humiliation and hurt as Eleanor told me I was there to unpack the shopping and peel eggs, then the alarm which gave way to quickening thrill when her friend had told the room he thought me desirable. My cheeks flushed red and I nodded.

Granfer smiled then covered his mouth to cough. When his hand dropped away I saw his papery skin was coated with a fine spray of blood spatters which mingled with the liver spots. He noticed me staring and dropped his hand, then shuffled into the bathroom and closed the door behind him.

I needed to get back to bed. I was feeling light-headed, which wasn't surprising given how little sleep I'd had. As I turned towards my box room, I was stopped by the sound of a key in the front door. I ran back to the banister and leant over it to see Mum hanging her bag on the hook and taking her jacket off.

'Hey,' I called down. 'Granfer said you wouldn't be back till two. Why didn't you tell—'

Her look stopped me mid-sentence. There was something wrong. Her eyes shifted from side to side and the fingers of one hand teased the hem of her sleeve.

'Are you okay?'

She didn't reply.

There was a letter in her other hand.

'Is that from Edie?'

'Tamsyn.' She hesitated. 'We need to talk.'

Alarm snatched at me. 'What is it?' She didn't answer, but lowered her eyes. 'Mum? Tell me.'

She lifted her head and nodded, taking a visible breath as she climbed the stairs towards me. She walked past me, into my box room, and sat on my bed. I followed her in and sat beside her. The room felt even smaller than usual, as if the walls had closed in on us, as if they were slowly squeezing the air out.

'You're scaring me, Mum.' All I could think about was my brother. That something had happened to him. The thought made me nauseous. 'Is Jago okay?'

'Jago?' She looked at me with a furrowed brow and then shook her head. 'Yes. Yes. He's fine. I mean, I think he's… It's not him. It's…'

'*What?*'

'I was at the Davenports'. And, well, I heard them talking. Arguing. She… She's not…'

'What is it, Mum?'

'Mrs Davenport…' Her face creased as she struggled to find the next word. 'She doesn't want us back at The Cliff House.'

I frowned. 'What do you mean?'

'You and I. We're not allowed back there.'

'Oh my God. What did you *do*?' I didn't even try to temper my angry accusation.

'I didn't—'

'What did you *do*?' I shouted it this time.

'Nothing, Tamsyn. I did nothing.'

'You must have!' My stomach churned. 'She was fine with me last night. She did my make-up. Lent me a shirt. Said I was an angel and a godsend and she didn't know what she would have done without me. The last thing she said to me was *thank you* and *do stay the night*. I haven't seen her since then. So it must be you. You *must* have done something.'

I don't know why I bent the truth. Why I didn't tell her how much Eleanor had hurt me or how she'd behaved or why I told her Eleanor had said thank you and asked me to stay the night. All I know is the thought of not going back to the house stripped my insides out like acid.

300

Mum chewed on her lower lip and looked out of the tiny window. Then she shook her head as if she had nothing else to lose. 'I overheard her accusing him of things.'

'What things?'

Mum looked at me straight in the eye.

'Mum. What *things*?'

'To do with you.'

My brain swirled.

'Me? What do you mean me? Mum, you're not making any sense.'

My mother appeared to break in half. Her shoulders stooped and her face drained of colour. 'She thinks you and Max are...' She hesitated again and I bit my tongue to stop myself shouting. 'That you're together.'

'I don't understand.'

'She accused him of having an affair – a relationship – with you,' she said, and looked at her hands.

An icy current shivered through me. I shook my head. Forced a laugh through my shock. '*What?* No. *No!* Of course we're not. I mean... that's crazy. I... I...' Panic seized me by the throat so I couldn't breathe. The idea that Eleanor suspected I was doing *that* with Max and banning me from the house because of it was paralysing. 'I need to go and tell her she's made a mistake. That it's not true!'

Mum's eyes widened. 'No. You aren't to go there. Do you hear me? The woman isn't stable. Please, Tam. I mean it. She's not right in the head. You should have seen how she was screeching. She even smashed up one of her own paintings. Things aren't right between them and they need to be left alone to sort it out. Don't go back. Okay? You don't want to cause any problems.'

She sighed and rubbed her face. 'God,' she muttered. 'They owe me nearly a month's money.'

My head roiled and I felt as if I might be sick. I tried to stand, but when I did my knees gave way and Mum moved to catch me. As she did she gasped.

'Sweetheart, you're so hot!' She laid the back of her hand on my forehead. 'Why didn't you tell me you weren't feeling well?'

But I couldn't speak. My mind was racing. I was weak with worry as I tried to work out why Eleanor would say and think those things.

'You need some Dispirin,' Mum said.

She placed the envelope on the table beside my bed and then left me alone.

I thought back to the party. Went over everything. Relived handing around drinks. That man saying those things. Max being kind. Making me feel better. It must have been the moment she saw us in the kitchen. Jumped to the wrong conclusion. My lungs constricted as I had a vivid recollection of the raven on the roof, its black marble eyes tunnelling into me. My vision swirled. I looked down at the envelope beside my bed. Edie's handwriting moved in and out of focus. My hand quivered as I reached out for it.

Mum came back in. She held two glasses, one murky with Dispirin, one clear. I tucked the letter beneath my pillow. She passed me the glass of cloudy water, Dispirin granules sitting in a fine layer at the bottom like silt, and I swallowed it down, then allowed her to help me into bed. She leant over and put the second glass on the bedside table. I watched as its surface wavered in search of stillness.

'Try to get some sleep,' she said. 'I'll be up to check on you in a bit.'

As soon as she left I reached beneath my pillow for the envelope.

Dear Tamsyn.

I'm so sorry. Didn't I tell you she was a lunatic??! Don't worry about anything she says. I know it's not true. You can't come here anymore, but I want to see you and make sure you're alright. Shall we meet at Cape Cornwall this afternoon? I'll be there at three o'clock.
 Please come!!!

All my love, Edie.

You can't come here anymore.

Seeing it in black and white, knowing Mum wasn't lying, made me feel like dying. My body seized up, the tips of my fingers and toes became numb as my lungs clamped. My breathing tightened and panic took hold of me. I thought of my father and me swimming that day. His laugh. The feel of him as I'd looped my arms around his neck and he'd swum me through the water. The last moments before my world was torn apart. The time I'd spent at The Cliff House had made these last few weeks the happiest I could remember since he drowned. I couldn't let her keep me from it. I had to make her understand nothing was going on with Max and me. The thought of not being there physically hurt, an inexplicable throb in the pit of my stomach, my head aching as if a blade was piercing it.

Edie.

Edie would help me make things better. The letter was a life raft. She still wanted to see me. I imagined her sitting down to write it, folding the sheet of paper carefully, then slipping it into the envelope. I saw her kissing the letter as she sealed it, then giving it to my mother and begging her to deliver it.

I read the letter again, concentrating on each word, on each letter, each punctuation mark.

All my love, Edie.

I stared at those words. Read them over and over and over. It was going to be fine. I'd see her. Talk to her. Explain. Then she'd tell Eleanor it was all a horrible mistake and they'd laugh at the silly misunderstanding and invite me over for a barbecue and a manicure and a swim.

I still had Edie.

It was going to be fine.

CHAPTER THIRTY-SEVEN

Tamsyn
August 1986

At a quarter to three I got out of bed and drew my curtains closed to make the room dimmer. The Dispirin had done the trick and eased both my nausea and my pounding head. I put my pillows under my duvet and arranged the bedcovers to make it look like I was still there, sleeping peacefully. Mum was in Granfer's room, busying about, making his bed and picking up his clothes. The door was a little ajar. I waited until I was sure she wouldn't spot me then I crept downstairs and out of the house.

Edie was waiting for me on the wall. She wore a white T-shirt and black trousers with a pair of men's braces, and held a cigarette burning in her fingers, but she didn't seem to be smoking it. She was like a statue, her eyes fixed on the waves crashing in and out over the grey boulders below her.

I walked up to her without calling out and was almost upon her before she realised I was there. She smiled at me but I could tell she was sad. Her eyes were red from crying, with a smudge of black mascara where she'd tried, but failed, to wipe away the run.

'I'm sorry,' she said. 'I've had enough. I hate it there. It's like hell.'

I reached out to touch her, dropping my arm when the pain shot down it from my shoulder. 'Don't be sorry. It's a misunderstanding, honest. We'll tell her it's okay. We can explain.' I smiled to reassure her. 'Don't worry.'

Edie swung her legs around and jumped down from the wall. 'Are you feeling okay? You look like a ghost.'

'Tired, that's all.'

'Shall we walk to the mine?'

I'd taken two more painkillers before I left, but even so, the going was harder than usual. I was short of breath and my legs were like jelly. I felt so poorly. I just wanted to lie down and sleep. But there was no way I was leaving her. Edie was my only connection to the house and I'd have died rather than let her out of my sights.

When we rounded the bend in the path, the ruins at Botallack came into view.

'They look like they might fall down any moment, don't they?'

'They won't. They've been there forever.'

We walked past the old metal sign with rusted nails telling us it was dangerous and to keep out. The ruins stood out against the sky; the sections of archways, the brick piers, the chimney shafts reaching up to the sky like forgotten sentries. Some of the walls held graffiti, names daubed across the stone, teenage love declared in rebellious etchings. The sun was hidden behind thick white cloud that hung low in the sky, and there was a fine layer of mist which hovered over the sea and caressed the coastline with gentle fingers.

'It's beautiful, isn't it?' she said. 'It's not hard to imagine there are spirits watching us.'

We walked along the narrow footpath that led to the engine house. The drop to the side of us was even more dramatic than usual. The wind and sea roared and looking down on the seething water made my head swirl.

'I wonder how many people have jumped,' she mused.

We turned and walked up through the ruins away from the sea.

'Come,' I said. 'I'll show you my favourite place here.'

I led her up through a low archway to a small enclosed area. Within the four crumbling walls which, like the engine house, had no roof, was a perfect carpet of soft grass. It was sheltered here, protected from the roar of the sea and wind. I sat down with relief and we lay back on the grass and stared upwards. The heavy white was now patched with darker clouds. The sky was still. Nothing moved save for the occasional bird flying overhead, too far above us to be identified.

Edie and I lay close. I turned my head to look at her, closing my eyes briefly to steady the swirl of faintness that came with the movement. I studied her profile. Her blemish-free forehead running into her perfect nose, upturned at the end, the silver stud like a full stop. Then the rise of her lips. My heart beat hard and my body flared with heat. I felt her hand reach for mine. Or was it me who reached for hers?

All my love, Edie.

'She means it, you know.' Her voice made me jump. She turned her head to face me. 'My mother doesn't want you anywhere near the house. I heard my dad arguing with her. I even tried. I told her she was crazy, but the silly cow was having none of it. She doesn't want any of you back there again. Not even your brother.'

'But if you try again. Explain to her.'

Edie rubbed her face and passed her hands over her forehead and hair.

'You know,' she said. 'She hit me last week.'

'*Hit* you?'

'Slapped me on the hand. It left finger marks. The next morning she couldn't remember a thing.'

Edie sat up and picked a blade of grass. Then she held it up in front of her face and studied it, rotating it slowly, tipping her head to look at it from every angle.

'Sometimes I think about her funeral and wonder if I'd even cry or not.'

I had a flash of Eleanor's face, drained of blood, her lifeless eyes staring through me. She was mouthing something at me. But I couldn't make out what she was saying. I told her to tell me again. Strained to hear. But nothing. No sound. Just her pallid face staring.

Tamsyn?

It was Edie's voice. In the distance.

'Tamsyn?'

She came into focus, emerging through the mist, her brow knotted, her face only a few inches from mine. 'Christ, are you okay? What the hell happened? You're burning up.' She pulled me in towards her. Held me tightly, one hand on the back of my head, her fingers scrunched into my hair. I was warm and safe, as if I was back at The Cliff House, lying beside the pool, the waves breaking on the rocks in time with her heartbeat which I felt through her T-shirt. Something inside me stirred. A radiating heat.

'It's okay,' she whispered.

All my love, Edie.

I looked up at her and she smiled. And then I moved closer and pressed my lips to hers. My stomach surged at the feel of her mouth on mine. The world slipped away as if we were floating. I imagined us in the pool at The Cliff House. Nobody there but us. The water so still, not a ripple, the two of us reflected in its black mirrored surface.

But then Edie took an intake of breath.

She pushed me away.

'No,' she breathed.

I watched with horror as her expression changed from shock to disbelief. Her hand flew to her mouth. Her head shook back and forth. All her warmth evaporated as she recoiled and the moment shattered like a fallen glass.

'What are you doing?' Her voice was strangled.

Fear flooded me.

She stood and wrapped her arms around her middle as if she were cold.

I scrambled to my feet. A pain skewed my shoulder and shot around my body.

'You said. You said *all my love*,' I whispered.

'What?'

'*All my love, Edie.*'

I stepped towards her, but she retreated. My world was darkening, the edges shrinking in on me. I saw The Cliff House racing away at a dizzying speed. I reached out to grab it, but my hand closed around nothing.

'I'm not like that. I like men. Boys. I'm not... that way.'

Edie's hands seemed to tighten around herself.

And then a raven cawed nearby.

I snapped my head around. Where was it hiding? It was somewhere there. Concealed amid the ruins. Watching from a glassless window. Or the top of a crumbling wall.

My shoulder burned. The tattooed cross pounded as if it might explode.

'I'm sorry,' I said. 'I…'

She bit her bottom lip and lifted her hand as if she was going to take my arm. I pulled away before she could make contact.

Then I ran.

'Tamsyn!' Her voice was high-pitched and loud and the birds hidden in the bushes flew up in panic. 'Stop!'

But I didn't stop. My lungs burnt as I ran. The gorse and brambles that bordered the path tore at my skin. My body dripped with sweat. My body screamed with complaint but I didn't listen to it, I pushed on.

She yelled my name, but it was faint, I'd put enough distance between us. I turned inland, over a stile and along a footpath that took me through farmland back towards St Just. It wasn't a path she'd know and I was certain she wouldn't follow.

'Tamsyn!' Her call fainter again.

When I was sure I'd lost her, I slowed my pace and came to a halt. I put my shaking hands over my eyes, pressed the heels of my palms hard into my sockets and tried to block out her horror. I relived our mouths touching and shuddered.

What the hell had I done?

CHAPTER THIRTY-EIGHT

Tamsyn
August 1986

The doctor sat on the edge of my bed, but addressed my mother who stood behind him.

Too many people in the room. Too cramped. Not enough air.

'It's a dangerous infection. Is she allergic to penicillin?'

I'd collapsed on the doorstep, my mother said. Jago heard a bang against the door and opened it to see me laid out on the ground and burning up like a furnace.

As Mum and the doctor talked their voices drifted in and out of my mind as if somebody was fiddling with the volume on a radio.

'Tamsyn? Did you hear me?'

I opened my eyes. The doctor's face was close to my own. He was a kind man with soft grey hair. He was the doctor who'd come to help Mum after my father died, prescribed her some tablets which I overheard him telling Granfer would dull her grief and help her sleep. She refused to take them.

I don't want to dull it. I want to feel it. I want to feel it all.

'We need to clean the site up, Tamsyn. You need to roll over.'

I did as I was told. Moved limbs filled with lead slowly and heavily.

I drifted away again but a pain like hot knives being driven into me brought me back.

'Bloody hell,' I heard my mother say. 'When did she get that?'

'It looks home done. Or if not then the person who did it should be locked up.'

I was aware of Jago standing at the door. Then soft voices. What were they saying?

The doctor took hold of my hand. 'Tamsyn, you need to sleep now. The antibiotics will work quickly, but you need sleep. Your body's exhausted from fighting the infection.'

He stood. Spoke to my mother. The two of them silhouettes through my half-closed eyelashes. 'Double dose now. Wake her for one before you go to bed. Then four times a day after food for the next seven days. If the temperature climbs any higher I want you to take her straight to Treliske. Don't hesitate. Keep the fluid intake up and give her only light food – chicken soup is good. She's to stay in bed for at least five days. On no account let her get up. And no visitors other than the family. It's important she rests. That infection is bad, another day or two and we'd have sepsis on our hands. We could have lost her...'

I must have drifted off to sleep because I was woken by Mum sitting on the edge of my bed with a glass of water and a pill in her hand. 'Tamsyn,' she whispered. 'Wake up, love. You have to take this.'

I opened my mouth and allowed her to put her hand behind my neck to support my head. She put the capsule on my tongue then the water to my lips. I swallowed the pill and collapsed back on the pillow.

'A tattoo?' she said. 'I can't believe you'd do something so stupid. Scar your body like that. Put your life at risk as well. It was that bloody Edie Davenport, wasn't it? I know it was her. The whole family is bad news. Why did you let her do that to you?'

She straightened my duvet. Passed her hand over my forehead. Stroked the side of my face. Whispered words into my ear. Then she stood and I was vaguely aware of her folding clothes, tidying things in my room, drawing the curtains.

I closed my eyes. My mind floated and sleep wrapped itself around me…

Moments later the door opened and Edie stood in the doorway. She was a dark silhouette with the light behind her. She held something out to me.

What is it?

A tape. For you. Because I love you. It's called The Cliff House and I chose the songs because they remind me of the house so you can always feel like you're there. So you can be close to your father. So you can have a home again.

She smiled.

I know how much you love the house.

Her smile slipped away like sand through a fist and a veil of fear descended over her. She'd seen something over my shoulder. I tried to turn my head but it was stuck rigid. I couldn't move. The whites of Edie's eyes grew wide as I stared at her. I squinted hard, focused on the bottomless black pools of her pupils, trying to see what was reflected in them.

Edie stepped back. She moved silently. Trying not to be seen. Wanting to hide, to get away from whatever it was that loomed. A shadow moved over me, darkening the air above my eyes like a rain cloud passing overhead. And there she was. Eleanor Davenport. She walked slowly towards me. I tried to scream, terrified of what she might do when she recognised me. But then I saw she was smiling. Her eyes were warm. Her hair was like a golden halo around her face. I tried to reach up to her, but my hands were pinned to my sides, swaddled, invisible bandages tight around me. She became cross with me then. Angry I wasn't greeting her properly with a kiss. How rude! Her face darkened. Blacker and blacker. Her nose and mouth deformed, stretching and contorting. Her eyes shrunk to small black beads which shone with a glint of light in their centre. Her blonde hair fell out in chunks, which tumbled to the floor like manna, and black needles began to push out from her scalp, her face, her limbs. The needles bloomed into feathers. Hundreds of black feathers bursting out like bot flies all over her. Her arms were changing shape, thickening and enlarging, until in one swift movement they sprung outwards, her sinewed limbs now mighty wings.

They spread. Beat the air.

Then she flew at me, her raven's beak wide, her eyes boring into me…

'Hush, Tamsyn.'

I woke with a start. My body was drenched with sweat. Heart pounding. 'It's okay, sweetheart. You've had a nightmare.'

Mum was in her dressing gown. Her hair mussed up from sleep. Eyes blinking into the light. She took my hand, lifted it to her mouth and kissed it.

'Will you stay with me tonight?' I asked her, gripping hold of her, terrified Eleanor would come for me in my sleep again.

'Hush, it's okay, of course I'll stay.' Then she lifted her feet

314

onto my bed and lay beside me stroking my head. 'I used to do this when you had bad dreams as a child.'

'It was Dad who came to me, wasn't it?'

'No, me mostly. He probably did once or twice though.' And she kissed the top of my head and held me until I fell into a smooth and dreamless sleep. 'But mostly it was me.'

CHAPTER THIRTY-NINE

Edie
August 1986

Edie stood outside the shop in St Just and took a couple of deep breaths, readying herself to face Tamsyn. There was no sign of her when she pushed open the door, just an old man in a striped apron, who flashed her his twinkly eyes and gave a cheery good morning.

'Are you Ted?'

'That's me!' he said, as if he'd won a prize.

'My name's Edie Davenport—'

'Ahhh, you'll be after Tamsyn, then?'

Edie looked at him in surprise then nodded. 'Yes. Is she here? She works here on Monday mornings, doesn't she?'

'Not today, love. She's poorly. Off the week her mum said.'

'Oh, I see.' Edie recalled Tamsyn's face when she'd pulled away from her at the tin mine. She wished she'd done something different. Reacted better. It had been such a shock. She should have seen it coming, but she'd been so wound up with her mother, with how bad things had been since the morning after the party, she'd been caught off-guard. The house had been a nightmare, filled with screeching, sobbing, slammed doors, her parents' friends leaving quickly and quietly, whilst exchanging looks. Then, of course, the relentless drinking until her mother collapsed in a heap on the sofa.

God, how could she have been so blind to the signs? Why did Tamsyn have to fall in love with her?

'Can you tell me where she lives? I'd really like to see her.'

'Of course, love. It's 17 Queen Street, just off the Cape Cornwall Road. It's the one with the light blue door and the pretty window boxes.'

'Thank you.'

'Not at all,' he said, then added, 'She said you were nice.'

Edie found the house quite easily. It was a narrow road with terraced houses on both sides. Bins in the small front yards. Iron pedestrian gates to most of the houses and front doors in a rainbow of colours. Though in need of painting, Tamsyn's house was neat and tidy from the outside. There was a short pathway that led from the pavement to the doorstep, which was cracked and uneven, but swept clean and free of weeds. There was a small white-framed window to her right with a window box filled with red flowers she didn't know the name of.

She stood on the doorstep and battled the nerves which dogged her. She had no idea what she was going to say and part of her wanted to turn and run away. But she knew she needed to check on Tamsyn. Her hand trembled horribly when she raised it to knock.

When she heard footsteps approaching the door she took a deep breath, ready to blurt out an apology for reacting so badly. But it wasn't Tamsyn who opened the door. It was Jago and her stomach twisted.

His eyes dropped to the floor to avoid looking at her.

'Hi. Is…' She hesitated, wrong-footed by his disregard. 'Is Tamsyn in?'

'She's not allowed to see anyone.'

'Is she okay?'

He raised his head and looked at her. 'No, she's really sick. With an infection.'

Edie remembered how hot she had been, how her eyes had moved in and out of focus, how she had lost consciousness for a few moments before she'd tried to kiss her.

'The tattoo went bad.'

'Oh my God,' she said, covering her mouth with her hand. 'I'm so sorry.' She didn't know what else to say. 'Will she be okay?'

'She will be now.'

Edie stared at him. His arm that rested against the door was circled with leather and his muscles were accentuated by his tight black T-shirt. He was unbearably good-looking and she realised how much she'd missed seeing him every day.

'And I definitely can't say a quick hello to her?'

'Not for a week.'

Edie nodded. She was about to turn away, but then stopped herself, nerves tumbling again. 'Will you tell her I said sorry. And not just for the tattoo.'

'Why? What did you do?'

She hesitated again as she saw a flash of Tamsyn's distraught face. 'Something happened. I handled it wrong and hurt her. I didn't mean to.'

He shrugged. 'Don't worry. She gets upset. It's sort of her thing.'

His voice was gentle but there was a clear note of protectiveness. Edie pulled at her sleeve and cleared her throat. 'I should get back.'

He nodded and held her stare as she took a couple of steps backwards. He didn't move and it was only when she turned away that she heard the door close.

As Edie walked back down Queen Street she considered returning. What excuse could she have to knock again? To ask him something – anything – so she could look at him some more.

She turned onto the main road that led back to the cliff path at Cape Cornwall. The waves beat out a rhythmic thump in the distance. The gulls cried. She looked up. Squinted into the sun. Watched one of them circling high in the sky.

'Hey,' said a voice.

She opened her eyes and looked to her side, but the figure was lost in momentary sun-blindness. She shielded her face and Jago came into focus. He stopped, bent his head, and lit a cigarette.

Her heart skipped a beat.

'Do you want a lift back on the bike? Save you the walk.'

She thought of her mother, of how she looked down on anybody who owned a motorbike, and smiled. 'Yes,' she said. 'I'd love that.'

'I'll finish my smoke first. You want one?' He held out his tobacco and she took it. 'Mum won't let me smoke in the cottage. Says it's not good for my grandad's lungs.'

Edie looked out across the sea. The sun bounced off the water in a corridor of light and fell across a boat so it glowed like a beacon.

'What's up with his lungs?' she asked as she sprinkled tobacco along the crease of a cigarette paper.

'Silicosis.'

'What's that?'

'It's fucking nasty. From the mines. Means he breathed in too much dust and shit. It's what'll kill him.' She handed him back his tobacco and he slipped it into the back pocket of his jeans. 'Fucking mines,' he whispered under his breath.

'Sounds horrible.' She rolled the cigarette and ran her tongue along the paper.

Jago lit it for her and looked back out to sea. 'We all have to go. He just knows what'll take him.'

'Is he scared?'

Jago sucked heavily on the cigarette and shrugged. 'Don't know. Maybe. I know I'm scared of finding him. Every day I think I'll go up there and he'll be dead.'

Edie kept her gaze locked on the horizon in the distance.

'Everybody should see at least one dead body in their lifetime,' she said.

He snorted. 'Man, that's fucked up.'

She glanced at him and caught his smile.

'Are you laughing at me?' She smiled too, relieved her nerves had finally begun to ebb.

'No. It's just…' He hesitated. 'You're different. We don't get many girls round this way who dress in black and want to see a dead body.'

'Nice girls then.'

He shook his head. 'They're boring. Like everything else around here.' He dropped his cigarette and trod it into the ground. 'I'll get the bike and meet you back here.'

A few minutes later he was revving the engine beside her. She hitched her skirt up and swung her leg over the seat of the bike. When she wrapped her arms around his waist, her body fizzed at the feel of his stomach, hard and muscular, beneath his T-shirt. She rested her chin against him and breathed in. He smelt amazing, musky with deodorant and smoke, fresh sweat and the hint of joss sticks.

He let the throttle go and with a roar they sped off. When they reached the open road – moors on one side, farmland on the other – she shouted for him to go faster. The wind raced past her ears. She tipped her head back and screamed, loving the feeling of freedom coursing through her veins. At the top of the hill he pulled into a gravelled lay-by and stilled the engine.

'Oh my God,' she said. 'So incredible! If this bike were mine I'd keep going. I just wouldn't stop. Not ever. I'd keep riding, as fast as I could, until I was five hundred miles away from it all.'

She climbed off the bike and held her arms out to the side, turned around and around, her palms outstretched, laughing as she spun. When she stopped she found he was smiling at her. She smiled back then walked over to the bike and stroked it. She looked down at her hand on the leather seat. A couple of inches from his. Her fingers were slight in comparison, her skin pale against his, which were stained yellow where he held his cigarettes. There was a ring on his middle finger, wide and silver, marked with Celtic shapes. His wrist was narrow but strong, the tendons clearly visible.

She inched her finger closer, until it grazed him, lightly, barely at all.

Neither of them breathed. Then his finger lifted so it hovered over hers then lowered slowly. She didn't move. Didn't want to break the spell. He stroked her. Electricity raced up her hand and arm and over her neck and shoulders.

She raised her face and looked at him. His eyes flicked left and right over hers. Then he moved his hand to cup her cheek.

'What about Tamsyn?' she whispered, leaning her face into his hand.

'What about her?'

Edie hesitated. 'She has a crush on me. She kissed me. That's why I came to check on her.'

Jago nodded. He didn't look surprised.

'I don't want to hurt her any more than I have.'

'She won't find out.'

He bent his head to kiss her and she gripped the bike, worrying her knees might give way, worrying how childish she'd appear if they did.

She opened her mouth. The tip of his tongue touched hers. His lips were soft. His breath tinged with smoke. His hand went to the back of her head. Pulled her tight to him. His other hand held hers. It was like nothing she'd felt before. Every part of her body tingled. He pulled away from her and smiled, then stroked her hair out of her eyes. She leant against his hand and smiled back.

CHAPTER FORTY

Tamsyn
August 1986

I locked the door so Mum couldn't come in and ran the hot tap. While the bath filled, I stood in front of the mirror and undressed, then turned my shoulder towards the mirror and picked at the edge of the dressing which Mum had reapplied the day before. I wasn't allowed to get the tattoo wet, not while it was recovering, so after I'd had a peek, seen the redness was subsiding and the gunk had disappeared, I pressed the dressing back down to make sure it didn't get splashed.

The water was boiling but I liked the sting of it. I lowered myself down, forcing my body into the scalding water in an effort to rid my mind of Edie's horrified face. I lay back in the heat and closed my eyes. She'd been my last hope of staying close to the house and now she hated me too and would never want to see me again. I felt sick, bile scraping the back of my throat. She'd tell her parents I'd been breaking into their house. They'd demand Mum's key back, change the locks, be ready to call the police at the first sight of me. What had I been thinking? And why – oh, God, why – had I kissed her?

After my bath I wrapped my hair in a towel and tied my dressing gown tight around my waist then unlocked the bathroom door.

Granfer's strained breathing pushed through the paper-thin walls. I poked my head around his door to check he was okay.

'Ah, hello... love. You feeling... all right?'

I nodded. Though it was a lie. My temperature might have gone back to normal, but I felt anything but all right. 'You?'

'A bit sore... today...' And he gestured at his chest.

I rubbed his hand and pulled over the stool, then tapped the jigsaw table. 'Come on, let's help you get this bugger finished.'

A while later, as we were sorting pieces, he said, 'She came here... you know... to see you...'

'Who?'

'The girl... from the white... house.'

'She was here? When?'

Surely he was wrong? Edie had been at the house? This meant everything. Maybe she wasn't angry with me? Maybe Eleanor had changed her mind? Maybe she'd come over to invite me back?

'Are you sure? It was definitely her?'

'She was... like... you said.'

I waited while he caught his breath.

'Short white hair. All... in... black.'

'When?'

'Beginning of the... week. You... were in bed...'

'What did she say? Did you speak to her?'

'Jago... did. Told her you... were sleeping. I heard... her say tell her... I'm sorry...'

My heart leapt. Everything was going to be okay! I jumped up and ran back to my box room, covered my face with both hands, and sobbed with overwhelming relief.

CHAPTER FORTY-ONE

Jago
August 1986

He folds the money and slips it into his back pocket then checks the street irrationally for his mum. Mind you, it's not just her he's worried about. He can feel his father's judgement from beyond the grave. His disappointment.

You bastard, he thinks.

Edie is leaning against the bike, smoking. Looking at her brings a hot rush of pleasure. White-blonde hair framing her face. Eyes blackened. An exotic punk panda. Since their first kiss she is all he can think about. He longs to touch her, to hold her against him, to explore every inch of her.

When she sees him walking back, her face lights up. Her enthusiasm dulls the shame of the cash in his pocket. He swallows, takes a breath to calm himself, to temper the craving which has hold of his whole body. He can't push it. Can't scare her. He knows it's only a matter of time before she works out he's not good enough.

Just like her mother said.

'So this is Penzance,' she says, scanning up and down Market Jew Street.

He smiles. 'Yup. Impressive, huh?'

The smile falls off her face. She fixes her eyes on him, looks up through lowered eyelashes. Her hand drifts to her upper arm and she rubs it.

His skin bristles.

The seagulls sitting on the roof of the town hall screech at each other as he climbs onto the bike and turns the ignition. She discards her cigarette in the gutter and climbs up behind him. Her arms reach around his middle and she rests her chin on his shoulder. He can feel the warmth of her breath on his neck and it's almost too much to bear.

They drive up towards Madron and on to Pendeen. When they reach the open stretch of farmland he lets go of the throttle and pushes the bike as fast as it will go. She tightens her grip on him, her hands slip beneath his T-shirt, and she presses her lips to his neck, before tipping her head back and crying out with exhilaration.

She yells something but her words are lost in the roar of the engine and whipping wind.

For the first time in years he remembers what it feels like to be happy; not the fleeting superficial happiness that comes with a spliff or a pint with his mates, but proper deep-down happiness. He briefly considers swerving hard to the left and careening headlong into the dry-stone wall to freeze the moment forever.

He doesn't take the bike through the gate to The Cliff House, but stops outside, a little way up the lane. He kicks the rest into position. Stills the engine. She climbs off and faces him, glances self-consciously at the ground, reaches out to pull on his T-shirt playfully.

'See you tomorrow?' he asks.

She shakes her head and for a moment he braces, ready to hear her tell him it's over before it's even properly begun.

But she doesn't end it.

'I want to see you later.' She takes his hand and pulls it to her mouth, opens her lips and gently bites the tip of his index finger.

His body explodes and when she touches her tongue to him his head swims. 'When?' he says with a strangled voice.

'Tonight. On the footpath in the dip beyond the gate, where we can't be seen from the house. Nine o'clock? I'll say I'm going up to bed. Not that they'll care. Eleanor will be passed out by then and Max will be shut away in his study.'

He nods.

He imagines taking her in his arms then and there. Pushing her top up. Pressing his mouth against her breasts. Lying her down and pushing himself into her. No. Don't think like that. Too fast. Don't scare her. His hand trembles as he lifts it to her cheek and a slow smile spreads over her face. She lays her hand on his thigh, high, near his crotch, and her skin warms him through the straining denim.

She drops her teasing hand and her eyes flash mischievously. He waits for her to step away, then revs the bike a couple of times, before kicking back the stand. He turns the bike and glances back over his shoulder for a final glimpse of her. As he does something catches his eye in the upstairs window.

A figure is watching them.

It's Eleanor Davenport and her face is set cold as stone.

CHAPTER FORTY-TWO

Edie
August 1986

'You know, Edith, I've just about had enough of this.'

Eleanor was at the top of the stairs, smoking, her eyes needling Edie.

Edie's breath caught in the back of her throat. 'Enough of what?'

'You.' Eleanor's eyes were wild and her lips thin as she drew on her gold-filtered cigarette in angry snatches. 'Making a fool of yourself. Of all of us. With that boy.'

Edie opened her mouth but no words came out. Her brain raced. She had a flash of her hand on Jago's trousers, her tongue tracing his lips. Eleanor must have seen them from the upstairs window; her face stung with heat.

'Your father thought it would be good for you to get away from London. Ha!' Eleanor shook her head with contempt. 'And look? Next thing we know you're keeping company with the great unwashed.'

'Shut up,' Edie whispered, her eyes prickling.

'I don't care how much your father loves it here, you and I are leaving Cornwall. I'm not staying here to wait for you to get pregnant by some unemployed halfwit no doubt up to his eyeballs on drugs. You're behaving like a spoilt brat and you continue to be an utter embarrassment to us, Edith. You should be ashamed of yourself.'

Edie stared up at her mother, muscles quivering with bottled anger. There was so much she wanted to shout back. Her mother's hypocrisy was staggering, but the vitriol in her eyes was like acid and sutured Edie's mouth closed. As she stood there she felt as if she were melting. How had they come to this point? When did her mother stop loving her?

Edie felt helpless. She didn't want this. She wished they were like a normal child and parent. Like Tamsyn and Angie. She'd seen the way Angie looked at her daughter, heard the warmth in Tamsyn's voice when she spoke about her mother, envied the way she respected her and cared about upsetting her. Edie would trade everything of hers which Tamsyn coveted for a relationship with her mother that was half as good as the one they had.

'You've nothing to say for yourself?' Eleanor drew on her cigarette and then blinked slowly. 'None of your usual excuses or sarcastic jibes?'

Edie lowered her head to hide her trembling chin and gathering tears.

'We're leaving at the end of the week. I'm taking you back to London. You're going to go back to school and get your A levels. You're going to start dressing properly, you'll take the crap off your eyes and throw that vile thing in your nose away. And then you'll start mixing with people who are worthy of your time and standing. *You* might want to throw your life away screwing hopeless losers, but you'll be doing it over my dead body.'

CHAPTER FORTY-THREE

Tamsyn
August 1986

I sat on my bed and willed the house to quieten.

I listened to Mum brushing her teeth and moving around on the landing. My grandad's light clicked off, then there were soft moans as he got himself into bed. My brother was out, of course. He was barely with us nowadays and I know it pained Mum, that she was forced to constantly bite her tongue, swallowing back a barrage of questions. Where have you been? Why weren't you back when you said you'd be? Any news on a job?

I heard Mum's footfalls on the stairs and the sitting room door closing. Then the house fell still. Only the odd creak broke the silence. I thought of Dad's stories about the Knockers, the piskies who lurked in the mineshafts and rapped on the supports and beams to warn of disaster. Had the Knockers come to our house to *tap-tap-tap* a caution?

No, not Knockers.

Just cooling rafters.

I dressed quickly and went down the stairs being careful not to make a sound. In the kitchen I reached for the tin on top of the fridge and searched for the key to The Cliff House. It wasn't there. I opened the fridge so I could check the tin in its light, but there was no sign of the key. I swore under my breath as my body thrummed with anxious energy. Mum's bag was hanging on the hook in the hall. I kept my eyes bolted to the sitting room door as I rummaged quietly inside it. My fingers found the small plastic fob with the key attached at the bottom of the bag and, as I grasped it, my body flooded with relief.

The night hung with a thick mist which gave the surroundings I knew so well an eerie sense of unease. Noise was muffled, except my footsteps, which rang on the road as I walked down to the Cape. The moon was full, but diffused, restricting my vision to no more than ten feet of murky dimness. When I turned onto the cliff path I was unable to see the sea to my right, but could hear it. The mist travelled fast, blown by the wind, billowing around me like smoke from a bonfire.

My nerves tumbled as I walked. I was excited and terrified at the thought of facing Edie. I had to keep reminding myself that she wanted to see me. To say sorry. That she'd come when I was poorly and been turned away. Eleanor and Max would be asleep. I'd wait until I was certain. I couldn't risk running into either of them until I'd seen Edie and made sure everything was back to normal. The thought of that kiss still made me cringe. I would have to laugh it off when I saw her, blame the fever and hallucinations, tell her I could hardly remember doing it. Apologise profusely. Beg her to forget all about it.

The mist thinned as I neared the house. Its white shape loomed in the dim light. Pulled me closer. With each step my anxiety seemed to lessen. I opened the gate, making sure not to creak the hinges, and as I stepped onto the lawn my eyes welled with tears.

It was as if I'd arrived home.

CHAPTER FORTY-FOUR

Jago
August 1986

Silence while they walk. The mist comes in with the dusk. Wraps around them like a blanket.

Edie walks beside him. She takes his hand as they climb away from the path up onto the part of the cliff where his father used to birdwatch. Her skin is soft with expensive creams and privilege. Jago is tight with desire. There have been girls before. But not like her.

'I thought you didn't want to be seen.'

She shrugs. 'You can't see anything through this mist, and anyway, I don't care anymore. They can get their kicks if they want to.'

But he leads her round the back of the rock so they'll still be hidden when the mist clears.

He sits down and she sits beside him. He strokes her cheek. She rests her forehead against his. He tilts his head so he can kiss her. He feels free. Like a boy again. The weight of the world lifted off his shoulders. All he's aware of is his heart hammering and the ache in the centre of him which makes him want to consume her whole.

He strokes her cheek. Kisses the tip of her nose. Her forehead.

Her chin. She closes her eyes, waits for him to kiss her, her mouth a perfect Cupid's bow like the lips a child would draw on a princess, curved and coloured in carefully with a rose-pink pencil. He presses his mouth to them.

They lie down at the base of the rock and kiss with eager lips. They are so immersed in each other that when they finally draw apart they discover night has fallen around them. It's dark and they laugh and wonder aloud how they didn't even notice.

Then she leans forward. Her mouth by his ear. Whispered breath warm on his skin. 'Jay?'

'Yes,' he murmurs.

'I'd like to have sex with you.'

He doesn't answer in case he misheard her.

'Do you want to as well?'

He hesitates, not because he doesn't want to, but because he's worried he'll sound too keen and betray the fact that making love to her is all he's thought about since he first laid eyes on her. 'Yes,' he rasps.

When they kiss again, there's an overwhelming urgency in both of them. His hands push up under her shirt. Up towards her breasts. No bra. Her nipples stiffen under his touch. His body jolts.

'Stop,' she says. He drops his hands from her, leans back, opens his mouth to apologise for moving too fast. She stills him with her finger against his lips. 'Not here.'

Then she laughs and it sounds like a peal of bells.

They stand. She takes his hand and they walk quickly along the path. The mist swirls around them and the sea roars. Fingers stroking, playing. His stomach starts to boil with nerves and anticipation, and as it does self-doubt seeps into him.

Eleanor Davenport's voice rings in his ears as she pushed the fence money into his hands. Told him not to come back. Told him he wasn't good enough.

I can see why she'd be tempted.

The strong white walls of her house emerge out of the mist which has started to fade and catch the muted moonlight. Edie pulls him down towards the gate.

'Not your house,' he says. 'Your mother. I—'

'It'll be okay.'

He stops. Pulls her back. 'If she finds out she'll hit the roof. She told me not to come back. Told my mum and sister to keep away. She doesn't want any of us around.' He remembers her face at the window. Her eyes thick with malice. 'I think she saw us earlier.'

'She did and I don't care. I mean, what can she do? I'm not a child anymore. She can fuck off to hell and stay there for all I care.'

Talk of Eleanor, the thought of her discovering them, dulls the moment. He reaches into his pocket and pulls out his tobacco pouch, opens it and retrieves a ready-rolled cigarette. He straightens it, brushing off the stray strands of tobacco, then puts the end in his mouth and lights up.

'Seriously. I don't care. It doesn't matter to me whose son you are or what job you do or don't do,' she said. '*Fuck* her. So it pisses her off? Good. I'm done giving a shit what she thinks.'

He draws the smoke into his lungs and exhales slowly.

She holds her hand out for the cigarette and takes a drag when he passes it to her. 'Her opinion is literally meaningless.' She passes it back to him. 'And anyway, they won't see us, they'll be asleep by now.'

He takes a last smoke of the cigarette then drops it. The ember glows in the dark and he treads it out with his boot.

They duck down, keeping low to the bramble hedge that runs along the front wall of The Cliff House. She smothers a laugh and he tells her to hush and she laughs again. They pause at the gate. Peer over the top.

'I told you,' she whispers. 'They've gone up.'

'Are you sure?'

'The living room lights are off and the one in his study. Their bedroom too.'

'But what if we wake them?'

She stands on tiptoes to kiss him. 'We're not going in the house,' she whispers. 'We won't wake them.'

She walks through the gate and he follows, reaches for her waist, rests his fingers against her and feels the heat from her body running into his. His body aches with longing. When they reach the terrace, she pulls him over to the pool. She stops and undoes her skirt. Steps out of it. Then takes her shirt off. She giggles softly as she sits down on the edge of the pool. Her legs dangle in the black water. He glances up at the house. Searches the windows for watching faces.

He walks over to her and she reaches up and pulls gently on the waistband of his jeans. Desire fires through him. His fingers clench and breath comes in shorter snatches.

She eases herself into the water and disappears beneath the surface. When she reappears her hair is slicked back. The water reaches her ribcage. She beckons to him.

'Is it cold?' He doesn't swim much anymore. Not since his father drowned. He eyes the blackness warily, his head reeling as adrenalin and lust pump through him.

She smiles and shakes her head. The mist has become sparse and patchy and the moon reflecting off the water throws enough light on her for him to see the outline of her breasts. He undresses and lowers himself into the pool. She was lying about it not being cold, but he doesn't care. His feet touch the floor and he wades over to her. Puts his hands on her skin which is peppered with goosebumps. He kisses her on the lips, then ducks his head and kisses each of her perfect nipples in turn. She strokes his shoulders then pushes back from him, fumbles beneath the water. Her hand emerges holding her underwear, which she throws onto the terrace.

His body fires again.

In the dark his senses are heightened. Soft breaths come in and out of her. He can smell her shampoo. Her make-up and perfume. Her skin is warm against his. She wraps her legs around his middle. Her pubic hair brushes against him and he stifles a moan.

'Jesus,' he whispers. 'Your parents—'

'Won't see us.'

'And if they do?'

'I told you. I don't care.'

She leans backwards. Her body floats on the surface of the water, breasts proud, he runs his hand from her abdomen up and over her chest and throat. Then she rights herself and takes his hand to pull him down beneath the surface. His heart thumps. For a moment he feels fearful but then her body envelops him. In the silence her lips find his. Her tongue is insistent. He puts his hand on her lower back and brings her closer to him. He wishes they could stay like this forever, suspended in the water, nothing else but the two of them. When they can't stay down any longer they break the surface.

'Have you done this before?' he whispers. He girds himself for the answer. He wants to be her first but at the same time feels the weight of that responsibility.

There's a hesitation. Then she says, 'Once.'

His body tenses with irrational jealousy.

'But I hated it. It hurt and when I told him to stop he was too caught up in what he was doing to hear me.'

The jealousy quickly turns to anger and he knows that if that man were here now he'd punch his lights out.

'It didn't feel,' she hesitates again, 'like this.'

'Like what?'

She laughs softly. Kisses him. Takes his hand and presses it between her legs with an urgency that paralyses him.

'You're sure?' His voice cracks with needing her.

'Are you?'

'Yes, of course, but we don't have to. There's no hurry. We can wait.'

She tightens her arms around him and nibbles his earlobe. Whispers hot breath against his cold skin. 'I can't.'

Then from somewhere nearby there's a snap. The sound of a breaking twig or a branch. He stops kissing her. Looks behind him in the direction of the noise. 'What was that?'

'Nothing,' she says. 'You're hearing things.' She cajoles him with her hand on the side of his face, turning him back to her, and he forces away the feeling that somebody is watching them.

Her face is serious for a moment, then she takes hold of him and guides him into her, and he moans softly.

Afterwards they stand entwined. Her arms tight around his shoulders. The water is cold and they are both shivering, her teeth chattering softly.

'Are you okay?' he asks.

'Yes,' she replies. 'Are you?'

He kisses her again by way of an answer.

'I love you,' she says.

He hesitates. Feels as if his chest is being cut open to expose his heart. He's never said those words to a girl before. What will it mean if he does? He decides not to care.

'I love you too.'

He looks up at the house. 'Which room is yours? I want to be able to imagine you sleeping.'

She kisses him and then points to her bedroom window.

They swim over to the steps. She climbs out first. He follows. As he does he hears a noise. Not an animal or a bird. A person. A sob or a faint shout? He listens. But the noise doesn't come again. When Edie presses her warm lips between his shoulder blades the noise is forgotten.

She finds a damp towel on one of the sun loungers and places it on the grass. They lie down on it. Their fingers play lightly with each other. Her head rests on his chest and her free hand trails his stomach.

'We should run away.'

'Run away?'

She nods.

'Isn't that what children do?'

She bats him gently. 'I mean it. I thought getting expelled would be the end of it. That I could leave school and get on with my life but they want to kidnap me and make me take exams I don't need.'

'How did you get expelled anyway?'

She shrugs. 'It wasn't hard. Not after Eleanor slapped Veronica Young-Newell at speech day.'

He laughs.

'Seriously,' she replied. 'You can't even imagine. After that it was easy. Graffiti in the loos was the final straw.'

'What did you write?'

'I couldn't think of anything clever so in the end I just wrote *Fuck you all, bitches*.'

With the mist finally lifted, her features are clear in the moonlight and he wonders at her beauty as he traces the line of her nose and mouth with his finger.

'Seriously, Jay. I want to go.' She sits up and reaches for her top and slips it back on. 'I've got friends in London. We could sleep on a floor for a while. Get jobs. Then a flat—'

He gives a bitter snort. 'Get jobs? Just like that?'

'Yes. Jobs. London isn't like down here. There are jobs. Lots of them. Waitressing, office work, building sites.'

'And what would we do for money while we looked for work?' he says. 'You can't just head up to London without cash.'

'I've got money!' She grabs his hand. 'A savings account. There's lots in it. Enough to get us settled.'

He doesn't reply and he sees her look of disappointment.

'I'm not saying we have to stay together,' she says.

'It's not that.'

She lies down on his chest again. 'What then?'

He pictures packing a bag. Shoving clothes, his lighter, his pouch of tobacco into it. Sees himself walking down the stairs. His mum asleep. Granfer too. Tamsyn on the top stair watching him abandon them.

'I can't leave my family.'

'You *can*. It's your life. You said there's nothing here for you.'

'I promised my dad I'd look after them. When we buried him. I promised.'

'Your dad's dead.'

He is silent.

She manoeuvres herself to look at him, hands on his chest, chin on her hands. 'You can't spend your whole life trying to keep a promise to your dead father. They'll be okay. Your mum and grandad and Tamsyn. They will. You have to be okay too.'

He strokes her cheek with the tip of his finger.

'I promised,' he says quietly. 'I can't leave them.'

CHAPTER FORTY-FIVE

Tamsyn
August 1986

I crept as close as I could. My breath stilled. Shapes and whispered voices in the darkness.

My blood solidified and I dug my fingers into my palms. Focused on the two people in the water. Voices I recognised. And sounds I didn't.

Godawful sounds that made me feel sick.

I crept closer still. As I did I stepped on a twig and he turned his head towards the noise. I froze. There was no doubt who they were and my body felt as if it was dissolving. He stopped searching the shadows for me. I took another step towards the pool, gaping and black. I walked as if I were crossing a thin sheet of glass. Quietly and carefully, keeping myself concealed in the shadows. The damp air wrapped around me. My eyes were trained on the two in the pool until at last I could make them out and there was no doubt.

My hand shot to my mouth to stop myself gasping out loud. I felt my skin burning red and my knees buckled. Their skin glistened as if they were slicked with oil. Him and her. Edie and my brother. Naked. Her back arched. His hands on her waist, moving her back and forth. The water made gentle undulations, reflecting the moon, in time with their movements. He leant forward. Pressed his face to the space between her breasts. They blurred again. Not the mist this time, but angry tears. Why were they doing that? I didn't understand. How had this happened? I hated them both and I wanted them out of the pool. How dare they? How dare they do that in my pool?

Get out. Get out. Get out.

I stayed longer than I should have done. Frozen in horror, desperate not to be seeing what I was seeing, yet unable to tear my eyes off them. Eventually, I forced myself away, then dazed and confused, crept silently back through the shadows and down towards the gate. With each step the image of them together hit me like a blow to the stomach. When I made it onto the path I broke into a run, tripping and stumbling over rocks and tufts of grass. I couldn't stop myself crying, though I tried, not altogether successfully, to muffle my sobs until I was far enough away that I could collapse on the path and draw my knees in tight.

It was as if each of them had stabbed me through the heart.

CHAPTER FORTY-SIX

Angie
August 1986

She was feeling weary, lids heavy, limbs creaky. Joints like a pensioner. Surely she shouldn't feel this old and stiff at her age. Stress, perhaps. She was still spitting with rage about what Eleanor Davenport had accused Tamsyn of. It was unforgivable. And then to forbid her from showing her face at the house? Heartless. She was a prize cow. Surely as an adult she could see how delicate Tamsyn was. How finely balanced. It was irresponsible of her to fly so fast and loose with the feelings of a child, to draw Tamsyn into their lives, then pull away like a rug from beneath her.

She laid some of the blame at Rob's feet. Why he'd built it up in her mind as some sort of fairy-tale castle was beyond her. Shoving that damn house into her head and heart as if it was perfect.

'Perfect, my arse,' she muttered, as she vigorously scraped old batter off the fryers.

Gareth was in the office above the shop. It was a small room with two desks, one which he'd moved in for her a few weeks ago. *You need a break from cleaning and serving*, he'd told her. So now once a week she helped with the books or other bits of admin he found for her. She was currently typing names and telephone numbers of their suppliers and customers into a new machine. A personal computer, Gareth had told her proudly. Apparently it was the answer to all the world's problems. When she asked what problems, he'd answered ominously, face serious: *Paper. If we don't use machines in thirty years' time they'll be no trees left anywhere.* Computers, he'd said, were the future. She wasn't so sure. It seemed ever so time-consuming to have to type it all in.

Angie turned the fryers on and stared down at the tiny bubbles of heat forming in the orange oil.

'Angie?'

Gareth was watching her from the doorway.

'Would you eat lunch with me?'

'But what about the shop?'

'Rose'll be in soon. She's happy to cover for a while.'

Angie hesitated.

'I'll still pay you.'

'You can't pay me to have lunch with you.'

'If I could, you'd be a millionaire.'

She smiled.

They walked down to the Old Success and sat outside and ordered half a lager each and two cheese Ploughman's. The sun was hot. It had been a glorious few weeks, with hardly any rain, which was great for business and kept Sennen buzzing. Tourists ambled up and down the streets and the car parks were overflowing. The beach, too, was full. People cheek by jowl. Towels, inflatables, buckets and spades, crabbing nets, cool boxes filled with sandwiches in tin foil, a patchwork of picnic rugs across the yellow sand.

Angie smiled as she watched two children dash down to the break of the waves only to squeal as they touched the icy water then turn to hare back up the beach.

'I miss mine being small,' she said.

'They don't care for me much, do they?'

She considered denying it, but in the end patted his hand. 'Don't take it personally. They don't understand.' She hesitated. 'They miss their dad, that's all. The family isn't the same without him. It's incomplete. Like a jigsaw puzzle that's missing a bit.'

He pushed his plate aside and leant forward. 'I want to ask you something.' He took a deep breath. 'I've been thinking and I changed my mind. When we kissed—'

'Gareth, I—'

'No,' he said. 'Let me finish. I know I'm not perfect, but maybe perfect isn't what you need? Maybe a bit less than perfect is okay?' He paused and took a breath. 'Marry me, Angie. I love you and I promise I'll do all I can to make you happy.'

'Marry you?' Her mouth fell open and she furrowed her brow. 'But... no. I mean, I can't. The kids. They don't want another dad.'

'I don't want to be their dad.' He rested his hand on hers. 'I want to be *your* husband.'

She was about to speak, but he stopped her.

'Just think on it, will you? At least do that for me.'

They walked in silence back towards the chip shop. Her insides were like a washing machine, tossing and flipping, rolling everything he'd said around her with a confusing mix of emotions. Part of her couldn't imagine replacing Rob – and,

God forbid, being intimate with another man – but then there was another part of her which was hollowed out with loneliness. She longed for somebody she could pinch a chip off or take a walk on the beach with. It wouldn't be long and the children would marry and move away. The silicosis would eventually come for Granfer. Then what? Just memories of Rob for company?

Before she caught the bus home she took a walk along the seafront to the lifeboat station. The yard to the side of it was a concreted area patched with seaweed holding fishing paraphernalia such as lobster pots, blue and green nets, floats slicked in algae, and small boats in desperate need of painting which had seemingly been there for decades. Two men with fishing rods sat on stools on the seawall sharing a packed tea and easy silence, and a woman stood in front of an easel, painting the sea in misleadingly garish colours.

Angie walked into the boathouse and made sure to keep her eyes averted from the waiting lifeboat propped on the angled ramp, ready to launch as soon as it was called. She walked to the memorial wall and looked over the array of small brass plaques which held the names of all those lost and the dates the sea claimed them.

She rested her hand against his. Traced the letters of his name cut into the metal. She thought of him that night. Saw his face as he bent to kiss her. His whispered words reassuring her. Telling her – as he always did – not to worry. Telling her he'd be back in her arms before she knew it.

In her fantasy world he did come home. And in the same fantasy world he was waiting at home for her now. A takeaway on the table. Red wine poured into two glasses.

'What are we celebrating?' she whispered, resting her cheek against the cool brass plaque.

Being alive, Ange. We're celebrating being alive.

It had been past four a.m. when she heard her son creep back into the house, so she was surprised to find him in the kitchen when she came down, already dressed, and standing at the cooker, stirring a pan whilst whistling brightly.

'You're up? I didn't think I'd see you until the middle of the afternoon.' She was unable to conceal her surprise. 'And making breakfast?'

He smiled.

'A smile too. Goodness, child, is it my birthday?'

'There's cash under the toaster,' he said. 'And I put extra butter in the eggs. Like Dad used to.'

'Thanks for the money. The Davenports owe me quite a bit.' She smiled. 'I loved your dad's eggs.'

Her son looked down at the pan doubtfully.

'I'll love yours too,' she assured him.

'Mum...' He hesitated. 'I'm sorry.'

'For what?'

He removed the pan from the gas and turned the flame off. 'For being useless. I'm going to do better. Get a job and look after you all.'

'Jago Tresize, you don't ever – *ever* – say you're sorry to me.' She walked over to him and placed her hand against his cheek. 'You have nothing to be sorry about.'

He dropped his eyes and shook his head. 'I should be helping but instead I make you worry.'

'I'm your mother. Worrying is what I do.'

He broke her heart. She wished he was still small enough for her to wrap him in her arms and kiss him all over until he begged her to stop.

'Listen, you,' she said. 'After your dad died, I wouldn't even have got out of bed each day if it wasn't for you and your sister. Do you understand? You helped me more than you'll ever know just by being there.'

They were interrupted by Tamsyn appearing in the doorway in her dressing gown, arms crossed, face like a storm. Angie smiled at him and patted his shoulder.

'Morning, love,' Angie said to her daughter. 'Jago's cooked breakfast.'

She glanced at him then back at Angie. 'I'm not hungry.'

'He's done eggs.'

'I *said* I'm not hungry.' She fixed her brother with a fiery glare. 'Maybe Edie Davenport could come over instead? I'm sure she's famished this morning.'

Tamsyn's expression was defiant and challenging. Her mouth twitched. Her eyes had narrowed to angry slits.

'Shut up, Tamsyn,' said her son with enough force for Angie to know that whatever they were talking about was significant.

'And if I *don't*?'

He needled his eyes at her, chin quivering.

'What's this about?' Angie asked. 'Tam?'

Tamsyn's face flared hotly and she scowled at Jago, who turned away from them and concentrated on stirring the contents of the pan.

'Jago?'

'Nothing,' he muttered.

'Yeah,' Tamsyn spat. 'Well, it didn't *look* like nothing last night. I *saw* you. In the pool. Apparently you like *swimming* again.'

Jago banged the pan down. 'For fuck's sake!' He spun around and glared at his sister, mouthed swear words, body rigid with sudden rage. 'You fucking spied on us?'

'Why? Why would you do that?' Tamsyn's eyes welled with tears. 'Isn't it enough you take up all Mum's worrying so she doesn't have time for me? Now you have to steal my only friend away too?'

Angie inhaled sharply at Tamsyn's words. She wanted to tell her it wasn't true, that she had time for both of them. She moved to her daughter's side and reached out to her, but Tamsyn swiped her hand away.

She stepped closer to her brother, head angled upwards so she was looking him in the face. 'I know what you're up to, you know. You don't want me there, do you? You want the house for yourself. It was you who made up those lies about me and Max, wasn't it? You who told Eleanor.'

'What the fuck are—'

'So I'd be out of the way. So you could screw Edie without me *bothering* you.'

Angie's stomach seized.

'Oh, Jago. No.'

He turned on her, his anger burning through his earlier softness. '*Oh, Jago, no* what?'

'You and the Davenport girl? Tell me that's not true.'

He didn't reply. Tamsyn crossed her arms again and leant back against the worktop, her rage seemingly subsided and in its place a resigned despondency.

'Of all the girls you could go with?'

'Why do you even care?'

'I *care* because that family is a bloody nightmare. I don't want either of you to have anything to do with any of them. And, if you want the truth, once Mrs Davenport has calmed down and got this stupid nonsense about Tamsyn out of her head – which, Tamsyn, of *course* Jago had nothing to do with – I was hoping I might get my job back.' She glanced at her daughter who glowered and kicked the floor with her heel. 'Or at least get paid what they owe me. But if you and Edie are—' She broke off and put her hand up against her forehead as a sudden panic grabbed her. 'Christ, is she even old enough?'

He rolled his eyes. 'Seventeen.'

'That's one thing at least.' She sighed. 'But why her?' She knew as the words left her mouth that it was a ridiculous question. As if teenagers ever thought these things through. 'God only knows what that woman will do when she finds out.'

'I was hoping she wouldn't.' He threw Tamsyn a filthy look.

'People always find out.'

'So what if she does?'

'She'll hit the roof.'

'Because I'm not good enough?'

Angie stared at him. She didn't speak. It was only a hesitation but it was enough. His face hardened and he shook his head.

Of course you're good enough.

That's all she'd needed to say.

He snorted bitterly. 'Fuck this,' he breathed. Then he stormed out of the kitchen, punching the wall with his fist as he left.

'Jago!' she called.

'I'm due at the yard.'

'Don't leave. Come back and talk.' But he was already opening the backdoor. 'Jago—'

'I said I'm due at the yard!'

Then the door slammed.

'Bloody hell,' she said under her breath, as the sound of his motorbike cut through the house. She ran out the back to the gate which led out onto the rear access whilst screaming his name. But he didn't stop and she helplessly watched him accelerating away from her.

Angie walked back inside. Her legs trembled and tears stung her eyes.

'You okay, love?' she said as she walked back into the kitchen.

Tamsyn pursed her lips and nodded. She still looked so ill, skin ashen, bruised smudges beneath her eyes, lank hair in need of a wash.

'I'm sorry you feel I've not been there for you. I am though. Really.'

Tamsyn flinched when Angie tried to touch her. Crossed her arms tighter. Drew away.

'I know this stuff with the Davenports is hard, but remember, I believe you. I know you and Max aren't… Well, you know.'

And then Tamsyn began to sob. Her body shuddered uncontrollably. Angie reached for her but, as she did, Tamsyn pulled away as if she'd been electrocuted, then tore out of the kitchen and up to her room.

Angie wanted to kill Eleanor Davenport. How could she do that to a child? She stood in the silence of the kitchen and listened to the echo of both her children's hurt and confusion. Then, she felt herself harden. Screw her. Angie was glad her hoity-toity daughter had fallen for her beautiful boy. How dare the stupid cow say he wasn't good enough? He was a hundred times better than any of their morally bankrupt family. Angie hoped Eleanor did find out the two of them were together. She hoped the woman choked on it. She was a silly bitch who treated them all like dirt.

Enough was enough.

Angie marched into the hall and grabbed her bag from the hook. Then she walked to the phone box and dialled the chip shop.

'It's me,' she said, when Gareth answered. 'Any chance you could drive me up to the Davenports' place?'

She waited for him on the corner and twenty-five minutes later they were pulling up in front of The Cliff House.

'Wait in the car,' she told him. 'This won't take long.'

Her nerves jangled like crazy as she raised her hand to ring the doorbell.

The door opened. As soon as Eleanor saw her she folded her arms and looked down the length of her nose at her.

Angie held out the key. 'I came to give you this back.'

Eleanor reached out to take it, but Angie closed her fist.

'And you owe me three weeks' wages plus the overtime.'

Eleanor snorted. 'And good morning to you too. Actually,' she said with a slow smile and a slur that hinted she might already have been drinking, 'I'm glad you're here.'

'Oh, really?' Angie tried to sound brave, but there was something in Eleanor's face that made her uneasy.

'You might be able to save me a call to the police.'

Angie opened her mouth in surprise. 'The police?'

Eleanor narrowed her eyes. 'To report a theft.'

'What?' Angie's heart jumped into her mouth. 'What theft? What are you talking about?'

'A valuable piece of jewellery. A gold and ruby bracelet. It's gone missing. You and your children are the only *unknowns* who've been here. And, let's face it, any of you could have done it. That son of yours has been snooping around, and you and Tamsyn had ample opportunity to take it.'

Angie tried to hold herself upright as her mind raced. When she spoke she kept her voice as level as she could manage. 'None of us has taken anything.'

Eleanor leant forward. 'Are you *sure*?'

Angie hesitated. Her thoughts became muddy. She glanced back at Gareth who was sitting in the car with a newspaper resting on the steering wheel. He turned his head and caught her looking and gave her a questioning thumbs-up. Flustered, she nodded, and he went back to his paper.

'I probably should have asked your son about it when he dropped Edith home on that horrific death-trap of his yesterday.'

'But he was working yester—' She stopped herself.

Eleanor gave a triumphant smile. 'I suggest you go home, Angie. Talk to your son. Ask him where my bracelet is then bring it back to me.'

The door of Gareth's car opened and closed behind her.

'You okay, Angie?' he called over.

Eleanor looked at him over Angie's shoulder and sneered. 'Christ, you're a load of inbreds down here, aren't you? Now remove yourself from my property and get my bracelet back from your thieving son.' Then she stepped back into the house and slammed the door.

Gareth opened the passenger door for Angie.

'You're shaking like a leaf, love,' he said as he helped her in. 'What happened?'

'I need to talk to Jago.' Her voice trembled with shock. 'Can you take me up to Rick Statton's yard? It's just the other side of Halsetown.'

Bobby Statton and Jago had been friends at school. Bobby's dad, Rick, owned a salvage yard. Though the boys knew each other, and Rick's dad had played football for West Penwith with Granfer, she didn't know Rick personally so wasn't surprised to see him staring at her without recognition as she climbed out of Gareth's car.

She crossed the yard which was rammed with an assortment of items: piles of fire grates and mantelpieces, old doors stacked like a deck of cards, baths that were stained and cracked, and a mountain of wooden chairs with turned legs that towered so high they threatened to topple.

'Can I help?' said Rick. He took off his cap and scratched his head.

'I'm Angie. Angie Tresize.'

His face broke into a smile. 'Of course you are. Sorry, Angie. It's been a while. How've you been keeping?'

She nodded, her eyes searching the yard for her son.

'Is he here?' she said. 'I need a quick word.'

'Is who here?'

Her stomach turned over. 'Jago,' she said, biting back desperate tears. 'He... he said he was working today.'

Rick furrowed his brow. 'Jago? Working here?'

Angie's tears brimmed over and she wiped them away with the back of her hand.

Rick's discomfort was clear as he shifted on his feet, and fiddled with his cap.

'Maybe somewhere else? He's not working here.'

'You mean today?' She was grasping at straws, pleading with him to smile, bat her arm, tell her he was joking and the boy was out back.

'Never worked here. He comes to pick Bob up on the bike every now and then, to go to the pub or what-have-you.' He hesitated. 'Everything okay?'

She forced a smile and shook her head. 'Yes, everything's fine. I must have got the wrong end of the stick. Misheard him. My mistake.'

He nodded with sympathy, parent to parent, the look on his face saying *ah, these kids of ours are little buggers, aren't they?*

'If I see him,' Rick said. 'I'll tell him you're after him.'

Angie nodded and walked back to the car. As Gareth drove her home she stared out of the window, unable to respond when he tried to talk to her.

All she could think of was the cash tucked under the toaster and all those times Jago told her he'd been at the yard or talked about Rick or moaned about how tired he was.

'Oh, Jago,' she breathed. 'What on earth have you done?'

CHAPTER FORTY-SEVEN

Jago
August 1986

She's waiting for him on the stairs when he walks in. Sitting on the second step. Hands folded into her lap. Her face is seething with anger and it throws him.

'I'm sorry,' he says. 'I should have told you about her. I—'

'I went to Rick's to look for you.'

His heart jumps into his throat.

'Well?'

He can't speak.

'You've nothing to say?'

He scratches hard at his lower arm, focuses on the thin leather cord Edie knotted around his wrist before he left her to walk home at dawn that morning.

'Eleanor's lost a bracelet.' His mother's lips twitch with rage. 'Says it's been stolen.'

He doesn't understand why she's looking at him like she is.

'Where's the money coming from, Jago?'

Her accusation hits him full on.

'Is that why you've gone after their daughter? So you can *steal* from them? Pawn their stuff for a fistful of tenners to stick beneath the toaster?'

Her words slice him like razor blades.

Her eyes narrow. 'Well?'

He blinks at her. Winded. 'I didn't—'

'You lied to me. You told me you were working at the yard but you weren't. You've never done a day there. But you give me cash. Jewellery goes missing from the Davenports. You're seen hanging around the house exactly when it was taken.' She pinches the bridge of her nose. Her voice drops. Her eyes close and she winces. 'Did I *ever* send you to school in dirty or torn uniform? Without the right PE kit? You might not have had fancy trainers but I fed you well, cut your hair nice, polished your shoes every Sunday night so you wouldn't look like the poor kids. I never took charity. I never broke the law. I worked any job I could find so we could hold our heads high when your dad died. And now *this*? Jago…? How *could* you?'

This hurts more than anything has hurt before, like a knife in his gut. 'You think that little of me?' he says at last.

'What am I supposed to think?'

'You're supposed to know I'd never steal. You're supposed to trust me.'

'How can I trust you when you lie?'

He absorbs her disappointment. Her judgement. The look on her face that tells him she knows now she was always right about him. That he'll never amount to anything. That he'll shiver in his dead father's shadow forever.

He turns his back on her and walks out of the house.

He parks his bike out of sight of the house and walks the last bit. When he gets to the gate he crouches to conceal himself behind the dry-stone wall. Then he watches. When he's sure nobody is around, he keeps low to the ground and scoots around the side of the house. He peers around the corner carefully in case they are on the terrace, but the garden and pool are deserted.

He stands below her window. Bends. Picks up few pebbles from the earth in the flower bed then throws them one by one so they tap on the glass. Nothing. He bends for more. Prays she's in her room. Throws another pebble.

Then her face appears at the glass. She looks down and sees him. Lifts up the latch and pushes the window open.

'Front door,' she whispers.

He nods and walks back along the side of the house then hovers at the corner until he sees the door open. When she sees him she lifts a finger to her lips. He gestures towards the gate. She nods and they scurry quickly to the gate and out onto the lane.

They don't speak until they reach his bike. He glances back to make sure nobody has followed them. Then he kisses her, cups her face with both hands and presses his lips to hers. She kisses him back with urgency. Her hands go under his shirt. Nails dig into him. He hears a noise and pulls away from her. Wipes his mouth. A walker rounds the bend with a rough-coated collie dog trotting happily beside him. The dog sniffs Edie and she reaches down to pat its head.

'Afternoon,' says the man. 'Beautiful day, isn't it?'

Edie and Jago exchange grins then climb on to the bike and the engine screams to life.

'Where shall we go?' he asks.

'The engine house.'

He nods and revs the throttle, releasing it to the tune of Edie's laughter.

They park the bike in the car park at the top of the cliff, then scramble down the path to the ruined mine. Inside the engine house they fall on each other. Tear at each other's clothes. Collapse back on the grassy platform. He unbuttons his jeans. Presses his mouth to the curve of her neck as he unclips her bra. She slips it off her shoulders and discards it, then pulls his head down to her chest. He kisses each breast in turn and she moans. His lust fires.

The sex is quick and, for him at least, angry. Emotion erupts in a torrent as his mother's accusation rings in his ears.

'Are you okay?' she whispers afterwards as they lie looking up through the ruined roof.

White clouds pass overhead. The sky behind them is touched with blue and gulls call to each other as they fly in sweeping arcs.

'Do you still want to leave?' he asks, turning his head to look at her.

'What do you mean?'

He raises himself on one elbow. 'To London. On the bike. With me?'

'You'll come?'

He nods.

'But your family?'

He sees his mother's cold, hard face. The hatred in his sister's voice. 'I'm done with them.'

'Really?'

'Yes.' He strokes a lock of her fringe from her forehead, plays with it between his thumb and forefinger. 'There's nothing here for me anymore.'

CHAPTER FORTY-EIGHT

Tamsyn
August 1986

Mum was sitting at the kitchen table with her head in her hands. When I walked in she glanced back at me. The raw pain hovering in her reddened eyes shocked me. My stomach turned over and over again. I sat in the chair opposite her. My whole body shook with nausea.

'I heard you fighting.'

She looked down at the piece of sodden, ragged tissue she was holding. 'He doesn't work at the yard.'

I swallowed. 'I know.'

'What do you mean you know?'

'I know he wasn't going to the yard.'

Her eyes flick back and forth over my face in confusion. 'But I remember you telling me that's where he was. Lots of times.'

I nodded, my throat constricting with guilt.

'He gives me money, Tamsyn. Cash. Where's he getting it from? Then some jewellery goes missing from the Davenports' house?' She rubs her forehead with a tense, white-knuckled hand. 'Why are you covering for him?'

Still I couldn't speak.

'Tamsyn. Please. I've had enough of being lied to! Tell me where he's getting the money from.'

'Signing on,' I whispered. I watched her face crumple with confusion.

'What?'

'The dole.'

'The dole?'

I nodded.

'But… I don't understand.' Her face drained of colour. 'Why didn't he just tell me?'

'He knew how disappointed Dad would have been. You, too. Said Dad would have hated it and called him a sponger and had no respect for him. He said it was just for a bit. Until he found another job. He made me promise not to tell you because he didn't want you to think badly of him.'

Mum flinched as if I'd hit her.

'Jago didn't steal anything.'

Mum stood. Her chair scraped loudly on the linoleum. She was muttering. Her hand tapping her thigh repeatedly.

'There's something I need to tell you,' I said.

'Not now.' She turned and walked out of the kitchen and towards the front door. 'I need to find him.'

'Mum!' I called after her. 'Mum! I need to—'

But she was out the door and gone.

I sat in the empty, silent kitchen and stared at the tin on the top of the fridge. How had it all gone so wrong? How had things changed in such a short time? Only a matter of days before I'd been part of the Davenport family. Part of The Cliff House. It was perfect. But then it all spiralled out of control. Everything caved in. Eleanor told vicious lies about me. I kissed Edie. Got sick. Mum kissed Gareth. Jago screwed Edie in the pool. And I was forbidden to set foot in the one place which made me happy.

Standing there in the kitchen, I was paralysed with desolate loneliness. The ache was acute. Every part of me wanted to get up to the house. I pictured myself walking through the gate. Imagined the calmness that would settle over me.

I walked into the hall and used every inch of willpower to turn away from the front door. The binoculars in the bag drew me like a magnet. I felt the phantom coolness of the metal against my face. I forced myself to climb the stairs. Every step away from the house was hard as I battled what felt like a pack of vicious dogs. This must be what being an addict felt like. I gritted my teeth. Counted my steps to the box room.

I closed the door and sat on the bed. My scrapbook rested on the duvet in front of me. I reached out. Placed my hand on it. Traced my fingers over the letters of the writing on its front.

The Cliff House.

Not the same as being there. But all I had. I took a deep breath. Opened the first page. Lightly touched the crispy piece of gunnera I'd torn from one of the leaves the first time I took the key. I recalled how peaceful it had been. Still and calm. Just me and the house and my memories of Dad. On the next page was the foil from the champagne cork from that first meal with the Davenports. Then the pressed daisy, its tiny dried petals surrounding the yellow centre like muted sun rays. The piece of sea glass attached with sellotape, grains of Gwenver sand stuck to its underside. Around the edges I'd doodled a universe of stars. I turned the page and stared at the sketch I'd drawn, the little boy being pulled from the sea, head lolled back, arm hanging, seaweed between his blue-tinged lips. Beside it, folded neatly, the cutting from *The Cornishman* showing the boy and the lifeguard. The next page held the index card from the mix tape Edie had made me. I paused, wincing as I recalled the hurt in Jago's voice when Mum confronted him about the money, then turned the page. Two tears fell onto the sugar paper and soaked into it like blooming flowers.

The bracelet was frozen in its sellotape coating. An uneven circle of gold. Rubies like drops of blood. I picked at the tape with my nail until the chain was free. I held it in my hand. Felt Eleanor's heat on it. Heard an echo of her laughing at the party. I raised it to my nose and picked up the scent of perfume mixed with cigarettes. I slipped it into my pocket. Nerves ricocheted around my body as I pictured Eleanor's face when I gave it back to her.

'I was only borrowing it,' I whispered. 'I saw it on the floor and—'

Then a shout ripped through the house. It was Granfer.

'Angie!' he called. Voice tight, guttural, laced with desperate panic.

I jumped off my bed, knocking the scrapbook to the floor. There was a loud crash from his room. I flung open my door and ran across the corridor. He was collapsed, his table upended, jigsaw pieces scattered across his carpet like fallen autumn leaves. He whimpered like a wounded animal.

'Mum!' I cried, praying she was back. 'Mum!'

I dropped to my knees beside him. His face was contorted in pain. Eyes wide with fear. He breathed as if someone had their hand over his mouth. Blood spattered his face and pyjamas and coloured his teeth so he looked like a wolf who'd eaten a lamb. His skin was a deep shade of purple and his forehead glistened with sweat.

'I… can't…' It was all he managed.

'Mum! Jago!' I screamed so loud it raked my throat.

Granfer grabbed at my arm with one hand and banged his chest weakly with the other, his fingers twisted into rigid claws.

'It's okay,' I said, knowing it was anything but. 'It's okay.'

I had to get a grip. I took a few deep breaths and gritted my teeth, then eased Granfer backwards. I reached for a pillow from his bed and slid it beneath his head. Then I stood and grabbed his oxygen tank, which I dragged over to him. I unravelled the tubing and fixed the mask over his nose and mouth. As he breathed, the mask misted with blood as if somebody had spray-painted it scarlet.

He jabbed the air in front of his face. He wanted to talk. I lifted the mask onto his forehead and as I did his mouth erupted with blood and spittle and minuscule particles of floating silica. He made a gurgling noise like he'd been stabbed through the heart and I turned my head away from him as fresh tears rolled down my face.

'Pain… chest. My…'

I swiped fresh tears away. Tears were no good to anybody. 'Don't talk, Granfer. Just breathe.' I stroked his hand. 'There's only you and me here. I've got to go to the callbox to ring for an ambulance. I'll be back before you know it. You're not going to die. You're not.' Yet even as I said the words I feared I was going to lose him.

His hand clamped around mine. His nails dug into my skin as he shook his head.

'I'll only be a few minutes.' I uncurled his fingers from my hand, then ran from the room, taking the stairs two at a time. I sprinted to the corner, opened the callbox and snatched at the phone. I was barely able to turn the dial for shaking.

'Nine, nine, nine. What's your emergency please?'

'Ambulance…' I said. 'I need… an ambulance.'

Somehow I managed to answer her questions. My name. His name. Our address. The date he was born. When she asked me what was wrong with him all I could say was, 'Blood. There's so much blood.'

'Don't worry, Tamsyn. We're going to help him. The ambulance is on its way. Help will be with you soon. Do you want me to stay on the phone with you until it gets there?'

'No,' I said. 'No, I need to get back to him.'

I put the phone down then rested my head against the receiver. I didn't want to go back. I wanted to stay in the phone box, where I was safe, where I didn't have to watch Granfer die.

'Don't be dead,' I whispered as I walked back. 'Please don't be dead.'

When I reached the door, gaping open as I'd left it, all I could see was the dark, cramped hallway. The stairs rose away from me. I listened but there was no sound. I tried to step inside but I couldn't move. I was frozen. I didn't want to see him dead. I didn't want to see his blood-soaked lifeless body. As I stood frozen to the spot I saw myself, aged ten, sitting at the top of the stairs looking down on the collapsed figure of my mother, her body wracked with sobs, the man in the yellow raincoat weighing her down with his heavy hand.

I have no idea how long it was before the wail of sirens finally approached our road. I waved frantically, tears prickling my eyes as relief flooded me.

'Up there!' I said, pointing into the house. 'He's up there.'

They ran inside, but I didn't follow them. I sat on the wall, numbed, arms clasped around my body, as I listened to their urgent voices, their footsteps, and the crackle of radios. It felt like hours before two men finally emerged from the house carrying my grandad on a stretcher. As they passed me I stared at him, flat and still, pale-faced, covered with a blanket, green canvas straps tying him down. The mask over his face misted and cleared. Still alive. But only just.

'Miss?' I looked up at the man. His eyes were kind. Crinkled at the corners. 'If you could step back now? We need to get him in the ambulance.'

I nodded then bent to kiss Granfer on the top of his head. He smelt musty and sweet and I wondered if this was what people smelt like before they died.

'Do you want to wait here?'

I shook my head vigorously, eyeing the house. 'Can I stay with him?'

They let me travel with them in the ambulance. I stared at the activity with thickening dread. It was like a horror film. They spoke loudly at Granfer. Pulled his eyelids up, shone a torch in his eyes, smacked his hand, checked dials and tubes and machines.

'Please don't die. Please don't die,' I whispered over and over again.

'You'll need to wait out here,' said one of the ambulance men as they wheeled Granfer through plastic double doors when we pulled up outside Accident and Emergency. 'Is there someone you can call?'

I nodded mutely and watched them disappear through the doors.

The phone was in the main reception and I walked over to it in a daze, ignoring the sympathetic looks of those waiting.

The room was large and plastic, lit harshly, filled with people with stricken faces, broken arms, bleeding cuts, old people with rainbow bruises on their papery skin, a woman trying to console a screeching, red-faced baby.

When I got to the phone, I raised a finger to call the chip shop but my mind went blank. What was the number? I rested my head against the receiver. I tried to remember but everything was blurred. The only number I had in my head was *three, four, eight, three.*

Three, four, eight, three.

I saw the phone sitting on the table in the hallway. I saw Edie's handwriting. Remembered how I'd felt when I'd read that first note from her. The joy. The ecstatic pleasure that had coursed through me.

Penzance 3483.

As I dialled the operator my heart quivered like a terrified rabbit. A few moments later there was ringing. Max's voice briefly. Then another voice.

'Will you accept a reverse charge call from Tamsyn Tresize?'

'Yes,' said Max without hesitation. 'I will.'

My insides collapsed with a sudden release and I moved the mouthpiece away from me so he wouldn't hear me sobbing.

'Tamsyn?' He waited. 'Tamsyn? Are you all right? What's happened?'

'It's my grandad...' I said after too long a pause. 'He collapsed... I called an ambulance. I don't know where... Mum is. I'm... alone... here. I'm sorry I called. I didn't have... any other number.'

'Which hospital are you at?' The tone of his voice was firm and kind, and I imagined for a moment he was my father, there to take control. 'Tell me where you are.'

'I'm at Treliske,' I said, managing to keep my tears in check. 'In the A&E waiting room.'

'I'm leaving now.'

'Max?'

'Yes.'

'I can't remember the number for where Mum works. Can you look it up in the *Yellow Pages*? Spence's Fish Shop in Sennen. Can you ask a man called Gareth to find my mum and tell her?'

'Of course.'

He put the phone down and a flat unbroken tone took the place of his reassuring voice. 'Thank you,' I whispered.

I waited on one of the seats in the corner, hands clasped, knees together, my head aching from crying and worry, eyes bolted to the clock as the minutes dragged on.

It was nearly an hour before I heard his voice. 'Tamsyn?'

Max was crisp and clean in his pressed jeans and blue leather shoes, a white button-up shirt, hair brushed back. He stood out like a shining beacon amid the worry and stench of the waiting room. A paralysing relief consumed me, as if I'd scrambled, exhausted, onto a piece of wreckage in the sea, and had to lie still for a while to catch my breath. He sat and put his arm around my shoulders and I curled into him, relaxing as his warmth bled into me. He smelt of The Cliff House and I drew him in like smelling salts.

'Has anybody given you an update on your grandfather?' he asked gently.

I shook my head.

'Wait here and I'll ask.'

I reached for him to stop him going, but noticed a smear of blood on my hand, and pulled my hand back, spat on it, then hastily rubbed the mark away with my sleeve.

I sat back on my chair and watched Max talking to the woman behind the desk. She nodded. Flicked through some notes on a blue clipboard. Spoke more words. Then shook her head when he said something in reply. I tore my eyes off their conversation. I didn't want to find out that Granfer was dead by catching her look of regret.

A few minutes later he sat back down beside me and handed me a polystyrene cup. 'I put three sugars in it. For the shock.'

'My grandad would like this. He loves sugar but we have to hide it from Mum because she worries about his insides rotting.' I smiled through fresh tears.

'He sounds like quite a character.'

There was a small commotion as two people ran into the waiting room. It was my mother and Gareth. She was agitated, tense and pale. Gareth went to the lady at the desk. She pointed over at Max and I. Mum asked her something, but she shook her head.

Mum then turned and walked over to me, arms outstretched. 'Are you okay? God, what's happened?'

'He couldn't breathe.' My voice cracked. 'There was... so much... blood. He's going to die, Mum. There was so much blood.'

'Hush, love,' she soothed. 'We'll have an update soon. He's a fighter, your Granfer.' She wrapped her arms around me and I listened to her talking with Max and Gareth over my head.

'Where were you?' I asked her when they'd fallen quiet again. 'I called for you again and again.'

'Oh, angel, I'm so sorry. I was at the church. Thought that's maybe where your brother had gone. He wasn't there, but I stayed for a bit to tidy up your dad's grave, then walked down

374

to the Cape,' she hesitated, 'I was upset, angry with myself, thought the air would do me good. Gareth found me on the lane and we came straight here. I'm—'

Max interrupted her. 'Unless you need me, Angie, I was thinking I'd head back. If you're staying here, and Tamsyn would prefer to be at home, I don't mind running her back. You might not hear anything for a while and it's pretty dismal here.'

'But isn't it out of—'

I had a vivid flashback of Granfer's mouth frothing with spit and blood. The scarlet stains on the bedclothes. His jigsaw scattered across his floor.

'No,' I pulled away from my mother. 'I'm not going back there.'

'Why don't you come home with me then? Your mother can pick you up when she's ready.'

I looked up at him and nodded.

My mother protested.

'Please, Mum?'

'But what about Mrs Davenport? No. Tam, please stay with me.'

'That mustn't concern you,' said Max, who'd obviously heard her. 'I'll look after Tamsyn. Nothing will upset her. Eleanor won't be a problem. Tamsyn? What do you want to do? Stay here with your mother?'

There was only one place I wanted to be.

'No,' I said quietly. 'I want to come back with you.'

At that moment the nurse approached us. 'Mrs Tresize? Can we speak with you?'

My mother became flustered. Looking between me and the nurse.

Max rested his hand on her arm. 'You go. She'll be fine. I'll look after her.'

Mum hesitated for a moment before nodding quickly. 'Thank you,' she said as she hurried after the nurse. 'I'll call as soon as we know anything.'

Max then smiled at me. 'I'll get the car,' he said gently. 'Meet me out front in a couple of minutes.'

I nodded.

I watched him walk out of the revolving door. Mum came back to me. Her face pale.

'He's dead, isn't he?'

Her face crumpled. 'He's not in a good way, but he's hanging on for now. He's in the best place and that's down to you. If you hadn't…' She lifted the back of her hand to her mouth, regained her composure, nodded to give herself strength.

Gareth walked towards us. I willed him to stop, but he didn't. He kept coming. Came right up to her. Whispered something in her ear. She nodded. Then he reached for her hand and squeezed it. I'd have told him to leave her alone, but I noticed her squeeze him back, so instead I walked away from them, pushed through the door and waited outside for Max's car.

CHAPTER FORTY-NINE

Tamsyn
August 1986

I leant against the window of the car and closed my eyes. I thrust my shoulder hard against the glass, putting pressure on the tattoo. I had a recollection of Edie's hand on my skin, steadying herself as she pressed the needle into me, the drops of black ink mingling with my blood and fusing with my body.

The indicator ticked and I opened my eyes. Watched Max's hand on the gear stick, strong and deliberate. I lifted my gaze to the rear-view mirror and found him looking at me. He smiled.

The car turned off the main road and headed onto the lane, unmade with potholes that jolted the car. Before we arrived at the house, he leant over and touched my knee. Patted it. His hand was firm and reassuring and made me miss my dad.

We pulled in to The Cliff House and he stilled the engine. Max shifted in his seat to face me and I mirrored him.

'Are you all right?'

I nodded.

Then he reached out and touched my hair, stroked it over my shoulder. 'He'll be fine,' he said. 'I'm sure of it.' And it took me a moment to realise who he meant.

'I hope so,' I said.

He dropped his hand from my hair. I got out of the car and followed Max to the front door. It closed behind me with a thud. The silence in the house was immediate and enveloping. There was a smell of old food and damp clothes. The atmosphere was heavy, similar to the air before a summer storm, thick with a growing sense of unease. The house didn't feel the same. There was a hostility to it. No. There couldn't be. It was just a house. Bricks and mortar. White paint and expansive glass.

Max put his keys on the hall table and walked through to the kitchen. I hovered by the door and listened to him filling the kettle, opening cupboards, the sounds of cups being deposited, jars being opened.

'Tea?' he called back to me.

I walked over to the kitchen doorway. My arms tightly crossed around me. He glanced up at me and I nodded, even though I didn't want any tea, even though I knew it would cool in the mug until a grey disc formed on its surface. I noticed the kitchen and gasped. No wonder the place smelt.

Max made an apologetic face.

'Not much cleaning's been done since…' He hesitated. 'Well, since your mother last came.'

He walked into the sitting room and I followed and was confronted with the same chaos. Its museum-calm was infected by dirty glasses, mugs, clothes, wet towels, even bottles and napkins and plates, all left over from the party more than a week before. The remains of the tiny egg were still trodden into the rug and one of the large canvasses was off the wall, leaning against the sideboard, a gaping ragged hole in its centre.

I jumped when I saw her.

She lay on the white leather settee, sleeping, one leg bent, the other trailing the floor, hand a few inches from a near-empty bottle of whisky which lay on its side. Her other hand lightly clasped a glass that rested on her stomach. Her mouth was open, make-up smudged down her cheeks, her hair in disarray.

He came up behind me, took in the sight of his wife, and muttered under his breath.

'Why don't you take a seat.' He gestured for me to sit in the chair in the corner. 'I'll help Eleanor upstairs. She's not been feeling well.'

I watched him pick up the bottle and carefully uncurl her fingers from the glass and place both on the coffee table. Then he bent and lifted her. Carried her exactly as he had the night Mum kissed Gareth and I'd gone to watch the house from my spot on the cliffside. Her head fell back, mouth gaping, eyes half open with the whites revealed. She didn't deserve him. She didn't deserve the house. None of it. She was spoilt and ungrateful and poisoned this beautiful place with every breath she exhaled.

Max and Eleanor disappeared up the stairs. I listened to his footsteps above, the door to their room creaking a little as he pushed it open. I turned to look out of the window. The table on the terrace was still covered with everything from the party. Amid the chaos, the pool was perfect. Flat and calm with the light bouncing off it so it sparkled. I imagined diving into it. Imagined how still it would be beneath the surface and how closely the water would hold me. As I thought of it I remembered Edie and my brother writhing in the water. My skin flushed hot. I dug my fingernails into my palms and forced the image back into the shadows.

A few minutes later he came down. He held a sweatshirt and tracksuit bottoms which I recognised as Eleanor's. 'I thought you might like some clean clothes.' I glanced down at mine which were covered in blood.

He stepped closer and gripped my upper arm. 'Try not to worry,' he said. 'Why don't you change in my study while I finish making the tea?'

When he smiled the uneasy atmosphere in the house began to subside.

His study was quiet and cool. The desk was empty apart from his typewriter. A piece of paper was turned into its roller. I imagined him writing when I called him. Standing up to answer the phone mid-word. Grabbing his keys and coming straight out to help me.

I walked over to the French doors that looked over the swimming pool, the sea and the horizon in the distance. The lock turned easily. I swung the doors wide open and breathed the air in. I saw us then, me and my father, the ghosts of us sitting up on the cliff beside the rock, half shielded in the grasses. We shared the binoculars. Our bodies pressed against each other. As I watched he stood. Strode back down towards the path. I saw myself, ten years old, skipping after him with my hair floating out behind me like the tail of a chestnut pony. He opened the gate and the hinges creaked.

Are we allowed?

Nobody's home.

Are you sure?

We walked up the lawn towards the pool, which shone like a sheet of polished ebony. He stopped and grinned. Took off his soft grey T-shirt.

What are you doing?

380

You mean what are we *doing? We, my lovely, are going for a swim.*

But we'll get put in prison.

There's nobody here. Just you and me. Nobody will know.

I smiled as I recalled him dive-bombing into the pool. Water splashing up around him like an enormous flower. He emerged and stroked his hair off his face. Beaming widely. He beckoned to me.

Come on then! It's perfect.

The terrace rang with the sound of us playing like two seals in the ocean. Afterwards we lay on the paving stones to dry off. We held hands. Watched the sky darkening as the weather closed in.

A few hours later he'd be dead.

I stepped out of Max's study and approached the poolside. The water was still. Like glass. Not even the whisper of a breeze to ruffle its surface. I took off my top with my grandad's blood on it and pulled off my jeans then stepped onto the first step. Ripples spread outwards from where I had disturbed the pool, fading as they moved towards the walls, no more than wavering light and shadow by the time they touched. Silently I walked down the steps until my feet touched the floor. I pushed off, dipping down beneath the water to glide through it. For a moment or two I felt safe. But then from nowhere I was hit with a barrage of images. Edie and Jago fucking. Eleanor cackling as she cut the man's clothes off. The little boy on the beach, purple skin, limp hands. My father's face struggling to breathe, tiny bubbles escaping his mouth and nose as he tried to shout my name. The raven with strands of torn chick clamped in its beak. I felt something watching me then. The raven?

In my head or real?

Real. I could feel it. It was there.

It was watching…

In an instant panic engulfed me. Constricted my lungs. My fingers and toes grew numb and, disorientated, I lost my bearings in the black water. I tried to find the bottom of the pool but my feet kicked against nothing. Everything burnt. I opened my mouth to scream and water flooded in. A shadow moved. A figure took shape. It was him. I reached out. My feet finally found the bottom and I shoved hard to break the surface. There was a splash. A flash of bubbling white and he was there. He grasped hold of me. Pulled me up. Oxygen filled my lungs, soothing the burn like calamine, as he wrapped his arms around me to stop me flailing.

'I've got you,' he said, gasping for breath himself. 'You're safe.'

I lay back against him and stared at the sky. No raven. Just seagulls circling slowly.

When we got to the steps Max took my arm and helped me out. When I was clear of the water my knees buckled. He caught me and held me tightly, as my head swam and spots of light danced behind my eyes.

'Keep breathing. Deep and slow. You panicked. You need to get oxygen into your body.'

He pulled me closer and rubbed my shoulder. I squeezed my eyes shut and pretended he was Dad, allowed myself to breathe in a parallel world where he hadn't drowned and we lived in this house, our family intact, shiny with happiness.

'I'm sorry I left you alone,' he said. His voice dragged me away from my reverie. 'But your mother called from the hospital.

Your grandfather is out of the woods. He has to stay in for a while, but he's going to be okay.'

Overcome with sudden relief, my body collapsed and as I exhaled I threw my arms around him. 'Really?' I laughed, my eyes welling with tears. 'Thank you!'

'Let's get you a towel and that cup of tea, shall we?'

He pressed his sleeve gently against my face to blot my tears. I laughed again and gripped his hand and he smiled at me.

Then a bloodcurdling scream tore through me.

CHAPTER FIFTY

Edie
August 1986

'I can't believe we're really going to do this.'

Her body thrummed with excitement. She was finally escaping the mind-numbing dullness of her gilded life with its rotten core.

Out of sight of the house, they leant back on the dry-stone wall and rolled cigarettes.

'You seem quiet,' she said as she watched him lick the paper. 'You're not having second thoughts, are you?'

He shook his head. 'I want to leave as much as you do.'

But he didn't look excited. He looked sad. So she threw her arms around his neck and bit the edge of his earlobe. 'All we're going to do is have sex. Everywhere. All the time.'

He smiled and she laughed.

It was as if she'd been dead up until now and at last her life was about to begin.

They finished their cigarettes and threw them into the gorse behind the wall. 'Don't bring much,' he said. 'We can't fit a lot on the bike.'

'I only need my building society book. I'll grab some clothes from the London house.'

'Do you know where we'll go after that?'

She laughed. 'Not at all! Isn't it exciting? I can't wait to get on the road!' She kissed him.

'After we've got your stuff I need to make a stop at mine. I can't leave without saying goodbye. I shouldn't have lied to her. I can see why she thought what she did.'

Edie raised her eyebrows.

'Don't look at me like that. She's my mum and I love her. I want to see her before I leave.'

'What if she tries to stop you?'

'She won't. She and my dad got together at our age. She'll be happy for us.'

'Well we're definitely not telling mine.'

'You sure?'

'Positive. They'll tie me up and make me take A levels and go to university and be a lawyer or something respectable like that.'

'A lawyer?' He laughed.

She frowned. 'I could be a lawyer.' Then she smiled. 'I can be anything I want.'

'Come on then, Miss I-Could-Be-A-Lawyer, let's grab your stuff and get going.'

They left the bike in a farm gateway and walked down the lane. She jumped onto him and he carried her piggy-back, while she nuzzled his neck.

'Car's here,' she whispered as they reached the house. He lowered her down. 'We need to be quiet.'

He nodded.

They made sure nobody was around then walked to the front door. She slipped her key in the lock and held her breath as she turned it. She could hear noises coming from her parents' room. Her father talking. Pained moaning from her mother.

'Come on,' she mouthed and beckoned him up to her room.

He sat on her bed while she threw a few things into a small bag. She retrieved her Halifax savings book from her bedside table and waved it in Jago's face excitedly. He grabbed her wrist and pulled her to him, wrapping his arms around her as she bent to kiss him. They fell backwards onto the bed and kissed harder. The excitement they both felt making every touch electric.

And then there was a piercing screech from the terrace. The two of them pulled apart quickly. Jago jumped off the bed and went to the window. Edie peered over his shoulder. Tamsyn was near the swimming pool. She was wet and dressed only in her underwear. Max had one arm around her shoulder. The other hand was raised like a policeman halting traffic. Eleanor stood a little way away from them, dishevelled and creased and screaming like a banshee.

'Holy shit,' Jago muttered.

He ran for the door.

'No, Jay.' Edie grabbed his hand. 'Leave them. Don't get involved. Let's just go. My father will calm Eleanor down. He's used to dealing with her when she's in a state.'

'But Tam's down there.'

'She's fine,' she said, picking up the bag she'd just packed. 'Let's just leave. Please. I don't want them to stop us going.'

He wrenched himself from her grasp and tore out of the room. She called after him but he was already down the stairs. She swore loudly and slammed the bag back down on the bed.

CHAPTER FIFTY-ONE

Tamsyn
August 1986

Everything moved in slow motion. Eleanor stood in front of us with her face split into shards of rage. The most godawful noise came out of her.

'What's that bitch doing here?' she shrieked. 'You promised me, Max. You said nothing was going on!'

'And I was telling—'

'Shut *up*! You fucking bastard. How could you do it to me again? And with a *child*? With a fucking child?'

Eleanor turned the full weight of her fury on me. I shrunk behind Max.

'You *whore*.' She spat the words at me as if she were firing darts. 'You think I'm stupid? Is that what you think? Treating me like a village idiot? Thinking you can steal him away from me?'

My heart pumped and I gripped Max's arm. I felt his hand on my leg, pushing me behind him. Eleanor swore again then stumbled to the table and began rifling through the mess of plates and glasses, half-eaten food and bottles. With an air of triumph she snatched something up, turned towards us, her face wild.

It was the knife. The one she'd used to cut the man's underwear off before they threw him in the pool at her party.

Max swore. Then stepped towards her. 'Eleanor—'

'She's a little *whore*,' she spat. Her savage words made me flinch and I stepped closer to Max again.

'That's enough now,' he said.

'You *lied*!'

'I didn't lie.' His voice was calm and level like someone in a film talking someone off the roof of a tower block.

'You said you weren't fucking her!' As she spoke she brandished the knife at me. 'Yet here you are. Right in front of my eyes. But you still try and tell me nothing's going on? Do you really think I'm that stupid?'

I held onto Max. Though his clothes were sodden his body was warm through his cotton shirt where we touched.

'Put the knife down,' Max said. '*Eleanor*. Listen to me. Put the knife down and I'll—'

'You'll what? She's got no fucking clothes on. I saw you *kiss* her.'

'I didn't kiss her.' His voice began to lose its cool. Raising incrementally as his frustrations grew. 'She's had a traumatic time. She was in trouble in the water—'

Her face twisted as rage continued to consume her. 'So traumatised she was able to laugh? You think I was born yesterday?'

'He didn't do anything,' I whispered.

'Excuse me?' Her anger burned into me.

'It was… I was… upset. But my grandad… He's okay…'

'*Upset?*'

I eyed the knife as she waved it chaotically. Her hair was mussed up and her eyes rolled and even from where I was, I could smell the fumes coming off her. How different she was from the woman I envied through my binoculars.

How fake life can be. Lies suffocating truths every moment of every day.

I glanced up at the spot where I watched from the cliff and saw two birds circling. They were silhouetted against the sun and it was impossible to tell what they were. It was then my brother burst out of the house and onto the terrace.

'Jago!' I cried. I wanted to break from Max and run to my brother but I was too scared of Eleanor to move.

'Tam, are you okay?' Though he spoke to me he stared at Eleanor.

'Eleanor,' Max said. 'Please, this is madness. Put the knife down.'

Then her face clouded over with confusion. She looked down at her hand and seemed surprised to see the knife. Her muscles relaxed as her tension visibly eased. She took a couple of unsteady steps towards the pool then her knees buckled. As they did her fingers loosened and the knife fell, clattering against the terrace. She crumpled, dropped to her knees, her head in her hands. 'I'm… I…'

'You're all right, Eleanor.' Max's soothing voice talked over her feeble whimpering.

'All *right*?' It was Edie. 'Are you *insane*?' She walked towards her mother and stood over her. 'Jesus, look at yourself. You're pathetic.'

'Edith,' said Max, in a low warning rumble. 'Your mother's tired. She's feeling unwell. She needs to sleep.'

'Tired and unwell?' Edie laughed bitterly. 'She's a fucking junkie.'

'Edith, this is not the time.'

Edie turned on her father then. 'Why are you always making

excuses for her? You think that helps her? Is letting her drink herself into a coma every day then carrying her up to bed so much easier than helping her? Do you care about her at all?'

A strangled broken sob came out of Eleanor then.

Edie began to cry bitter tears which she swiped at with the back of her hand. 'Do you know what it's like living with an alcoholic mother? Being sent away at eight years old and the last thing I remember being the fumes on your breath when you tell me to stop crying and be brave? Hating school but feeling relieved to get back because watching you drink yourself stupid was living hell? Never knowing which version of my mother I'd get?'

Eleanor lifted her head and looked at Edie with red-rimmed, puffy eyes.

'Alcohol stole my mother. Every memory I have of you comes with the stench of it.' Tears spilled down Edie's face, dragging her mascara into long black lines. 'All I ever wanted was a normal mum. Someone who brought me soup when I was ill or gave me advice about boys. A mother who worried about me. Not the other way round. I *hate* that I wasted so much of my childhood terrified, picking up leaflets on addiction from the doctor, trying to find AA meetings to fix you, just to have you shout at me. Because you don't want fixing, do you, Eleanor?'

'Edith—'

'I don't want to hear it, Max.' Her voice was softer. Resigned. 'It doesn't matter anymore. You can do what you want. You can let her drink herself to death for all I care because I'm finished here.'

'What do you—'

'I'm leaving.'

'Leaving?' said Max.

'With Jay.'

I inhaled sharply and looked at my brother, but his face registered no surprise or protest.

'We're leaving this afternoon. I've packed my bags and you can't stop me.'

Eleanor slowly focused her faltering gaze on Jago.

'With him? An unemployed thief? After everything we've given you and all the privilege you've had, you're running off with a gutter-rat.'

I thought of the bracelet in the pocket of my jeans which lay in a heap beside the pool. 'He's not a—'

But Edie shouted over me. 'God, you're a hateful bitch. I never want to see you again. Please feel free to drink yourself to death and when you do I won't care. You're a selfish, spoilt cow and I *hate* you.'

She turned herself into Jago's arms as he came to her side.

Eleanor looked wildly around. Her eyes seemed to find me, travelled the length of my semi-naked body, before lurching forwards onto her hands. I watched her fingers scrape the ground, then one hand patted the stones, feeling for the knife. When she found it her fingers closed around the handle, tightening as she lifted her head. Then she looked straight at Edie. Pointed the knife. Raised her other hand and turned it to expose the translucent skin on her inner arm, blue veins running just beneath her creamy skin. She hovered the knife above it.

'Why wait for the alcohol to do it?' she whispered.

I watched in horror as she pressed the blade against her skin.

'Eleanor!' cried Max. He took a step towards her with

his hand outstretched. My skin cooled quickly where his had touched me. 'Eleanor?' Another step. 'Put the knife down.'

'Mum, no!' Edie was white with fear. 'Don't. It's not funny. Put the knife down. Please! I don't hate you. Stop it! I love you. I do!'

And Eleanor pushed the knife harder still against her skin until I saw a line of blood appear on her skin.

Edie screamed.

'No!' my brother shouted as he ran over to Eleanor. 'Don't!'

Jago lunged at her, grabbing the hand which held the knife, swiping it away from her exposed wrist. Eleanor pulled herself to her feet. The two of them seemed to be dancing. The noise on the terrace was replaced with a low hum, a ringing in my ears, and I felt myself floating out of my body as I had done whilst talking to Max beside the barbecue, when we'd first properly met. It was as if I was watching the scene from the rock, sitting beside my father, binoculars pressed to my eyes.

It was quite beautiful as they moved, embracing each other, their arms entwined, at least it was, until I saw her face twisted into a grotesque mask, eyes widening, mouth torn in a silent scream, and his which mirrored it. And then my brother staggered backwards. His arms opened wide. His head tipped as he looked down. As I followed his gaze I was catapulted back to the terrace. Noise and commotion hit me suddenly as if a television had been switched onto full volume.

Edie was screaming. She ran to him as he tumbled forwards onto his knees. His stomach was soaked with red, blood seeping into the fabric of his T-shirt. His eyes found mine and he shook his head helplessly. Edie pulled him to her. His bloody hand reached up and grabbed her shoulder. Max dropped down beside them. I was rigid, trapped in my frozen body, as I watched him push Edie to one side. Max pulled his sweater off. Balled it. Pressed it against Jago's stomach. Eleanor caught my eye, clawing herself away from them as if she were dying in the desert, knife in her hand, face painted in horror.

My eyes were drawn back to my brother. Blood had pooled on the terrace. It ran between the paving stones, along the gaps between, dripping into the pool. I watched the drops falling, tapping like a metronome, ripples in ever-increasing circles as his blood dispersed in the inky water.

CHAPTER FIFTY-TWO

Angie
August 1986

Nobody answered her repeated knocks. She glanced back at Gareth who shrugged and stepped backwards to look up at the windows.

Then they heard raised voices coming from the terrace behind the house. She swore, angry that Max hadn't kept his word to keep her daughter away from that mad cow. She reached for the handle and pulled open the door. As she did a scream ripped through the house. She could see them through the window in the living room. They were gathered on the terrace. All of them. Something was wrong. She ran out through the open door and tried to take everything in.

Tamsyn was standing in her underwear, hair wet, skin white with cold. Eleanor was on her knees, rocking like a boat on the sea, a knife on the paving stones beside her. There was blood on her hands.

Whose blood?

Max was crouched down. His face was wracked with concern. In his hand he held a light green sweater against the person who lay on the floor. Edie was there too, shaking as if an electric charge was passing through her. Angie walked closer. Her gaze

397

was locked on the unmoving figure on the floor. The familiar clothes and boots. Familiar hazel hair.

'An accident,' Max said. His voice faint. 'A terrible accident.'

Horror tumbled her insides, twisting and tightening them like a garotte.

'No,' she whispered. 'No. Please, God. No.'

She was aware of Gareth trying to hold her back. She shook him off. She thought she heard Tamsyn calling her name. Max said more words. These ones she didn't hear. All she was aware of was the blood soaking her son's T-shirt, soaking the sweater pressed against his stomach, pooling on the floor beside him.

She dropped to her knees. Shoved Max out of the way. Grabbed her boy around the shoulders and lifted him up to her. Pressed her lips against his cheek. Edie wailed in the background. Gareth shouted at Max demanding to know where the phone was. Tamsyn sobbed.

Jago's eyes were open. They fixed on her. Dipped in and out of focus. She reached for his hand and held it. Her tears fell on his skin and she gently wiped them away with her thumb. He opened his mouth a fraction, but no words came out.

'My lovely boy, you're going to be okay,' Angie whispered into his ear. 'You can't leave me. Do you hear me?'

She leant forward and rested her head on his. Clutched him tight to her. Closed her eyes.

As she did she heard another voice. Eleanor's. Quietly crying. Words punctuating her sobs.

I didn't mean to. I didn't. I'm sorry. I'm so sorry.

Later – she had no idea how long it had been – she felt hands on her. Strangers. Strong men easing her fingers from her son.

'No!' she shouted, smacking them away. 'He's my boy. He's my boy.'

But the strangers spoke in firm voices. Told her she had to let them near him.

'Mum,' said Tamsyn's voice beside her. 'They need to look after him.'

And so she released him and sat back on her haunches. Tipped her head back. Circling birds above her. Black. Not gulls. Maybe choughs or maybe ravens. Rob would know.

Gareth was beside her then. 'The police are here,' he said.

'He's going to be all right, isn't he?' She raised her hand to him. He grasped it. Nodded mutely. Then he sat down beside her and rubbed her to keep her warm.

Angie remembered Tamsyn and looked for her. Seeing her standing a little away from them, she beckoned to her. But her daughter didn't come. Instead she took hold of the tartan blanket, which someone – Max perhaps – had given her, and pulled it tighter around her shoulders.

CHAPTER FIFTY-THREE

Tamsyn
August 1986

Edie and Max stood nearby and talked in urgent whispers. Gareth sat with his arm around my mother. He seemed about to talk to me but the ambulance and police cars disturbed him as they screeched along the lane and pulled into the driveway.

I watched, numb, as for the second time that day one of the people I loved most in the world was lifted onto a stretcher. We followed as they carried him out to a waiting ambulance, its blue light turning silently like the lamp of a lighthouse.

'I don't want to go back to the hospital,' I said, my voice barely audible.

Mum faced me. Her fingers twisted around each other. Her face was pale as snowdrops. 'But I need you with me.'

I said nothing. Shook my head, didn't stop, just shook it. The ambulance men were rushing. Talking urgently. The door slammed shut on my brother and the engine started up. Mum looked panicked. Gareth stepped forward and as the ambulance drove off, its siren bursting into life, he pulled a pen and an old receipt out of his jacket pocket. 'Here's the number of the hospital,' he said as he scrawled on the scrap of paper. 'If you need to, dial this and ask for your mother. They'll get a message to her.'

I took hold of the receipt and scrunched it into my hand.

'I'll look after her,' Gareth said quietly.

I glanced at Mum, pale and shellshocked, then nodded.

'We'll see you at home.'

Images of Granfer's blood spattering the walls and floor battered me. My skin crawled at the thought of the loss that pervaded the air in that cold and claustrophobic house. 'I'm not going back there.'

Max joined us. 'I've explained it was an accident but the police want statements from us all. They said we could go to the station, either later today or in the morning.'

Edie went to the hospital with Mum in Gareth's car. She pulled at her sleeve repeatedly, her face wracked with fear, skin so pale she looked like the dead. Perhaps she really did love him? Though as I stared at her through the window I saw her swear silently, her expression twitching with anger, which led me to suspect Edie Davenport's reasons for running away had little to do with feelings for my brother and everything to do with what Edie Davenport wanted for herself.

When the two policemen led Eleanor away from The Cliff House I watched from the threshold of the front door. They didn't cuff her or even hold onto her, she just walked between them as if they were all going for a summer's day stroll. As they reached the car she glanced back towards the house and we held each other's gaze for a moment or two and I knew from her eyes that if she could she'd run back for the knife and drive it into my heart. I didn't drop my head or look away, but stared back at her, my face impassive. One of the policemen said something to her, then held open the back passenger door. She drew her attention off me and thanked him, before climbing unsteadily into the car.

I walked into the house and closed the door and leant against it for a moment or two. Max was out on the terrace. He was sitting at the table, looking out over the sea, one leg crossed over the other, blue leather shoes cradling his feet. I pushed off the door and went into the kitchen, picked up some dirty plates and walked them to the sink.

It didn't take long to get the kitchen clean. Not only was it therapeutic but it also gave me the feeling that somehow re-establishing order meant something bigger. New slates. Fresh starts. And it kept my mind busy.

When everything was washed and dried, the rubbish binned, a cloth with Jif rubbed around the worktop to make it shine, I flicked the kettle on.

'We never had that cup of tea,' I said as I put the mug down on the terrace table. 'It's got three sugars in.'

I sat in the chair beside him and pulled my knees up to my chest then rested my chin on them.

'Thank you.' He turned the mug a quarter rotation. Then turned it again. 'She used to be so much fun, you know. Life and soul of the party. But something happened. I've done things I'm not proud of. She's right about that.' He ran his finger around the rim of the mug once, then laid his hand flat on the table. He looked out over the sea. 'It's beautiful here, isn't it? I loved it here from the moment I saw it. This is what I want. I don't know what Eleanor wants but I do know it's not this. And I also know it's not me. Our love has faded and now, well, we're both stuck with each other, wanting different things. Miserable.' He caught himself then. Glanced at me with a tight embarrassed smile. 'Sorry. You don't need to hear all this.'

I leant over and rested my hand on his, curled my fingers around him and squeezed. He returned his gaze to the sea and for a long while we sat there like that in silence.

CHAPTER FIFTY-FOUR

Tamsyn
September 1986

I spent my days watching from the rock.

When I was in the house, when I wasn't out on the cliff, I confined myself to my box room. I'd covered the bed with the tartan blanket from Max's study, the one he'd draped around my shoulders to keep me warm, and every night I slept in the tracksuit he'd leant me, ignoring the staleness which soon seeped out of it. I decorated the walls of my room with the pages torn from my scrapbook: the dried gunnera, the daisy, the sea glass and the rest. The only thing I didn't stick up was the bracelet, which I kept beneath my pillow. To help me sleep I'd grasp hold of it and think of The Cliff House as I touched each ruby in turn like a Catholic praying a rosary.

Jago remained on the ward. The knife hadn't ruptured any vital organs, though only missed his spleen by quarter of an inch. He was lucky, they said. A miracle, they said. Every night I went to bed and expected to wake up to the news he'd died. Without him the house was unbearable. Mum worried continuously, chewing her fingers to shreds, slamming pots and pans around in the kitchen as she muttered about *that mental bitch*. Granfer lay in bed, grumbling about not being able to do his jigsaw and begging for sugar. And then there was Gareth, there all the time, wherever I went. So each morning I'd pack food into my bag and set off down to Cape Cornwall. I'd walk with my face set, feet trudging the path without pause, and when I got to the rock, I'd settle down on my patch of salty grass, the old purple chocolate wrapper long since blown away, and press the binoculars to my face.

The incident was pronounced accidental by the police. It wasn't pre-meditated; if Jago hadn't tried to be the hero nothing would have happened. Eleanor was full of remorse and felt desperate at the situation. The extravagant basket of fruit the Davenports sent to the hospital would have fed the whole of St Just. The gift made Mum even angrier and if I hadn't stopped her she'd have chucked the whole thing in the bin untouched. The fruit was delicious, though. I peeled an apple and cut it into eighths then offered her a slice. But she wouldn't touch it. Wouldn't even look at it.

Two weeks afterwards I sat on the cliff as usual. Dusk was falling in a glorious sunset. The sky, luminous with bright pinks and oranges, was reflected in the windows of The Cliff House as if it were ablaze inside. The ache from my exile thrummed in my stomach. It was as if I'd been cast out of Eden and there was nothing I could do to get myself back.

Eleanor sat on the terrace, still beautiful of course, but stripped of fine clothes and shiny silken hair she looked dishevelled and uncared for as she smoked cigarettes and stared at nothing. I could see Max and Edie inside. They stood in front of the living room window. The light was on and through the binoculars I could see them perfectly. They were talking. Her head hung low. She looked younger and had lost weight, which I didn't think was possible. Her black clothes and make-up and jewellery were gone. Instead she wore jeans and a light blue denim jacket. Her hair was pulled back into a short ponytail, an inch of brown hair visible at the roots. Every now and then she would shake or nod her head, her mouth downturned at the edges, eyes blinking slowly.

Max turned away from Edie. There was a sense of sadness in the way he moved through the sitting room. He came out onto the terrace and crossed over to Eleanor. I imagined his soothing voice, comforting her, reassuring her he was there for her as he'd reassured me. She looked up at him and I imagined her saying sorry, promising to clean up her act, stop drinking, be the mother and wife they both needed. I had to stop myself shrieking down to warn him not to believe her. She was lying and didn't deserve his kindness. It was her who was the bitch, the slut, the whore, who'd left my brother in a pool of his own blood.

Edie walked out of the house and joined them. She faced her mother. I concentrated hard on her lips as they moved.

'What are you saying?' I whispered under my breath.

Edie's face was twisted and ugly. Her hard, narrowed eyes brimmed with contemptuous tears. She shook her head disdainfully, pointed a finger, jabbed the air near her mother in accusation. Then she shouted, gesticulated wildly and kicked a chair over. Her mother winced. Edie turned on her heel and stormed back into the house. I followed her up the stairs. Lost her as she reached the landing and moved out of sight. I shifted the binoculars over to her bedroom window. She marched in and began roughly shoving things into a bag, sobbing as she did so.

She stopped suddenly as if someone had interrupted her. I waited for either Max or Eleanor to enter the room. But they didn't.

Edie slowly lowered her bag. Looked up. Out of the window. Straight at me.

My heart thumped. Then, as I watched, Edie raised her hand. Something stopped me throwing myself to the ground. Perhaps it was the look on her face, a mix of sadness and regret but with a calm air of acceptance. Instead of hiding, I raised my own hand. Edie gave a thin half-smile before hefting her bag onto her shoulder and walking out of her room. At the bottom of the stairs I expected to see her turning towards the terrace, but she turned the opposite way, towards the front door. It opened and closed in a flash of evening light and she was gone.

Eleanor and Max were still on the terrace, standing, facing each other. She moved towards him and tried to put her arms around him. He pushed her away and shook his head. When she tried again, he turned his back on her and walked into the house, went into his study and closed the door behind him.

Eleanor collapsed onto the chair. Her shoulders heaved up and down, wracked with sobs it seemed, though I couldn't be certain. Soon she half stood and reached out for a bottle on the table. Her fingers closed around it and she sat back heavily, unscrewing the lid and tipping it to her lips, her face contorted with pain. She placed the bottle back on the table, then struggled to retrieve something from her pocket which she placed beside the alcohol.

Her small brown bottle of pills.

For a while she stared at it in some sort of motionless trance, then in one sudden movement leant forward and snatched it up. She twisted it open and upended it into her hand, shaking the bottle vigorously. I watched as she painstakingly laid a line of yellow pills in front of her. She then appeared to count them, touching each one lightly with the tip of her finger, her mouth moving almost imperceptibly.

'Seventeen,' I whispered. 'There are seventeen.'

She picked two of the pills up, put them in her mouth, and washed them down with more alcohol.

I scanned the binoculars over to Max's study, to the French windows on the far side of the house, but the curtains were drawn, a dim light hazing the fabric. The internal door, too, was closed. My heart quickened.

Eleanor moved and caught my attention. Again she'd reached forward. This time she collected up a number of pills and dropped them into her cupped hand, tiny yellow eggs in a trembling nest. Swiftly she threw her hand up and swallowed them.

'Too many. You're taking too many.'

As I realised what I was watching, what she was doing, my body grew rigid. I pressed the binoculars so hard against my face it began to hurt. I should stop her. I knew that. I should yell out. Run along the path and through the gate and up the lawn, screaming her name and shouting for Max. I should have talked to her. Told her not to. Told her this wasn't the answer.

But I didn't.

I sat and watched her swallow the pills in twos and threes. This woman who accused me of things I didn't do. Who thrust a knife into my brother. Who kept me from the house. She didn't deserve any of what she had. Her life was perfect yet she spat in its face. As I watched her I saw the deep unhappiness Jago, my mother and Edie had spoken of. How had I been so blind to it before? Eleanor Davenport was broken, rotten inside, past helping. It wasn't my place to stop her. It was kinder to let her go, like a sick and dying animal. So I watched as she delivered the last of the pills to her mouth and then with a shaking hand she upended the bottle and drained it.

The terrace was veiled with dusk, caught in that moment of soft grey light before darkness fully sets in. Eleanor stood. Her chair fell backwards and she took two staggered steps. As she stumbled the bottle slipped from her hand and smashed on the paving stones. She took another step. Her knees buckled, but like a battle-weary soldier she drew herself up again and walked closer to the pool. She knelt, her hands gripping the edge of the paving stones. She leant over the water and looked into it as if she were searching for something beneath the surface. Then she lifted her head. The wind took her hair. I could see her in profile. Her face was wracked with pain. As I watched her mouth moved. No sound. Not from where I was. Then her mouth moved again. I closed my eyes and concentrated, trying to turn down the volume of the sea and wind. And then I heard it. A faint shout.

'Max!'

I scanned the house for movement. But there was nothing.

She dragged herself upwards. One foot. Then the other. Unsteady like a newborn foal. Once on her feet she took a step towards the house.

But then she missed her footing. Misjudged the paving stone, her foot catching only half of it. I watched as she stumbled and grabbed at nothing in an attempt to regain her balance. Her arms windmilled and for a moment she seemed to hang in the air, time stilled, then she hit the water.

I dropped the binoculars and moved over the tufted grasses

to rejoin the footpath. When I reached the gate I paused to catch my breath, hesitating as my hand rested on the cold iron.

Are we allowed?

My father nodded and smiled.

The gate creaked open as I went through it. The lawn was soft beneath my feet. I didn't run. I walked. Enjoying the sensation of the grass underfoot once again. When I reached the terrace I glanced up at the house to check Max's study door was still closed. It was, so I walked to the edge of the pool and looked down.

She floated just below the surface of the water. Her hand reached upwards, fingers outstretched. Her eyes were open and unblinking, a sparse trail of bubbles escaping from her mouth and nose. As I stared down at her, her empty gaze seemed to focus for a moment. Her mouth stretched fractionally wider as if trying to talk to me. Her hand twitched and clawed the water.

Was she still alive?

Then something whispered in the wind. A gentle calling. I looked away from her, raised my head, stared up at the house. Warmth radiated through me. There was no place else I felt this safe and happy. This was where I wanted to be. Nowhere else. Just here.

When I eventually looked back down at the pool, her eyes had glassed over, unseeing now, staring at nothing. She hung suspended in the black water like an art installation. Peaceful and calm, hair floating out from her head like summer-gold seaweed, her skin tinged a shimmering green in the blackness.

'You'll be happier now,' I told her. 'At peace. It will all be fine now.'

Everything around me fell silent. The wind dropped. The waves quietened. The only sound was the plaintive caw of a raven in the distance.

Real or imagined?

I could no longer tell.

CHAPTER FIFTY-FIVE

Present Day

*S*he sits on the chair in the corner of our bedroom. She is dressed in a royal blue kaftan tied with a matching sash. On her manicured feet are a pair of golden sandals.

I want to ask her – again – why she's here. But I don't need to. I know the answer.

She's here because she is the price I have to pay.

Eleanor is motionless as she watches me. I close my eyes and remind myself she's made up, a figment of my imagination. But when I look again she's still watching me.

'No,' I whisper. 'You aren't real. You're just in my head.'

She smiles brightly.

'Leave me alone.'

'How's your brother?' Her singsong voice cuts through the silence.

'He's good.'

My brother visits me once a month on a Sunday. He drives down from Falmouth. Sometimes he brings his children who bounce around him like puppies. Sometimes he comes alone. We meet at Sennen and buy a takeaway coffee, then walk from the car park to the far reach of Gwenver, turn and walk back.

When the children come – two girls and a boy – they beg him to throw stones with them. I smile as I watch them because every few goes he lets them throw the furthest. His wife never joins us. She and I don't get on. Once I overheard them talking. It was Christmas Day. She was angry. I hadn't liked the dinner she cooked so I left it. Politely, knife and fork neatly together, plate pushed a little away from me. Apparently this was rude enough to mean I would never be welcome again. She told him I needed help. I wanted to burst in and ask her who doesn't need help, but I bit my tongue and stayed put.

'And Edie?'

'She was in touch last year.'

'Is she well?'

A look of sadness passes over her face like the shadow of a cloud. I wish I were able to tell her she is well. The truth is I can't. The last we heard from her was a postcard, written to tell us she'd had a second son and they were moving from central Melbourne to the suburbs to give the boys a better standard of living, in a house with a garden in an area with a sense of community. She said she would forward the new address but never did. The card shared only the scantest of facts – didn't even give the name of the baby – but if I had to hazard a guess, I'd say she was well. So I nod.

'Do you think she misses me?'

'I'm sure she does.'

My own mother is still alive. I rarely see her. We speak occasionally on the phone but it isn't the same as seeing her in person. She won't visit. She makes up an array of elaborate excuses but the simple truth is she doesn't know what to say to us or how to be comfortable here. She doesn't understand. We unnerve her.

414

I saw Ted last week. He was visiting his son who now runs the shop. He was old and frail, hands knotted with arthritis, but his eyes still twinkled. He told me Gareth bloody Spence recently married. His new bride, twice divorced, is from Swansea and makes curtains for a living, which, according to Ted, are fancy ones for London folk with frills and lace and nonsense like that. I didn't ask Ted how he knows all this. Of course, he asked after my mother and I told him she was doing well.

I walk over to the wardrobe and retrieve the silk scarf. I wrap it around my body, tie it like she used to. As I do the smell descends around me. Thick and putrid and horribly familiar. My skin bristles and I close my eyes.

It isn't real, I tell myself again. Eleanor. The smell. Her voice. None of it. The doctor had told me severe anxiety may cause all manner of hallucinations. Then she asked me about my father's death and I could tell what she was getting at.

Grief had ruined me.

I sense Eleanor approaching. Feel her standing behind me. Her breath is icy on the back of my neck. I tense. Ready myself to face her. When I do I inhale sharply and my hands clench at my sides. She is behind me, her face reflected in the mirror, half-rotted, bloated, the skin patchy and bleached, lips tinged blue. Her eyes are glassy and her sodden hair hangs in rats' tails.

'The scarf suits you.'

My eyes prickle with tears.

'And the bracelet too.'

I don't reply. Sometimes I wonder if it's worth it. But then again it's not as if I had any choice. This was the path I chose. The only way I could see.

This house.

The Cliff House.

Looking back it's hard to say exactly why I fell so in love with The Cliff House. Can anyone put their finger on why they fall in love? Like any affair it starts somewhere, a spark of attraction or an emotional connection, and then comes the gradual deepening of affection. A growing sense of security. An ache in the pit of the stomach which comes with being separated. Occasionally love darkens. Addiction blurs the line between love and obsession. It would be simple to say the house was where I felt my father the strongest. Or that I was seduced by the lifestyle it promised. Or that it became an escape from my sadness and emotional confusion. Or, perhaps, I was just a teenage girl who felt a little lost until she stepped through the gate at the bottom of a beautiful garden. A teenage girl who wanted a different life. A life this house promised her.

However it started, whatever the reason, The Cliff House consumed me.

'So,' she says. 'Are you swimming today?'

'Yes,' I reply, managing to keep my voice steady. 'I am.'

'That's good,' she says. 'I love to watch you swim.'

Epilogue

I watch him walk through the living room from a sun lounger on the terrace.

I spy. With my little eye.

The air is cool. Summer evenings turning chill as September takes hold. I reach for the flute of champagne and hold it up to the light to watch the tiny bubbles race to the top. The glass is chipped at the rim so I am careful to drink from the other side. Nothing is as flawless as it was. Though perhaps I'm mistaken. Perhaps it was always like this and I just didn't see it.

The sea is calm today, flat, like a millpond. The gulls wheel with purpose, searching the water, hunting for fish swimming close to the surface.

The house holds me tightly. Its whiteness bold against the moorland backdrop. It doesn't belong in this coastal place, but it has claimed it as its own.

As I have claimed it.

On October third, my seventeenth birthday, my alarm woke me early. The house was still asleep as I quickly pulled on my mother's rainbow dress. I brushed my hair and applied mascara and a blush of lipstick. Mum was in the sitting room, curtains closed, the shape of her in the fold-up bed visible in the dawning light. There was a present on the kitchen table, wrapped in shiny paper, beside three envelopes with my mother's writing on them and a chocolate cake covered with a domed fly net. Leaving everything on the table untouched, I grabbed my coat from the hook and opened the front door.

When I reached the rock I sat down to watch the house and wait. As soon as he appeared on the stairs I removed my coat and left it. Then I walked down to the path and through the creaking gate, across the lawn and up to the terrace. I faced the house, ignoring the chill, which covered my skin with goosebumps. When he came out of the kitchen he noticed me at once. My heart pounded as he unlocked the door. He walked onto the terrace and asked if I was all right. I told him it was my birthday and that I was more than old enough to leave home. Then I asked him if I could I stay for a while. He protested feebly, but I silenced him and told him he didn't have to worry. I'd sleep in Edie's room and, of course, would cook and clean to pay my way. I walked slowly towards him, using my body as I'd seen Edie do, and promised it would all be okay.

And it was.

Now, many years passed, Max comes out onto the terrace with the drink he's just made. His hair is thinning, mostly white, fine and easily lifted by the onshore breeze. He limps a little, one knee not so good. He sits back down on his chair and rests the glass on the table beside the dog-eared bird book, the shadow of a single perfect tea-ring on its cover. He reaches for the binoculars and scans the sky, ready, I know, to call me when he spots something I'd like. On his feet are the same soft blue Italian leather shoes he's always had. They are faded and worn now, but still his favourite.

He and I. Locked in this place together. Happy enough.

The sunlight catches the facets cut into his glass. I listen to the clink of ice cubes as he picks it up every now and then to drink. I lower the sunglasses on the top of my head, briefly lift my face into the last rays of the day, the dying sun still warm on my skin.

Then I stand.

I walk over to the pool. The paving stones are cracked and uneven, weeds pushing through between. The plants around us are overgrown and lawless. The brilliant white of the house has faded to a greenish-grey with lichen and salty dirt blown up by the winds.

I untie the silk scarf and let it fall to the floor. It flutters in the wind as if breathing. I step down onto the first step. Then the second. The third. As always I try not to disturb the water. It needs to be still. To reflect my face in the darkness. A black mirror hiding my secrets beneath its polished surface.

Sometimes I wonder what I'd have done if she'd fought more. If she'd managed to kick for the surface. Taken a desperate breath of air. I like to think I'd have leant over and grasped her hand or jumped in and pulled her to the steps. But there's a part of me that knows better. Part of me knows exactly what I'd have done. That I'd have calmly pushed her down. Held her head beneath the surface. Made certain she took her final breath and filled her lungs with water.

It's the part of me that knows I was always supposed to be here.

I stretch out and push off. In a few strokes I reach the end. I rest on the edge of the pool and stare out across the sea to the horizon. The light catches my bracelet and I look down at it.

Beautiful rubies encircle my wrist. Perfect drops of blood cradled safely in a gilded casing.

I turn and glide back through the silken water. I absorb it all, the gulls, the sound of the breaking waves, the unruly garden and overgrown grass which surround this magnificent place.

The Cliff House.

My home.

I glance at him. He smiles and I smile back.

'I spy,' I say quietly.

Something beginning with P.

Max lifts his drink and sips and I duck my head beneath the water to drift through the silence.

I spy perfection.

Acknowledgements

My gratitude goes to the incredibly talented team at HQ. Your professionalism, enthusiasm, and warmth has been unerring. Thanks to Lisa Milton for your support and kind words. This book would not exist without my editor Kate Mills who was there from the very beginning of the story. The Sennen setting owes a lot to our shared love of this stunning stretch of Cornish coastline. A brilliant and insightful editor, you understood everything I was trying to achieve and made each step of this journey a pleasure. Thank you.

Heartfelt thanks to my agent, and dear friend, Broo Doherty. I can't imagine writing anything without your constant encouragement and counsel. Thanks also go to the team at DHH Literary Agency for cheerleading and good humour. Thank you to Lucy Atkins for helping me see a way through the story when it was looking very murky indeed and to Alexandra Benedict who was there with the right words and invaluable editorial advice when I was ready to throw the manuscript on the fire. Thanks to Sara Crane and Paul Swallow for your eagle eyes, and to Cosima Wagner and Sian Johnson, my early readers, for your encouragement and positive feedback. Thank you to Dieter Newell for generously supporting CLIC Sargent and bidding to name one of the characters.

While writing this book, and for various reasons, I relied tremendously on the friendship and camaraderie of fellow writers. I would like to take this opportunity to thank you all. I will remember every word of support, every joke and witticism, every nod of understanding and bolstering act of kindness. Special mention must go to those who were always on the end of the phone: Susi, Tammy, Clare, Hannah and Lucy. Thank you. And to Jenny who sent me her number and told me to call her at 7 in the morning whilst she stood in a motorway service station and basically sorted my head out.

Thank you, of course, to those who have read this book. You make it all worthwhile. Thank you to the bloggers. You give your time and passion to the support of books and writers you love and your tireless championing is greatly appreciated.

Lastly, my family. As ever a tower of strength. My sister. My parents (to whom this book is dedicated). My dog who kept my feet warm while writing. My cat who kept my lap warm at the same time. My three incredible daughters who make me so proud and always manage to put a smile on my face. And, then, my husband. Without you, lovely man, there would be no words. With all my love as ever.

Gripped by *The Cliff House*?

The Storm

The next harrowing thriller by
Amanda Jennings is coming soon!

Read on for an exclusive extract.

PROLOGUE

The chill December wind blows in gusts, turning drizzle to slivers of glass and scoring the sea with angry white slashes. A boat emerges through the dawn mist like a ghostly galleon. The man at the helm is still and rigid. He cuts the engine and the small vessel drifts into dock. He moves to the side of the boat and bends for a coiled rope, which he throws over a bollard with ease. He pulls the rope tight and secures it at the cleat. His movements are sure, his features set in sombre concentration. The man reaches down and takes hold of the boat's hose and, grim-faced, he washes the deck down. All the surfaces and edges and crevices. He takes great care.

He climbs out of the boat and begins to walk up the jetty. But he stops halfway and his head and shoulders slump forward like a marionette with snapped strings. For a few moments he is motionless, spent, his arms hanging limp at his sides, but then he rallies, straightens his back, forces himself along the gangway past the discarded fishing nets and stacked crates patched with algae and salt stains. Each step is heavy with the air of a condemned man approaching the gallows.

He thinks the port is deserted. He thinks he's alone with only the waking seagulls and the echo of his laboured footsteps for company. But he's wrong.

He isn't alone.

There is somebody watching.

CHAPTER ONE

Hannah

In the early days, when memories of that night ambushed me at every opportunity, routine was my lifeline. Routine gave me a set of stepping stones over the quicksand. It got me through my days without thinking. Thinking wasn't good for me. Thinking was where the madness lay.

These days, fifteen years on, I rely less on routine. I've let go of the smaller things. I no longer wear navy on a Monday, for example, or pull my hair – twisted clockwise, using seven pins – into a tight bun on a Thursday. The bigger jobs, the weekly chores, still have their set days, more, I think, because I find it comforting rather than necessary. Today is a Tuesday, so after I've walked the dog, I'll catch the 10.07 bus into Penzance to meet Vicky, spend an hour with her, shop for what I need that day, then catch the 14.13 home, and make our supper. I cook from scratch every day. On a Tuesday I make something with lamb. For ease, I rotate three of Nathan's favourites: shepherd's pie, Lancashire hotpot, moussaka.

Today it's shepherd's pie.

'Come on then,' I say to the dog.

Cass enjoys routine as much as I do and has been waiting at the back door, her eyes bolted to me, since Alex left for school.

3

When I lift her lead from the hook she jumps up and spins excited circles around me. I swear this dog smiles proper smiles. Her face breaks in two, white teeth on show, eyes crinkled with joyful anticipation.

'Silly dog,' I whisper, as she bounds out of the back door and along the gravel path which folds around the house. When she gets to the gate she stops and glances back at me, jogging on the spot with impatience.

Cass is a tricoloured collie-cross from the animal rescue in Truro. She has odd eyes, one brown, the other – a wall eye – the colour of glacier ice, the pale blue accentuated by the pirate's patch of black fur which surrounds it. When we aren't walking, she spends her time curled up in her basket in the kitchen or stretched out on the front doorstep, paws neatly crossed, watching the world with her dewy mismatched eyes. Nathan took some convincing. I begged for years. A home isn't a home without a dog, I'd said. Thankfully he was swayed by the 'a large country house needs a dog' argument I pushed. I'm not exaggerating when I say that before Cass arrived to keep me company, the never-ending hours spent in this suffocating place were torture. Nathan has never taken to her, but she's clever and keeps herself inconspicuous when he's around.

The gate clicks shut behind us and I breathe in deeply, relishing, as I do every day, the immediate sense of freedom. I loathe the house. Disquiet ferments in its shadows and the air inside is heavy as if each molecule is formed from lead. To the outside world Trevose House is impressive, huge and undeniably beautiful, a grand building which passersby take note of. I watch them sometimes, from the window on the first floor landing, concealed from sight behind the musty damask

4

curtains. Walkers on the lane who slow down to take a better look, occasionally stop and lean casually over the wall to point out features and nod with appreciation. Some take photographs on their phone. Perhaps for Instagram. Hashtag *housegoals*. Sometimes, if I'm outside, hanging the laundry or pinning back raspberry canes, they might catch sight of me and blush, ashamed of their snooping, hastily informing me how lovely my home is as if this will excuse their intrusion. A curt nod and no attempt to engage invariably sends them scurrying away and I become no more than an easily dismissed entry etched into the diary of their day, *the dour owner of that beautiful house we walked past.*

Trevose House, near New Mill, with iron gates which close with a clang and lock with a large key more at home on the belt of a gaoler. Two stone pillars stand guard either side. The granite walls are studded with a line of sash windows and three wide steps lead up to a grand doorway beside which the date of construction – 1753 – is carved into the seal-grey stone. The house was the principal dwelling on land profitably run by the Cardew family for generations. That was, until Nathan's father got involved. Charles Cardew was a poker-loving drunk who, between inheriting the estate in his mid-thirties and killing himself at fifty-two, sold most of it off in chunks to pay gambling debts. Three hundred acres or so, four farm workers' cottages, and a number of characterful barns which, as Nathan often tells me bitterly, could have been converted into lucrative holiday rentals.

Nathan has no fond memories of his father and rarely mentions him with anything other than contempt in his voice. According to my mother, Charles was a *drog-polat* – a rascal – with a twinkle in his eye. He spent most of his time in the pubs of Penzance and Newlyn, buying drinks for the locals and losing his money to anybody willing to sit down and play cards with him. He shot himself in the face in the study at Trevose House on Nathan's thirteenth birthday. Nathan and his sister, Kerensa, who was seventeen, found him. It turned out the debts he'd run up were far worse than he'd let on and, after she'd replaced the carpet in the study, it fell to Nathan's mother to clear up the financial mess he'd left behind. Sylvia Cardew had, in her own words, *no time for fools, gluttons, the idle or weak,* and slowly but surely she managed to sort out the chaos. Kerensa ran away from home soon after Charles killed himself and – if *sotto voce* local rumours were to be believed – died from a heroin overdose in a squalid bedsit in Hastings eight months later. Though Nathan doesn't talk about his sister, there's a photograph of her in a silver frame on his desk, taken when she was about fifteen or sixteen. She sits in the garden of Trevose, holding a blade of grass, smiling at something, or someone, unseen beyond the camera. Her hair is plaited into a loose braid and she's dressed in a long flowery skirt and muslin shirt. Bare feet. A silver ring on her middle toe. She wears no make-up and her face is dusted with freckles, her eyes shining with joyful abandon. I think I would have liked her.

Sylvia Cardew didn't stay in Cornwall. She once told me, lips pursed, nose wrinkled as if smelling something vile, that she'd never got on with the county – *too parochial, too backward* – but I'm certain it was scandal and snide whispers that drove her away. Whatever the reason, the curtains at Trevose House were drawn and the furniture sheeted, and she and Nathan, aged fifteen, moved to a mews house with neat window boxes in Kensington. When Nathan and I married, she bequeathed him their holiday home as a wedding gift. It was riddled with ghosts she wanted nothing more to do with, so instead gave them to me.

'Live in it. Sell it. Burn it to the godforsaken ground for all I care.'

My mother-in-law is the type of woman who chills the air when she enters a room. God knows what it must have been like having her as a mother. Thankfully she refuses to see me. On our first meeting, over tea served from a paper-thin china teapot decorated with gold patterning, she smiled and said lightly, 'I would have expected Nathan to choose someone quite different. More bookish. Brighter. With a degree in a modern language, perhaps, or the history of art. Still,' she went on, sipping her tea, 'one can never know what happens behind a closed bedroom door. I am sure you are *excellent* at what you do. It's just a shame my son wasn't more careful. Shotgun weddings lack class.'

On the rare occasions Nathan needs to see her, he makes the journey to London alone, but never stays more than an hour or two. Serves her right. She's a stuck-up cow. The only thing I wish is she'd taken her husband's ghost with her. He's there wherever I go in the house. As I walk from room to room I can feel him watching me, his face blown apart, an unidentifiable mush leering at me from every corner. I pleaded with Nathan to sell up, but he wouldn't hear of it. What man wants to live in the house where his father committed suicide?

It's not all bad. The inside of the house might give me the shivers but I adore the garden. The plot is enclosed by a drystone wall that plays host to an array of colourful flowers between

May and October. Beyond the boundary we're surrounded by farmland and in the summer months, when the cows are on the pasture, I lean on the wall and watch them, content and languid as they graze, flicking their tails at the flies which irritate their gentle eyes. The air hangs with their scent, but occasionally, if I'm lucky, an onshore breeze will bring up the smell of the sea and with it the heady memories of my childhood.

There's a substantial lawn which takes over two hours to mow. I do it on a Friday because Nathan likes it nice for the weekend. Huge flowerbeds brim over with rhododendrons, camellias, azaleas and agapanthus, and in the far corner is a regimented vegetable patch, put in by Nathan and covered over with netting to keep off the birds. He restored the Victorian greenhouse a number of years ago and now spends his time nurturing his tomatoes and cucumbers, red peppers and courgettes, protecting them from thieving rodents and brushing their skins clean of greenfly and dust. He digs powdered ox blood into the compost and repots the delicate seedlings, handling each one as if made of glass.

Mum and Dad made their first trip to the house soon after we arrived back from our honeymoon in the Dordogne. Mum had dressed Dad in a tie I didn't know he owned which he apparently kept for *funerals and the like*. The two of them sat on the edge of the sofa, hands clasped in their laps, spines starched rigid, shifting in their seats like fidgeting children in church. Mum cleared her throat constantly, which made me want to scream, whilst Dad tapped out some sort of SOS in Morse code with his freshly polished shoe, knowing full well the funeral tie was fooling nobody. Despite their discomfort a mantle of pride hung over them both. At one point Mum lost control and a beaming smile erupted on her face as she nudged Dad's knee and exclaimed in her broad Cornish accent, 'Oh, Harry, can you believe it? Our *melder*, lady of the manor!'

I remember being dazed and confused, as if waking from an operation, anaesthesia clogging my veins. Where the hell was I? How on earth had I got there? *Stop it*, I wanted to shriek at them. *Stop being so impressed. You've nothing to be impressed by.* It was as if I were no longer their daughter, but had emerged altered from a cocoon, an unrecognisable stranger sitting opposite them.

A few weeks later I'd mentioned this to Mum. Her smile, warm and kind, made my heart ache. 'That's normal, *melder*.' Her voice was silky with love. 'You *are* a different person now. You're Mrs Nathan Cardew.' Then she glanced at my stomach, which had begun to swell against the cotton of my skirt refusing to stay concealed any longer. 'And you've got the *babi* to think about now.'

After our walk, I change quickly, drag a brush through my hair, and kiss Cass before walking briskly down to wait for the bus. The bus stop is no more sophisticated than a laminated timetable nailed to a telegraph pole, riddled with woodworm, on the overgrown verge. It's about a quarter of a mile from the house. I always leave plenty of time to walk down and, as usual, am ten minutes early. I lean back against the telegraph pole and tip my face into the warmth of the sun. For a moment I allow my mind to drift to where it's desperate to be.

With you.

We are on the beach at Godrevy. The sky is the colour of cornflowers, the wind cold and fresh, the mid-October sunshine is bright. Your hand is warm and holds mine tightly as if you're worried I might blow away. I'm talking too much. About everything and nothing. Suddenly self-conscious, I stop myself and look up at you.

You smile. *Carry on*, you say.

I'm not boring you?

Boring me? You laugh and it sounds like music. *How could you ever bore me?*

It's low tide. The beach is deserted but for a man sweeping a metal detector like a metronome over the ribbed sand. I can smell the mussel-cloaked rocks. The sea. Drying seaweed. You unpack the picnic you made. Thin squares of electric pink ham on sliced white, spread with margarine.

Mum would call you a criminal for not using butter.

Your sheepish smile melts my heart. Your body is hard and muscular. Not an ounce of fat. The feel of it excites me as I lean against you.

I'm sorry, you say.

It's delicious, I whisper. *Best sandwich I ever tasted.*

We talk. Drink Fosters. Smoke roll-ups and kiss. We don't notice the tide coming in until the sea skims our toes. We're trapped. We laugh. Jump up. Hold hands and wade through the icy water to reach the path. I stumble, giddy from the lager and kissing, and you catch my elbow.

Saved you, you say.

I miss you.

I had no idea how important these moments would become. At the time it was just a picnic on the beach. With a boy I was falling in love with. Something fun to do at the weekend. We had no idea how fleeting our happiness would be. We took love for granted. We imagined we'd always be free. But now the memory of that picnic on Godrevy is a scrap of precious fabric I cling to like a child with their blanket, comforting and safe, ragged with overuse. I remember the heat of him. I can taste the cigarettes on his breath. As I let his lips linger on mine, my pulse quickens. I recall the smell of him. The feel of his skin against mine. The sound of his voice as he whispered in my ear.

It only takes a moment for grief to take over. My stomach pitches with loss and the image of him dissolves, leaving the space where he was desolate and empty. Regret seeps into every nook of me.

If only I could replay that night. Do things differently. Alter our course.

If only.

I hear the bus wending its way along the lane and push myself off the telegraph pole. It draws to a halt and the door opens with a hydraulic sigh. The driver, who's been driving this route for years, greets me like a friend. I count my fare out. I no longer apologise for the coppers. He waits patiently as I drop them into the dish and thanks me when I'm done.

I don't know his name and the only words we've exchanged are the occasional comment on the weather and a 'Happy Christmas' or 'Happy New Year' when seasonally appropriate. I always sit close enough to watch his face in the rearview mirror. He wears his happiness like a medal of honour. Right there, on show, unashamedly proud of it. He is one of those people who whistles a tune. Sometimes he'll spontaneously smile and when he does, it makes me glow as I imagine he's recalling something funny or touching. Perhaps he's thinking of his wife and children clamouring around him when he gets home from shuttling backwards and forwards between Land's End and Penzance. I imagine he has a simple life. An allotment. A comfortable, threadbare armchair he'll never throw out. I find imagining this man in a life of contentment comforting. My Tuesday bus journey is something I look forward to. On the rare Tuesdays when there's an unknown at the wheel, I can become inexplicably agitated, as if my world has tipped and I'm sliding towards the edge.

Like I said, routine helps.

ONE PLACE. MANY STORIES

Bold, innovative and
empowering publishing.

FOLLOW US ON:

@HQStories